#7

Garner, H.
Death in Don Mills.

MYSTER.

895

DEATH
in
DON
MILLS

DEATH in DON MILLS

a murder mystery by

HUGH GARNER

McGRAW-HILL RYERSON LIMITED
Toronto   Montreal   New York   London

DEATH IN DON MILLS
Copyright © Hugh Garner, 1975
All rights reserved No part of this publication
may be reproduced, stored in a retrieval system,
or transmitted in any form or by any means,
electronic, mechanical, photocopying, recording,
or otherwise, without the prior written permission
of McGraw-Hill Ryerson Limited.

ISBN 0-07-082178-x

1 2 3 4 5 6 7 8 9 10 JD 4 3 2 1 0 9 8 7 6 5
Printed and bound in Canada

The characters in this book are completely
fictional, with the exception of some well-
known members of the citizenry who are
used to give the book authenticity. There is
no such address as 1049 Don Mills Road,
but there are a great many apartment houses
in metropolitan Toronto that resemble it and
are occupied by the same kind of tenants.

Chapter 1

George Bullay finished his soft-boiled egg and one slice of buttered wholewheat toast. After masticating his food thoroughly he washed the last bite down with a gulp of his tea, which had cooled. At the age of fifty-eight George was taking no unnecessary chances with his health, and he not only did what the doctor ordered but what he was also advised to do by *Reader's Digest*, the medical columns of the Toronto newspapers, and *People's Health* magazine.

With his half-grapefruit, every-second-day boiled egg (too much egg yolk added cholesterol to aging arteries) and toast digesting comfortably, he lighted his first cigarette of the day and puffed on it between sips of tea. For the past several years he had rationed himself to ten daily cigarettes, after trying to switch to a pipe or cigars at the beginning of the lung cancer scare.

Dolly Bullay, his childless wife of fifteen years, entered the living room and glanced across to where her husband was seated at the dinette table. She was fully dressed in a light summer dress, white flats on her feet, her legs bare and her brown hair combed frizzily to hide its thinning.

She crossed the room, planted a wispy kiss on George's forehead, and said, "Don't forget to take out the garbage, dear, when you leave for the office."

"I won't forget."

I'm coaching the sprinters of the girls' track team at four, so I may be a little late getting home. Take the package of frozen chicken breasts out of the icebox and let them thaw on the sink counter, too."

"Yes, dear."

"Bye," Dolly said as she left the apartment to catch the Don Mills bus.

"Bye, Dolly."

George sat back and enjoyed his cigarette. During the past fifteen years he had never regretted his marriage to Dolly, two years his junior, though they had been in their early forties before they married, each for the first time. Their failure to have a child had been one of his deficiencies, for a medical test had proved he was sterile. It had been a shock to George to discover this, but Dolly had accepted it philosophically and, as he sometimes suspected, happily. She had never said so but he had reasoned she had been afraid of having her first baby at the age of forty-one.

He glanced at his watch and saw that it was exactly eight-twenty. He had timed his morning rush-hour drive to his office in the west end of the city shortly after they had moved into the apartment house. He knew it took him between thirty and thirty-five minutes to get there by nine o'clock.

When his cigarette had burned to within a half-inch of the filter tip he butted it in an ashtray, cleared the breakfast dishes from the dinette table and placed them beside the sink. Then he took the cellophane bag of chicken breasts from the fridge and put it on the plate that had held their morning toast, shoving it to a spot beside the other dirty dishes. He returned to the dinette and wiped the patterned oilcloth table cover with a damp dishcloth, then glanced through the high-set small window at the rush-hour traffic building up in the southbound lanes of Don Mills Road.

In the bathroom George washed his hands and splashed cold water on his mouth and chin. The FM radio station's weather report had said the June day was to be clear and warm with lower humidity, 75 degrees in the city and 70 in the suburbs. A change from the storm-filled humid weather that had advanced up the Mississippi and Ohio valleys from the Gulf of Mexico over the past three days.

George Bullay checked the contents of his pockets, making sure he had his wallet, key-case and reading glasses, pulled on a light woollen sport jacket, took the

2

supermarket bag of garbage from the trash can beneath the sink, folded up last evening's paper and placed it under his arm, double-locked the apartment door and set off along the hallway. His destination was the garbage disposal closet located three-quarters of the way to the rear of the building. His own one-bedroom apartment had a choice location at the northwest front on the sixth floor of the seven-story apartment house.

He glanced at the door of the apartment opposite his own, remembering the sounds of dry retching he had heard from there the previous evening. The woman who occupied the apartment, about forty years of age he would say, was on a smile-and-a-word-of-greeting friendliness with him, though she and Dolly didn't speak to each other at all. The apartment next door to his, a "bachelor," was the home of a now-unmarried man with a name George could never remember, whom he thought to be a Scandinavian. The other apartments he passed, on both sides of the corridor and both east and west of the two center elevators, were occupied by single or married tenants that, with one or two exceptions, he scarcely met or knew.

George carried his bag of garbage and bundle of newspapers past the elevators towards the door to the garbage disposal closet. This tiny alcove with its spring door was set into the wall of No. 609, a one-bedroom "compact" apartment tenanted by an elderly gentleman named Raymark Osler. Mr. Osler it seemed, from the infrequent short conversations George had had with him, was a sort of blacksheep member of an old, impeccable Toronto Establishment family, and had lived in the Don Mills neighborhood when it was rolling farm country, seven and a half miles from downtown. Ray Osler had intimated he was a widower.

George shifted the paper sack of garbage to his left hand and used his right to open the door and switch on the closet light so he could see the metal door of the garbage chute on the rear wall. He pressed on the light, took one step inside the closet, and recoiled in horror, dropping both the bag of garbage and the newspapers to the tiled-linoleum floor. The naked body of Zelda Greenless, who lived across the hall from him in 602,

3

occupied a sitting posture in a corner, the head fallen onto the knees and the carved, colored hilt of a decorative knife protruding from beneath her shoulder blades.

As he raced back to his own apartment, fumbling with the two keys necessary to open the door of 601, George Bullay's thoughts were a crazy quilt of fear and shock at the obvious murder. He also felt a queer prurient satisfaction at having at last viewed the nude body of Zelda Greenless. He had often made her the secret partner in his sexual fantasies, since catching her, about six months before, being felt up by a long-haired hippie on the turn of the front apartment stairway between the fifth and sixth floors. He was also peevishly angry that she would be the cause of his lateness that day at the office of Tangle Toys Limited, where he had been office manager for the past ten years with no lateness or absenteeism at all.

After finally opening the door to his apartment he fell into a chair, picked up the phone from a side table, and dialed "0" for the operator. When there was no dial tone or other sound from the receiver he noticed he was holding down the buttons on the top of the phone with his elbow. "Damn!" he muttered, using the unpracticed oath.

He picked up the phone book and glanced at the inside front cover. A headline in heavy type read,

EMERGENCY CALLS IN
METROPOLITAN TORONTO

and under it in boldface type were the instructions, **Dial 361-1111 or you may dial "0" (zero) and say, "This is an emergency." The operator will attempt to connect you with the required number.** George dialed the number and a female voice answered, "Yes?"

"Police!" George shouted, amazed he hadn't stammered.

A gruff male voice answered.

"I'm reporting a murder," George said.

"A murder?"

"Yes, a dead woman with a knife in her back."

"The address?"

4

"Ten-forty-nine Don Mills Road. Doncentre Apartments, sixth floor."

"Hold it a moment please." There was a click on the line.

George felt like hanging up and staying anonymous, but on second thought realized this would be foolish. While waiting for the male voice again he stood up, holding the phone to his ear, and quietly shut the apartment door, which he had neglected to do when he entered.

The same male voice—a policeman's?—asked, "What is *your* name and address, sir?"

George told him.

"Do you know the dead woman?"

"Yes, Zelda Greenless. She lives in the apartment opposite my own, number six-o-two. No, I live—my wife and I live in six-o-one. Yes, at ten-forty-nine Don Mills. Opposite the Don Mills Shopping Centre."

"The police will be there in a minute. Will you keep people away from the body, Mr.—how do you spell your name again? "*B-u-l-l-a-y*? Okay, thank you." There was a click at the other end of the line.

Constable Hugh Chesley, six months on the Metropolitan Toronto Police Force, high school graduate (Eastern High School of Commerce), seven-month married man, sat at the wheel of squad car No. 3302 around the corner from Don Mills on Barber Greene Road. For twenty minutes he'd been watching the heavy 8 to 9 A.M. traffic pouring down the slight hill that rose between the traffic lights at Barber Greene and those at The Donway to the north. The Don Mills morning rush-hour traffic was reinforced by that from Don Valley Village a mile north, and traffic that had taken the Don Mills cloverleaf from the freeway, plus the stuff off the cross-streets, York Mills Road and Lawrence Avenue.

Constable Chesley was surprised to hear his car number called through the slight crackle of his dashboard speaker, and even more surprised when the voice he heard was Desk Sergeant Granby's at the station.

Usually it was one of the other junior officers who handled the phones and radio transmissions from his precinct station, unless it was the traffic division.

"Investigate reported corpse on sixth floor, Doncentre Apartments, ten-four-nine Don Mills Road," the voice said.

"Car thirty-three-o-two. Right. Now at Barber Greene and Don Mills Roads. Over and out."

Officer Chesley put the idling car in gear, turned on his roof flasher, and eased himself through the red stoplight and into the downhill traffic, which halted with skids and a squealing of outraged brakes. He turned north on Don Mills, shot the squad car to fifty up the hill to the Doncentre Apartments, two blocks north.

Chapter 2

Shortly before 9 A.M. Inspector of Detectives Walter McDumont reached his third floor corner office of the Metropolitan Toronto Homicide and Missing Persons Bureau on north Jarvis Street. He glanced idly at a thin pile of reports that lay on his desk, took off his suit coat, and changed the desk calendar to read Thursday, June 13.

He first read the reports of Detectives Lorne Gardner and Willis Arnop, who had been on the 6 P.M. to 2 A.M. shift the evening before. They had been investigating the death of a John Doe wino whose body had been found in a west-central city back alley south of the Ontario Art Gallery. Though the body had been massively bruised and a severe beating had been indicated, the coroner's autopsy report that accompanied those of the detectives stated the man had died not as the result of a beating but from strangulation caused by partial regurgitation of solid foods into the pharynx while in alcoholic coma. It was the coroner's belief that the numerous bruises and contusions on the body had been caused over a period of several days by frequent falls.

The inspector was happy with this, for of all the murders his squad investigated the ones involving unknown winos, transients, prostitutes and drug addicts were the hardest to follow up. The people who made up the city's lumpen proletariat were a secretive, squalid section of the citizenry who had a hate for, and a code of stubborn silence towards, all policemen.

McDumont picked up the report left by the midnight to 8 A.M. team. Detective Sergeant Edward Soley and his teammate, Detective Bill McQuaig, had investigated

7

the discovery of a young girl's body at the rear of the street-floor passageway of a rooming house in the Annex neighborhood of the city. The girl had been a well-known heroin addict around Yorkville Village, the wife of a U.S. Army deserter who had fled to Canada in 1969 from Fort Sam Houston, Texas. The couple had been separated for the past year, the husband having given himself up to the U.S. Army in Buffalo, New York, the previous September. There had been no sign of violence, and the body had been taken to the Lombard St. morgue for an autopsy. Sergeant Soley had written in pencil at the bottom of his typed report, "McQuaig and I think the girl died of a drug overdose, but we'll have to wait for the coroner's report."

The phone rang, and the inspector picked it up. The voice on the line identified its owner as Inspector Ernie Willis of No. 33 station, Don Mills.

"Hi, Ernie," McDumont said. "What are you reporting, a stolen bicycle?"

"Cut it out, you smartass headquarters stiff," Ernie answered. "You know we have as much crime up here as you guys have downtown. Enough anyway to keep two men on the phones most of the day."

"Just kidding, Ernie," McDumont said, laughing.

Inspector Willis's voice was suddenly serious. "We've got a murder up here, Walter. A young woman found a short while ago in a garbage disposal closet of an apartment house with a knife in her back. I have two squad cars on the scene and a pair of divisional detectives."

The Homicide Squad inspector asked the address, wrote it down on a desk pad, said, "Okay, Ernie, I'll send up a team right away," hung up and walked quickly to the door of his small office.

He looked into the squad room for Detective Sergeant John Stuart and his partner Sam Chisolm, one of the 8 A.M. to 4 P.M. teams, before he remembered they were both due in court that morning for the prelim hearing of a kid accused of murdering the manager of a North Bathurst jug milk store, during a holdup. He hurried through the main office, glancing into each of several small offices along the west wall. In the last

8

one he spied Detective Bill Zotas, who was writing a report.

"Bill, we've got a stabbing death up in Don Mills," the inspector said.

Without a word the detective gathered up the pages of his report and shoved them into the top drawer of the desk, then took his sport coat from the back of his chair and put it on. McDumont was favorably impressed; he'd had a recent acquiescence from the Police Commission in a request that his squad be increased from fourteen men to twenty, due to the sharp increase in street crimes, and Zotas was one of five young detectives he'd hand-picked from the headquarters detective pool. They didn't know it but they were being judged for permanent jobs on the homicide squad.

"Go out back and get one of our cars," the inspector told him. "Better get one of the Chevys; that goddam Plymouth might leave us stranded on the parkway."

"Right, Inspector," Zotas said as he pushed past McDumont in the doorway.

"Bring it around to the front door; I'll be with you in a minute."

"Right," the young man said over his disappearing shoulder.

McDumont went back to his office, took his revolver and holster from the bottom drawer of the filing cabinet, threaded the holster through his belt until it rested far back on his left hip, the pistol butt facing forward, and buckled the belt again. He pulled on his suit coat, picked up a blank report pad from the top of his desk and took off down the main office.

As he passed his secretary's desk he told Marge Craiglie where he was going and told her to give the word to Staff Superintendent Randall Ford as soon as he came in. Marge quit plucking a vagrant eyebrow and stared up at him. Her small purse mirror was propped against a two-inch-thick file.

"What'll I tell Grant and Wilson when they come on duty at ten?"

"Tell them to keep on whatever they're working on —it's that Etobicoke wife-husband shooting, isn't it?"

"Yes."

9

"You can get me through Number Thirty-three Division if I'm wanted. I'll phone in later."

The inspector walked quickly from the office, nodded to three or four detectives he met along the hallway, and hurried down the two flights of stairs. The Homicide Squad car was waiting at the curb, and it was a Ford.

As he let himself into the front passenger seat beside the young detective at the wheel McDumont said, "I thought I told you to bring a Chevy."

"It had a flat, Inspector. There's a man there from the police garage changing it now. I checked out the trunk on this one, and it has a crime kit."

"Okay. Make a U turn onto the Mount Pleasant Extension."

Zotas gave him a quick questioning glance but did as he was told, cutting off an old woman driving north in a Toyota. She bewailed their reckless illegal U-turn with a long angry pressing of her falsetto horn. "She wants to get us pinched," the inspector said, settling back in his seat as the young driver swung off Jarvis onto the Extension and pushed the car up to fifty, ten miles above the limit.

The young policeman drove skilfully, weaving back and forth from one lane to the other as they sped north through Rosedale and the light northbound traffic. The southbound lanes were choked with incoming cars. "The nine-thirty executive set," the inspector commented, glancing at his watch as his driver smiled.

After they crossed St. Clair, the car still holding to its fifty-mile speed though it was a thirty-mile zone, McDumont said, "What nationality are you, Bill, Greek?"

"No. My parents came out here in 'thirty-nine from Macedonia. My mother's a Montenegran, so I really don't know what *I* am."

"Do you speak any other languages?"

"Not very well. I can get by in coffee-shop Greek, and I understand some conversational Balkan languages."

"How old are you?"

10

"Thirty-one, Inspector. I was born here, out in the West End, on Crawford Street."

"I'm an East Ender," the inspector said, before subtracting 31 from 74. Jesus, this young guy had only been born in 1943. It was hard to believe there were detectives on the Metro force who were only being born when he was a corporal in the 48th Highlanders in Italy. "What's your birthday?"

"July twenty-fifth."

July twenty-fifth? That was just about the time his battalion was beaten in their attack on Agira in Sicily by the Fifteenth Panzer Grenadiers. That was where Alex Duncan and Geordy Moffat, both Toronto policemen, had bought it. He opened his mouth to tell this to the young man at his side, but changed his mind. It would have seemed a pretty cornball statement to his young partner he thought. Instead he looked through the window into Mount Pleasant Cemetery and said, "I'm a crazy old Scotsman," in his still distinctive Dumfries burr.

"I know, Inspector," his driver said, smiling. Then wiping off his smile he added, "That is, I know you're Scotch. I didn't mean you were crazy."

The inspector grinned and said, "Run that old bastard down," as a gray-haired jaywalker carrying an attaché case crossed against the lights at Davisville Avenue.

Zotas didn't run him down but drilled the big car so close to the jaywalker's heels that he probably gave a shove to the old guy's first coronary.

From there to Eglinton, through the shopping section of Mount Pleasant, the D-car was forced back almost to the thirty-mile speed limit by streetcar islands, pedestrian crossings and street-parked cars. Neither policeman spoke until they were well east on Eglinton. In the meantime McDumont's thoughts were filled with other things.

Driving past Mount Pleasant Cemetery had reminded the inspector of the recent death of Inspector Bud McCabe of one of the suburban precincts, with whom he'd been friends since they'd both walked a beat. Lately his friends and acquaintances seemed to be dying like flies, which he supposed was a normal adjunct to the aging process. Which reminded him, he should look into the burial society business. It wouldn't be right to leave Jean with a big funeral bill when he packed it in, especially since cemetery plots had increased in price about twice as much as other real estate.

As they drove east through what had once been Leaside the inspector thought of the recent sudden increase in street crimes, especially murder. A great deal of the blame, both from the police department and the public, was laid on the increase in youthful transients and American immigrants, but he didn't buy this entirely. It was true that petty thefts, rapes, indecent assaults, common assaults and purse-snatchings were up, but so were most other crimes. The widening acceptance of soft drugs such as marijuana and hashish had brought its own problems, but these he was quite willing to leave to the Police Youth Bureaus, the precinct forces and the Royal Canadian Mounted Police.

Most of the increase in killings was due solely to the increase in the metropolitan population, and gang killings and those tied in with the distribution of hard drugs like heroin and cocaine were far more prevalent in Montreal and Detroit than in Toronto. Most of this city's street killings could be blamed on alcohol, either as a contributing factor to the actions of the murderer or as a cause of the victim's inability to defend himself. Some were skid-row murders, unpremeditated, the weapon either a brick or a heavy instrument, some as a corollary to the theft of a bit of cash or a pension check, and others seemingly idiosyncratic.

They passed a yellow police scout car on Eglinton, and McDumont noticed that its uniformed officer was driving bareheaded, something the young policemen had picked up from American television shows. Of course some of them were probably afraid of losing their hair.

He had to agree with the Police Association that one man to a police car was dangerous, especially at night.

This North Toronto neighborhood had few police cars, being a relatively stable residential area which before municipal amalgamation had been almost a town by itself. Now the outer suburbs had moved five miles north.

West of Leslie Street Eglinton Avenue widened into four lanes with a forty-mile speed limit, running downhill and then up again to the Leslie Street traffic lights, between an industrial area on the south that had once been an airfield from which Canada's first air-mail flight had originated when the inspector was a boy. McDumont remembered it, and the Canada Wire and Cable Company plant to the south of the field that had then been Durant Motors. You're older than you think, he reminded himself.

Past the residential area on the north of the road the road dipped to a confluence of two deep ravines— the ravines a topographical oddity of the city dating back to the retreat of the glaciers during the ice age. The northern ravine made a park abutting on the north-side road allowance of Eglinton, and had divided the street in two before being filled in to allow the joining of the east-west artery after the Second World War. A number of streets had undergone this joining, forming wide traffic arteries that now crossed east-west and north-south through the 240-square-mile city. Inspector McDumont remembered the day, more than forty years before, when he had run with sobbing breath across the fields and through the ravines they were now driving over, in a high school six-mile cross-country race. My God, he'd huff and puff even walking it today.

They passed the Inn-on-the-Park, which always reminded the inspector of the name of a Yorkville Avenue coffeehouse that in a thumb-to-nose gesture of youthful hippie incongruity had named itself The Inn-on-the-Parking-Lot. They drove under the CPR mainline bridge. The young detective had the car up to fifty-five now on the divided six-lane road.

McDumont nodded in the direction of the south side of the road. "You ever been to the Science Centre there, Bill?" he asked.

"Yes, I took my six-year-old twins there one Sunday last year."

"Twins eh? That's nice. Girls or boys?"

"One of each," Zotas said.

"I've never been there yet, but I guess it's nice for the kids."

"They enjoyed it."

The young man swung the car into a left turn when the lights came on to flashing green at the Don Mills intersection, giving them a right-of-way against the halted westbound traffic. The inspector was staring over his shoulder to the left where the IBM plant stretched its length north along Don Mills.

"Why didn't we take the Don Valley Parkway, Inspector?" Zotas asked.

"They're repaving the northbound lanes under the Leaside Bridge. I noticed it driving to work this morning. Since we moved the headquarters up to Jarvis Street I've been coming in along Lawrence and south down the Parkway to Bloor Street."

"Oh."

The inspector was thinking of a tall building they'd passed on the southeast corner of Eglinton that bore a large sign, FORESTERS. When he'd been a boy the workingmen and members of the lower middle class had had their own clubs, orders and associations: Foresters, Odd Fellows, Loyal Orange Order, Masons, Knights of Columbus, Sons of England—Now they were fast-disappearing shadows of their former selves, anachronisms as he'd be when he was pensioned off. No wonder the younger generation didn't cotton to people his age. Not that I'm fading away to a shadow yet, he said to himself, shifting his bulk on the car seat as they sped north.

They jumped red lights at Wynford Drive and again at Green Belt, and sped over the rise to The Donway where the traffic lanes were filled with cars waiting for the lights to change. When the traffic began to move the inspector told his driver to creep up to the curb lane. He stared through the right-hand window at the façades of the six- and seven-story apartment buildings that lined the east side of the street, trying to catch

14

their numbers. The first one he caught was No. 1055, the Envoy apartments, with north of it the Mayflower and Tomonaco at 1057 and 1059. "Dammit!" If he'd had his mind on what he was doing, instead of thinking back on the Saturday night dances at the old Odd Fellows Hall down on Broadview Avenue, he wouldn't have missed the apartment house. He pulled a piece of paper from his pocket and glanced at the number he'd scribbled on it, 1049.

"Make a right turn along Lawrence and back down The Donway," he said to Zotas.

When they were back on Don Mills again the young detective asked, "What's the number again, Inspector?"

It wasn't necessary for the inspector to answer, for there were two yellow No. 33 Division squad cars parked in front of the southernmost apartment house, a new-looking seven-story job. McDumont knew that his driver had spotted them the first time round, but decided to say nothing about his own day-dreaming. Detective Zotas pulled the D-car into the curb behind them.

The inspector stepped out of the car and waited on the sidewalk for his driver. As they started up the walk to the front door of the apartment house McDumont pointed to a new Plymouth Fury with police licence plates parked in the side driveway of the building.

"How come, Inspector, we have to drive these aging heaps downtown while these guys in the suburbs get new cars?" Zotas asked.

"Downtown we're fuzz or pigs," the inspector answered, "but up here we have to protect our image. You ever seen the thirty-third precinct station?"

The young detective nodded.

"It's a Holiday Inn. If they've got a sewage disposal plant up here it probably looks and smells like Helena Rubenstein's. Incidentally, Bill, you're a good driver. We did the six miles from headquarters in ten minutes."

They entered the vestibule of the Doncentre Apartments, and the inspector searched for the superintendent's button below the intercom grid on the wall. He had just spied it, "Zutach, Apt. 110," when the door leading to the foyer was opened by a fat little woman, who stood there in a housedress wringing her hands.

"Thank you," Zotas said. "Police."

The woman nodded but made no reply.

They crossed to the pair of elevator doors and the inspector pressed the Up button. One of the elevators was at the seventh floor and the other at the sixth. The foyer was furnished in a combination of *moderne* and mock-antique furniture, a false chest of drawers, a commode, ancient-looking side tables each bearing a long slim lamp, and a contemporary oversize green sofa with two matching armchairs. Each article of furniture was secured by lengths of chain to the floor.

Neither detective spoke as they watched the elevator descend from the seventh floor. The one at six remained where it was. When the elevator doors opened an elderly woman wheeling a bundle-buggy got out, smiled and nodded at the policemen, and crossed the foyer to the front door. McDumont pressed the sixth-floor button, and the detectives were wafted silently to the scene of the crime.

The rear of the hallway on the sixth floor looked crowded to the detectives as they emerged from the elevator, and the inspector made a mental count of those standing in front of the garbage disposal closet. Two were uniformed policemen, two looked to be divisional detectives, and a little man leaning against the wall, with a green trash-disposal bag in his arms, was obviously an apartment tenant.

When they reached the group McDumont said to nobody in particular, "I'm Inspector McDumont of Homicide, and this is my partner Bill Zotas."

One of the two tall men in civvies introduced himself as Sergeant Brad Semons of No. 33 Division, and his partner as Detective Arthur Ellys. The inspector shook hands with them both before he turned to the uniformed men. "Who was first on the scene?" he asked.

"I was, Inspector," said the younger of the two. "Hugh Chesley."

"What was going on around here when you arrived?"

"This gentleman—" pointing to the little man against the wall—"Mr. George Bullay from six-o-one, was

16

standing where he is now. He was the citizen who put in the call."

McDumont nodded, then pulled open the door to the disposal closet. He stared inside for some time, then motioned to Bill Zotas to join him. Both detectives stood at the wide-open door, looking down at the naked female corpse in the corner, and at the floor which was littered with spilled garbage and newspapers. The decorative hilt of a knife stuck out from the dead woman's back, showing about an inch of blade.

"Did anyone touch the body?" the inspector asked, closing the door and turning to the other men.

"No," the divisional sergeant answered.

"Did you, Mr. —?" he asked the white and shaken figure who was still standing in the same position as if glued to the wall.

"No, sir. As soon as I saw Miss Greenless lying— sitting there dead,—I ran back to my apartment and called the police."

"What apartment did she live in?"

"Six-o-two, Inspector, at the front of the building," said Semons, consulting his notebook.

"Across the hall from me," George Bullay offered.

"Okay." The homicide squad inspector turned to the divisional detectives and asked, "What's been done so far?"

"Nothing much," Semons said. "I questioned Mr. Bullay as soon as we arrived. A man and wife from six-o-five came out of their apartment to take the elevator—." He glanced at his notebook. "Mr. and Mrs. Derymore. I asked them to go back to their suite and phone their employers that they would be held up this morning. I thought you'd want to question everyone on the floor."

"Yeah. Good." McDumont turned again to the little tenant. "Did you know the dead woman, sir?"

"Just to say hello to, you might say."

"Huh-huh. Did you ever know her to walk along the length of the floor naked to put out her trash?"

The little man shook his head.

The inspector asked Semons, "How do you construct the crime, Sergeant?"

17

"Well, like you I guess. It looks as if she came to put out her garbage and old newspapers—naked as you say—and was stabbed in the back while she was doing it."

George Bullay said, "That garbage on the floor is mine. I dropped it when I saw the body in the corner."

McDumont turned and faced the little man. "Then the spilled garbage wasn't hers?"

"No, sir. I spilled it myself. The newspapers too. There was nothing—except Miss Greenless—on the floor of the closet when I opened the door."

"Was the light in the closet on, Mr.—Mr. Bullay?"

"No, sir, it was out."

"What time was this?"

"About twenty-five past eight."

"What makes you so sure of the time?"

"I always leave my apartment then. It takes me between thirty and thirty five minutes to get to the office."

"Where's that?"

"I'm the office manager of Tangle Toys Limited, out in the west end of the city, Dufferin Street."

"And you drive to work?"

"Yes, sir."

"You keep your car in the underground garage?"

"This apartment building has no underground parking. I park at the rear of the building."

"What route do you take to work?"

"North on Don Mills to Lawrence, then west to Leslie, north onto the freeway, and west again to Dufferin."

The inspector noticed that although the little man answered his questions quickly and sensibly he was obviously under a heavy strain, trembling and his face drained of color. "Just a couple more questions, Mr. Bullay."

The man nodded.

"You say that's your spilled garbage in the closet?"

He nodded again.

"What's that you're holding in your arms then?"

The little man looked up, essaying a thin smile. "Oh. This bag is—it belongs to the woman in six-o-four. After

18

I phoned the police I came back here, as somebody at the police station told me to do, and when she came down the hall carrying this disposal bag I took it from her. She was holding it out at arm's length, afraid I guess to dirty her dress."

"I see. And she went to work?"

"She took the elevator. Dolly and I don't know her very well. I suppose she works."

"Then what did you do?"

"I just stood here until the officer—" he nodded his head in the direction of Officer Chesley, "came up here."

Chesley nodded his confirmation.

"All right, Mr. Bullay, that'll be all for now. You can go back to your apartment. Please stay there until we come and ask you a few more questions later."

George held out the green plastic disposal bag. "What'll I do with this?"

"Just leave it there against the wall."

Bullay did as he was told, and after placing the bag on the floor he stumbled along the hall on his short legs. Just as he passed the elevator doors one of them opened and a man wearing a sport shirt and slacks emerged from an elevator followed by a tall, stooped, rumpled figure wearing an untidy business suit.

"Hello, Doc," McDumont said to the tall elderly man.

"Hello, Walter. What're you doing out on a case? Have a fight with Marge Craiglie? Why don't people get shivved at a reasonable time, or at least get found during the course of a shift? I was just getting ready to go home for some much-needed sleep when the call came in. If you people had waited ten more minutes it would have been Dr. Maitland's baby, not mine."

"Sorry, Doc," the inspector said to the duty coroner. He introduced him to the divisional dectectives. "This is Dr. Edmund Mainguy from the Coroners' Office."

Sergeant Semons said, "Hello, Doctor." His partner said, "Detective Ellys, Doc."

"Where's the body?" the doctor asked.

McDumont opened the closet door and pointed inside.

The doctor pushed past him and, being careful not to disturb the spilled paper bag of trash and newspapers on the floor, made a cursory examination of the corpse. He took a plastic reel of tape from his pocket, decided he didn't need it, and put it back. He tried to lift the dead woman's head from where it was resting on her knees, but was unable to do so. He bent over and sniffed the mouth and nostrils of the corpse. He examined both hands and the soles of the dead woman's feet, studied the knife handle and the woman's back again carefully, tested the give of the arms as he tried to raise them, then, just as carefully as he had entered the closet, he backed out of it and began making notes on a pad he took from his pocket.

"What time was the body found, Walter?" Dr. Mainguy asked the inspector.

"Eight-twenty-five, the man who found it said."

"Mmmph." The doctor jotted down the time on his pad. "Has she any relatives, a husband, in the apartment block?"

The younger man who had accompanied the doctor from the elevator, and who had been staring at the body from behind the detectives, said, "She live alone. In six-o-two. Her name Zelda Greenless."

"Who are you?" the inspector asked him.

"I'm superintendent. Anton Zutach." It was apparent by his use of English that he was a European immigrant. "Z-u-t-a-c-h."

"Where is your apartment, Mr. Zutach?" McDumont asked him.

"Not Zutach, sir, but prounouced Zutak. I am occupant of number one-ten on main floor."

"When did you last see Miss Greenless?"

The superintendent thought for a moment. "Today Thursday, no?"

The inspector nodded.

"Maybe Monday, Tuesday. Saw her in lobby while I was wash tilework."

"And you haven't seen her since?"

"No, sir."

"You live in one-ten you say?"

"Yessir."

20

"Okay, Mr. Zutach," McDumont said, pronouncing the name correctly this time. "We'll be down to see you directly." He pointed to the elevators, dismissing the man.

"Sir."

"Yes?"

"Her name is *Missus* Greenless," the man said.

"Do you know where her husband lives?"

"Sout' America, Brazil, she once tol' me. She is divorce. Mr. Greenless is engineer."

Before the inspector could ask him anything else one of the elevator doors opened again and two young men from IDENT, the Police Criminal Identification Bureau, approached the small knot of men in the hallway. One of them carried a Speed Graphic camera, and had a light meter and 35mm. camera slung from his shoulder; the other carried a small black leather satchel. They nodded to the policemen, and one of them said, "Hi, Doc," and "Hi, Inspector," to Dr. Mainguy and Walter McDumont.

The apartment superintendent took the elevator the IDENT men had just vacated.

The man with the camera checked the instrument, placed a flash-bulb in its holder, and began photographing the corpse and the interior of the disposal closet. His partner brushed powder on the inside doorknob, staring at it intently to see if any usable fingerprints came up. He brushed powder along the handle of the metal garbage chute on the wall, and on the handle of the knife protruding from the dead woman's back.

While the bureau men were doing this the inspector sent Detective Zotas down to their car to fetch some things from the large fiberboard box carried in the trunks of Homicide D-cars, called a "crime kit."

An old woman peeked around the door frame of apartment 607, across from the elevators, but quickly pulled her head in when she saw the policemen staring at her.

When the bureau men were finished with the garbage closet, McDumont sent them along the hall, telling the fingerprint man to dust the doorknob of

21

apartment 602. Then he sent one of the uniformed men to get the superintendent and his keys, wondering why he'd dismissed the man before he'd opened the door to the dead woman's apartment. Daydreaming his way past the house when they'd arrived, then this. He'd have to watch himself; the rustiness of age was beginning to show.

By ten-thirty Zelda Greenless's body had been placed in a plastic body bag by the inspector and his young partner, samples of her blood taken and placed in glass vials, the knife removed from the wound in her back, photographs taken of the body in its original position and of the interior of the disposal closet, measurements taken, and the body removed in the police death wagon to the morgue, where Dr. Mainguy, still grumbling over his loss of sleep, would perform an autopsy.

When every shred of newspaper and spilled garbage had been placed by the detectives in a green disposal bag similar to the one previously held by George Bullay, the bag was taken downstairs and placed in the trunk of the Homicide Squad car, along with the vials of blood and a vial holding a short piece of unmatching hair found on the dead woman's neck.

The inspector sent the two divisional detectives and the second uniformed officer to question everyone they could find at home in the apartments on the first five floors and on the seventh floor of the house. Accompanied by the apartment superintendent, the coroner and the IDENT men, he and Detective Zotas then admitted themselves to apartment 602.

Chapter 3

The hall door of apartment 602 opened into a short hallway leading to the living room at the front of the building, with the bedroom and bathroom opening from it. The living room was furnished rather sparsely according to the preconceived notions of Don Mills held by Detective Inspector McDumont, who had expected either upwardly mobile Bloor Street Scandinavian or mock-middle-class proletarian garishness.

The floor was covered with slightly worn scarlet broadloom around which were ranged a department-store-catalogue sofa, two matching chairs and an ottoman in black simulated leather. Between these were interspersed walnut veneer end tables, a liquor cabinet and an octagonal stand holding a green glass hookah with three very long cloth-covered flexible smoking tubes piled beside it. The end tables and the cabinet, which divided the larger furniture like commas, each held either a small *objet d'art* figurine or a table lamp. The lampshades were red sackcloth. A nineteen-inch black-and-white TV set on a moveable stand was crowded into a corner, its cable TV lead-in stapled around one wall beneath a narrow radiator, above the floor and along the top of the baseboard. It had been installed before the room was painted, for excepting the yard or so of its length coiled behind the set it was painted red, the same color as the walls.

The west wall was taken up with a door (leading to the front balcony) and two large flanking windows reaching from a point waist-high to the tall detectives up to the ceiling, and covered with red rattan drapes, which were drawn. A square four-legged cocktail table stood in the middle of the floor, holding a half-empty uncorked vodka bottle and two empty Five-and-Ten tumblers. A small portable hi-fi set with a transparent dome and pair of moveable boxed speakers were crowded on the floor beneath one of the small tables. The rack beneath the TV set held a half-dozen 33 ⅓ r.p.m. record albums.

"Get the inside knob of the door," the inspector told the IDENT man with the fingerprint equipment, also the door edge inside and out. Then get the liquor bottle and glasses." He turned to the man with the camera. "Take a general shot from the doorway, one of the hookah there, and a picture of the vodka bottle and glasses."

McDumont walked to one of the front windows and pushed back the drapes, gazing out over the plaza parking lot that stretched from the street back to a large supermarket. When he was joined by his young partner and the coroner he glanced back over his shoulder and asked, "What do you make of it?"

Dr. Mainguy, still staring through the window, said, "It's handy to the liquor store."

Bill Zotas said, "It looks like Fu Manchu's rec. room."

"Or a Sicilian whorehouse," the inspector said.

The doctor turned and looked over the room. "The stuff's a little too well matched and expensive for a hippie pad, yet a little off-center for this neighborhood. If you want a thumbnail description of the tenant I'd say she was a neurotic female wierdo."

"Bill?" asked the inspector.

Detective Zotas straightened up from a crouched position he had taken to look at the small hi-fi and record player.

"What do you think of the woman who lived here?"

"No comment yet, Inspector."

The inspector led the two men out of range of the photographer's camera, which was aimed at the cock-tail table. "Do either of you notice the same thing I do?" he asked.

Both Mainguy and Zotas turned their heads as they examined the furniture again.

"There's no pictures on the walls," McDumont said.

"Maybe our Mrs. Greenless got her jollies from the lively arts rather than the visual," the coroner said.

The inspector crossed the room and reached up to the wall above the sofa, pointing out a painted-over picture hook of the stick-on type. "Take some impressions around this hook, Don," he said to the fingerprint man. "It's a heavy type, and high enough to have held a large picture. Because of the depth of the hook, the string or wire must have been removed by hand."

Bill Zotas's impression of a homicide inspector who had allowed him to drive past the scene of a murder changed to one of slightly awed semi-respect.

McDumont asked the building superintendent, who had been standing almost forgotten by the others in the doorway, "What kind of picture did Mrs. Greenless have hanging here, Mr. Zutach?"

The man shrugged. "Jus' a picsha of mounting an' forest, eh?"

"Mountain and forest. When did you see it last?"

"Las' time I'm in dis room. Mont' ago."

"A month ago?"

"No, maybe six mont' ago; when painters come to decorate."

The inspector entered the dinette, separated from the living room by an arched open wall. The tiny dining space was furnished with an inexpensive suite of table, four leather-upholstered mate's chairs, and a sideboard, the hutch of which was used as a bookcase. On the dinette table was a cheap vase holding a clutch of imitation pussy willows.

McDumont, followed closely by the young detective and the coroner, entered the small kitchen through the connecting doorway, leaving the IDENT men and the apartment superintendent in the living room.

The tiny kitchen held a matching yellow electric four-burner stove and refrigerator, a too-short sink counter, a stainless steel sink, and a yellow-painted pedal garbage container. The short sink counter was literally covered with empty vodka, gin and scotch bottles and unwashed glasses of various sizes.

McDumont looked at his partner.

"Either a monumental binge or a house party for fifty guests," Zotas said.

The inspector walked over and stared down at the four burners on the stove, which were unwashed and bore varicolored food spills. What the hell happened to the pots and pans, he wondered.

"Don!" the inspector called.

When the fingerprint man entered the kitchen Mc-Dumont told him to pick up every print he could from every bottle and glass in the kitchen. Then he added, "Brush the handle of the fridge and the ones on the stove, both oven and pan drawer."

"Right, Inspector."

The policemen, doctor and the superintendent walked back along the narrow hallway and entered the bedroom. It also was carpeted in the same crimson broadloom as the living room. Taking up most of the floor and leaving only a narrow strip of floor on either side of it was the largest Continental bed any of them had ever seen, of normal length but tremendous width.

"Christ, it's at least nine feet wide!" exclaimed Zotas from the doorway.

"Just the thing for an orgy," mumbled the doctor.

Inspector McDumont eased himself between one of the walls and the bed, shuffled sideways to its head, and pulled the covers from where they lay in unmade abandon on the pillows. Only one of the bolster-like long pillows bore the identation of a head. "It looks as if she was sleeping alone during her binge," he said.

"Or she and her partner slept pretty close," his young partner ventured.

"Wouldn't you?" asked the old doctor. "I know I would have."

"Let's not jump to the conclusion that she either slept alone or with a partner," said the inspector. "And we don't know yet whether her bedmate was male or female."

"I never seen her wid a girl," said Anton Zutach.

As if they'd forgotten his presence the other three men looked around at him.

26

"I'll question you later, Mr. Zutach," McDumont said.

"Yes, sir."

"This bed could sleep five easily," Dr. Mainguy said, shaking his head.

Detective Zotas picked something up from the floor on the side of the bed opposite to that occupied by the inspector, and dropped it into his pocket. Then he and the inspector pulled the top sheet and coverlet down to the foot of the bed, and they and the doctor stared hard at the bottom sheet before throwing the bed-clothes back in an approximation of where they had found them.

The IDENT man with the cameras appeared in the doorway.

"Take a shot of this bed, Russ," the inspector said. "How's Don doing with the prints?"

"He'll be finished soon, I think. I've caught all those he's found so far."

The four other men returned to the living room, from which they could see the flash of bulbs from the bedroom.

"Did you get some good prints, Don?" McDumont asked the fingerprint man.

"Plenty, Inspector, but probably all belonging to Mrs. Greenless. There were none on the doorknobs, either inside or out."

"How about the door itself?"

The man shook his head. "All wiped clean."

"The bottles and glasses?"

"Plenty."

When the bureau man had gone into the bedroom the inspector walked along the hall to the bathroom door, standing in the doorway and looking the room over. The shower curtain, blue with a design of yellow clowns' heads, was pulled together towards the middle of the curtain rod. A bathmat of the same design as the shower curtain had been tossed in a heap on the floor beside the bathtub. The plastic toilet cover and seat were up, leaning against the water tank. The mirrored door of the medicine cabinet above the wash-bowl was open a half-inch or so.

"Don!"

"Yes, Inspector?"

"Bring your stuff in here a minute, will you?"

When the young man arrived McDumont said, "See if you can pick up anything from the medicine cabinet."

The IDENT man sprayed the mirror, then searched it closely with a magnifying glass. "Nothing at all, Inspector. It's been wiped clean."

"Shit!" McDumont exclaimed. "Try the flushing handle on the toilet."

When the young man brushed the stainless steel handle an almost perfect print showed up in the powder, clear enough to be seen with the naked eye.

"Good job, Don! What does it look like to you?"

"A thumbprint, probably a man's."

"That's our first break."

"It looks like a left thumb, probably made by a person standing up facing the toilet bowl."

"By the guy who left the toilet seat up?"

The young man smiled. "Inspector, *you're* the detective."

"Get Russ in here right now to photograph it before somebody else uses the toilet."

The inspector returned to the living room.

Detective Bill Zotas had unscrewed the bowl from the top of the hookah, and had placed it in one of his plastic bags. He was also stacking the bottles and glasses from the sink counter into a cardboard box he'd found holding vegetables under the sink.

"What do you think of the lady's taste in booze, Doc?" McDumont asked the coroner, who had been looking over the contents of a kitchen cupboard.

"Plebeian," Mainguy answered. "Vodka and Seven-Up and gin and the same mix." He pointed to the trash container. "There's two nonreturnable Diet Seven-Up bottles in the can there. Also a returnable ginger ale bottle."

"Don't touch them," the inspector warned as he went to the doorway and shouted, "Don, did you get the bottles in the garbage can?"

The IDENT man's voice came back from the bathroom. "Yep. We got the can too."

"Okay." Detective Inspector McDumont took the bottles from the trash can and read the brand names. Diet Seven-Up, Canada Dry Ginger Ale."

"Here's a Diet Pepsi bottle that was behind the empty liquor bottles," Bill Zotas said.

"I guess that would be mixed with the scotch, wouldn't it, Doc?"

"Only by a pervert," the coroner said. "Although the scotch is a brand that no scotch-drinker ever heard of, except one bottle."

"What's that?"

The coroner lifted a Johnny Walker Red Label bottle from the cardboard box and held it up for the inspector to see.

"What does it all mean to you, Doc?"

The doctor finished scratching his chest and said, "First, the liquor wasn't all bought by one person. Second, I don't think the deceased drank scotch—" He shuddered. "With Pepsi or without it. Thirdly, before her drinking was finished she ran out of mixes and cut her vodka with tap water."

"How do you know?"

"The bottle on the small table in the living room is a brand of cheap vodka that hasn't been closer to Russia than I have, and both glasses beside it have lipstick marks—"

"Proving?"

"Proving nothing, but it's my guess that she shared her last shots of vodka and water with another woman."

"How do you know it was vodka and water?"

"By a very slight taste of it on my tongue. I also took what was left in the bottom of one of the glasses while you were in the bathroom." He held up a stoppered glass vial.

"But how does that prove she didn't drink scotch?" the inspector asked.

The doctor pointed to the counter top on which was revealed, now that most of the bottles had been cleaned off, a scotch whisky bottle with an inch and a half of liquor in it. "No scotch drinker would have switched to a heathen potable like vodka and Seven-Up while there was a couple of shots of scotch left."

The inspector laughed. "You should have joined the force, Doc."

"Not enough dough in it, and you guys can't bill your patients. Now, if you two can carry out your investigation without my help I'll go on back to the morgue—pardon me, coroners' building—why the hell do they need a euphemism for morgue?—and see what I can find out about the untimely death of Mrs. Zelda Greenless."

"She was stabbed in the back," Zotas said.

"True."

"Well?"

"Goodbye for now, gentlemen."

The old doctor, looking stooped and decrepit, shambled to the apartment door and let himself out.

McDumont went into the bedroom, where he talked for a moment or two with the young men from the Police Identification Bureau. After they too had left he returned to the living room and sat down. He took out his notebook and made entries in it for several minutes. When he finished he kept the open notebook in his hand and told the apartment superintendent to sit down on the couch.

"Your name is Anton Zutach?"

"Yes, sir."

"And you're the superintendent of this apartment house, the—?"

"Doncentre."

"Yes," the inspector said, checking a page in his notebook. "How long have you worked here, Mr. Zutach?"

"Since building open. A year, a little over dat."

"And how long did Mrs. Greenless live here?"

"Since dat time building open."

"Did Mr. Greenless ever live here?"

"No. I never see. Zelda tol' me he work in Sout' America for oil company."

"Did you know Mrs. Greenless well?"

"Excuse please?"

"Were you a good friend of Mrs. Greenless?"

"No. I ony know her like I know odder peoples in house."

The inspector said, "But you *did* know her enough to call her Zelda?"

"Eh?" The superintendent hazarded a wan smile. "She call me Anton, I call her Zelda."

"So you were pretty good friends?"

"Same as wid udder peoples."

"Do you call all the tenants by their first names?"

"Some. I—."

"Who else, for instance?"

The man hestitated.

"Do you call Mr. Bullay—" McDumont consulted his notebook. "Do you call the man across the hall George?"

"No—sir."

"What do you call him?"

"Mr. Bullay."

"So Zelda Greenless was more of a friend than George Bullay?"

"I don't—yes."

"Did you visit her often?"

"No. Las' time was when I unplug sink. Wit' wire snake, you know."

"When was that?"

"Weeks, maybe two mont' ago."

"And that was the last time you saw her?"

"No, I seen her udder time. In foyer, when she pay rent, in parking lot—"

"You told me earlier that you last saw her six months ago, when the painters came to decorate?"

"No, sir! I tol' you I seen picha on wall here den."

The inspector consulted his notes. "Sorry, so you did. But you didn't see the picture when you came *two* months ago to unplug her sink?"

"I wasn't look for it den. Maybe see it, maybe no."

"Who was Mrs. Greenless's best friend in the house?"

"Excuse me?"

The inspector repeated the question.

"She have friend nex' door, Miss Jacton. Don't know odder friend."

"Does Miss Jacton live alone too?"

"No, wit' her 'usban'."

"Oh, her name is *Mrs.* Jacton then?"

"No, her 'usban' name is Mr. McMulley."

McDumont and Zotas exchanged glances.

"Is Miss Jacton in now?"

"I don't t'ink so. She go to work."

"What country do you come from, Mr. Zutach?"

"Hungary, but I am Serb. I am works manager of textile cooperative before Hungarian revolution of fifty-six, in Budapest." (He pronounced it *pesht.*) "Escape to Austria, then come to Toronto."

"You are a citizen?"

"Yes, sir!" His face lighted up. "I become citizen las' week, in Federal Building on St. Clair Avenue. Judge Anderson court. June eight, nineteen an' seventy-four."

"Okay, Mr. Zutach. You're married?"

"Yes. I got wife, Xenia, an' son, Rudolph, two year. Rudolph born in Canada."

The inspector nodded. "You have a master key for every apartment in the building?"

"Yes, sir." Zutach pulled a heavy key-ring from his pocket and held it up for the detectives to see. "I got key for apartment, front an' back door, boiler room, locker room—"

"Does every apartment have a locker?"

"Yes."

"Where was Zelda Greenless's locker?"

"In storage room at back of dis floor. Every apartment have locker in storage room on its floor, eh?"

"Outside of yourself did anybody else have a key to this apartment?"

The superintendent smiled from one detective to the other, then shrugged. "I not know dat, sir. Every tenant get key to apartment, den some of dem get udder key made for dere 'usban', wife. Over in hardware store in Don Mill Centre."

There was a knock on the door, and Detective Zotas shouted, "Come in'"

The divisional detectives, Semons and Ellys, entered.

"Where is the uniformed man?" McDumont asked.

"Downstairs somewhere, Inspector," Semons answered.

"Did you cover every floor of the house?"

32

"Yep. It didn't take long; most tenants have gone to work."

"Did you cover this floor too?"

"Yes." Semons looked at Ellys.

"I told you the first five floors and the seventh," the inspector said. "I want to do this floor myself."

"Sorry, Inspector," said Detective Ellys. "I covered this floor. It took longer than the others—most other people in the building didn't even know the dead woman—so Brad here," pointing to his partner, "helped me out."

"Who did you talk to on this floor?"

Ellys opened his notebook and began to read, "I talked with Mrs. Norma Dryburg in apartment 607. Mrs. Dryburg told me that—"

"Hold it, Ellys," the inspector said. He motioned with his head in Anton Zutach's direction. "Just give me the names of the people you talked to."

"Well, Mrs. Dryburg—" He shuffled back through the pages of his book. "Mr. and Mrs. Derymore in six-o-five. Mrs. Doris Hardley and her son Dwayne in six-o-six. Mr. Raymark Osler in six-o-nine. And Mr. George Bullay across the hall. They're the only ones who seem to be in. The Derymores are mad as hell, Inspector."

"Let 'em be," said McDumont standing up. He said, "Mr. Zutach, take us along to the locker room, will you?"

"To storage room?"

"Whatever you call it."

The inspector stood up, and waving the others ahead of him followed them to the door. He made sure the door was unlocked, closed it behind him, and called the uniformed officer who'd been first on the scene, and who was still standing against the wall near the garbage disposal closet. "Keep everyone out of this apartment, will you—"

"Hugh Chesley."

"Okay, Hugh, and that means *everybody*."

"Yes, Inspector."

When the group reached the storage room Zutach opened the door and the five men stepped inside. There was a passageway between two lines of individual lockers, divided one from the other by widely spaced wooden slats with doors of the same construction. Most were secured with a padlock.

Some lockers were jammed full of furniture while others contained a bicycle, trunks, rope-tied cardboard boxes, washing machines, rolled-up rugs, skis, a surfboard and outboard motor, snowtires and unrecognizable junk. Others were almost empty, and it was one of these Zutach pointed out when the inspector asked him which one belonged to apartment 602. Staring through the space between the wooden slats the inspector made out an old round-topped tin trunk and a papier-mâché dress form on a wooden stand. He crouched down and shoved his arm between the slats, dragging his finger through the dust on the floor. Seemingly satisfied he looked around the floor between the feet of the other men, and said, "Okay, that's all in here for now." Before following the others into the hall he tested the Yale padlock on the locker door, which was locked.

When they drew abreast of the elevators Inspector McDumont said to the superintendent, "Okay, Mr. Zutach, that's all right now. I'll send for you if I need you again."

"Yes, sir."

"You're not going anywhere today, are you?"

"No, sir."

The four detectives went on along the hallway towards the front of the building.

Chapter 4

"I see you're still here, Chesley," Detective Inspector McDumont said to the uniformed officer standing at the door of 602.

"You told me to keep everybody out."

"And did you?"

"Yes."

"Okay. You can go back to your car and report in to division."

"Yes, Inspector. I guess I've done enough taking charge and protecting the scene."

The inspector stifled a smile. "I see you're up on the manual."

"I try to be."

"You did a good job," the inspector said, letting himself into the dead woman's apartment, followed by the three detectives.

They all sat down in the living room, and the inspector gave them permission to smoke, taking a package of straight gaspers out of his jacket pocket and lighting up. The only other smoker was Semons. McDumont asked the two divisional detectives to tell him what they'd found out.

"Nothing much, Inspector," said Brad Semons. "The people I talked to on the other floors heard nothing out of the ordinary yesterday, and most of them had never even heard of Zelda Greenless."

"How about you?" the inspector asked the other detective.

"Just about the same thing."

"You're Arthur Ellys?"

The man nodded.

"And you questioned the tenants who are in on this floor?"

"That's right, Inspector."

"What did *they* have to say?"

Detective Ellys flipped the pages of his notebook. "Mrs. Norma Dryburg in 607 is a sixty-ish widow, very talkative. She said, in effect, that the dead woman was a bum, and she wasn't surprised she'd been stabbed. She said she'd heard nothing last night, and couldn't have even if she'd wanted to for the noise from the apartment across the hall from her. It's a two-bedroom apartment occupied by a man named Cecil Gilcrest. Hers is a bachelor apartment. Apparently, or at least according to the Dryburg woman, this guy holds frequent noisy parties."

"Why does Mrs. Dryburg think Zelda Greenless was a bum?"

"She wouldn't elaborate. I got the idea she thinks most younger women are bums."

"Okay, go on."

"Albert and Freda Derymore in six-o-five hadn't heard anything, and said they didn't know the dead woman at all." He looked up; the inspector nodded and waved his hand to go on. "Mrs. Doris Hardley in six-o-six said just about the same thing—that is about not knowing the dead woman. Her husband, Craig, is at work. She's alone in the place with her son Dwayne—that's *D-w-a-y-n-e*. He was asleep—I saw him but I didn't wake him."

"How old is Dwayne?"

"I didn't ask his mother, but I know the kid from seeing him around the shopping center. I'd say seventeen or eighteen."

"Okay."

"Mr. Raymark Osler in six-o-nine—the garbage disposal closet inserts itself into his apartment between his bathroom and linen closet—it's a one-bedroom compact. He came to the door in his pajamas. He's a pretty-old man and slightly deaf. He's quite a character around Don Mills, and has been featured in the local weekly paper. He used to own some land around here that was bought up by Don Mills Development when the subdivision was planned. He comes from an old Toronto family, legal profession mostly, but he's a sort of family dropout. He used to live up the street in the Mayflower Apartments before this place was built. He lives a pretty spartan life as a kind of rich recluse."

"What did he have to say?"

"He knew Zelda Greenless, and was pretty broken up when I told him what had happened to her. He hadn't heard anything last night though."

"Who else did you talk to?"

"Just George Bullay across the hall. He seems too upset right now to be questioned much."

The inspector butted his cigarette and stood up. "Okay, you two, you can go back and report in to Inspector Willis. When I'm talking to him I'll tell him you both did a good job. Hold on to your notes, and I'd appreciate it if you'd send a carbon copy of them down to me at headquarters. Tell that young fellow Chesley to do the same."

The two divisional men stood up, nodded to the inspector and Zotas and left the apartment.

When they'd gone McDumont phoned the homicide squad office and asked Marge Craiglie to put Sergeant of Detective Eric Manders on the line. "Hello, Eric, anything you want to tell me?"

"No, Walter."

"Okay. What men have you got there now?"

"Jack Lee, and George Wilson, and Perry Smith. Tony Colabra phoned in sick, Asian flu or something."

"Any of the new men?"

"Two."

"So Jack Lee's the only sergeant we've got?"

"Yes, Walter. He's starting his holidays tomorrow. He's already booked a BOAC flight to London for tomorrow night with his wife and daughter."

"Yeah, that's right. Eric, can you send the two new men up here? I've got Detective Bill Zotas here with me. I'll take the case for the rest of the day at least, and as soon as we can we'll put a sergeant on it. Drop in and tell Superintendent Ford, will you?"

"Okay, Walter."

"Take care of the store, Eric."

As soon as he'd hung up the phone, the inspector dialed again and said, "Jean, I won't be home for supper . . . Don Mills . . . You'll read about it in tonight's *Star* . . . No, a young woman . . . Stabbed . . . I'll call you this afternoon . . . You can get me through Thirty-three Division . . . Yes, good-bye."

After putting down the phone McDumont turned to his young partner and asked, "What did you pick up from the bedroom floor, Bill?"

Surprised and nonplussed for a moment Zotas remembered, and pulled a new paper-wrapped condom from his pocket and handed it over to the inspector.

"You should have left this until the IDENT boys brushed it for prints."

"Gee, I'm sorry, Ins—"

"It's all right. Now go down and stir up the superintendent and have him show you where the garbage comes out of the basement garbage chute. If it hasn't been shovelled up yet try to find out who was the last person on this floor to dump a bag or box of trash down the chute. Look for names and addresses on envelopes, shopping slips, things like that. Understand?"

"Right, Inspector." Zotas left.

When he was alone Inspector McDumont walked into the bathroom and opened the medicine cabinet, making notes of all the prescription drugs it contained. Then he searched the kitchen and a broom closet, reading the ingredients on the boxes and bottles of laundry materials, cleansers, polishes, detergents, and even those cn a can of floor wax. He then looked through the food in the fridge, and took several food cans from a cupboard above the stove and studied them carefully before placing them back on their shelves. Returning to the bathroom he searched the almost empty cupboard under the vanity, finally standing up wearing a puzzled frown.

Bill Zotas returned in less than an hour, his sleeves rolled up and his collar undone. He was holding his hands away from his clothes.

"How did you make out, Bill?" the inspector asked. Then before Zotas could answer he said, "Go and wash up first."

When the young detective had gone to the bathroom the inspector took a pair of scissors he'd found previously in a kitchen drawer and cut two small patches from the pile of the living room rug alongside one of the chairs. He placed the cut and slightly stained fibers into a small vial from the crime kit and placed it in his jacket pocket.

Zotas returned from the bathroom and handed Mc-Dumont several greasy-looking pieces of paper, an envelope, and two small sections of a laminated plastic card.

The inspector turned over one of the pieces of paper, which was pasted to a small square of light cardboard, a department store delivery slip from the T. Eaton Co. The name and address on it was that of Mr. Piet Langenzent, Apt. 603, 1049 Don Mills Rd. The inspector wrote the name and apartment number in his notebook, placing the delivery slip inside the book's back cover.

"Was this near the top of the pile of garbage?"

"Yes, but it was impossible to tell whether or not it came from one of the last bundles to come down the chute. Zutach told me he doesn't change carts—"

"Change carts?"

"Apparently there's a metropolitan bylaw or something that prevents new apartment houses burning their garbage as the older houses do. Now the garbage chutes end on a level with the first floor and the garbage is wheeled out to the rear of the building where a private garbage collector picks up the metal container and leaves an empty one in its place. It's an antipollution measure."

"I learn something new every day," the inspector said.

"Zutach's present garbage disposal cart is still only half full, so he doesn't have to put a new cart under the bottom of the chute until tomorrow at the earliest."

McDumont nodded, turning the other pieces of paper in his hands. The untorn envelope was from a letter addressed to a woman on the second floor. The inspector disregarded it, and tried to fit together the two pieces of laminated plastic. They formed a bank's credit card, called Shop-Easy, issued jointly by three Canadian banks and honored in many stores and eating places throughout the city, and presumably the whole country.

"Where was this Shop-Easy card, Bill?"

Zotas, who had been inspecting his soiled shoes and socks, said, "That was a little farther down in the cart, Inspector."

"Come here." The inspector led the way into the kitchen, and took the trash basket from beneath the sink. He removed several crushed newspaper pages from it, noted that the dates on them were several days back, and spread one of them on the floor. He handed the others to Detective Zotas and said, "Clean off your socks and shoes with these." Then he emptied the contents of the pedal-can onto the spread sheet of newspaper.

Poking about in it with his ballpoint pen, as Zotas looked on, he separated egg shells, the contents of some ashtrays, a bacon wrapper, an empty Tampax box, two half-eaten pork chops, tea bags, liquor bottle screwtops, coffee grounds, pieces of a broken tumbler, and a minutely-torn note on pink bond paper, of a type usually found in a woman's letter set. The minute scraps of paper had been printed over with a black felt pen. McDumont collected every scrap of the pink paper and placed them in a careful pile on the kitchen floor.

As he bundled the rest of the garbage into the sheet of newspaper McDumont said, "Now clean off your shoes, and then go and throw this bundle down the garbage chute before it begins to stink." The young detective began cleaning his shoes as the inspector placed the tiny pieces of torn paper into an envelope, one of many containing bills and notices, that he took from an inside pocket. He first glanced at the original contents of the envelope, an advertising come-on for flight insurance from American Express, before inserting it into the bundle of garbage.

When Zotas returned to the apartment he found the inspector sitting on the couch and talking into the telephone, the two halves of the laminated plastic card on the small table beside the phone.

"No, Jocko, we've nothing more than the woman's

name, and the fact that she was stabbed. . . My guess it was last night, but you'll have to check that with Mr. Mainguy after he performs his post-mortem. . . Not that I know of up to now . . . yes, a fancy sort of decorative knife. . . A decorative handle covered with Egyptian hieroglyphics. . . I've only had a high school education too; get a christly dictionary. . . Maybe they're not Egyptian. . . Maybe Syrian or Druid; anyway it was probably made in Japan. . . Tell 'em the usual; we're following several leads. . . What? I know goddam well all murder victims, all female murder victims, are beautiful, but this one really was. . . Jesus, I saw her naked, didn't I? Late thirties, that's right. At my age any woman under sixty-five is beautiful—no, I haven't found a single picture yet. For chrissakes we only came on the case at nine-thirty. . . Yes, later this afternoon. Okay, Jocko."

After he'd hung up the phone McDumont said, "That was the *Star*."

"How did they know about it already?" Zotas asked.

"It's their job to know. Jocko just got the name of the victim from Marge Craiglie or Eric Manders, or maybe from Ernie Willis up here at Thirty-three, then called her number in the phone book. There's nothing mysterious or cloak-and-dagger about the way police reporters work, or detectives either, except in books. It's just looking around, listening and digging up things,"

The young detective nodded.

"And using your intuition, suspicions and common sense," the inspector added.

He fitted the two pieces of laminated plastic together, then stared down at the incomplete charge card, trying to decipher the name. He shook his head, then looked up at Zotas and said, "You want to try your luck?" He moved along the couch, giving the detective his seat against the table.

Bill Zotas tore a page from his notebook, placed it on the table top, then fitted the two parts of the card as closely together as possible while leaving the missing space between them. The card fitted together perfectly at the top. He took out a ballpoint pen and began to reconstruct the missing letters and figures on the notebook paper from what was left of them on the plastic card.

To hide his admiration for the other's ingenuity McDumont said, "Of course this will probably turn out to be all bullshit. We'll come up with the name of a Mrs. Vanderbilt on the fourth floor, or even if it's one of the dead woman's neighbors, what does it prove?"

"That's what *I* was wondering," the young detective said.

"Go on anyway."

Zotas continued the laminated lines with his pen on the paper, and finally part of a name was reconstructed: W LER D MOM ILFY. He had better luck with the card number, 5 3 088 301 B.

The inspector read, "WILEBED or WALERED or something else, MOM—MOMFILFY." He took his own wallet from his pocket and looked at his credit cards. "Here's my Esso card. My name is spelled MCDUMONT, with a capital C. Now supposing that O between the two M's was a C, it would be MCM. . . something. MCMILFY. No. Supposing the I isn't an I at all, what could it be?"

"It could be a J."

"Or another L!"

"Yes. McM llfy."

The inspector said, "Wait a minute!" He consulted his notebook. "McMulley! The F isn't an F at all but an E. Zutach told me that the man in the next apartment is named McMulley. We can make that, eh?"

"I can make McMulley but not—what's his first name?"

"Wilfred."

"I can make WILFRED."

"It's his card all right, but maybe he spells it WILFRID, with an I between the R and the D. Anyway, it's him. Good work, Bill."

The inspector picked up the phone and called Eric Manders down at the squad office. He gave the Sergeant of Detectives the partial and possible number of the Shop-Easy card and asked him to check out the name and address of the owner. They talked for another minute or two about squad business before the inspector hung up.

McDumont sat fingering the packaged condom Zotas had picked up from the bedroom floor. "I wish we'd got a print from this."

"Sorry, Inspector."

"Hell, you've got to learn. We'll find out who owned it."

"I didn't think anybody wore those any more."

"Not many married men do; not since the birth control pill. There's a lot of clap around, they tell me. It's on the increase again. Maybe the guy who owned it was using it for the reasons they used to put on the tins in my younger days. 'For the prevention of disease only.' Boy, what a line of bullshit that was!" He undid the paper cover and unrolled the rubber. "It's so fine," he said. "In the army the safes they gave us were as thick as bloody inner-tubes."

Zotas laughed, as the inspector rerolled the rubber and placed it back in its package.

"I suppose you're wondering why I sent you into the basement to check the garbage?"

"No."

Surprised, the inspector asked, "Why do you think I did it then?"

"Well, there wasn't much stuff in the trash can here. Maybe you thought there'd be something from this apartment."

"That would probably have helped us all right, but my main reason was to try and discover who was the last person on this floor to use the garbage shute. When we find out what time they used it—for instance Mc-Mulley and Langenzent, we'll know the body wasn't put there before they emptied their garbage."

"Unless one of them took his garbage down to the chute, found the woman there and stabbed her."

The inspector lighted a cigarette, then shook his head. "In the first place, Mrs. Greenless wasn't stabbed in the garbage closet; secondly, I don't think—even as drunk as she must have been yesterday—she was in the habit of walking the length of the hallway naked;

and thirdly, nobody followed her there, found that knife or took it with him, and then dumped the contents of a garbage bag."

"Why would somebody cut up a credit card, Inspector?"

McDumont looked up in surprise. "Haven't you ever done it?" he asked.

"No."

The inspector wondered if he was the only person in town who constantly received unsclicited credit cards in the mail. Maybe because he'd kept a good credit rating over the years. Zotas, being much younger, probably hadn't yet reached the phony pinnacle of middle class respectability, or had the kind of address that put his name on charity sucker lists and into potential credit-card customer files. He laughed. "Hell, Bill, I've chopped up a dozen unasked-for credit cards over the past couple of years, Chargex, Gulf Oil—"

"I carry a Gulf card."

"Did you request it?"

"Sure."

"So you're not intending to cut that one up, right?"

Zotas nodded.

"But supposing some outfit sent you, let's say, a Shell Oil card? Would you keep it?"

"Maybe, maybe not."

"If you didn't want it, what would you do with it?"

"Mail it back?"

"*You* might, but most people, if they're smart, would just get rid of it. The best way to do it, to keep it from falling into some crooked bastard's hands (maybe somebody working with a girl in the credit card office— ask some of the guys on the fraud squad sometime about white-collar criminals) would be to destroy it, so it couldn't be used. The best way to destroy a laminated plastic card is to cut it with scissors into small pieces. Personally, unlike McMulley next door, I cut such cards into so many pieces you'd never be able to find them all, even in a garbage bag." He laughed again. "Not only would it be impossible to glue them together but it would take a credit card fraud a day to even assemble my jigsaw puzzle."

"I'll remember that."

"Sometime when we're not so busy ask me how to write a cheque that's nearly impossible for anyone to raise."

"I'll do that, Inspector," the young man said, smiling. Then he asked, "Where was the dead woman killed?"

"Right in here, I think."

"How come there's no blood?"

"Good question. There was a bit, if you remember, congealed at the side of the wound. I think I found a couple of drops on the floor over there." He took out the vial and held it up. "Let's presume for now that the person who stabbed her mopped up the rest."

The inspector stood up. "We've got a lot to do. The first thing I want done is for you to go downstairs and get from Zutach a list of all the people who live on this floor, and their apartment numbers. When the two other new men in the squad arrive I'll send one down to get everybody's name and apartment number in the house. We'll question the ones on this floor, who are in, this afternoon." He glanced at his watch. "It's almost noon, so after you get the list just hang on to it. In the meantime you can go across to the plaza and grab a lunch. While you're over there drop this key—" He handed the key to apartment 602 to the detective. "—into the hardware store, and get a couple of duplicates made."

"Okay, Inspector. *Two* duplicates?"

"Yeah. Incidentally, find out from Zutach who the owners of the building are."

The young inspector stood up.

There was a knock at the door, and McDumont barked, "Come in!"

It was the second uniformed officer, who both detectives had almost forgotten was still in the building. He was young, with sideburns as long as police regulations allowed, and just over the minimum height for a Toronto policeman.

"Christ, we almost forgot you," the inspector said. "What's your name?"

"Harvey Miller, Inspector."

"You seem to have done a pretty thorough job. How many people did you find to question?"

"A couple of dozen anyway."

The inspector told Detective Zotas he could go.

When they were alone McDumont told the uniformed officer to sit down. "Okay, Miller, don't give me all the details, but keep your notes. Have them typed up; they'll be needed probably at the trial. What did you find out about Zelda Greenless?"

"Nothing much. Most of those I questioned were old—"

"Biddies?"

The officer smiled. "Right on. Hardly any of them knew the dead woman, and most went into panic when I told them she'd been murdered."

The inspector frowned. "You should have said she'd been in an accident or something. Anyway, go on."

"One of the very few who had even heard of her was a man called Gerald Robinson, in his sixties." He took his book from his uniform shirt pocket and looked in it. "Sixty-eight years old. Retired from his public school principal's job three years ago. He taught at and was principal of Annette Street, Lord Dufferin, Kew Beach and Hester How Public Schools. His last job was principal at Park School—"

"I used to go there," the inspector interrupted. He told the young officer that Park and Dufferin schools, before they prefaced Dufferin with the word "Lord," were the original Cabbagetown schools of his childhood, and that Shuter Street in his day had been named Sydenham.

The officer went on, "Mr. Robinson told me he'd suspected for a long time that Zelda Greenless was either a prostitute or a drug dealer. He said he'd heard funny things coming through the ceiling of his apartment, which is right under this one—"

"What kind of funny things?"

"Dancing, bumps as if people had fallen on the floor, crazy laughing as he called it, and sometimes too-loud rock music. About a month ago there'd been a constant buzzing, like people all talking at once or humming. To him, he said, it sounded like ten Allen Ginsbergs mumbling "om." Whoever Allen Ginsberg is."

"I know who he is," McDumont said.

"Robinson said the woman was in a good position to

get drugs, because she worked in a doctor's office down at One, Medical Place."

"Where's that?"

"Down on Wynford Drive, first north of Eglinton running east."

"Okay. Did he know what doctor she worked for?"

"Yes." He read from his notes: "Dr. Morris Franczic, a urologist. He's Robinson's doctor. Robinson kept me an extra five minutes talking about his prostate trouble."

McDumont laughed. "Him too?" Sobering up he said, "Go on."

"Robinson said he'd heard a lot of retching from the bathroom up here. It wasn't the first time though. He'd heard it before, except it didn't go on all day practically."

"Yesterday?"

"Yes."

"Did he hear anything last night?"

"He didn't come in until late. He goes to the bingo games in the recreational center across the road. He didn't hear anything more from up here after he arrived home."

The inspector copied down the name of the urologist and his address. "Okay, Miller, you've done a good job, and I'll mention it to Inspector Willis when I go over to the station. Is your car still outside?"

"No. When I phoned in to Division from one of the downstairs apartments, Sergeant Granby, the desk sergeant, told me he was sending over another man to take over the car."

"Can you get over to the station without it?"

"Sure, Inspector. It's just across the shopping plaza. No problem."

"Okay, Miller, you can report in. Tell Inspector Willis I've got some more of my own men coming up here, and I thank him and the men of his division for their cooperation."

"Will do, Inspector."

The officer stood up, returned his notebook to his shirt pocket, and let himself out of the apartment.

McDumont also stood up and stared out of the living room window at the cars entering and leaving the large parking space in front of the supermarket in the plaza across the road. Most of them were small cars, Volkswagens, ancient Vauxhalls, new Pintos, Firebirds and Fiats, with a few secondhand bigger cars. The "second" cars of the Don Mills lower middle class, bought for two-car status and to take care of wifely errands while the young or no-longer-young husbands drove the larger, newer family car downtown to work.

He saw Miller cross Don Mills Road at a pedestrian crossing, cross the parking lot to the vicinity of the government liquor store and disappear into the shopping center. After the police officer had gone he watched the young housewives getting in and out of their cars, many of them accompanied by small children. Some of the women wore dresses, but most were wearing slacks, Levis or hot pants. The occasional one still wore her hair in curlers or in an uncombed bird's nest. They looked no different to the inspector than the female pedestrian shoppers on Cabbagetown's Parliament Street would have, had he been viewing them at this moment. Without realizing it the country had become egalitarian and socialistic, while still trying to preserve the pretence of class and socioeconomic differences in life styles. After a working lifetime of watching people from the point of view of a policeman, McDumont was no longer fooled by their outward trappings, which were only a credit card or a time payment removed, one from the other.

He threw himself into one of the armchairs and collected his thoughts about the case up to now. First, Zelda Greenless had been murdered, but not only by being stabbed in the back. There was the possibility that she hadn't been murdered at all of course; but until he received confirmation one way or the other from Dr. Mainguy or the forensic laboratory he was going to look upon it as murder and not accidental or natural death by involuntary inspiration of foreign matter into the esophagus, or other causes following a lengthy alcoholic binge.

All right, if the Greenless woman had been murdered —and it hadn't been by a knife wound as both he and old Mainguy knew—how had it been carried out? Not by manual strangulation, suffocation, carbon monoxide poisoning, beating, drowning—then what? A poison of some sort, maybe an overdose of a narcotic (accidental or predetermined), barbiturate poisoning (almost always suicidal or accidental), or what? McDumont arbitrarily ruled out accidental food poisoning such as botulism, basing his belief on the lack of food remains in the apartment. He had been unable to find any barbiturates such as Seconal, Nembutal or Amytal, or any container that had held them.

All right, the woman had been poisoned, by herself or by somebody else; but by what poison? That would have to wait for the results of the post-mortem and the analysis of stomach contents and other medical analyses. Poison was a female murder weapon, but not always.

Was the murderer the owner of the second set of lipstick stains on the tumblers taken away by the coroner? Possibly. Maybe. If so, had the female murderer then ignored the evidence of her own presence with the dead woman before her death, leaving behind the visual evidence of her being there in the print of her lips on the drinking glass? Not likely.

Had a female murderer, after poisoning the woman she was drinking with, then have been capable of carrying Zelda Greenless's body along the apartment hallway and placing it in the garbage disposal closet? Not unless she was an amazon. And what would be her reason anyway? Because she looked upon the dead woman as garbage, and wanted to prove it symbolically? No. Too risky; theatrical to the point of vaudeville.

All right. Two women had been drinking together. Then one had left. Zelda Greenless had been left alone. Somebody had entered the apartment and had poisoned her by implanting or pouring a poison into her drink. Then he—it had to be a he—had stabbed her corpse in the back with a knife, carried it down the hall to the garbage chute and propped it in a corner. Why?

Was it a lover who had discovered that Zelda was unfaithful to him? Did he discover her in a lesbian situation with her female drinking companion, or more likely find out about it after her female companion had left? Was the poisoning deliberate and the stabbing an afterthought? Was the poison in the apartment when the stabber arrived? Could be, but not likely, unless the stabber removed the bottle or container when he left. Was the knife in the apartment? Did it belong to Zelda Greenless, or was it brought with him—or her—by the stabber? The latter was unlikely because of possible identification through the knife, but not impossible; sometimes a murderer deliberately used a weapon that would incriminate him for reasons as far apart as a death wish and bravado.

But that was enough pre-evidential conjecture, McDumont thought, remembering the phrase from a long-ago course at the FBI Academy. Right now he had to find out *who* Zelda Greenless was, *who* her possible friends and enemies were, *what* the neighbors had heard or seen relating to apartment 602 over the past few days and especially the night before, *what* had been the actual means of her death, and *who*, if it was a second person, had bothered to stab her dead body and sit it in the hallway closet.

He also had to match a thumbprint taken from the flushing handle of the toilet, and match its being there with the fact that so many possible prints, from the medicine cabinet, from the door and doorknobs, and other places around the flat, had been wiped clean.

First the *who* of Zelda Greenless.

Chapter 5

The occupant of apartment 602 had been a clean, neat woman, despite her proclivity for, or eccentricity in, far-out furniture. There were outlines of stains on the linoleum tile of the kitchen floor, and a few separate light brown stains around the base of the toilet bowl—all of which might have been caused by cleaned-up vomit. The drawers and cupboards throughout the apartment were clean and their contents neatly arranged, and the floor rugs were just slightly soiled, as if from just one monumental drinking bout.

Detective Inspector McDumont read the book titles on the shelves of the hutch in the dining room. There were several *Reader's Digest* Condensed Books, several cookbooks, one of which was *The Alice B. Toklas Cookbook*, some obviously secondhand bound copies of *National Geographic*, bought, he supposed, for decorative purposes and to fill out the upper shelf, four Book-of-the-Month Club best-sellers of a few years before, *The Female Eunuch* in hard covers, and some pseudo-medical paperbacks on sex, male-female relations, and Women's Lib. Along the bottom shelf were J. R. R. Tolkien's *The Lord of the Rings*, *Outlines of Scientology*, *The Catcher in the Rye*, Tom Wolfe's *The Electric Kool-Aid Acid Test*, *The Fruits of Philosophy* by Annie Besant, and *Isis Unveiled* by Madame Blavatsky.

What did Zelda Greenless's choice of reading prove? McDumont returned to the chair in the living room more puzzled than ever about the dead woman. He knew that some of the books, Tolkien's and Tom Wolfe's for instance, as well as *The Catcher in the Rye*, were those usually found on the bookshelves of a much younger reader. The names Annie Besant and Madame Blavatsky surfaced in his memory from somewhere, but he couldn't remember what religious group or philosophy they had written about. Scientology was a comparatively new movement started by somebody— what the hell was his name? Hubbard, that was it, Hubbard. They'd once had a downtown office on Yonge Street south of Bloor, maybe still had. There'd been a lot of screwballs who'd joined the movement, and it seemed to him some of them had sued Hubbard for large donations they'd made to it. The joiners were the same kind of nitwits who had rushed to join an alleged political movement called Technocracy after the war. He remembered investigating a couple of their meetings when he'd been a rookie detective in the headquartters pool. Jesus, you could start a voluntary emasculation society and have idiots rush to join it!

The two new probationary homicide detectives arrived, and the inspector had to ask them their names. They gave them as Tom Smith and Clarence Roundy, the latter a black Jamaican. When they were sent to his squad he'd been impressed by some plainclothes work the black detective had done in Yorkville Village and around the downtown Spadina Avenue area, among his fellow blacks. When he interviewed him he'd discovered that Roundy had been a detective sergeant in Kingston, Jamaica.

He gave Roundy the vial holding the rug samples, and told him to take the Ford D-car back to headquarters, remove the tagged evidence from the crime kit and give it to Eric Manders to send to the crime lab, then come back to Don Mills. He sent Smith down to the car with Roundy, with instructions to bring back the knife used in the stabbing.

When they'd gone he phoned the morgue and spoke to Dr. Mainguy.

"Walter McDumont, Ed. When are you going to perform the autopsy?"

"This evening. I've got to grab some sleep first."

"It's a poisoning, isn't it?"

The old doctor laughed. "How in hell did you know?"

"I didn't think the stabbing killed her. By the lack of blood I'd say she was stabbed after she was dead."

"You're smartening up in your old age, Walter. I expect to find that the point of the dagger went into the pleura and collapsed a few lobes of the left lung, but that's about all. I don't think there'll be any pleurorrhea either, not much anyway."

"Speak English, Ed."

"There wouldn't—won't be much effusion of blood into the pleural cavity—that is, between the membranes that enfold the lungs."

"Have you any idea what she was poisoned with?"

"No, and I won't have until the toxicologist at the Forensic Science Centre does his tests on the contents of the viscera I'll ship to him. That means the lady's guts."

"I know what it means, you vulgar old abortionist."

"Abortions aren't vulgar any more, Walter, if they ever were."

"Listen, Ed, let's keep the poisoning out of it for a while, eh? I'm not even mentioning it to my men. I want the murderer to go on the assumption the police think she died of the stab wound. We'll be ostensibly looking for the stabber."

"Okay. I'll do what I can."

"Would the person who poisoned the woman also stab her?"

"Maybe, Walter, if he—or she—hated Zelda that much."

"Do *you* think it was the same person?"

"I'm inclined to doubt it, Walter."

McDumont heard the apartment door open, and Detective Smith entered the living room, carrying the ornamental dagger with the police tag fastened around the handle.

The inspector turned back to the phone. "Thanks, Ed. I can't talk any more right now."

"You'll get my autopsy report in the morning, Walter, and, I hope, the report from the Forensic Lab sometime tomorrow."

"Thanks, Ed."

McDumont hung up the phone, and turned the knife

over in his hands. It was a mock-oriental thing with an intricately stamped plastic handle colored to imitate ebony or mahogany. The handle was four inches long and its half-inch-wide blade six inches long. The inspector had the feeling as he gazed at it that the blade had been shortened considerably, for the haft and blade were completely out of proportion to each other. Both sides of the blade had been recently honed to a razor sharpness, and the end of the blade honed to a long point. He tested the bending properties of the steel and found it difficult to bend at all.

If Zelda Greenless had been first poisoned, as both he and the coroner were almost sure she was, why had she later been stabbed and placed in the garbage closet? Wanting more time to think things out he said to Detective Smith, a balding man who looked like a fattened former 400-meter man, "Tom, I want you to look through the dresser and highboy in the bedroom, also the clothes closet, and bring out here any box or boxes containing letters, private papers, photos, photograph albums, anything at all of that kind of thing. If you find any hidden pills, medicine bottles, or stashes of hash or pot, bring them out too."

When the detective had gone McDumont began asking himself the same questions he'd been asking himself ever since he arrived on the case. Why would her killer, or somebody else, stab the Greenless woman after she was dead? Was the stabbing a psycho-symbolic gesture by her killer, as the placing of the body in the garbage disposal closet seemed to be? Why would either her poisoner or her stabber—considering they might be two different people—have carried a corpse along the length of an apartment house hallway during an evening or in the early hours of the morning when they might have been so easily discovered? He looked at a page in his notebook. Cecil Gilcrest in No. 608 had thrown a noisy party the evening before, according to Mrs. Dryburg across the hall from him. What time had it broken up, and who was there? Why in the sweet name of Jesus would a killer take such chances as being caught with the body after a murder when the obvious thing would have been to leave it in the apartment? And *how* had he—the inspector was almost certain by now that the murderer was a male, even if the murder weapon was female—carried the body along the hall? Supposing rigor mortis had already set in? How would *he* have transported the body to the garbage closet if *he'd* been the murderer? Carry it in front of him, over his shoulder? The truth suddenly hit him; he'd have wheeled it along the hall on a handcart or something, maybe covered with a blanket! He picked up the phone book to ask Zutach if there was such a thing in the apartment house when the phone rang.

It was Eric Manders asking him what he should tell the newspapermen, who were clamoring for information; some of them threatening to go out to the apartment house.

"Tell them, Eric, that first off any son of a bitch who comes out here before my investigation is finished will be on my permanent hate list, and will be unwelcome at any homicide in the future. Then tell them that the body of a woman—the nude body of a woman—identified as Zelda Greenless of 1049 Don Mills Road, Don Mills, was discovered early this morning in her apartment building by another tenant. No, never mind his name yet. Mrs. Greenless, apparently in her late thirties or early forties, had been stabbed in the back with an imitation oriental dagger. The police are carrying out a thorough investigation at this time. No, up to now no photographs are available; we haven't found any. Details and photographs will be released to the press as soon as they're available. Oh yes, Eric, did you get the name of the Shop-Easy card owner or recipient? Yeah, just a minute while I write it down. Go on. Wilfrid McMulley. Yeah, spelt W-I-L-F-R-I-D, yeah, M-small C-M-U-L-L-E-Y. Apartment 604, 1049 Don Mills Road. The serial number on the card is 513 dash 088 dash 301 dash B. Yep, go on. Who sent it to him and when? Shop-Easy Incorporated, yes, and they have a tie-in with some Canadian chartered banks, yes. Are they countrywide? From Ontario to the West Coast, yes. And they mailed it to McMulley on June tenth? Okay, Eric, anything else? Right. Hold the fort, Eric; I won't be back today. Okay."

The inspector paused at the bedroom door and told

Detective Smith that he was going downstairs for a minute. He'd lock the door after him. He noticed that the detective had already made a small pile of things from the closet on the top of the bed.

On the main floor he knocked on the door of No. 110, and the same little woman who had let him into the house earlier answered the door.

"Mrs. Zutach?"

She smiled and nodded.

"Is your husband in?"

She shook her head and pointed to the rear exit door, which was only a few feet away from the doorway to the Zutach apartment. "Anton outside," she said, smiling and showing a stainless steel eyetooth.

"Okay, thank you," said the inspector, already striding in the direction of the door with the red Exit light above it. He hurried down the few steps to an outside door at the foot of the building's rear stairs and found himself in the parking lot. Anton Zutach was tramping down the garbage in a large metal container with wheels which had the words NORTOWN SANITARY ENGINEERING stencelled on its side. McDumont stood for a minute on the outside steps and watched the little building superintendent frantically stamping down the garbage. To the inspector it looked as if he was trying to hide or bury something. He strolled over and stood beside the garbage cart.

When Zutach noticed him standing there he visibly recoiled against the side of the container, staring in frightened astonishment at the big policeman.

"Trying to hide something, Anton?" the inspector asked.

"No, no try hide noddings. Pack garbage for pickup eh?"

"I thought you weren't getting this picked up until tomorrow?" the inspector asked, walking to the side of the heavy steel wagon and staring into it. The tramped-down contents of the container were made up of everything from nonreturnable milk jugs to flattened cardboard cartons all mixed in an indescribable mess with vegetable parings, egg shells, thrown-out food scraps, newspapers and magazines, and in one corner something that looked like the edge of an old woollen blanket that was still uncovered.

"What's that?" the inspector asked, pointing to the piece of blanket.

The superintendent shrugged. "Noddings. Jus' old junk, eh? Sometink tenant t'row down chute, eh?"

"Pull it up and let's have a look at it." The inspector noticed now that the man had changed his shoes for a pair of knee-length rubber boots into which his pants had been tucked.

"What pull, inspector?"

"Pull up that blanket and let's have a look at it. That's what you were trying to hide, wasn't it?"

The little man almost screamed with nervousness. "Is noddings."

"Pull it up!" McDumont circled the container until he stood within reach of Zutach's legs. "Come on, goddam it, pull it up!"

Slowly and reluctantly, fighting his fear, Zutach began scraping the garbage back with his foot from around the corner of the blanket.

"Come on! Grab the goddam thing with your hands and pull it out!"

The superintendent's obvious fear of the inspector overcame his reluctance and with much straining he took hold of the corner of the blanket and pulled. Slowly, as the covering of garbage fell away, more and more of a yellow woollen blanket came into view. Near the middle of it was a small slit surrounded by a brown uneven stain that McDumont knew was blood. When the whole blanket, with its stamped-in fruit and vegetable peelings, was free of its former covering the little apartment-house janitor held it up by its sides so that the top quarter of it folded over and covered the stain.

"Shake all that crap off it, Zutach, and bring it down here," the inspector ordered, and the little man brushed most of the stuck-on garbage off with his hands. Then he threw the blanket over the side of the cart to the pavement of the parking lot and climbed down himself.

McDumont nodded towards the blanket, which was

still in good condition except for the one small slit and its surrounding bloodstain. "Pick it up and let's take it up to Apartment six-o-two," said the inspector. The superintendent rolled the yellow blanket into a ball and, followed closely by the big policeman, entered the apartment house.

Detective Smith opened the door to McDumont's knock, and the inspector followed Zutach into the living room.

"Open that thing up and lay it on the floor," the inspector said, and Zutach, visibly trembling, spread the yellow blanket on the red broadloom. The detective moved the cocktail table a couple of feet to make room for the blanket to be spread to its full length and width.

"What do you think that stain is, Zutach?" asked the inspector.

The superintendent, now beyond speech, shook his head.

"What do *you* think it is, Tom?" McDumont asked the detective.

"Blood."

"Right. And the slit in the middle of the stain?"

Smith walked onto the blanket and stared closely at the narrow slit. "I'd say it was the entry point for a sharp instrument that caused the bloodstain."

"A knife say?"

"Probably."

"Would you say the person who lost the blood on the blanket was alive or dead when stabbed?"

The detective gave the inspector a surprised glance. "I wouldn't know that, Inspector."

"I can't say for sure, but I think it's venous blood," the inspector said. "We'll know more about it after it's been examined down at the Forensic Lab." He turned suddenly on the balls of his feet and asked the trembling little man who was staring in frightened fascination at the bloodstain, "Is this your blanket, Zutach?"

The superintendent stepped back into the doorway and without raising his eyes screamed, "No! I not own dat! No, no, no!"

"You ever see it before?"

"Never!" He crossed himself in the Eastern Orthodox manner. "No, inspector, I swear to you dis, I never seen it before, on the body of my dead mudder!"

There was a knock on the door, and the inspector angrily pushed himself past the superintendent and opened the door. Bill Zotas was standing in the hallway, holding up a pair of apartment keys. The inspector slammed the apartment door behind him and led the young detective along the corridor to the rear stairwell. In a low voice he filled Zotas in on what had been happening during his absence at the shopping plaza, especially about his finding the incriminating blanket and Zutach's attempts to bury it deep in the trash cart.

"Are you going to run Zutach in?"

"No, not yet anyway. There's a hell of a lot more we've got to learn about this thing before we snap any suspects at all. That little son of a bitch is scared out of his wits about something, and I'm not sure it's necessarily being charged with murder. Right now I haven't enough to hold him on a smoke pollution warrant anyway. From now on you're no longer Bill Zotas but Bill Jones. Got it?"

"Sure, Inspector, but—"

"I could send our scared little friend Anton down to Jarvis Street and let the boys give him an interrogation session, but I don't want to do that. Instead I'm going to send him back to his own apartment with you as a sit-in watchdog. You're a Welshman or Englishman named Jones, Bill Jones. You don't understand a word that the Zutachs might say to one another, but you listen. This is your chance to become an amateur actor. Whatever language they speak in you'll probably be able to catch the drift of it, but at the same time you don't let them suspect you understand a word, got it?"

The detective nodded.

"Phone your wife, say 'This is Bill,' or whatever you say at times like these, and tell her you won't be home maybe until late tonight or maybe not until tomorrow morning. This'll convince the Zutachs that we're going to keep them under close surveillance. Now I'll have somebody spell you off for meals, tell your wife on your one phone call home that you can't let her call *you*, understand?"

59

Zotas nodded.

"If you have to call me or anybody else do it through our own office, as Detective Bill Jones. I'll fill in Eric Manders that Detective Bill Jones is actually Detective Bill Zotas."

"Right, Inspector."

"Just keep your ears open, and if you want to jot down a name or anything like that go and do it in the john, but don't take too many notes or pisses or both or Anton and Xenia will wise up. Have you enough cigarettes for the afternoon?"

"I've got this," Bill answered, pulling a pipe out of his pocket.

"Good. Lots of tobacco?"

"Enough."

"All right. I'll go back and scare the living Jesus out of that poor little Zutach by telling him we've decided to snap him on a suspected murder charge—he's already swearing his innocence on the body of his dead mother—then you come to the door—incidentally give me the pair of apartment keys." Zotas handed them to the inspector. "You come to the door, let's say in five minutes, and I'll have a change of heart and tell Zutach I'm gonna let him stay at home for now but Detective Jones is going to stay with him until further notice."

"Okay."

"In the meantime sit out here out of sight till it's time to come down to six-o-two."

"Right, Inspector."

McDumont swung on his heel and went back into the hallway.

Back in Zelda Greenless's apartment McDumont began putting pressure on the superintendent to tell him why he was trying to hide the blanket, and threatening him with a "suspected murder" charge. "Your new citizenship won't do you much good sitting down in your cell in K.P., Kingston Penitentiary, Zutach. Even if it isn't your blanket it belongs to somebody you're trying to protect, maybe for money, eh?"

"No, inspector, I swear—"

"I'll do all the goddam swearing around here, and there's nothing makes me swear as much as a little son of a bitch like you who won't help us in an investigation, understand? What's more I think you and Zelda Greenless had something going on between you. Maybe Xenia could tell us more about that; there's no better detective in the world than a little wife who's convinced her husband's screwing around with a younger, prettier woman. And maybe Judge—who was it, Anderson you said?—could take away your citizenship just as easy as he gave it to you. Did you know that?"

"I know citizenship act pretty good."

"Then you'll be able to read it over and over down in the Don Jail while you're waiting to be deported back to—"

"Jugoslavia."

"You were probably a Nazi informer or a member of, what did you call yourselves, the *Chetniks*? Maybe Tito's secret police would like to get their hands on you, then you'll wish you were back here stompin' garbage, eh?"

"I 'ad noddings to do wit' Zelda Greenless's deat'. I swear—"

"I've told you, Zutach, I'll do all the bloody swearing around here."

There was a knock at the door and McDumont hurried to answer it. He came back to the living room followed by Bill Zotas. "You made it pretty fast, Bill," he said to Zotas. Then turning to the superintendent he said, "You met Bill Jones here this morning. He's going to take you down to police headquarters for questioning. And remember it's a hell of a lot easier to stay out of police buildings than to get out once we get you in." Turning to Detective Zotas again he said, "Cuff him with his hands behind his back and sit him next to you in the front seat."

Zutach panicked as he saw Zotas unhook his handcuffs from the back of his belt. "Inspector, please, let me make phone call to Xenia!"

"You'll be allowed one phone call from headquarters. We don't want any brouhahas around here when we're taking you out. Anyway your wife and son will be

61

taken care of. Maybe the apartment owners will hire a nice strong young man for your job. By the way, who owns this high-priced tenement anyway?"

"Martin-Rubins Development on Bloor Street West. Call Jerry Martin an' ask him about me; he'll tell you everyt'ings."

McDumont finished writing down the name of the apartment owners in his notebook. "You can call anybody you want, *once*, from headquarters. Maybe this Mr. Martin will get you a lawyer or furnish bail, if it's allowed. Cuff him, Jonesy."

The little man fell to his knees and grabbed McDumont around the knees. "Please don't do dis to me, Inspector. I know noddings about no murder."

"You can tell that to the judge at your arraignment. Or later to the Jugoslav secret police."

The little man's voice cracked as he said, "How could I be a traitor in war when I am only little boy then!" There were tears running down his cheeks as he looked up at the inspector, hanging on to McDumont's knees as if his life depended on not letting go. "In war wit' Germans my fadder fight two years in mountings wit' Communist partisans, in Bosnia."

Detective Smith walked back into the bedroom.

McDumont, as if relenting, said, "Listen, Anton, I'm going to give you a chance to help us." The grip around his knees slackened. "Get up." Zutach, afraid that even a slight show of disobedience might make the inspector change his mind again, clambered quickly to his feet. "For now, I'm going to let you stay here at home with your wife and son, understand?" Zutach reached for McDumont's hand, but the inspector pulled it away. "I want you to do your regular work around the place, but for the next day or two to try and stay in your apartment." The superintendent wiped his eyes on his shirt cuff and smiled and nodded. "Detective Bill Jones here will stay with you to keep an eye on you." Zutach smiled at the young detective, nodding eagerly. McDumont turned to Bill Zotas and said, "Bill, you keep your eye on this man until you're relieved. Except for a real emergency he's not to leave his apartment."

"Right, Inspector," Zotas said, hanging his handcuffs on the back of his belt again.

"You know what I just told Detective Jones?" McDumont asked the building superintendent.

"Sure, Inspector, I unnerstan'."

"All right, you two, go downstairs and wait things out until we finally figure out what we're going to do." He turned his back on them and looked out the window as they left the room. When he heard the hall doorway shut behind them he went into the bedroom where Tom Smith was busy in the clothes closet. Piled together on the bed were a photograph album, several letters in slit-open envelopes, a check book issued by the Don Mills branch of the Royal Bank of Canada, some cosmetic advertising brochures, a year's warranty on a TV picture tube from a TV-radio repair shop in Scarborough, a small cheaply framed photograph of a much younger Zelda Greenless, a pad of physician's prescription forms, and a page torn from a Toronto hippie publication, *Guerilla*. Inspector McDumont noted the doctor's name and address from the prescription blanks: Dr. Morris Franczic, Urologist, One Medical Place, Wynford Drive, Don Mills. The page from the semi-underground paper contained a list of free clinics which treated bad drug trips and venereal diseases.

Detective Smith backed out of the walk-in closet. "You know something, Inspector, you kept calling Bill Zotas "Jones" all the time."

"You should be a detective," McDumont answered dryly.

Squelched, Detective Smith said, "Look at this, Inspector." He was carrying a plain cardboard box half filled with condoms, each of which was individually wrapped as was the one picked off the floor by Bill Zotas earlier.

McDumont took the box and ruffled through its contents. "My God, there's enough safes here to outfit an infantry platoon on wartime leave in a Lancashire mill town. Our Mrs. Greenless mustn't have heard of The Pill."

63

"There seems to be about four dozen left, which means another four dozen have been used."

"One thing sure, our Zelda wasn't frustrated for tail," McDumont said. "Is there anything else in there?"

"I found the box of rubbers on the closet shelf," Smith answered. "It's filled with pieces of luggage and a couple of wig cases, Inspector. I'll look through them."

"Okay, Tom," the inspector said, ashamed now of the sarcasm he'd used to Smith when the other had brought up the change in Bill Zotas's name; hell anybody would have been nonplussed. He was glad that Smith had had the sense to keep it to himself at the time. He watched as Smith brought out the pieces of luggage and searched them each carefully before closing them again. The detective also removed a blonde and a red wig from the wig boxes, shaking them and combing through the hair with his fingers.

Smith began carrying the luggage back into the closet when suddenly he shouted, "Here's something!" and backed into the bedroom carrying a twelve-by-three-by three-inch metal box of the type some people use to keep valuable papers in. He handed it to the inspector, who found it was flimsily secured with a cheap spring lock.

"These things are sometimes a protection against fire but in a good blaze they melt," McDumont said. "They're not worth a pinch of coon shit against burglars, but you'd be surprised how many idiots think they are. Any kid could open this with the end of a metal coat hanger. This is the quickest way though." He placed the box on its side on the dresser and struck it sharply with the edge of his fist near the lock. The lid flew open, spilling out its contents.

"Make a list of everything as I read them to you," he said to the detective.

"Right." Smith sat down on the edge of the oversize bed and waited, pen poised above his notebook.

"Bank savings deposit book, Royal Bank, Don Mills Branch, number 2 dash 7661, balance on June 11, 1974, $287.37. Last deposit, $50.00, on June 4, 1974.

64

Last withdrawal, $20.00, June 7, 1974. Got it?"

"Yes."

"Here's another. Bank book, nonchecking account, Coxwell and O'Connor Branch, Royal Bank, number 626 dash 1175, balance $7,111 and no cents, dated April 8, 1974. Only deposit made same date, that's the seven grand and change. No other deposits and no withdrawals."

"Okay, Inspector."

"Two birth certificates, first one issued to Grace and Charles Stanton in the name of Zelda Grace Stanton, born August 6, 1936, in Crow Lake, Ontario. That must be the dead woman's, making her, let's see, just short of thirty-eight years old."

"Right."

"Second birth certificate, issued to Zelda Grace Stanton and Lawrence Charles Musgrove—"

"How do you spell that last name, Inspector?"

"*M-u-s-g-r-o-v-e.*"

"Okay."

The baby's name is Lawrence Charles Musgrove Stanton, born February 15, 1950, Toronto, Ontario."

"That's all?"

"Yes. Here's a death certificate, a cemetery plot receipt for the Crow Lake Protestant Cemetery, undertaker's receipt, and a receipt from the Hospital for Sick Children, Toronto, all stapled together. The death certificate, for Lawrence Charles Musgrove Stanton, made out and signed by Dr. Arthur Gueller, September—"

"How do you spell the doctor's name, Inspector?"

"*G-u-e-l-l-e-r.*"

"Got it."

"—September 2, 1950. Cause of death pneumonia and pulmonary stenosis. The undertaker's, cemetery and hospital receipts all have September 1950 dates."

The detective looked up.

"What do these things add up to, to you, Tom?"

"Well," began the detective, staring at his notes, "I'd say that the slain woman (McDumont smirked at the other's use of "slain") was born in Crow Lake, Ontario in 1936, and had a baby born in 1950—"

"When she was only fourteen years old."

"Yes."

"Go on."

"The baby died in September of the same year, after living for only—" he counted on his fingers, "—six and a half months."

"Was the mother married?"

"The baby was registered in her maiden name."

"Right, with the father's name also, and the baby named after him. Today's birth certificates don't show legitimacy or illegitimacy, thank God for the sake of the kids, but in those dark ages they still did. Do you think Musgrove was the father's name?"

"It could be, but it might be her—the mother's mother's maiden name."

"You mean the baby's maternal grandmother's maiden name?"

"Yes, Miss Stanton's mother's."

"It could be I guess, but I'm inclined to doubt that."

The inspector shuffled through several guarantees, for a steam iron, stereo set, set of electric hair curlers, some old rent receipts for an apartment on Gamble Avenue. "Mrs. Greenless used to live down on Gamble Avenue, that explains the bank account at Coxwell and O'Connor. Take this address down."

"Ready."

"Apartment 507, 126 Gamble Avenue."

"Right."

The inspector pulled a folded sheet of heavily embossed paper from the diminishing pile of documents and opened it up. "Take this down, Tom."

"Okay."

"Wedding certificate, dated May 23, 1968, marriage of Zelda Grace Stanton to Edgar Stewart Greenless, signed by the Reverend Paul Fannon of St. Barnabas-on-the-Cross Anglican Church, and witnessed by George—somebody, I can't make out the signature, and Eleanor Jacton, That's the woman in the next apartment!"

Chapter 6

Inspector McDumont read out the descriptions of the other documents that had been stored in the small steel box: the apartment lease, automobile purchase order, car insurance certificate, and the final date of the receipt from the Gamble Avenue apartment house. After Detective Smith had carefully listed them all in his notebook the inspector placed all the documents back in the box, locked it again with the heavy pressure of the palm of his hand, and placed it under his arm. He glanced at his watch and said, "Roundy should be back here any minute. He and I'll go down to Wynford Drive and see Zelda's boss, and maybe on to the Gamble Avenue apartment house. You stay here, Tom, and take any phone calls. Tell the caller you're the superintendent or something. Try to get their name and phone number. By this time the noon edition of the *Star*'ll be out, and plenty of people will know about the stabbing." Without being obvious about it he constantly referred to the murder as a stabbing, just to plant in everyone's mind, including the minds of his own men, that the knife wound had been the cause of the murder.

"Okay, Inspector," Smith said.

"Go and roll up that yellow blanket in the living room so that the knife hole and the small bloodstain don't show."

Alone in the bedroom the inspector began leafing through the photograph album, seeing pictures of Zelda Greenless as a child, a snapshot of her as a very young girl holding her baby in her arms, photos of people he took to be her parents or other relatives; and farther back in the book studio photos and snapshots of Zelda, other young women and men, and still farther back a better class of snapshot, probably shot with a 35 mm camera in her own apartment—according to the furniture background—of several teen-aged boys and very young men. Occasionally he removed a photo or snapshot from its corner tabs, and was pleased to see that Mrs. Greenless's sense of orderliness was not confined to her housekeeping; the back of each picture bore the name of the subject and the date the picture was taken.

Detective Smith came to the bedroom door just as there was a knock on the hall door, and at a nod from McDumont went to answer it. He came back followed by Detective Roundy.

The inspector looked up. "Did you deliver all the stuff to Sergeant of Detectives Manders?"

"Yes, Inspector."

"What do your friends call you, Clarence, Clare or what?"

"They call me anything they want to, Inspector. That is my friends do. Others have called me even more." His black face split into a wide white-toothed grin.

The inspector grinned up at him. "It was a legitimate question, Roundy. I don't know you new men well enough to have gotten onto a first name basis yet that's all. Until today I didn't know Smith's first name was Tom."

Still grinning Roundy said, "Well, Inspector, my wife still calls me Clarence, as do my parents back in Jamaica. The boys in the detective pool, some of them at least, have shortened it to Clary."

"Which do you prefer?"

"I think I prefer Clary on the job."

"Okay then, Clary, we're gonna go down south of here to a block of doctors' offices where the dead woman worked, and see her boss. Then we'll probably drop down to an apartment house on Gamble Avenue— I know where it is—and talk to the superintendent there." He looked at Detective Smith to include him in what he was about to say. "Almost before we really start looking for the murderer we have to find out who the murdered person is. Up to now I've got only a few unconnected ideas. I'm telling you two, though you

68

may know these things already, some things it's necessary to know in the Homicide Squad. That's the end of your schooling for now."

Both detectives smiled and nodded.

"Tom, you carry on as I told you to. Detective Sergeant Alvin Prust and his partner Larry Helmont are on the four-to-midnight swing this week, and Eric Manders is sending them up here as soon as they report in. Tell Prust to send Helmont down to the superintendent's apartment as soon as they arrive, to spell off Bill Zotas. Tell him too that Zotas's name has been changed for the time being to Jones, and that it's very important that he remain Jones for now. Okay?"

"Okay, Inspector."

"I want Bill Zotas to call 33 Division for a squad car to take him down to police headquarters, where I'll see him as soon as Clary and I are finished up in this part of town. Okay?"

Smith nodded.

The inspector picked up the photograph album, the steel document box and the cardboard box of condoms and walked to the door. "Get me that yellow blanket too," he said to Smith.

With the stuff piled in his arms McDumont, along with Roundy, headed for the elevator. "Goddamit!" the inspector swore while they waited for the elevator to come up. "I forgot to give Smith a key to the apartment." He handed over the boxes, album and blanket to Roundy, and told him to put them in the D-car on the floor behind the front seat. "Then lock the car, and go to apartment one-ten. Got it?"

"Yes," Roundy said, holding the elevator open with a foot.

"Remember that Zotas is Jones, but just call him Bill."

The black detective nodded.

Then I want you to ask the superintendent where his two-wheeled utility cart is. If he says there is none in the apartment house he's lying. When he tells you where it's kept or where it is at this moment go get it and bring it out to the car."

"Will do, Inspector."

The detective let himself into the elevator as the inspector returned to apartment 602. There he had no difficulty opening the door with one of the keys he'd had made, entering to find himself facing a poised Detective Smith, who was standing against the wall next to the door ready to grab whoever it was who'd unlocked it.

"Here, Tom," McDumont said, handing him the key. While he was at it he tried the other key, which opened and locked the door as easily as the first one. "When Sergeant Prust comes up here give him the key, and tell him to stay in the apartment until I call him, will you?"

"Sure, Inspector."

"There's a half-jar of instant coffee in one of the kitchen cupboards and a can of Carnation in the fridge. I forget where the sugar is, but there's a bowl of it somewhere. Make yourself a coffee if you want. Nobody in this apartment's gonna need it any more."

"Okay, Inspector."

McDumont turned and hurried to the back stairs instead of the elevators, and down them to the parking lot. He saw that Roundy had placed the things on the car floor behind the front seat, and tested every door to see that all were locked. Then he walked down the driveway almost to the sidewalk and stared across the busy street, its northbound lanes beginning to fill up with late afternoon traffic.

The Don Mills Road, and everything that bordered on it or surrounded it, had been metamorphosed out of all recognition since the day in 1926 or '27 when he as a tall skinny kid in a gym suit, thirteen years old, had run along there in the high school's annual cross-country race. He remembered the exhaustion he'd felt for the first couple of miles, up through the empty fields between Danforth Avenue and O'Connor Drive, then dipping down through the Don Valley ravine and across the small concrete bridge that crossed the river. North of the valley had been a series of farms, among them a huge dairy farm with "Donalda Farms" lettered on one of its beautifully built outbuildings, and large pastures filled with knee-high clover and alfalfa that almost hid the herds of Guernsey dairy cows.

He'd forgotten now where Donalda Farms had been, whether it was this far north on the road, or south where the high-rise and town-house development called Flemingdon Park now stood. And he'd also forgotten where a small group of race officials, a teacher and some students, had directed the runners west through a series of pastures to what must have been the steep ravine they now called Wilket Creek Park. Maybe his memory was playing him tricks, and they'd turned east somewhere up here and followed a branch of the Don River down to and under the old CPR trestle bridge south of what was now the Eglinton extension. Anyhow he remembered running under the trestle bridge, where he passed four or five exhausted runners, and across an empty field where the old airfield had been located, passing more runners on the way.

His memories triggered the old forgotten memory banks inside his now-graying head, and he suddenly remembered passing the race's favorite, sitting on the curb on Laird Drive, when it was one of the town of Leaside's main industrial streets. He smiled to himself at the memory, at the smart-ass richer-than-he-was favorite of the race, collapsed in front of the old Durant Motors factory. And now the good-looking, tennis-playing kid's name was released to him: Bradley Hardy, who lived somewhere in The Beaches district, and got on well with the high school girls because he could not only outdress any other kid in the school but because he was un-shy with girls and able to flatter them and entertain them with his smalltalk.

Jesus Christ, Bradley Hardy! A name he'd forgotten for over forty-five years. He remembered now he'd always thought of the guy as having two last names.

And now he remembered passing him, still running at an easy lope, his second wind long in his possession, and looking down at the winded Hardy and saying derisively through his own labored breathing, "What's the matter, slack-ass, this a bit harder than tennis?"

He'd passed a lot more exhausted runners, some who were gamely trying to go on and others who had given up and were sitting on the curbs of the street that passed the old Thorncliffe Race Track, and on the bridge railings of the still-standing Leaside Bridge.

71

He'd forgotten now whether he'd come in second, third or fourth in the race, but he remembered too the pride of a thirteen-year-old undernourished kid who'd beaten most of the fifty-odd runners who'd started out to run the six-mile race. He remembered that the winner was another poverty-stricken kid from his old neighborhood, a short Italian who'd gone to St. Anne's parochial school on Bolton Avenue before going on to the public technical high school. Jimmy. Jimmy something. Anyway it'd been a victory of the Plebes over the Patricians.

"Inspector."

McDumont swung around and saw Detective Roundy standing beside the Homicide car with a small red-painted handcart.

"Good work, Clary," the inspector said as he reached the other's side. "Where was it?"

"In the superintendent's basement utility room," Roundy answered in his precise West Indian sing-song.

"Throw it in the trunk, Clary."

When they were both seated in the car the inspector said to the detective, "About twenty yards down the street is an entrance and exit to the shopping plaza. The northbound traffic's being held up by the lights at The Donway. Just go south in the northbound lanes and swing through the gap in the center strip to the southbound. I want to catch that doctor before he quits for the day."

The detective did as he was ordered, and they passed through the gap in the raised center strip. Just then a big rich car, maybe an Imperial, Cadillac or Lincoln, things were happing too fast for McDumont to know or care what its make was, came beetling out of the shopping plaza and they almost crashed into its left front side. Detective Roundy braked their car, but the other didn't push ahead into the northbound lanes, but halted in front of them, blocking their progress. The inspector rolled down his side window.

The driver of the other car, a fat man with his balding hair styled and brushed forward in a Caesar haircut, said, "What do you people think you're doing, coming down the wrong side of the road and then swinging into this lane!" He was just angry and drunk enough to be spoiling for an argument. Some southbound traffic, a taxi, a rented panel truck, and three or four more cars behind them, were being held up, and somebody far back in the line began hitting his horn peevishly.

"Sorry, Mac," the inspector said. "Nobody hit anybody, so why the hell don't you just go on where you're going."

"I'm not moving until I tell you what I think of dangerous drivers," Caesar said. "And I want your number too so that I can report you."

The inspector said, "There's our number on the front licence plate unless you're too lushed to read it."

Caesar took out a little black notebook and scribbled their number down.

"Now I want to see that—that person's driving licence," he said, pointing at Detective Roundy.

The inspector turned to his partner and said, "Get out and show the son of a bitch your driver's licence—" He winked. "And everything else in your wallet."

"It'll be my pleasure, Inspector."

Roundy got out of his side of the car and walked over to the other driver's car, taking his wallet out of an inside pocket of his suit coat. Even as the detective approached his car, old Caesar was still full of drunken insults.

"I suppose you're this man's chauffeur?" he asked the approaching black. "It's *his* ownership I'm really interested in."

Detective Roundy reached the open window of the big car and stuck both his face and his wallet through it. Caesar put on his reading glasses and began to write down Roundy's name and address from his driver's permit. The cars being held up behind them started up a clamor of impatient horn-blowing.

Detective Roundy took back his wallet, and turning to the inspector said, "This man's drunk, Inspector. What will we do with him?"

"For starters show him your police badge, and tell him who we are."

73

The detective did this, as the fat man's mouth dropped open and his jowls began to quiver.

"I'm—sorry, Inspector," the man said, looking and trying to smile at McDumont."

"You're too late, Mac," the inspector shouted above the cacophony of horns behind them. He said to Detective Roundy, "Have him back that heap into the parking lot, and we'll follow." The detective said something to the man and pointed back into the parking lot. He put his wallet back in his pocket and they followed the weaving big car into the lot, bringing to an end the cacophony of the horns. Caesar managed to back into a parking space without hitting any cars, and they drew up in front of him, the inspector stepping out of the D-car and walking over to the other driver's window.

"Step out here, you," McDumont said.

"Listen, Inspector, I told you I was sorry. I'm a lawyer."

"Fine. Let's see *your* driver's permit and ownership card now."

The man handed his wallet through the open window.

"Get out!" McDumont ordered. "Get out, before I charge you with interfering with the police!"

The man stumbled out into the parking lot.

The inspector handed him back his wallet. "Take out your driver's permit and ownership slip," he said. He noticed that Caesar's hair was abundant over his collar, a compensation of balding men who like to show that if they can't grow hair where it's needed they can sure grow it where it's not.

Inspector McDumont read the man's name and address on his permits. "Funny, but I sort of thought your name might be Bradley Hardy," he said.

"Why?"

"Forget it, it's an inside joke. Where do you live?"

"High Point Road, it says so on my permit."

"I know, I can read. I wanted to know if you remembered." The inspector reached into the car and took the keys from the transmission.

"You can't treat me as a—a—"

"As a common drunk? You bet your ass, Mister, I

can. You see that white line over there, the one that runs between the four empty parking spaces. You go over and walk it."

"I'll do nothing of the sort! And furthermore I've got influence with the police. Assistant Chief Plandy is practically a neighbor of mine."

"I'll ask Joe Plandy about that tomorrow. In the meantime go and walk that white line."

"I told you I'll do nothing of the sort. You can't humiliate a decent taxpaying citizen. Look at that crowd of punks standing there and laughing at me! Christ, I'll have your badge for this!"

"I'll give you two alternatives. Either you walk that white line or we'll book you for drunk driving, and you won't go over to No. 33 precinct house for your Breathalyzer test but down to Regent Street Station. If you're sober you've got nothing to worry about, but if you're drunk I'll tell the desk sergeant down at Regent Street to keep you in the drunk tank until you sober up, then send you over to one of the downtown detoxification centers."

"Listen, Inspector, for God's sake!"

There was a crowd of eight or ten blue-denimed teen-agers standing in a group about four parked cars away. It was hard to tell which of them were boys and which were girls, but they were staggering around as if drunk and puffing out their cheeks in imitation of the man McDumont was talking to.

"I'm a homicide inspector," McDumont said. "My partner, Detective Roundy, and I are working on a recent murder case. You've already cost us ten minutes of valuable time. You say you're a lawyer, so you know what the penalty is for interfering with the police in their line of duty. Now go and walk that line or get into our car."

The man, mumbling drunken imprecations and threats under his breath, turned reluctantly and walked, doing his damndest not to stagger, to the white dividing line McDumont had pointed out to him.

The inspector told Detective Roundy, handing him the car keys, to search the seats and the glove compartment for liquor, then lock the car. He walked over and took up a position at the end of the white line. "Okay, Mac, walk it," he said.

With the group of middle-class hippie kids hooting at him and imitating his stumbling attempts to walk the line, from which he kept veering to the left, the fat man finally reached the end. The inspector motioned to him to stay there, then turned and waited for Clary Roundy to finish his search of the car. Finally the detective reached under the right-hand bucket seat and brought out an expensive bottle of scotch, half consumed.

"Lock the car, Clary, and come over here," McDumont shouted to him.

When the detective arrived at his side, the inspector motioned to the drunken man to walk the line towards them. He began fine, but about five steps from where he'd begun he veered several feet off the line to his left. He made as if to get back on it, then gave up, and ignoring the line came towards them. His fat face was now livid, and part of his Caesar hairdo had fallen over one ear, revealing his baldness.

Without a word Roundy took him by the arm and led him to the D-car, putting him into the back seat. The inspector got in, and they drove around the parking lot, back onto Don Mills Road, and headed up the Donway West towards No. 33 police station.

"I've got plenty to tell my friends about you," the drunken man snarled from where he was lying on the back seat out of sight of people they passed. "You can't come up here and throw your goddam weight around with people like me. Don't worry, you bastard, you'll wish you'd never treated me like a Queen Street wino."

"No, Mac, I'll never wish that," McDumont said, turning around and pinning the drunk with unblinking eyes. "In that big car of yours you could kill a dozen kids driving home from wherever you've been; a Queen Street wino can't run over anybody but himself as he staggers home to his room or flophouse, that's if he's allowed to make it that far. You may think you're King Shit living on a street full of two-hundred-grand houses, along with your architects, lawyer friends, sons of millionaires and guys who made a fortune out of

76

real estate deals, but you're worse than any downtown drunk. You're worse because you are much more of a menace to ordinary people walking the streets, and because you're a lawyer who knows damn well when he's breaking the law."

"Bullshit," the drunk mumbled.

"And don't throw your wealth or the street you live on at me. I don't give a damn if you live on Trefann Street or have just bought Casa Loma. I had a suspect in a case a few years back, a Chinese whoremaster, who lived over in the Bayview district where you do, and last winter we had two plainclothes officers killed by a psychopath up near York Mills. A criminal is a criminal to me whether he wears a blue collar, a white collar, or a back-to-front clerical collar, and over the years I've snapped plenty of each of them."

"Jesus Christ, Inspector, you're not classing *me* as a criminal are you?" He tried to laugh, almost choked, and had to sit up in the seat.

"What the hell do you class as a criminal then? You're drunk, you're driving a man-killing bomb, you're in possession of an open and half-consumed bottle of liquor, which is a criminal offence under the Liquor Control Act, and you've interfered with two officers in the line of duty. Doesn't that make you a criminal, or do you think a guy with a law degree and probably a Q.C. attached to his name can't commit a crime?"

Clary swung the car into the front parking lot of No. 33 Division police station, and with the inspector carrying the half-empty scotch bottle they entered the building.

They took their drunk straight to the office of the divisional inspector, Ernest Willis.

"What the hell's this, Walter," the shirtsleeved inspector asked as they entered his office, and the drunken lawyer leaned insolently against a wall.

"This is one of your local lushes, Ernie. We picked him up driving out of the Don Mills Plaza parking lot —not *in* the parking lot but out on Don Mills Road." He threw the man's driver's licence and vehicle permit onto the uniformed inspector's desk. "Detective Roundy here—oh, Clary meet Inspector Ernie Willis." The inspector stood up behind his desk and shook the black detective's hand. "Detective Roundy dug this bottle from under this joker's front seat." He placed the half-bottle of Chivas Regal on the desk.

Willis had been reading the name and address on the permits. He stood up and taking McDumont by the arm led him out to his outer office, shutting his own office door behind him. His secretary's desk was empty.

"Listen, Walter, do you know just who this guy is?" Ernie asked.

"Who is he?"

"Well first of all he's one of the richest corporation lawyers in the city."

"Check. What else?"

"He's running for the opposition party in a North Toronto riding in the next federal election, with a hell of a good chance of getting in."

"Check. What else?"

"He's already turned down a county judgeship."

"Check, and fuck 'im. Do you know what he is to me, Ernie? He's a rich son of a bitch who thinks his social position and his money will either buy him out of jack-pots other guys go to jail for, or he'll scare ordinary policemen out of pinching him. I'm charging him on three counts, drunk driving—which I realize will prob-ably be reduced to impaired driving by whoever tries him—with a breach of the Liquor Control Act for the open bottle of scotch in the car, and for interfering with two homicide detectives that he delayed while they were engaged in their regular duty, namely check-ing out a murder case in your division, Ernie."

"Jesus, Walter, he can make it tough on you."

"If he tries I'll make it tough on him, if I have to stake out that goddam mansion on High Point Road myself for a month."

"What do you want me to do with him?"

"Ask him to take a Breathalyzer first. If he refuses, mark it on your blotter. Then let him call a lawyer, but after he's made the call throw him into a cell until the lawyer arrives with whatever bail you want to set, or whatever. Tell his lawyer about the three charges, and that Roundy and I had him try to walk a line in the plaza parking lot, which he couldn't do."

"God, Walter, I'm up for my pension next year."

"I know you are, Ernie, and I sympathize with you. Put all the blame on me, but there'll be no dropping of charges, or anything like that, no matter who he is. He's been insulting both me and Clary Roundy since we met him a half hour ago. He's just lucky he didn't get too goddam smart and call Roundy a nigger or something, because I'd have had to drive him up behind some factory building in one of this place's industrial sections and let Clary beat the hell out of him. Now remember what I've told you, Ernie. Roundy and I'll be down at the drunk court at Regent Street in the morning, and we'll expect to see that newly rich shyster there among the Queen Street winos and the other poor lushes that he despises so much. Okay?"

"Okay, Walter," Inspector Willis said, with a shrug of resignation.

McDumont pulled out his notebook and glanced back through its pages. "I'd like to use this phone to call a Dr. Morris Franczic down at that medical place on Wynford Drive."

"Sure. Go ahead, Walter. In the meantime I'll ask him to take a breathalyzer. Just take the phone off the hook and one of the boys behind the desk will get you your doctor."

Inspector McDumont spelled out the doctor's name, and gave his address to a young policeman who was manning the station phones. When he was connected with Dr. Franczic he gave the doctor his name and rank in the police force and told him that he was coming down to talk to him.

"Certainly, Inspector, I'll wait here for you. I was just leaving, but I'll wait."

"I'm sorry, Doctor, but I've been held up. Perhaps you'd better phone home and tell your wife you may be a half hour late for dinner or something."

"Yes, Inspector, thank you. I shall. I suppose this is connected with the death of Mrs. Greenless?"

"Yes it is."

"My wife heard it on the radio this afternoon and phoned me."

"Yes. We'll talk about that when I arrive at your office, Doctor."

"Fine, Inspector, I'll be here."

When McDumont entered Inspector Willis's office again he found the drunk lolling in a chair, not quite as drunk as when they'd scooped him but still drunk enough to be insulting and belligerent.

"Well, here's our friend McDumont, superfuzz and friend of the downtrodden. The guy who's going to find himself off the force within the month and retired on half pay." He laughed a particularly nasty laugh. McDumont noticed that his vanity had caused him to comb his hair since McDumont had left the office. The big inspector walked across the room, pulled the drunk out of the chair by his wide green-and-white foulard necktie, and shoved him back against the wall. Then McDumont parted the drunk's hair with a hamlike hand. "What the hell're you trying to do, grow bangs?" he asked him.

The drunk, visibly shaken by the first manhandling he'd probably received since Upper Canada College, was afraid to answer.

McDumont turned to Ernie Willis. "Did this fat slob refuse the Breathalyzer, Ernie?"

"Yes, it's his right to if he wishes."

McDumont pulled the man's car keys out of a side pocket and handed them to Inspector Willis. "Here's his car keys, Ernie, but breathalyzer test or not the man's drunk and in no condition to drive his car. We'll leave Julius Caesar here with you to with whatever you do to drunken slobs around here. Come on, Clary, we've got more important things to do."

With a nod to the uniformed inspector, McDumont and Roundy left the office. When they reached the door from the outer office to the hallway, the inspector said, "Wait here a minute, Clary," and returned and poked his head into the divisional inspector's office again. The drunk was again sitting in the chair, combing his hair forward, and Willis was sitting across the desk from him looking almost apologetic.

"Hey, you!" McDumont barked, making the drunk spring to his feet like a private caught sitting on the edge of his bed during officer-of-the-day barracks inspection. "Don't forget, my partner and I'll expect to see you tomorrow in Regent Street drunk court. Make sure you're there or I'll have them pick you up on a bench warrant. Understand?"

The drunk gave a slight inclination of his head.

Without looking at Willis again Inspector McDumont joined his partner and they went out to their car.

Chapter 7

The inspector and detective pulled up and parked on Wynford Drive in front of the medical building. A commissionaire came running out from the building and shouted, "Hey, you can't park there!" The detectives climbed out of the car and walked up to the excited little man.

"You can't park there on the street, you know," the commissionaire said.

McDumont answered, "Police," and the commissionaire closed his mouth quickly.

"Where's Doctor—?" Glancing at his notes. "Where's Dr. Morris Franczic's office?"

"Second floor, at the back. Follow me, officers," the commissionaire said. After holding the door open for them he went on, "There's an elevator along that hallway there."

"Where's the stairs?" McDumont asked.

"Through that door there."

As they hurried up the stairs McDumont said, somewhat out of breath, "I take stairs as often as I can. It's good for reducing the hips, and God knows after sitting at a desk most of the past seven years I need to reduce them."

Roundy laughed.

They walked down a north-south corridor, reading the doctors' names on the doors they passed. At the back of the building the sign on a door read, "Dr. Morris Franczic, Urologist."

Roundy knocked on the door, and the two men entered a well-furnished waiting room with green leather divans around the walls, separated by end tables and a tall magazine rack full of slightly dog-eared magazines.

A small man wearing a gray glen-check suit and black suede shoes appeared in the doorway of an office near the sliding glass panel of a secretary's office.

"Dr. Franczic?"

"Yes, gentlemen. You are the police?"

"That's right," McDumont answered.

"Please come in."

The two policemen followed the doctor into his private office. It was furnished with two overstuffed wing chairs, a small antique table holding an ash tray, and a huge desk that dwarfed the doctor when he sat down behind it. The doctor's chair was set before the room's window whose drapes were pulled back, giving a short view of a small industrial area of Don Mills. There was one picture on the east wall, a large oil of the ash-can school of art showing the rear of several slum houses and their backyards.

McDumont walked over and stared at the picture, then returned to the closest chair and sat down. He motioned Detective Roundy to sit in the other chair.

"That picture was painted by a friend of mine from the old country, Laszlo Rudnickas. He died last year."

"It reminds me of all my youthful backyards," the inspector said. "What country is your 'old country,' doctor?"

"Hungary."

"How long have you lived in Canada?"

"Since 1948."

"I'll lay it on the line, doctor. You knew that Zelda Greenless was dead, right?"

"Yes."

"How?"

"It's a little complicated. My wife phoned me and told me—"

"What time was this?"

"Ten. Ten-thirty this morning."

"Okay, go on."

"She had received a phone call from her friend Eleanor Jacton."

"The woman who lives next door to Zelda Green-less?"

"Yes. Miss Jacton had got the news over the phone from the apartment superintendent."

"Where did Miss Jacton phone from?"

"From the Bon Beauty Boutique, I guess. That's where she works."

"Where's that?"

"In the Don Mills Centre. She's a hairdresser. She's been doing my wife's hair for—well, for as long as she's been there."

"Why did she call your wife, do you suppose?"

"She knew, of course, that Zelda worked for me, and I was operating this morning. I guess that's why she called my house."

"Where do you operate?"

"The North York General."

"I see. How long has it been since Miss Greenless came to the office last?"

The doctor thought a moment. "A week, maybe a little longer."

"Who do you have taking her place?"

"A girl who works for a cardiologist on the first floor. He and his wife have gone on a vacation to South America. His answering service takes his calls and transfers them to a colleague. I've had the same girl before." He shrugged. "I've had plenty of part-time secretaries."

"What was Zelda Greenless' trouble?"

"She was an alcoholic."

"Why did you continue to employ her, Doctor, if she was away so often?"

Dr. Franczic shrugged again. "Actually she wasn't away from the job that often—"

"Inspector."

"Inspector. She had maybe two or three binges a year. She used to count it as her holiday time."

"She was paid while she was on a binge?"

"Of course. She was an excellent medical secretary, and she was valuable to me in her job. We all have weaknesses, and alcohol was hers. Besides I liked her as a woman."

"Just liked her?"

"Yes, Inspector. I wasn't in love with her, if that's what you're hinting at. I never visited her at her apartment, nor did she ever visit with my wife and me. My wife also liked her very much."

"Where do you live, doctor?"

"Sixty-seven Overton Crescent. Up in the northeast quadrant of Don Mills."

"Quadrant?"

"Yes. When this development was first built, in the early fifties, Don Mills was divided into four parts, or quadrants, with the Don Mills Centre forming the centre of the development. Your police station is in the northwest quadrant, just off the Donway West."

The inspector nodded. "The Don Mills Hilton," he said.

Dectective Roundy and Dr. Franczic laughed.

The doctor added, "Today what is called Don Mills, at least the postal district, has spread from Leslie Street on the west to Victoria Park Avenue on the east, and from Eglinton Avenue north to—I believe—Sheppard Avenue."

"There are new suburban developments in this city that are as foreign to me as Calcutta," the inspector mumbled. "Especially in the northwest part of the city."

"Where we are right now," said the doctor, rising and walking to the window, "is south of the southeast quadrant. This is one of the areas designated as an industrial zone. Look," he said, turning to the detectives.

Both got up and joined him at the window, both towering over the little man.

"See, there are a lot of small manufacturing and distribution plants north from here to Greenbelt. Pitney-Bowes, National Sales Incentives, companies like that. Across Don Mills Road itself, south of Barber Greene Road, are more plants—Longmans of Canada —and so on, and of course I.B.M. When you pay your telephone bill by mail it's addressed to Bell Canada in Don Mills, and across the street from this building are Imperial Oil and Shell offices which do your credit card accounting."

The three sat down again.

"Dr. Franczic, I must confess that I know very little yet about Zelda Greenless, that is from people who knew her. Right now I'm trying to build up an assessment of her character and habits. Not only don't I yet know who killed her, but who *she* was herself."

The doctor nodded.

"Was she ever treated for alcoholism?"

"I don't think so, that is, not in an institution or hospital. For a short time last fall she attended A.A. meetings at the Anglican Church of the Ascension. Then she dropped them."

"Was she ever treated by a private shrink?"

"A psychiatrist? As a matter of fact she was. By Dr. Hugh Rutsey up on the third flood of this building."

"I don't suppose he'd be in his office now?"

"He might be. He has patients throughout most evenings."

"Did you know that she had a baby when she was fourteen?"

The doctor looked from one detective to the other. "Yes. She told me that a long time ago."

"Did she have access to drugs here in the office?"

"Yes, some. I don't carry what you could call a pharmaceutical stock, but I have some."

"Any that are poisonous?"

Detective Roundy stared at the inspector.

"Was she killed by a poison?" the doctor asked.

"Actually no, she was stabbed in the back," the inspector said.

"Most of the drugs I have are not poisons, Inspector. I have some antibiotics, penicillin, tranquilizers. I receive a lot of samples from drug salesmen." He pulled open a drawer of his desk and dropped a small pile of drug samples onto his blotter. "I give my patients prescriptions, which they can have dispensed at the drugstore downstairs or wherever they like."

"Where do you keep your prescription pads?"

The doctor opened a bottom drawer of his desk. "In here."

"How many pads have you?"

"Oh, I'd say a dozen, Why?"

"You were not aware that Zelda Greenless had one of your prescription pads?"

The doctor's mouth dropped open. "If it wasn't *you* telling me this, Inspector, I wouldn't believe it! I'd have trusted her with anything in the office or dispensary. I certainly didn't know she had any of my prescription forms."

"Did you know anything about her sex life? From a purely medical point of view I mean? Did you as a doctor find any sexual aberrations in her conduct, or surmise any?"

The doctor stroked his chin. "You've got to believe me, Inspector, when I tell you I had no sexual congress with her at all, at any time. To me she was an efficient, likeable secretary. I would say, unless you can prove me wrong, that she was also heterosexual."

"Did she receive private phone calls here in your office?"

The doctor smiled. "Yes. They all do."

"Do you remember any in particular that seemed to bother her?"

The doctor shook his head.

"How about visitors? Did she have any male visitors here?"

"Only once that I recall. Last winter. A couple of young long-haired kids. I don't know their names."

"Did she ever mention a man named Musgrove?"

"No."

"Did you know that she was married once to a man named Edgar Greenless?"

"No, I didn't know that, Inspector."

The inspector stood up, his action followed by Detective Roundy. "Sorry to have kept you late for dinner, Doctor," the inspector said. "May I talk to you again if it's necessary?"

"Certainly, Inspector."

"Let me congratulate you on your English. You speak very well for—"

"A D.P. as they used to call us?" The doctor laughed.

"No, but as a foreigner to the language."

"My father was in the Hapsburg diplomatic service, and later in that of Hungary under Admiral Horthy. I

87

attended prep school for some years in England, where my father was an attaché."

"That explains it. Do you think Dr. Rutsey might be in his office?"

"I'll see for you." The doctor leafed through an address book, and dialed a number on his phone. "Hello . . . Dr. Rutsey? . . . Yes, fine, thank you I have a detective and a detective inspector from homicide down here . . . no, no charges of malfeasance or practicing euthanasia. It's about my secretary, Zelda Greenles . . . yes. She was murdered last night or this morning . . . no, it wouldn't be in the papers yet, unless it's in tonight's *Star*. Could these officers have a few words with you about Zelda? I am too; she was a fine woman and a fine secretary . . . all right, Doctor, I'll send them up."

Dr. Franczic said, "Dr. Rutsey will see you. He's in suite three-o-seven, just forward of this one on the center corridor, next floor up."

"Your relations with Rutsey sound pretty formal, Doctor."

"Yes, well in our trade he's a head-shrinker and I'm a plumber. We don't have much in common, that is in our patient relationships. Unless I happen to have to perform a prostatectomy on one of his neurotic patients we hardly ever see each other."

"Don't mention that word "prostatectomy" to me," the inspector said.

The doctor laughed. "It gets us all in the end, Inspector. Today it's a comparatively simple operation, no—"

"Don't tell me about it, Doctor."

"Who's treating you?"

"Dr. Wallace. Robbie Wallace out at Scarborough Centennial."

"He's a good man. Take a week off, Inspector, and get yourself reamed out."

"I'll stick to antibiotics for now, Doc. Come on, Clary, let's get the hell out of here!"

The two detectives found suite 307 without any difficulty, and entered the wide-open door. A tall young man with a long "styled" haircut, holding a Big Mac hamburger in one hand, came to the door of his office and waved them in. After he'd swallowed his mouthful of hamburger he said, "Sit down, gentlemen." He pointed to a rep-covered blue couch that stood across a corner of his office. He himself sat back in a blue Barcalounger and said, "I'm Hugh Rutsey."

"This is Detective Roundy, and I'm Detective Inspector Walter McDumont of the Metro Homicide Bureau. I think Dr. Franczic downstairs told you what this is all about."

The doctor jumped up from the lounger and shook hands with both police officers. Then he went back to his chair and said, "If you'll excuse me, officers, while I devour this hamburger. Take a look at the wall decorations if you like. They're all the work of psychotics. I bought them when I was doing time down at the Clarke Institute."

The detectives looked over a series of paintings, some quite good from their point of view, with others that were post-Grandma Moses primitives. A framed multicolored cat, done in small tiles pasted to a wooden background, caught the inspector's eye, and he stood admiring it.

By the time they sat down again the doctor was just washing the last bite of his hamburger down with coffee from a paper cup. He was wearing gray cord flare trousers, a dark brown shirt with the collar open to show a green ascot, and a fawn cardigan, unbuttoned.

There was no desk in the office, but on a small table beside the doctor's chair was a brown Permax file folder.

After throwing his wax paper and paper cup in the wastebasket in a corner of the room the doctor murmured an "Excuse me," and left his office. He returned and said, "Just had to rinse off my hands." He sat back in his chair, let it fall back into a reclining position, and said, "Let's go, gentlemen."

The inspector said, "I understand Zelda Greenless was a patient of yours once, Doctor?"

The doctor picked up the file folder and glanced at the papers it contained. "Twice," he answered. "She came to me for four visits last summer—psychotherapy—but gave them up. She came to me again later last year, in October."

"What for, Doctor?"

"The October visit was to ask me if I could get her into a clinic to dry out after a drinking bout, a heavy one. I told her I could probably get her a bed in the Homewood Sanitarium in Guelph, the Donwoods Clinic down in the city, or some other place, but she turned them down on the grounds that they might keep her too long. She told me she'd been drinking for ten days then, and didn't want to lose her job with the urologist downstairs."

"So what did you do?"

"I gave her a prescription for thirty caps of three-hundred-milligram Noludar sleeping pills—they're not a barbiturate; thirty caps of sodium Dilantin—that's an anticonvulsant; and thirty caps of twenty-five-milligram Librium, a tranquilizer. I told her she had the alternative of putting herself on the pills, especially the Dilantin if she thought she was going into the d.t.'s, had hallucinations or other such signs; or if she thought she could make it to go downtown, get half-drunk on draft beer in a hotel bar, go to a movie, take some more beer, eat something, go to another movie, then after killing the day with the draft beer to go home, take a Noludar and go to bed."

"Is that the kind of cure you give all your alcoholic patients, Doctor?" asked Detective Roundy.

"No, sir. Alcoholics aren't a homogeneous mass of nuts or self-indulgent idiots. Each one is different from the next, and each needs the kind of drying out that he or she can take. I don't believe in cold-turkey cures, and if the person is young, strong and has a modicum of will power, as Zelda had, I figured she could probably make it by tapering off on beer, some food and some movies. If not she could switch to the pills, at least the tranquilizers and the sleeping caps."

The detectives exchanged glances.

"I know what you're thinking, gentlemen. You're saying to yourselves, 'This shrink is a nut himself.' Right? I don't care what you're saying to yourselves.

Most of the medical profession hasn't a clue on how to treat an alcoholic, because the amount of time given to the treatment of alcoholism in medical school is so minuscule as to be almost nil. Most general practitioners, especially if they're nondrinkers themselves or so-called social drinkers, don't want to treat an alcoholic or somebody on a drug trip. They're a nuisance to them; they vomit in their waiting room, clown it up before the mothers and babies, are too talkative to the point of garrulousness, ask for dangerous combinations of drugs, and eventually drive the nice, decent little patients with their flu or broken ankles away from the doctor's practice.

"Gentlemen, most of what the public, the police *and* the medical profession know about alcohol or any other drug or narcotic is bullshit."

After a silent minute the inspector asked, "What were the psychotherapy visits about, Doctor?"

Rutsey looked up from his file. "Do you know anything about the woman named Zelda Greenless?"

The inspector said, "Not enough, Doctor. That's why we're here. I know she had a baby when she was fourteen, and that the baby died at the age of six months. I think its father was a much older guy called Musgrove. I also know that she was married once to a man called Edgar Greenless, that's where she got her name. Her maiden name was Zelda Stanton, and she was born in Crow Lake, Ontario, in 1936."

The doctor said, "Good, Inspector. We both know she was a binge-drinking alcoholic." He sat up. "Incidentally, she tapered off by herself—back to sobriety —on my beer-and-movies prescription. Except for the Noludar capsules she didn't have my drug prescription dispensed at all. My homeotherapy worked with her, and she was back in Dr. Franczic's office three days later." He reclined in the chair again. "Zelda Greenless was a poor, mentally ill woman, stemming back to the time she had a baby at the age of fourteen. She wasn't psychotic, but neurotically troubled from then on. What the ladies of Don Mills call, when they have a temporary lapse into neurasthenia, 'a nervous break-down.' In Zelda it was chronic. She could only ameliorate it with drinks or drugs. I don't know for sure but I think she'd been on a couple of speed trips, may have taken acid once or twice, but generally stuck to the legal narcotic, liquor."

"How about pot?" the inspector asked.

"It's endemic up here, Inspector. Nearly everybody over twelve has smoked the odd reefer."

"Her living room was furnished like a—a seraglio," the inspector said. "She had one of those hookahs, or whatever they're called, in her living room."

"I didn't know that, but it figured."

"Figured? How?"

"Zelda Greenless suffered from a sexual horror of older men. She preferred boys of an age that took her back to her teens, before the older man, Musgrove, put her in a family way and then deserted her and her baby. I think the hookah, and any pot you might have found around the place, was used mainly by the boys she associated with."

"We didn't find any pot—yet," said the inspector. "What we did find though were several dozen condoms in a box in her bedroom. What was the significance of them?"

"Medically I could say she had an unreasonable fear of the clap, and Dr. Franczic could tell you more about *that* than I can. I think he's got a statistical breakdown of the prevalence of gonorrhea in Don Mills, and a projection of its growth among the students in the neighborhood schools."

"What about syphilis?"

"Not as prevalent up here. There is some, of course."

"You said 'medically,' Doctor. Does that mean you also have a psychiatric theory about the condoms?"

"Not really. I think though that they tie in with Zelda's teen-age traits. During *my* teens (which weren't that long ago), and I'm sure it was true also in your teen years, the safe, rubber or condom was the recognized form of both birth control and disease prevention. It still is, or was, to Zelda Greenless. I think that probably her most troubling phobia was her fear of pregnancy. And with good bloody cause I'd say."

92

There was the sound of somebody entering the waiting room. The inspector stood up. "Thank you very much, Doctor."

The doctor, who had also stood up at the sound from the waiting room, shook hands with each of the detectives. "It was my pleasure, gentlemen. That is, to meet you, not to discuss that poor woman. Do you mind telling me how she was killed?"

"A knife in the back," the inspector said.

"She didn't deserve *that*," the young doctor said.

The detectives walked through the waiting room, each glancing at a prim-looking woman wearing over her head a scarf, which tended to hide her face. Her eyes were on the waiting-room rug.

When they were back in the car the inspector said to Clary Roundy, "Drive me up to the Don Mills Centre, Clary, and then take the car back to headquarters. I think Sergeant Manders will be still there, and he'll give you your evening's assignment. Tell him that I'm having supper up here. Put all the stuff that's in the trunk in my office—the blanket, steel box, everything."

"Okay, Inspector."

"And on your way back downtown drop into an apartment house at one-twenty-six Gamble Avenue. Zelda Greenless used to live there, and I think her girl friend Eleanor Jacton, who now lives next door to her up at the Doncentre Apartments did too. Find out from the superintendent or anybody else who lives in the house all you can about both women."

Roundy wrote their names in his notebook, and the Gamble Avenue address.

"The dead woman lived in apartment five-o-seven, so, if the super can't tell you anything about her, most likely somebody on the fifth floor can."

"Where's Gamble Avenue, Inspector?"

"I think your best bet, Clary, is to turn around in the Don Mills Centre and go south on Don Mills to O'Connor Drive, turn right on O'Connor to Donlands Avenue, and it's the third or fourth street down."

"Okay, Inpsector. I got it."

On the way up Don Mills Road the inspector told

the detective all he wanted from Gamble Avenue was a synopsis of the women's life styles, when and why they moved, and so on.

"Right," Roundy said.

The inspector got out of the car in the Don Mills Centre parking lot, and watched the Car as it swung south into the Don Mills Road traffic. Then he walked into the shopping center itself and into the Diana's Coach'n Four, a nice little restaurant owned by an old friend of his, George Boukydis, who had expanded his father's Diana Sweets restaurants from downtown into several suburban shopping centers. George owned another place in the Don Mills Centre, called Diana's Artifactory, which the inspector thought might be a sort of fancy pub, though he'd never visited it.

The maître d' welcomed him and led him to a corner table.

"Are you dining alone, sir?"

"Yes I am." As the man pulled back a chair for him. "First though I'm going to wash my hands."

"Very well, sir." The man pointed to the washrooms sign.

When he returned from the washroom the inspector ordered a Johnny Walker Black Label on the rocks. When it arrived he sipped his drink, taking in the customers who were scattered around the room. There were a few married couples, some touristy-looking people in sports clothes, and a couple of lone male diners. He realized it was still too early for the Don Mills dinner crowd.

The waiter came and placed a basket of bread and crackers on the table and a container of butter. "Do you want to give me your order now, sir?"

"Yes," McDumont answered in his Scots burr. "I'll have the chef's salad and a T-bone steak, rare, with a baked potato. I'll have butter with the potato, not sour cream."

"Yessir."

"Oh, and bring me my coffee with the salad, please."

The waiter left the table and the inspector finished his scotch-on-the-rocks.

After finishing his salad the inspector watched as

the waiter placed a wooden steak platter before him, flanked by a knife and fork with handles that were identical to the handle of the knife found in Zelda Greenless's back. He picked it up, gauged the serrated blade to be about eight inches long, studied the handle again and, now sure that the stabbing weapon had been cut down from one of the Coach'n Four's steak knives, pointed and honed into a deadly weapon by somebody who had stolen it from the restaurant, sat back and enjoyed his meal.

He turned down dessert, but asked the waiter to bring the maître d' over to his table.

"Is something wrong, sir?"

"No, son, your meal and service were excellent. What's the manager's name?"

"Mr. Corbett," the young waiter answered.

"Tell Mr. Corbett I'd like to talk to him for a minute, will you please? And bring me another coffee."

The waiter began to gather up the steak board and the cutlery, but the inspector said, "Leave the knife and fork here, son."

The waiter gave him a frightened look, but did as he was asked, clearing off the bread basket, butter dish and steak board.

In a couple of minutes the middle-aged maître d' came over and stood at the inspector's elbow. "I hope everything was satisfactory, sir?"

"It was great, Mr. Corbett. No complaints." The inspector showed the man his badge.

"Oh! Inspector, for a minute I thought you were from either the health department or the liquor commission."

"I'm sure a place like this doesn't get many visits from those people."

"You'd be surprised. Some of them can be pretty tacky. You refuse them a free sirloin, or they have an argument with the waiter, or they claim their Martini is short of a full shot of gin."

"Take a chair, Mr. Corbett. Can you spare me a couple of minutes?"

"Sure, Inspector," the man said, pulling back a chair.

The waiter brought McDumont's coffee.

95

"I'll have one too, George," the manager said. "And tell Luigi to take over the door for a while."

Both men were silent until the waiter had placed a coffee in front of the maître d' and had left the table.

The inspector picked up the steak knife. "Do you have many of these stolen?" he asked.

"Quite a few over the course of a year, Inspector. Sometimes as many as a half dozen a month, sometimes only one. I guess we lose maybe twenty pairs of knives and forks a year. They're very attractive. As you can see the handle is only plastic, but it looks and feels like genuine bone. The steel is extra strong Sheffield. I don't know where the boss buys them; from a New York importer I think. We have them in all the Diana's steak houses."

"Who steals them?"

The manager shrugged. "There's no pattern to restaurant or hotel thefts, Inspector. It could be a lady from Bayview, driving a Lincoln Continental and wearing a mink stole that would keep my family for three months. It could be a drunken businessman, or a tourist who pockets a knife and fork for souvenirs. A couple of years ago we had six pairs stolen, always on Sunday, by a colonel in the Salvation Army."

The inspector laughed.

"You don't believe that, Inspector?"

"Sure I believe it, Mr. Corbett. In my job I've met them all, from my own Scots Presbyterian clan to the Sally Ann and beyond it to every kind of nut-Jesus-freak in the book." The inspector sipped his coffee and asked, "Do you remember anyone specifically who only stole the knives, not the forks."

The manager thought for a moment. "Yessir. We found a knife missing about two months ago after a couple had left the restaurant. Of course we don't prosecute. These people know that. This man and his wife usually dropped in here every Saturday evening. Since one of them stole the knife I haven't seen them."

"You don't know their name?"

"No. We have hundreds of customers, regular and transient, every week, Inspector. But I'm sure they live quite close to this restaurant. They look fairly well-to-do, you know, dress good, are well-mannered."

"Huh-huh. How about young people? Do you remember any young people stealing knives?"

"Yes, last winter. It was a quiet evening, and we had a table full of them in the place. Some of them were pretty noisy. They were high, Inspector. You know, not on booze but on something. We finally had to turf them out. Just a bunch of smart-ass high school kids. They usually hang out over at the Artifactory, but maybe Bill Mayers, the manager over there, wouldn't let them in that night. I wouldn't have let them in here except they sneaked in while I was showing some people to a table. When I turned around they'd already seated themselves."

"What about the knives?" the inspector asked.

"Let's see, there were six of them, four boys, two girls. They hang around the Centre here all the time. There were four of the knives missing when we checked the table."

"Did they pay the bill?"

"Sure, but no tips for the waiter. These kids around here are spoiled silly by their parents. They've got more money to spend than I had when I was first married and bringing up a couple of babies. They're snotty little—"

"Bastards?"

"Right! They're snotty little spoiled middle-class bastards, Inspector."

"No argument. Do you know any one of the four boys?"

"I know them all by sight. I'll bet they're somewhere in the Centre right now. The leader seems to be a scruffy-looking jerk with frizzy hair worn in an Afro, though he's as white as you can be without bothering to wash. They call him 'Dreamer.' "

The inspector jotted the nickname in his notebook.

"Why 'Dreamer,' Mr. Corbett?"

"I dunno except that he's always on a high of some kind, a real speed freak."

"Okay, Mr. Corbett, thank you very much. I'm a friend of George Boukydis, I don't think he'd mind me taking this steak knife on loan you might say. I'll give you a receipt for it if you like."

"That won't be necessary, Inspector."

The inspector pulled a bill from his pocket and laid it on the table.

"The check's on the house, Inspector."

"No, Mr. Corbett, it's expense money. It comes from yours and Boukydis's taxes. I'll pay the tab."

"Come again anytime, Inspector," said the maître d', walking him to the front door. "Bring the wife. Some Sunday. I'll have the chef cook you up something real special."

"Thanks, Mr. Corbett. Maybe I'll take you up on that."

When he was outside the Inspector headed for a glassed-in telephone booth at a corner where two of the Centre's streets met. He called his office, and the phone was answered by Eric Manders.

"Hi, Eric. I'm staying up here in Don Mills until later in the evening . . . No, nothing that definite yet, but we're working on it. Has Clary Roundy arrived back yet? . . . no. Well he will. He's bringing a lot of stuff from the dead woman's apartment. Have him put everything in my office. I left him almost an hour ago, but he had an investigation to make in the East End . . . Yeh, connected with the Don Mills killing. You can re-assign him. I won't need Prust and Helmont up here tonight . . . Yeh, you don't need to stick around, Eric. Right, I'll see you in the morning . . . eh? Two of the new men, Bill Zotas and Tom Smith . . . Okay."

McDumont then called his own house. "Jean? Listen I'm going to be tied up most of the night, I expect . . . You say Beatrice is there with the kids . . . I see, Danny's on the night shift?. Okay, why don't you invite Beatrice and her family to stay there tonight? Okay. What! You've got to go 'cause you're watching *Maude* on TV . . . I said 'God forbid I'd interrupt such an event'. Listen, when I come home I'll let myself in and flake out on the living room sofa . . . Okay. Bye."

Inspector McDumont was smiling to himself as he left the phone booth. There was a gaggle of teen-agers standing in front of a small Greek coffee house. One of them was a scruffy-looking young man, maybe in his early twenties, unlike the others who were younger. He wore his long blond hair in a fright wig, and it

98

looked as if it had been bleached. Taking a good look at him before turning away the inspector thought, That must be Dreamer!

He strode across the parking lot with his steady policeman's stride, crossed Don Mills Road, and entered the front door of No. 1049.

Chapter 8

The inspector rang the buzzer of apartment 602 and the intercom was answered by Detective Tom Smith.

"Hi, Smitty. Walter McDumont."

"Okay, Inspector." The buzzer on the door opened the lock, and the inspector went up in one of the elevators to the sixth floor. He walked along the quiet empty corridor to 602 and found the door unlocked. As soon as he was inside the apartment he sat down in a chair and said to the probationary homicide detective, "Let's see, you're on the four to midnight shift aren't you, Tom?"

"Yes."

"Are you working on anything downtown?"

"No, Inspector. I've been going out on calls with Sergeant Prust and Larry Helmont all week."

"Okay. Did you make yourself a coffee?"

"A couple of them, Inspector."

"You found the sugar all right?"

"Yes. I found something else too." He took his handkerchief out of his jacket pocket and opened it up. There was a small oiled paper package holding something that looked like part of an Oxo cube. "Hash, Inspector. It was in the tea caddy under the tea bags."

"Good work, Tom. Put it back in your pocket. When you check in tonight, put it on my desk, will you? Were there any phone calls?"

"Just one, Inspector. It was a man, young I'd say, with a high squeaky voice. Sounded as if he was on a long run on speed or acid. Far, far out. I told him I was one of Zelda's friends, and when he asked to speak to her I told him she was at work. He asked me if there was any meth or M.D.A. in the apartment, and

I told him no. I asked him who was calling. He asked me why. I told him I wasn't talking or telling anything to somebody I didn't even know. Maybe he was the fuzz or something. He finished up saying, 'Tell Zelda that Dreamer called.' "

"Okay, Tom. I suppose you're hungry?"

"I could stand a sandwich."

"Okay, we'll get Bill Zotas up here, and the two of you can go across to the plaza and grab something to eat."

The inspector phoned the superintendent's apartment, and when Xenia Zutach answered the phone he asked to speak to Detective Jones.

"When Bill Zotas came on the line the inspector said, "Bill, this is McDumont upstairs in Zelda's apartment. Tell Zutach he's off the hook, and we're not going to keep him under surveillance any longer. Then come up here."

"Okay, Inspector."

In a few minutes Zotas arrived.

"Do you want to make yourself a coffee, Bill?"

"No thanks. I had some Jugoslav coffee downstairs. Have either of you ever had Croatian coffee?"

The inspector and Detective Smith both shook their heads.

"Jee-zus! No wonder my own parents emigrated to this country."

The other two laughed.

"I'm letting both you and Smith go to eat, Bill, but first tell me anything you learned downstairs."

"Well, first of all, Inspector, Anton Zutach is one scared little man. I don't know why—that is I know one reason he's scared, but it's not the main one. Secondly I found out that through Zutach claims to be a Serb he speaks Croatian to his wife."

"They didn't know you understood them, did they, Bill?" asked the inspector.

"No."

"Did they say anything significant?"

"Mrs. Zutach was plenty hot about something. She told her husband that the police would find out for sure about the painting."

"What did she mean?"

Zotas said, "I think they've got the painting that's missing from that wall there on *their* living room wall. I'm only guessing. Maybe I'm only guessing about the word 'painting' too; I'm not that good in the Jugoslavian languages."

"Okay, Bill."

"I got a list of everybody on this floor, Inspector. Apartment six-ten, at the back opposite the storage room, is vacant. Its last tenants were a Mr. and Mrs. Wesley Glennan. They left a month ago for Guyana as Church of Souls missionaries."

"Good."

Zotas pulled a sheet of 11-inch by 8½-inch white bond paper from his pocket and spread it out on the floor. "This is a plan of every floor but the main one in the apartment house. Specifically, this shows the names of all the tenants on this floor, and in most cases their occupations."

The inspector picked it up. "Good work, Bill. Now you two go over to the plaza and get yourselves a bite to eat."

"Okay, Inspector, we'll do that. But don't forget I'm *certain* that Zutach had more to do with this murder than he's letting on."

"I've made a mental note of it. I'll arrange for extra duty pay for you."

After the two detectives had gone McDumont looked over the sixth-floor plan, making mental notes of the apartments' occupants, and in some cases their occupations. He lighted a cigarette and while waiting for the detectives' return from the shopping center walked into the bedroom and searched carefully the drawers full of clothes in the dresser. He was getting old and careless, there was no doubt of that. *He* should have found the hashish in the tea caddy, but maybe it was just as well that Smitty had found it. It would give the young man some self-confidence, and that was something every detective needed. In the bottom of one of the drawers he felt two folded sheets of paper, and pulled them out. One was a city of Toronto assessment notice and the other was a year-old Urban Preliminary List of Electors, Don Mills Road. He carried them into

102

the living room and went through the names on the electors' list, comparing those on the sixth floor of number 1049 with the plan that Bill Zotas had drawn. They tallied perfectly, even to the names of the former occupants of 610, who were now in Guyana.

The apartment house was typical of most middle-class high-rise apartments. The occupations read: bookkeeper, hairdresser, manager, clerk, teacher (retired), buyer, accountant, printer, supervisor, telephone operator, housewife, saleslady, retired clergyman, educator (silly bugger, ashamed to call himself a teacher!), insurance adjuster, airline stewardess, auto parts manager, clothing salesman, secretary, dental nurse, shipping superintendent; and Zelda Greenless had listed herself as a doctor's secretary. A cross-section of some occupations of the Don Mills citizenry. He shoved the list into a pocket.

He took the Annie Besant book from its shelf and read enough of it to tell him she had been a theosophist. God, it took him back forty years to a time when he and a friend called Fred Martin had gone to a room on Charles Street West occupied by two girls they'd picked up in a Bloor Street Honeydew cafeteria. The girls had been theosophists, and had tried to proselytize them while he and Freddy had tried to seduce *them*. The hell of it was neither side had won. "Go back on your shelf, Mrs. Besant," McDumont said, shoving the book back into its place beside Madame Blavatsky. He turned away, saying under his breath, "Walter, my boy, you're going crackers, or senile." Funny though how he remembered even his youthful failures of forty years before.

McDumont took the steak knife from the Coach'n Four from his pocket and hefted it in his hand, finding its point of balance. He tried to bend the blade, but it was too strong to bend. Boukydis didn't only serve excellent steaks, he also used excellent china and cutlery. The inspector wondered to himself, first, why the four street kids from the shopping plaza had stolen the four steak knives (when they could buy good hunting knives in the Eaton's store practically next door to the restaurant), and second, what they'd done with them. Obviously somebody who had either stolen one of the knives, or had access to one, had shoved it into the back of the dead woman. The "why" he could leave until later, it was the "how" and "who" he was interested in at the present time.

With a smile he ruled out the Salvation Army colonel who had stolen six pairs of knives and forks. Obviously he was just a thief who wanted to impress his fellow Salvationists at steak-outs on his patio or something. Probably prayed like hell for forgiveness while he was using the knife or, later on, kneeling beside his bed. But what about all the other knives that had been stolen, by restaurant customers who weren't long-haired street kids? He couldn't afford to think about them.

The leader of the Don Mills Centre gang, Dreamer, didn't seem to be the one, but the inspector wasn't ruling him out. Normally a person who had had anything at all to do with a murder wouldn't phone the victim's home later and ask to speak to her. But how about a speed freak on a drug run? He wouldn't be acting normally anyhow, and the phone call that Tom Smith had taken might have been made to see if there was anyone in the apartment. If it had been empty he might have come up, presuming he had a key, and that was a likely presumption, to get the hashish that he knew was stored in the tea caddy. But then would he have given Smitty his name, or nickname? The inspector, for the time being, was ruling Dreamer out as the possible stabber.

That left the possible stabbers, and probably poisoners as well, as one of the two doctors, Franczic and Rutsey (who had easy access to poisons); the apartment house superintendent, Zutach, whom both he and Bill Zotas were suspicious of, he for finding him trying the bury the blanket that he was sure covered the body of Zelda Greenless when she was stabbed, and Zotas because he was sure the superintendent knew more about the murder than he was letting on; and—who else?

He lighted a new cigarette from the butt of the last one and sat thinking things out until the two young detectives returned.

"Where did you guys eat?" he asked them.

"A joint called The Coffee Spot," Zotas said. "Do you know, Inspector, that there's more than eighty stores and places of business in that plaza. I counted them when we were looking for the location of a place to eat, on the glassed-in directory at the corner just beyond the liquor store."

"I guess there would be. Did the joint serve decent food?"

"Middling," said Tom Smith. Bill here had a ham sandwich and I had fish-and-chips. Despite the name "Coffee Spot" it served lousy coffee."

"Kee-rist!" Zotas put in. "I haven't had a decent coffee all day!"

McDumont laughed. Then, butting his cigarette and becoming serious, he said, "Were there any kids hanging around outside the place? I guess it's that little Greek coffee joint up one of the short connecting streets?"

Smitty said, "Yeh, there was a small gang of young wierdos. They spotted us for fuzz right away."

"Did you notice one with a bleached blond Afro haircut?"

Both detectives nodded.

"His name is Dreamer, and he's the leader of the gang," the inspector said. "He's the guy who phoned here this afternoon, Smitty."

The probationary detective's estimation of the inspector went up at least a hundred per cent. He thought, Now how in the hell does the old man know that?

McDumont went on. "All right, both of you, here's where we stand right now. I'm certain that the dagger found in the corpse is a honed-down steak knife like this one." He took it out of his pocket again and showed the detectives. "It was stolen from the Coach'n Four restaurant in the shopping center. I don't know when or by whom. I'm not ruling out Zutach, Bill, especially after what you told me about your suspicions of him and the stolen painting. In fact, just from many years of experience, or maybe from an old man's stubbornness. I've got the feeling that the murderer of Zelda Greenless lives in this building. It can be either a man or a woman." He looked from one to the other. "Okay?"

They nodded.

"Starting right now we're going to question the people on this floor. Bill and I will start with the apartment across the hall, that'll be six-o-one occupied by the Bullays. You, Smitty, stand by the elevators and stop anybody from leaving this floor until we've questioned them all. You two will spell each other off taking turns coming with me to each of the apartments while the other watches the elevators. Okay?"

"Okay," said Detective Smith.

"Right, Inspector," Bill Zotas answered.

They let themselves into the long hallway, locking the apartment door behind them. Smith walked along and took his place outside the elevator doors.

At Zotas's knock the Bullays' door was opened by a prim-looking middle-aged woman.

"We're the police," the inspector said. "Could we have a few words with you?"

"Is it about the Greenless woman?"

"That's right."

"I have nothing to say about her."

"Are you Mrs. George Bullay? Dolly Bullay?" asked the inspector.

"I'm *Mrs. George* Bullay," the woman answered.

"Well then, you know it was your husband who found Mrs. Greenless's body. When we charge her murderer your husband will be a witness in court. You know that, don't you?"

"Why should decent respectable people get mixed up in a sordid mess like that woman's death? Believe me, if it had been I who had found the body I'd have ignored it and brought our trash right back here to the apartment."

"I'm sure you would," the inspector said. "Luckily your husband isn't stupid enough to do something like that. To not report a crime is a crime in itself, just for your information." The inspector looked down the hall. "Do you want all the neighbors to hear us, Mrs. Bullay, or would you sooner we stepped inside. We haven't got a warrant or anything, so you can refuse to let us in if you want to."

"I don't give a damn what the neighbors hear!"

The inspector raised his voice. "All right I'll do my questioning here at the door. The next time we come—and we will—I'll have a search warrant from a judge." He stared hard into the woman's face. "I know that you, Dolly Bullay, are a schoolteacher down at Berkeley Street Public School. At three-thirty, like the rest of your tribe, you beetle back to Don Mills, and you probably speak to women's groups about the unfortunate slum kids you have to teach, your speech liberally punctuated by your amateur sociological jargon like 'inner city,' 'programmed,' 'playback,' 'one-parent families,' and all the rest of that middle-class baloney. Right now though I want to know what you thought of Zelda Greenless?"

Dolly Bullay, whose face had become livid, answered, "I knew nothing about that woman! To me she was lower class scum like some of the parents I meet at Berkeley Street. And she wasn't a missus, she was an unmarried miss!"

"That's where you're wrong," the inspector said. He looked beyond the woman to her husband, George, who was sitting on the sofa biting his nails. "I have Mrs. Greenless's marriage licence in my office right now. I am certain *she* had one, but have you?"

The inspector turned on his heel and, followed by Bill Zotas, left the Bullays' doorway. The Bullays' door slammed behind them.

"Bill, change places with Smitty," the inspector said. Before Zotas left him he said, "I'm going to get a search warrant for the Bullays' apartment. That broad trying to put on the class! I had to stand her kind of bullshit when I was a kid, but I don't now. We'll turn that joint of theirs inside out so that they'll have to get a moving company to straighten it out again!"

When he was joined by Detective Smith the inspector knocked at No. 603. The door was opened by a tall, bald, middle-aged man.

"Are you Mr. Piet Langenzent, sir?" the inspector asked.

"Yes?"

"We're the police," the inspector said. "I suppose you knew there was a murder committed on this floor last night?"

"A murder! On this floor of this building!" If he was faking his surprise he was good at it.

"Yes. Mrs. Zelda Greenless across the hall in six-o-two."

"I didn't know, officers. Come in please."

"Thank you."

The two detectives followed the man down a narrow passage, from which opened doors to a kitchenette and a bathroom, and into a combination living room-bedroom furnished simply with a pull-out sofa bed, a couple of easy chairs and a kidney-shaped center table with a bowl of imitation flowers and grasses on it.

"Please sit down, officers," the host said, pointing to the two easy chairs.

"Thank you," said the inspector. "This is Detective Tom Smith and I'm Detective Inspector Walter McDumont of the Metro Homicide Squad."

Langenzent shook their hands and sat down on his bed sofa. He took a pack of cigarettes from an end table, and a lighter. "Cigarette, gentlemen?"

"Not for me, thanks," said Smith.

The inspector walked over, took a cigarette from the pack and leaned down as Langenzent lighted it with his butane lighter. On his way back to his chair he took note of some paintings and prints on the walls. They were all geometric in design. Half covering one wall was a large architectural drawing of some college buildings.

The inspector said, "I was just glancing at your paintings and that architect's drawing. I understand you're a landscape engineer?"

"That's right, sir."

"You're a bachelor?"

"Yes. And as you can see I live in a bachelor apartment. Could you tell me a little about the lady's death across the hall?"

"Only that she was stabbed in the back. Her body was found in the closet holding the garbage chute down the hall this morning. By Mr. George Bullay next door to you. Did you know Mrs. Greenless?"

"No, sir. Until now I didn't even know her name. I think I've seen her on a couple of occasions. Was she a social worker maybe?"

"No. Why do you ask?"

"Well, I saw her on at least two occasions going into her apartment with—well, with young hippies or whatever they call themselves now."

"When would that be, Mr. Langenzent?"

"Last winter sometime. You see, officers, during the winter months I do a lot of my work in a government office building downtown, and I'm around here more. In the warm weather I'm usually away, out on the projects that I have planned the winter before. As a matter of fact you were lucky to find me here tonight. I've been up in Ottawa for the past two weeks working on the grounds and campus of a new community college. I drove back this afternoon."

"You're dressed for going out I see," the inspector said. "I hope we're not keeping you?"

Langenzent glanced at his watch. "No, Inspector, I'm not late yet. I have a date." He laughed, showing his long white teeth. "Though I'm a bachelor I'm not a monk."

"And you never spoke to Mrs. Greenless?"

"Spoke with her? Oh yes, sure. Sometimes we went down in the elevator together. I usually speak to anyone I meet here in the house. Just to say hello, or make a comment on the weather. I don't really know anybody who lives here."

"Not even the Bullays next door?"

The man's face darkened. "I didn't know their name either until now. I said hello to the lady in six-o-one twice, but she didn't even have the courtesy to answer me. Maybe she doesn't like foreigners."

"What nationality are you, Mr. Langenzent?"

"I'm a Hollander. Dutch."

"I see," said the inspector, getting to his feet. "Don't worry about the woman next door, she's discourteous to everybody except perhaps the Vanderbilts, Astors and the Governor General of Canada. She's trying to hide the fact that she was born working class. I'd bet a

109

thousand dollars her old man was a day laborer. She's only a school teacher—public school—and her husband is the straw boss of the typing pool or something in a toy factory."

The tall Dutchman laughed. Then he said, "Her husband is a nice man, but—timid?"

The inspector nodded.

"Maybe it's ladies like her that make me glad I'm a bachelor."

"She's no lady, Mr. Langenzent. Now if you'll just give Detective Smith the particulars of your job, what government department you work for or hire out to, your office address and phone number, what job in Ottawa you're working on now, we'll let you go on your date."

"Thank you, Inspector. I'm going back to Ottawa tomorrow. Does it matter?"

"No, we'll get in touch with you if it's necessary."

While Piet Langenzent gave the information to Detective Smith, who wrote it down in his notebook, McDumont studied the architect's drawing on the wall.

On the way out he said, "And you came back this afternoon? Did you put anything down the garbage chute?"

"Just a Chicken Delight carton. That's what I had for supper."

"And nothing else?"

"No, nothing," he said, staring the inspector in the eye.

They said good-bye to him at the door.

Bill Zotas came along the hall. "I had to stop some people from leaving the building. Some smart-ass son of a bitch, his wife and their girl-haired son. From apartment six-o-six." The detective was seething with unsuppressed anger.

"Take it easy, Bill. I'll fix him."

"He said he's a personal friend of Deputy Chief McCallum."

"All right. When we get to his place I'll do the questioning. You stay out of it. You're too good a detective to get a demerit, and I'm too old to give a damn." He turned to Smith. "Tom, let those we've already questioned leave the building, but none of the others, especially those—" He glanced at the floor plan. "The Hardleys in six-o-six. That means by either elevator or stairs."

"Okay."

The inspector patted Zotas on the back. "Simmer down, Bill. Come on, we'll try apartment six-o-four."

As Detective Smith went to stand by the elevators, the inspector and Zotas went to 604, where the inspector knocked at the door.

It was opened by a man in his early thirties, his hair crew-cut.

"Police," the inspector said.

"Come in."

The two policemen followed the man into the living room, and took the chairs he pointed out to them.

The room was totally unlike any other living room they had seen so far in the apartment house. It was tastefully, even elegantly furnished in Scandinavian blond furniture. Even the bric-a-brac was elegant and the paintings on all four walls were beautiful and modern.

The inspector said, "You're Mr. Wilfrid McMulley, I take it? I'm Detective Inspector McDumont of the Metro Homicide Squad and this is my partner Detective Bill Zotas."

McMulley nodded and said, "Howdya do."

"Is Mrs. Jacton in?" the inspector asked, glancing at his floor plan.

"Yessir. She's lying down. She's taken Zelda's death pretty bad. They were long-time friends you know."

"Yes, we know that, Mr. McMulley. We won't bother her right now. Do you mind answering a few questions?"

"Not at all. Go ahead."

"We're not keeping you from supper or anything?"

"No."

"Do *you* usually put the garbage out, Mr. McMulley?"

"Sometimes. Sometimes Eleanor does."

"At what time? You know, is it in the morning, the evening, or when?"

111

"I guess it's when the bag gets full. It could be any time."

"Try to remember. Did you put it out yesterday?"

McMulley's face wrinkled up in a thinking frown. "Let's see, yes I did. After supper. Maybe seven o'clock. No, it'd be later than that. Let's say nine or half past."

"And Zelda Greenless's body was not in the garbage closet then?"

"Hell no! If it hadda been I'd a called the cops!" He said, "Excuse me, I meant I'd a called the police."

"It's all right, we've been called a lot worse than 'cops', Mr. McMulley. Was there anything unusual going on on this floor of the apartment house when you took out the garbage? Did you see anybody, anybody at all?"

"No."

"Did you hear anything unusual?"

"I dunno if you could call it unusual. Plenty of times some people have parties. They were having a doozer in the apartment opposite the garbage chute. I'll bet you could hear them clean up to York Mills Road."

The inspector glanced at his floor plan. "Would that be Cecil Gilcrest's apartment?"

McMulley counted with his finger. "I guess so. It'd be apartment six-o-eight."

"That'd be Gilcrest's."

"Outside a that, I didn't see nothing or hear nothing," McMulley said.

The inspector took out his notebook. "Tell me, Mr. McMulley, do you have any credit cards? Eaton's, Simpsons, gas cards, American Express, any credit cards at all?"

"Yeah. I have a Gulf gasoline credit account. Nothing else. Eleanor has both Eaton's and Simpsons cards, oh and a Diners Club card."

"Do you sometimes receive cards, like Bank Americard, Chargex, anything like that sent to you in the mail?"

"Not very often. I'm only a lineman with the North York Hydro Electric Commission you know."

"So you never get that kind of card mailed to you?"

"I didn't say that. As a matter of fact I got one a

couple of days ago. A Shop-Easy card, something like that."

"What did you do with it?"

"Well, see, it's like this. I like to pay cash for stuff, except maybe gasoline. I don't want no credit cards. I cut the card in half with the kitchen scissors and threw it in the garbage."

The inspector said, "We know you did. That's how we knew either you or Mrs. Jacton had put garbage out last night. We found it."

"Jeez, you guys don't fool around, do you?"

"Not when we're looking for a murderer. Do you think we could have a word with Mrs. Jacton? We won't be long, and we don't want to disturb her, but this is pretty important."

"I'll go and see if Eleanor's awake."

The short stocky McMulley disappeared down a hallway towards the bedrooms. Bill Zotas waved his arm over the room and pursed his lips in an expression that meant "pretty classy." The inspector nodded.

The policemen could hear a short low conversation from the bedrooms, then Wilf McMulley returned to the living room. "Eleanor'll just be a minute," he said. "She's fixing herself up a bit. She sure took Zelda's death hard."

"Did Eleanor visit Zelda last night?" McDumont asked.

"Yeah. As soon as she got home from work. She—"

A short pretty young woman in her late twenties entered the room. Both detectives stood up.

McMulley said, "Dear, this is Inspector—"

The inspector said, "I'm Inspector Walter McDumont of the homicide squad and this is my partner Detective Bill Zotas. We're sorry to interfere with you like this, at a time like this, but we're investigating the death of your friend Zelda Greenless."

Eleanor Jacton nodded, and sat down beside her common-law husband. Her face was red and puffed from crying, but even this didn't take away its prettiness. Her coal-black hair was cut fairly short and styled so that one side of it covered an ear. Like the murdered woman she was very attractive indeed. The

113

inspector wondered why so many good-looking women were divorcées.

"Mr. McMulley was telling us that you visited with Zelda last night after work?"

She nodded.

"How was she then?"

"She was sick, real sick, Inspector. You know that she drank quite heavily sometimes?"

"Yes."

"She'd been on this binge more than a week. My God, I've never seen her so sick." She began to sob, and McMulley put his arm around her. After she'd wiped her eyes she went on, "Drinking was a disease with her. She'd been to doctors—you know she worked for one?"

"Yes. We've been to see both Dr. Franczic and a psychiatrist, Dr. Hugh Rutsey."

"Doctor Franczic was very good to her. He'd let her take time off from work when she was on one of her drinking bouts, thinks like that. He recommended Dr. Rutsey to her, and he was the best of the doctors she'd seen."

"Who were the others?"

"I don't know. Honest. She'd visited other psychiatrists, but none of them had done her any good. There was one down at the Ontario Mental Hospital, a woman, that she saw for quite some time, and others, some of them after I met her and some before. None of them could cure her of her fears, real crazy nervous fears. Not that Zelda was crazy. Far from it, but she had these bad nervous spells. Some of them she got over herself and some she tried to shut out of her mind with liquor. I don't think there's a doctor in the world who could have helped her."

"What about Hugh Rutsey?"

"As I said, he was the best one she ever had. She didn't go to him for very long, but in the short time, in the few visits she had with him, he did her good. I could see the improvement myself. In the first place he didn't lie to her, and he made it easy for her to tell the truth to him. One time, when she was coming out of a binge—not as bad as this last one but almost—he made her cure herself. It may sound crazy, but I know he did it. He told her that she had to face up to the fact that she was an alcoholic, and that the medical profession didn't know much about alcoholism. He was inclined to think that in some people it was physical, a case of a meta—metaphysical—no, that's not it. A case of *metabolic* imbalance. In others it was psychological, which was her trouble. I think he said that there was a third kind of drunk who drank excessively, too much, because of cultural or behavioristic pressures." She smiled tearfully, and wiped her eyes again. "It's funny that I remember those big medical words, but Dr. Rutsey had written them down for her, and she repeated them to me several times. I think he might have been able to straighten her out if she'd let him. But she left him too soon."

"You said something, Mrs. Jacton, about Dr. Rutsey once bringing her out of one of her binges."

"Yes he did. She once went to him and he gave her prescriptions for some pills. He told her to take the pills—"

"What kind of pills?" the inspector asked.

"Oh, tranquilizers, sleeping pills, and another kind that was for her nerves I think. Anyway, she only bought the sleeping pills."

"Why?"

"Well, this sounds crazy, I guess, but as I said it cured her, and Dr. Rutsey was the only one who was ever able to do it. He told her to take a drink of liquor in the morning, to straighten her out. Then to go downtown and drink a few beers, then take in a picture show —to get her mind off herself, then drink enough beer to give her an appetite, go to a restaurant and eat something, anything—she hadn't eaten a bite for a week—and then, if she wanted to, to drink beer until it was time to come home, take a sleeping pill and go to bed."

"And it worked?"

"Yes it did. I talked to her when she arrived home that first night. She sat for a few minutes right where you're sitting, and she was tipsy all right but not blind crazy drunk like she'd been for over a week. The next day she did the same thing, and on the third day she might have had a shot or two of liquor but she was eating again. On the fourth day she went back to Dr. Franczic's office. I guess she was a little shaky, but the cure had worked."

"How often did she have these binges?"

"Maybe three or four times a year, sometimes more, sometimes less. She drank some at other times, but in a social kind of way."

"You said that Dr. Rutsey had told her that her drinking problem was caused by a psychological pressure?"

"Something like that. She was full of shame and hate for herself. She'd had a hell of a life, mister. You don't know what kind of a life that woman had had." She began to sob again, but recovered herself and dried her eyes.

"I think I know quite a bit about it," the inspector said. "She was put in a family way by an older man called Musgrove when she was only thirteen—"

"That's right. How'd you know that?"

The inspector raised his hands but said nothing. When he did speak he asked, "Who is Musgrove? Do you know where he lives? Has he had any contact with her?"

"No. She's never seen him since the night he made her pregnant. I think he lives here in the city, but I'm not even sure of that."

"Her baby died in the Sick Children's Hospital when it was about six-and-a-half months old?"

"Yes." Eleanor looked at Wilf, surprised that the police knew so much about her friend.

"I understand from Dr. Rutsey that from the time Musgrove made her pregnant she had a great fear of older men? That she hung around with young men and boys, some of them young enough to be her sons, from then on?"

Mrs. Jacton nodded.

"You met her, I believe, when you both lived in an apartment house down on Gamble Avenue?"

"Yes I did."

"I guess you were pretty young then?"

"I was. I was taking a hairdressing course at night, and working in a factory during the day. I'd only had

116

Grade Eleven in a secondary school, which is what they call technical schools now, and I'd wanted to be a designer. The courses they gave me at school were a waste of time. I moved into a bachelor apartment on Gamble Avenue."

"We know the house number. What apartment did you live in there?"

"You know—is it 'Inspector?' "

McDumont nodded.

"You know something, Inspector, I've forgotten the number of the apartment down there. Anyway it was on the same floor as Zelda's.

"The fifth."

"I guess so. Anyway, I got fired from my job, and I would have had to quit my hair-styling course, if Zelda hadn't helped me out."

"How did she help you out?"

"Food, money, the rent. For more than a month."

"Was she going with younger men down there?"

Mrs. Jacton hesitated. Then she said, "Yes she was."

The inspector said, "This may be embarrassing, Mrs. Jacton, but did you double date with Zelda with these younger men and boys?"

"Yes. Wilf here knows all about it, and I think you do too from the questions you've been asking me. Sure I dated boys down there, in fact I married one."

"What happened to that?"

"He screw—he went off with another girl, back to New Brunswick."

"Did Zelda take drugs then?"

"No, and she didn't take them here either. She smoked pot, that was all. Just to be social-like with the kids that visited her."

"We found some hash in her apartment. By weight I'd say maybe twenty dimes worth."

"She was holding it for one of those creeps."

"What creeps?"

"Those creeps that used to come and visit her. The gang from over in the Don Mills Centre."

"Like Dreamer?"

"Good God, is there nothing you guys don't know? Yeah. Creeps like Dreamer."

"Did some of those creeps—and I'm not arguing with you about the term because it fits them—sleep with Zelda?"

"Some of them did. I won't call her a nympho, but she was sexy."

"Did Dreamer?"

She gave a short hysterical laugh. "Hell no, Inspector. He was always too far out on speed and stuff to get it up for a woman." She looked from the inspector to Bill Zotas. "I'm sorry, gentlemen; I didn't mean to be vulgar. But when we're talking about vulgar people like Dreamer sometimes we use vulgar expressions."

"It's okay, Mrs. Jacton. Tell me, why, if Zelda Greenless was turned off by older men, did she marry Greenless?"

"I wondered about it plenty of times myself. I stood up for her at her wedding you know."

"We know that."

"I should have known you knew, Inspector." She gave a wan smile. "I think that Zelda hated the—the psychological bind she found herself in. Understand?"

McDumont nodded.

"I think that all her life, from the time that guy Musgrove ruined her—and I *do* mean ruined—I think she was searching for a release from her fears and self-hate. Greenless—he's dead now incidentally—was an older man, but a pretty nice guy. I think that Zelda got the idea that by getting married she could become respectable. Does that sound screwy?"

"No."

"I think she thought, at the time, that marriage to Greenless would allow her to forget her hang-ups, to forget the baby she'd lost, to forget that that bastard Musgrove had raped her when she was just a kid."

"Was it rape?"

"I don't know. Rape, seduction, call it anything you want. When an adult has intercourse with a girl of thirteen it's anything you want to call it."

"Right," the inspector said. "I just have a few more short questions to ask you, Mrs. Jacton. We have quite a few more people on this floor to question."

"All right."

"Had Zelda any relatives in Crow Lake, do you know?"

"I think she has an aunt and uncle up there."

"Is their name Stanton?"

"Yes. Her uncle is her father's brother. Peter Stanton."

The inspector wrote the name down in his notebook. Then he asked, "What time did you visit Zelda's apartment last evening?"

"Around seven."

"Did you join her in a drink?"

"No. I haven't had a drink for a couple of weeks."

"We found two tumblers, both bearing lipstick stains."

"I think they were both hers. I saw the other tumbler when I was in there. I think she was just too drunk to realize she'd been drinking out of one, and took down another."

"We're having them examined now. Was it likely she'd have another woman friend in there with her at all last evening?"

"I don't think so. I think I was the only woman friend she had." She broke out into loud sobbing, and it was a long time before Wilf McMulley could calm her down.

"How long did you stay with her?"

Mrs. Jacton looked at McMulley. "How long would it be, dear?"

"I'd say maybe half an hour."

"Maybe a little longer, Inspector," Mrs. Jacton said.

"And she was all right when you left her?"

"She was alive, but she wasn't all right. She's been sick as a dog all day. I cleaned up vomit in the bathroom. She would take a drink—"

"Of what?"

"I don't know, Inspector. She had a dozen empty bottles, and some with some booze in them, on the sink counter. I really don't know what she drank when I was there."

"Was it the same drink all the time? I mean, did she refill her glass at all?"

The woman thought a moment. "I can't swear to it,

Inspector, but I think she just sipped the same drink. She was just too sick to do anything else. She'd take a sip, gag, then sometimes seem to pass out for a couple of minutes, or run into the bathroom to throw up. God, I'd never seen anybody so sick in my life."

"What did you do about it?"

"I phoned Dr. Rutsey, but all I got was his answering service. I thought of getting a cab and taking Zelda up to the North York General, but she didn't want to go. I took the phone off the hook, laid her down on her bed and covered her, locked the door, and came in here.

"Did you return at all?"

"We left our own door slightly open until Wilf here went out, just in case any of those drug-shooting creeps came up, then I went back to see how Zelda was doing. She was still in bed, apparently asleep, except that she was breathing funny. Kind of gasping out each breath like."

"Where did you go out to, Wilf?" the inspector asked.

"Oh, just over to the Don Mills theatre. I'd seen the picture, so I went to the Artifactory and had a few beers."

"Were any of Zelda's young friends there?"

"I didn't see none of them. I only had a few beers with old man Osler in six-o-nine."

"You obviously have a key to Mrs. Greenless's apartment, haven't you, Mrs. Jacton?"

"Yes."

"Did anyone else have keys?"

"I think she gave keys to one or two boys. I warned her she was a fool to give them to them, but she wouldn't listen to me."

"Did you drop into Zelda's apartment again later last evening?"

"Yes. I guess it was about ten o'clock, after Wilf had come home from the plaza. I just looked through her bedroom doorway, and she was lying there quiet, sleeping good by then. The funny breathing had stopped. Then I put out all the lights, tiptoed out, and came back here."

"You have no idea then whether she was still alive or dead?"

"Good Lord no! I was sure she was asleep!"

"You put her to bed wearing her clothes. Was she still wearing them the last time you saw her last night?"

"I—I don't know, Inspector. She had the covers over her."

The inspector, followed by the dectective, stood up. "Thank you both. I may have to question both of you again; I hope you don't mind?"

Both Mrs. Jacton and McMulley shook their heads.

Inspector McDumont asked, "Did you notice a picture missing from one of the walls?"

"No," Eleanor Jacton answered.

"Okay. Good night then," McDumont said, heading for the door.

Bill Zotas said, "This is a beautiful living room, Mrs. Jacton."

"Thank you. I think I'd have made a good interior decorator if—well, just if. Instead I'm a hairdresser at the Bon Beauty Boutique."

"That probably makes the Don Mills women very happy," said McDumont.

He turned around at the door.

"Oh, by the way," the inspector said. He walked back into the apartment, followed by Bill Zotas, closing the door behind him. "Have either of you ever seen a knife with a handle like this one?" He pulled the steak knife from his pocket and hand it to Wilf McMulley.

McMulley examined the handle. "No, I never seen one like this."

"How about you, Mrs. Jacton?"

Eleanor took the knife from her common law husband and looked it over. "I saw one once, I think the handle was the same, but the blade wasn't so long and it was sharpened to a point."

"Where was this?"

"In Zelda's place."

"How long ago?"

"A couple of months ago I'd say."

"Did you ask Zelda about it?"

"Yes. I think she said it belonged to one of the gang, the Centre Gang as they call themselves. He'd left it

121

there, forgotten it. I think she told me some of the guys carried them as a kind of gang badge."

"How—in a sheath on the belt maybe?"

"I don't know that, Inspector."

"Something else I forgot. When did Mr. Greenless die, and what was his first name?"

"It was either late last February or early March. Zelda and I went to his funeral. As I told you, he was a nice guy. He was only forty-seven when he died. Heart attack. He'd worked for the TTC, a bus driver."

"And his first name?"

"Danny. Daniel Greenless."

"You don't remember the date? Do you remember the funeral parlor?"

"It was over on Yonge Street below Lawrence. I forgot the date. He was buried up on Kingston Road in that cemetery that doesn't allow gravestones."

"Resthaven Memorial Gardens?"

"Yes, that's it."

"Okay, thanks again." The inspector nodded to Wilfrid and Eleanor, and he and Bill Zotas went out into the hallway again. McDumont wrote some notes in his notebook.

Bill Smith joined them.

"How'd things go, Bill?" the inspector asked him.

"I let Piet Langenzent out, and the couple from the front apartment across from the dead woman."

"Yeah. The Bullays. Where were they going?"

"I don't know. They were dressed up. When they got into the elevator the woman said, "I guess this place'll be crawling with cops from now on.""

"She doesn't know the half of it," the inspector said.

"The kid from six-o-six came out, put some garbage down the chute, then tried to sneak down the back stairs. I stopped him, and sent him back to his apartment."

"Did he give you any lip?"

"No. He was quiet. He looked pretty scared about something."

"Maybe of his old man, or maybe something else. We'll leave the Hardleys until last. Okay, Smitty, let's try the Derymores in six-o-five."

Chapter 9

The door of 605 was opened to the end of its chain door-lock. A middle-aged woman wearing glasses and a zippered housecoat looked out. She had her hair done up in curlers.

"Mrs. Derymore? Freda Derymore?"

"Yes."

The inspector showed her his badge. "Police, Mrs. Derymore."

"Oh my!" The woman closed the door, unhooked the chain, and invited them in.

The living room floor was covered with wall-to-wall red pile carpeting, which ran back through a hall past the bathroom and bedrooms. The furniture was old but good and very conservative. A color TV was on, with the sound turned down. On the walls were typical shopping plaza reproductions of landscapes and seascapes. There were also some framed photographs—family photos of a father and mother and three small daughters—some of them individual snapshots, and one big studio-posed photograph of what the inspector took to be the parent Derymores when they were younger, flanked by a pair of young girls. There was a baby sitting on the mother's lap.

"Is this a family photo, Mrs. Derymore?" the inspector asked, pointing to the studio photograph on the wall.

"Yes. Those are my three daughters, Karen, Barbara and Eunice. We lived in our own house then, in Willowdale. My, when I think of it! It only cost us eight thousand dollars in those days, with an open mortgage. We were offered fourteen for it when Eunice left—she's the baby—and so we took it. Nowadays it's probably worth fifty thousand. My husband, Ab, had put a lot of work into it, hardwood flooring throughout, a garage, things like that. We were within walking distance of Yonge Street, just north of Finch. Ab hated the long drive to work in the rush hour. There was no Don Valley Parkway then, or the 401 freeway, of course. Now the subway runs all the way up Yonge. Even without it Ab could have gone down Bayview to 401 then over to the Parkway, or even driven down the Bayview Extension. I hate apartment houses; I wish I still had my garden and my pair of Welsh terriers."

"Is Mr. Derymore in?"

"No," she answered, looking crestfallen. "I'm expecting him soon though. He's doing an audit down at the bank."

The inspector looked at the voters' list he'd filched from Zelda's apartment. "He's an accountant at the Bank of Montreal at Richmond and Sherbourne Streets, I understand?"

"Yes, Chief Accountant."

"I understand you and your husband were pretty angry about being asked to stay in the apartment this morning by one of the detectives."

"Yes we were, sir. Albert had this auditing to do, and I had a particularly important visit to pay to a very disturbed child."

"What institution do you work for, Mrs. Derymore?"

"No institution, sir. I do voluntary visiting for our church. Mainly to counsel the mothers of disturbed children."

"What church is that?"

"Christian Science. We attend the Second Church out on the Danforth."

"I see. Mrs. Derymore, did you or your husband see or hear anything out-of-the-way last evening or during the night?"

"Nothing but that awful drinking party across the hall in Mr. Gilcrest's apartment. Apart from that, that is because of it, we wouldn't have heard an earthquake."

"You didn't *see* anything peculiar going on in the apartment corridor?"

"No, sir. Albert and I stayed right in here all evening."

"What time do you usually go to bed?"

"Right after the National News on the TV." As she spoke she looked at the TV set and saw that it was still turned on. She walked over and switched it off.

"Did you know the dead woman, Mrs. Greenless?"

"I chatted with her sometimes, in the hallway or the elevator. I understand her husband is a mining engineer or something in South America? Has he been notified?"

"I think that was a little exaggeration of Mrs. Greenless's. Her husband is dead."

Sorrowfully, the woman said, "Why would she lie to me? I once told her that our Karen was married to a General Motors executive in Rio de Janeiro, and she said her husband was in Venezuela or somewhere."

"Maybe it was just a bit of personal snobbery on her part. We all exaggerate ourselves a little sometimes."

Again sorrowfully she said, "Yes." Then, "I guess it doesn't matter much now that she's gone over to the other side."

The inspector stood up. "I guess that's all, Mrs. Derymore. If you hear of anything give me a call. I'm Walter McDumont of the Missing Persons and Homicide Division of the Metro Toronto Police."

"It seems funny putting Missing Persons in with the Homicides."

"Believe me, it's not always funny to us in Homicide, Mrs. Derymore."

"I always keep my door locked, double locked. Did you see the lock and chain?"

"Yes, they're good against amateur prowlers, but a good burglar can open a chain-locked door as easy as a can of sardines."

"Oh my! They can?"

"Yes. If you've got a length of string and a thumbtack I'll show you how they do it."

"Just a minute, sir." The woman went into her kitchen and came back with about a yard of parceling string. "I think Albert has some thumbtacks in his desk." She returned from one of the bedrooms with a brass-headed thumbtack. "Is this what you mean, sir?"

"Yes. That'll do nicely. Now, Detective Smith and I will go out into the hallway. You can presume that a burglar has something that will open any of the apartment doors in the building. They make keys by the dozen down in the joint—in the penitentiary. He might also be able to pick the lock of the chain-lock, but that's a little more difficult because of the way the lock faces up. Not at all impossible, but depending on the burglar's expertise. Now, we'll go outside and you lock both the door and the chain-lock. *I* don't happen to have a master key to open the regular door lock, but I'll open it too. Okay?"

"Okay, sir."

The two detectives went into the hallway, where Bill Zotas joined them. They heard Mrs. Derymore sliding the chain in its slot.

"If neither of you guys know how a chain-locked door is opened, watch this," the inspector said, taking his ID card from his pocket.

He opened the door lock easily with his stiff laminated ID card. Taking the piece of string he tied a running bowline on one end, reached inside and tightened the bowline around the small knob on the end of the chain in the slot, then letting the string hang he reached as far as he could inside the door, passed his hand across the brass slot to its inside end and as far past it as he could. He pressed the thumbtack into the wooden door half-way, leaving enough of the thumbtack's pointed pin exposed between the head and the door itself to allow him to circle the pin with the string, which he then pulled back outside. Pulling the door nearly closed, he pulled on the string, which, with the thumbtack as its pulley, gently pulled the chain knob back along its slot, so that it fell out. The door was open.

McDumont pushed open the door. "Hello, Mrs. Derymore, I'm your local burglary instructor," he said to the woman who stood in her hallway with her hand covering her mouth.

"My, oh my!" she exclaimed. "I thought those things were foolproof."

126

"Nothing is foolproof against a determined and efficient burglar, Mrs. Derymore. I'll leave the thumbtack and the string where they are, so you can show your husband when he comes home from the bank. Maybe you'd feel safer by buying another Welsh terrier."

"They won't allow pets in the house," Mrs. Derymore said.

"That's too bad. Okay, ma'am, you can lock it up again. We may want to question you or your husband again, but we'll wait until evening next time."

"Okay, sir." They heard her sliding the chain along its slot, then pulling it out with the string.

McDumont pulled the floor plan from his pocket, and said, "I think Mrs. Norma Dryburg in six-o-seven is next."

He and Bill Zotas went to the widow's door and knocked. "Anyone else try to leave the floor, Bill?" the inspector asked.

"No. I didn't see anybody, Inspector."

The inspector knocked on the door, harder this time."

There was no answer.

"She may be out," Zotas said.

"I hope not. I saw her this morning peeking out through the crack of the door. Quite an old lady, over seventy at least. They see a lot more than most younger people."

Zotas knocked, quite hard this time.

Mrs. Dryburg's door was not opened, but the door across the hall was. A paunchy young man, his hair uncombed, wearing yellow polo pajamas, or a yellow sweatsuit, stood in the open doorway of 608, in his hand a long glass filled with a colorless mixed drink. "Mrs. Dryburg doesn't answer her door after dark," he said.

"Which shows her common sense," said McDumont. "Are you Cecil Gilcrest?"

"I am, gentlemen. And, don't tell me, *you're* the police."

"Right on, Mac," Zotas said.

"Please come in."

They followed the pajama-clad young man into a living room that looked as if it had withstood the seige of the Alamo. There were bottles and glasses all over the large straw rug that covered the floor, beer-bottle caps and cigarette butts filled several ash-trays, and in a corner were propped a couple of colorful corduroy custions. The sofa cushions were lined up in a row on the dinette floor. A beautiful, almost photographic nude oil painting, stretched full length and facing the room, hung crookedly on the wall above the stripped-down sofa.

"Some party last night," McDumont said, moving a striped suit coat out of an easy chair and sitting down. The inspector pointed to a hassock, and motioned Detective Zotas to sit down on it. Their host threw a cushion onto the sofa springs and sat down there.

"I said, Mr. Gilcrest, you had quite a party last night."

"Sure did. Last one for a while. It'll take me a week to get back in shape."

"This is Detective Bill Zotas and I'm Detective Inspector McDumont of the police homicide bureau."

Gilcrest nodded. "Glad to have you aboard, gentlemen. You know who *I* am already. May I get you a drink?"

"No thanks," McDumont said.

"I suppose this is about the lady along the hall?"

"Yes."

"Ask me whatever you want." He held up the glass. "I'm only sipping this for medicinal purposes. Jeez, today I even hate the taste of it."

"Did you know Zelda Greenless?"

"Yes and no. I knew her to speak to but didn't know her well enough to proposition her."

"Would you have liked to?"

"Sure. A little older than me, I suspect, but still an attractive lady. Unattached attractive women are not a feature of this low high-rise rabbit warren, gentlemen."

"When did you see her last?"

"Maybe a week ago, at the elevators. We went down together. I thought she might work downtown, so I offered her a lift. She told me she worked in a doctor's office here in Don Mills, and walked to the office for her daily exercise."

"That was the first step in your get-acquainted campaign shot," said the inspector.

"Shot all to hell, Inspector. I mean she and I being neighbors and all it would have been handy. But you win some and lose some."

"Do you know Eleanor Jacton?"

"Not by name. Who's she?"

"The short dark-haired woman in apartment six-o-four."

"Just to say hello to. She's even prettier than Mrs. Greenless was. There is only one thing wrong with her."

"What's that?"

"Her husband. I'm a head taller than him but I wouldn't want to mix with him in a fight. He's a pretty husky guy who doesn't have to go to Vic Tanney's to stay in shape. I've met him sometimes in the hallway or the elevator. Looks like a U.S. Marine drill instructor, with his brushcut and everything." He took a long pull at his drink.

"What is that stuff?" Zotas asked.

"This?" He held up the glass. "This is three ounces of Smirnoff vodka, soda water and a dash of bitters."

"Are you an American, Mr. Gilcrest?" asked the inspector.

"Just Cec, please. Yes, but I've taken out Canadian citizenship."

"Why?"

"After I was discharged from the army my company sent me to Toronto, I liked it, so when five years had gone by I gave up my U.S. citizenship and became a Canadian."

McDumont asked, "Are you a salesman for a mining company?"

"Yes. Corinth Base Metals Mines, a company that's somewhere in the lower echelons of a conglomorate called Pacific Investments Inc."

"You sell base metals?"

"No, Inspector. All the base metals from two Ontario mines, one in Quebec and another in Manitoba, are

129

sold before they're taken from the mines. To Welsh-Hayrush Brass & Steel Products, Dayton, Ohio, another Pacific Investments Inc. company."

"Then what do you sell?"

"Good will, company relations, international co-operation."

"In other words public relations?"

"Yes, but Pacific Investments Inc. never uses the term. We're all called salesmen."

"Why?" the inspector asked.

"I don't really know, and I've never really asked. Some guy up at the top, or mabe in the advertising company that handles Pacific's account, thought we'd be better off known as salesmen. This is true of the States as well as Canada, Mexico, Morocco, Chile, and anywhere else Pacific has a corporate foot."

"Who's the top guy in the company?"

"Arnold Hayrush is president of Corinth Base Metals, Canada. He used to own Welsh-Hayrush Brass & Steel Products. He lives in Dayton, Ohio. As to who owns Pacific Investments Inc. it could be Howard Hughes, Cyrus Eaton or Bob Hope. I couldn't say, and I guess the U.S. Internal Revenue Dept. would have a hard time saying."

"Did you leave the apartment any time last evening or early this morning?"

"Yes, on a few occasions, usually to see guests to the elevator. Later on I was too drunk or too busy, or both, to bother."

"Did you see anything unusual out in the corridor, anything or anybody near Mrs. Greenless's apartment?"

"No."

"You saw nobody at all in the sixth floor corridor?"

"Yes, I saw little Anton Zutach pushing his hand-cart past my door. I was bidding goodnight to a lady guest, and she took a ride on it to the elevators."

"What was this particular lady guest's name?"

"I think it was Pat Enderby but I'm not sure." He took a long gulp of his vodka drink. "It might have been Monica, but I think it was Pat."

The inspector told Bill Zotas to take down the

names and addresses, then he asked Gilcrest for a list of the people who had attended his party the evening before.

"Well, there was Patricia Enderby. Just a minute." Cec Gilcrest jumped up, went into one of the two bedrooms in the apartment and came back with an address book. He turned some of the pages to those following the letter E. "Pat Enderby. She's a nurse at the East General Hospital on Coxwell Avenue in the city. She lives up the street in the Envoy Apartments. Just a couple of doors from here."

"Okay, Cec, go on."

"Ruby Susanna—"

"How do you spell that, Cec?" Bill Zotas asked.

Gilcrest spelled it. "Ruby is a schoolteacher at a neighborhood parochial school—you call them Separate Schools up here I think—Our Lady of Compassion Separate School. Sorry, the school is in Scarborough, not Don Mills. She lives on Broadpath Road. Don't know the number."

"Go on," said the inspector.

"There was Monica Smith. She's a public school teacher somewhere around here. Overland Drive Public School, I didn't know I'd written it down. She lives at nine Woodcliff Place, Don Mills."

"How old are these girls, Cec?"

"All above the age of consent. Pat is twenty-four, Ruby is twenty-seven or eight, Monica is twenty-two."

The inspector said, "Okay, who else was there?"

"There was Benton Graveros, whose address I don't know, but who lives in the city. I have the odd drink with him downtown at the Cav-A-Bob or the King Eddie Hotel."

"Where's the office of Corinth Base Metals Mines?"

"In the Royal Bank Building, King and Yonge."

"Okay, go on."

"Benton brought a French-Canadian guy with him, from Quebec City. His name was Paul-Emile Tremblay."

"Sounds like a cardinal," McDumont said. "Tremblay is the most common French-Canadian name,

131

Cecil. How could we get in touch with either one of these two men?"

"Tremblay I'm not sure of, but Graveros works at the stock exchange. He knows Craig Hardley along the hall."

"We haven't questioned the Hardleys yet. When we do I'll ask him. Were the Hardleys the only people from this apartment house who were invited to the party?"

"They weren't the only ones invited but they were the only ones who came. I'd also invited Mr. Raymark Osler across the hall. Very nice old gentleman, lived near here when it was farm country. Used to trap muskrats along the banks of the Don River. Knew Ernest Thompson Seton, your famous Canadian nature writer. Mr. Osler told me Seton had written his animal stories down in the Don Valley. I'd read them when I was a school kid."

"Where was that, Cec?"

"Plainfield, New Jersey. Born and raised there. So was Jack Benny's wife, Mary Livingstone. Only thing the town's famous for. Of course she was born a few years before my time."

"How old are you now, Cec?"

"Twenty-nine. I'll be thirty in August." He shook his head. "Goddam, it's hard to believe today that Seton could have written his animal stories down in the Don Valley. Now one side of it has the Bayview Extension and the other side the Don Valley Parkway."

"Was there anybody else in the apartment house that you invited to your party?"

"Yes. There was Leslie Gormley—that's a girl, twenty-five, in apartment three-o-one. We had a good thing going one time, but she called it off. Still friends though. She's going to marry a dentist. Saw through me; said I was an insincere gadabout. That's the term she used. She was right of course. She's a secretary to an insurance company exec. I told her to come and bring her dentist, but she turned me down."

"Anybody else?"

"Yes. John Kapett who lives in an apartment on the

seventh floor. He's manager of a paint company I think. Talked to him for an evening over at Diana's Artifactory in the plaza. Talked about base metals mostly. Seen him since on occasion going or coming on the elevators. He's an older man, maybe fifty."

"Anybody else?"

"There's always others, Inspector. You're introduced to them but you never remember their names. Maybe six or eight."

"Do you know what the apartment superintendent was doing with his handcart?"

"No. Didn't ask him. After Pat Enderby got off he wheeled it along the corridor to the front stairwell."

"I see. Okay, Cec, thanks for your cooperation."

"*Es nada*, Inspector. It was nothing."

"We'll be going now."

Cecil Gilcrest took the detectives to the door and bid them goodnight.

Inspector McDumont pulled the steak knife from his pocket. "Have you ever seen one of these before?"

Gilcrest took the knife in his hand and inspected it. "No, I don't think so, Inspector."

"Have you ever eaten at the Coach'n Four?"

"A few times. But believe me I wasn't paying much attention to the knives and forks. Is that where this knife came from?"

"Yes," the inspector said, opening the door.

"Don't tell me Mrs. Greenless was stabbed with one of those? That must have been hard to do."

"Not if the knife was sharpened and pointed, and honed like a razor."

The young man shook his head. "I'll be a son of a bitch!" he said.

"It's a cinch somebody is," McDumont said. He and Detective Zotas stepped into the corridor, and with a wave of his hand Gilcrest closed the door behind them.

Raymark Osler's door was opened almost as soon as the inspector knocked on it. The old man who faced them was short, wrinkled, and with a white fringe of hair surrounding his partly bald head. He hadn't shaved that day. He was wearing a pair of old but

133

well-cut charcoal gray Daks slacks, a Tattersall vest over a plaid green-and-gray shirt, and highly polished brown slip-on moccasins.

"Come in, officers," he said to the inspector and Detective Smith.

"How did you know we were policemen?" McDumont asked.

"The word 'officers' doesn't only apply to policemen," Osler said. "Anyhow, I've been listening to you coming this way down the hall. From your size and the way you're standing there I'd say you were policemen. Come in, come in."

The detectives followed the old man straight into his living room. It was furnished in old comfortable-looking leather furniture. There was an Aztec or Apache shawl or blanket thrown over the back of the sofa and a rather moth-eaten polar bear rug on the otherwise bare floor. The walls were hung with photographs, of people, animals, a small stream, landscapes. One wall bore a large oil painting of a young woman wearing a gown of a style out of date for forty years. Her hair was bobbed in a mid-Twenties cut.

"That's my wife," Osler said, flicking on a small electric light bulb on the bottom of the picture frame. "Her name was Ethel, and she died in childbirth in nineteen-thirty-two. I and a neighbor woman delivered the baby. Not any more than a mile from where we're standing now. Excuse me, gents. Sit down, sit down."

The detectives sat down on the sofa.

"I'm sorry to hear of your wife dying like that, Mr. Osler," McDumont said. "Did you save the baby?"

"Yes, a healthy baby boy. My poor wife died of puerperal fever, septicemia, what we called childbed fever then. Wouldn't have if I could have got her to a hospital. It was during the worst blizzard of that winter. I had to leave my wife in labor, and snowshoe from our place on one of the banks of the Don River to my nearest neighbor's, a good man called Martin MacKay, part Indian, who lived downstream about a mile. MacKay's wife came back with me to my place, both of us on snowshoes, while MacKay made it downstream and up the old Don Mills Road to what was even then O'Connor Drive. Mostly empty fields though, with the first working-class suburbanites living in the basement they'd been able to build before they went on relief when the Depression struck. Our doctor, Victor Johnston, a son of a bitch if there ever was one, wouldn't come up home on a pair of spare snowshoes MacKay had taken him. I and MacKay's good little wife delivered the baby ourselves. MacKay tried to get an ambulance, but none of them would come. I've had nothing to do with doctors or ambulances since. Poor Ethel was in agony for three days before she died, high fever, terrible pain, the veins in her legs all swollen, and her belly swollen and tender, the stink of it—Christ, I swore I'd run that Johnston out of town. And I did."

"How?" the inspector asked.

"I went to see Lady Kemp, my father had been a friend of her husband's, and I had her cut off the compensation cases from their factory—then it was known as the General Steel Wares, but as Kemp's by some people—that were going to that bastard Johnston. I'd articled in law and been called to the Ontario bar. Never practiced much though. The black sheep of the Osler clan. Five of them in *Who's Who* and four of the five are Q.C.'s. After St. Andrew's, Toronto University and Osgoode Hall law school I built a house up the Don River and settled down with Ethel to live a simple outdoor life. It worked fine too until Ethel was killed by that goddam quack's neglect. Had a pair of purebred Belgian Shepherds, King and Queen. There weren't too many of them in Canada in those days. Brought the baby up myself. Bought my milk from the head herdsman at Donalda Farm. Good pure Guernsey milk."

"What about Dr. Johnston?"

"I sued him on my own behalf, and Ethel's, but lost the case. Then I sued him for three men who had been injured at the General Steel Wares, and who were being done out of their compensation by that bastard Johnston. Won all three of the cases. One of them was an Italian who worked in the extrusion department. He's dead now, but I put him on easy street during the Depression. Another was a Macedonian who

135

through that quack's neglect lost his whole right arm. In those days there wasn't any penicillin, antibiotics or even sulfonamides. The man developed gangrene in his arm, which had to be amputated at the shoulder. He and his family moved out west somewhere. The third one was a Cockney, newly arrived from Over 'Ome. He was blinded in the grinding room. Won him a pension and he opened a newstand in the Union Station. He must be dead too; I haven't seen or heard of him in years. What beat Johnston was the legal costs. Even doctors didn't have much money during the Depression, and what with having to spend so much time in the courts and paying so much for lawyers it beat him out of his practice and put him on the bum. His wife left him, just as he'd taken mine away from me. He died in the Queen Street Mental Hospital —we called it Nine- Ninety-Nine or the Insane Asylum in those days. Celebrated his death when I heard of it by buying a gallon of Catawba wine and getting drunk with the MacKays and a couple of unemployed guys who were riding the freights. Some of the hoboes would walk up the CN tracks through the valley that runs under Eglinton Avenue now, east of the Don Valley Parkway, and catch the slow-climbing trains on the steep grade there."

"Where's your son these days?"

"He's practicing law out in British Columbia. Married with three nice children."

"And you brought him up yourself?"

"As a baby. When he was six I sent him to a one-room schoolhouse in the village where Victoria Park Avenue and Lawrence Avenue meet today. Later on he went to St. Andrew's, U of T and Osgoode Hall. One of my dogs, either King or Queen, would go to school with him and come home with him when school was finished for the day. He was as safe with one of the dogs guarding him as he would have been with a platoon of infantry. The country around here was half-wild in those days, especially down in the river valley. During the Depression we had squatters who moved into log cabins and tarpaper shacks down there. And there were always a lot of hoboes."

136

"I'm sorry to break into your reminiscences. Mr. Osler, but we're late now and have one more family to question on this floor. Where did you spend last evening? I understand you turned down an invitation to Gilcrest's party across the hall?"

"Yes, it was nice of him to invite me, but I'm too old for those young people's parties. I went over to the Artifactory and drank beer most of the evening. I was half sloshed when I staggered back here and turned in."

"What time would that be?"

"I have no idea. Elevenish I'd say."

"Who did you drink with over there?"

"A couple of different people. One of them used to be a groom in Eddie Taylor's Windfields Farm when it was functioning up on York Mills Road."

"E.P. Taylor's?"

"Yeah. I also drank for quite a while with a young man who lives along the hall. He's got an Irish name. He works for the North York Hydro Electric utility."

"Wilf McMulley?"

"That's him."

"After you got home did you see or hear anything different from the usual?"

"In the first place I was sloshed just enough not to see lightning or hear thunder, and in the second place I wouldn't have been able to anyway with the noise from Gilcrest's apartment. Talk about the rape of the Sabines! Not that I don't envy the young buggers."

Inspector McDumont took the steak knife from his pocket and showed it to Mr. Osler. "Have you ever seen a knife like this, sir?" he asked.

"A steak knife? Not that I recall."

The inspector put the knife back in his pocket again.

"What do you think of Anton Zutach, the super-intendent?"

"Well, he shovels the snow and keeps the halls clean. I don't think about him at all."

"What did you think of Zelda Greenless?"

"The murdered woman? I thought she was a pleasant girl. We chatted now and then."

"You couldn't hazard a guess who murdered her?"

"Ha! I'm a lawyer I told you. I don't make guesses about such things, and if I do I keep them to myself."

"We'll let you go back to your TV viewing."

"All right. I watch the late news on the CTV network, or part of it, then switch to Buffalo's Channel Two and watch Johnny Carson's monologue."

"Just the monologue?" asked Detective Smith.

"That's all. I don't like talk-show guests who are retired old actresses, should-be-retired young comics, or quack doctors peddling fad diets. Anyhow, by the time Carson's monologue is finished I'm ready for my bed."

"You know, Mr. Osler, we used to call the General Steel Wares plant at the corner of River and Gerrard streets 'Kemp's,' the inspector said. "I remember Lady Kemp's mansion, it was called Castle Frank, at the western end of the Bloor Street viaduct. They've torn it down now and replaced it with a high school."

"Right!" old man Osler agreed. "Did you live in that area?"

"No, a lot farther south than that. In Cabbagetown."

"Well, we used to share the same politicians with you," Osler said, laughing. "Not that many of them were any damn good."

"Where did you live, Mr. Osler?"

"Rosedale. Glen Road. That was before Ethel and I split from the social scene and built our cabin on the Don."

"It's been nice talking to you, sir," McDumont said.

"I'm sorry I had nothing to tell you. I would have if I had had any information."

"If you hear anything let us know," the inspector said. "Good night."

"Good night, officers."

When they joined Bill Zotas at the elevators the inspector said, "I'll have someone talk to the Dryburg woman tomorrow. Now we'll tackle the Hardleys. Remember what I told you, Bill, stay out of the questioning. You may as well come along too, Smitty."

McDumont and the two dectectives walked to the door of No. 606 and McDumont knocked on it forcibly with heel of his hand.

138

The door was opened by a middle-aged man whose hair was graying at the temples. He was wearing well-pressed trousers, a white shirt and a wide fancy neck-tie.

"Mr. Craig Hardley?"

"Yes."

"I guess you know who we are?"

"Of course I know. You've kept my wife Doris and me from attending a dinner at the Inn-on-the-Park."

"Sorry," the inspector said. "We're investigating the murder of a neighbor of yours."

"Well we don't know anything about it."

"Do you want to invite us in or would you sooner we questioned you out here in the hall?"

"Maybe the hall would be better."

"Suit yourself. Bring out your wife and son."

"Why them?"

"Make up your mind," the inspector said.

"Oh, come in then." Hardley walked along the short passageway into the living room.

The room was over-furnished, with souvenir knick-knacks from Key West to the Custer Battlefield. It seemed to the policemen that it was self-advertising like a motorist who covers his windows with decals from every place he's ever driven to.

Hardley didn't ask them to sit down. He said, "Let's get the questioning over. It shouldn't take too long."

"Where's your wife and son?"

"In bed."

"Get them up please."

"What! At this time of night?"

"Get them up," McDumont said, moving a step closer to the man, whose middle height was dwarfed by the tall policemen.

Hardley went along a hallway and said, "Doris, Dwayne, get up. The police want to ask us some questions about the Greenless woman."

The inspector let his glance flit over the bric-a-brac with something like a look of disgust on his face. When Hardley returned McDumont said, "Detective Zotas there told me you threatened to get in touch with a friend of yours, Deputy Chief McCallum. Have you called him yet?"

"He wouldn't be in his office this time of night. I'll call him tomorrow."

The inspector took a small address book from his pocket and looked up a name and phone number. Walking back to the telephone that stood on a small table in the outer hallway he picked up the phone and dialed a number. "Here's Deputy Chief McCallum's house, Hardley. Come and give him your complaints."

"I'm not going to talk to him tonight."

The inspector turned his back on the man. "Hello, Rob, did I get you up? . . . Walter McDumont . . . I'm in a man's apartment in Don Mills. He claims you're a friend of his . . . Craig Hardley . . . Yeah, *H-a-r-d-l-e-y* . . . You haven't. You don't . . . Okay, Rob, sorry to have bothered you." He laughed. "I didn't think so either, that's why I called his bluff . . . Okay. Good night."

Turning back to Hardley he said, "Deputy Chief McCallum never heard of you, Hardley. From here on in answer our questions politely and truthfully or we'll take you over to the station for questioning."

Mrs. Doris Hardley entered the living room, wearing a padded pink bathrobe. She sat down on a chair and stared at the floor. The Hardley's son, a good-looking teen-ager whose long blond hair turned his looks pretty, entered. He was wearing gray pajamas and a dressing gown.

"Okay, Hardley, you work at the stock exchange I believe. As a floor trader?"

"Yes."

"Who for?"

"Cline, Mills and Robertson."

"You look over the age limit for a floor trader, Hardley. I thought they were younger guys."

Hardley didn't answer, and the inspector knew he'd struck a raw nerve. The man's job, his collapsing aggressiveness, even the furnishings of the room, showed McDumont he was dealing with an angry, frustrated failure. McDumont motioned to Detective Smith to take down notes. The young detective took out his notebook.

"So you work now for Cline, Mills and Robertson? Who else have you worked for?"

"What's this got to do with the Greenless woman's death?"

"It's got a lot to do with you, and it's you I'm questioning. I asked you who else you've worked for?"

"Draper Dobie, Nesbitt Thomson, Gairdner & Company, Doherty McCuaig—"

"That's enough. Did you work for them all as a trader?"

"I used to work for James & Macy as a customers' man."

"Is a floor trader a promotion or demotion, Hardley?"

No answer.

"Okay, you there, son. What's *your* name?"

"Dwayne," the boy answered, his voice cracking.

"How do you spell it?"

"How many ways are there to spell a simple name!" his father exclaimed.

The inspector said. "Is it spelled *D-u-a-n-e*?"

"No, sir. *D-w-a-y-n-e.*"

"Okay. You were a friend of Zelda Greenless I've heard?"

"No he wasn't!" the boy's father answered desperately.

McDumont kept his eyes on the boy. "Weren't you a friend of hers, Dwayne?"

"Kind of. Like I knew her."

"Did you visit with her often?"

"Why should *he* have visited—" Hardley broke in.

"Right now I'm questioning your son. Don't worry, Hardley, your turn'll come. In the meantime just stay quiet."

"I want a lawyer."

"You haven't been charged with anything—yet. Get a lawyer if you want, but it'll just be money thrown down the drain." Turning to Dwayne he asked again, "How often did you visit her?"

The boy glanced at his father, who wasn't looking at him, then answered, "Sometimes."

"What does that mean, every day or evening, once a week, once a month?"

"A couple of times a week maybe."

Doris Hardley said, "You don't have to answer his questions, Dwayne."

The room seemed crowded, with the three big policemen standing in the middle of the floor.

"What did you visit her for?"

Hesitatingly the boy answered, "She—she always had—a few reefers around. Sometimes a little hash."

"That's all? Did she peddle the stuff?"

The boy shook his head. "No. Some of the guys stashed their—stuff at her place. She didn't peddle drugs."

Doris Hardley, almost screaming the words, cut in, "That Greenless woman was a dirty little whore!"

It had been so unexpected that all three policemen stared at her.

"You mean she was using her apartment as a bawdy house?" the inspector asked. "She was selling herself for money?"

"I don't think so. She had to give it away!" she said triumphantly.

"Then she *wasn't* a whore? She might have been promiscuous or foolish, or drunkenly free-wheeling, but being any of those things is not a crime, Mrs. Hardley. You've got to be more precise in what you call people."

"A woman her age, forty or so, taking young boys to bed. It—it was immoral and indecent!"

"You'd better lower your voice, Mrs. Hardley, or you'll have all the neighbors listening in."

"I don't give a good goddam!"

"Do you go out to work?"

"My wife has never had to work since we were married," Hardley said.

"Congratulations." The inspector turned once again to the pretty young son. "Did *you* ever go to bed with Zelda Greenless, Dwayne?"

After glancing at his mother and father the boy whispered, "No."

"In the past week?"

Another whispered "No, sir."

"Last night?"

"I demand a lawyer!" exclaimed Hardley.

"Okay," said the inspector. "If the three of you will get dressed we'll go down to headquarters. You can get a lawyer after we book you, your wife and your son, on suspicion of murder or aiding and abetting a murder." Turning to the boy again. "After your mother and father went down the hall to Cecil Gilcrest's party last evening, did you visit Zelda Greenless?"

"No."

"You're telling the truth now?"

"Yes."

The inspector pulled the packaged condom from his pocket, and holding it by one corner as if afraid of erasing fingerprints, showed it to the Hardley family. He said to the boy, "Was it you who took this from the box of condoms in Zelda's clothes closet?"

"No, sir."

"Do you know who it might have been?"

"Hardley said, "Why don't you ask that bunch of creeps in the Centre Gang. It was probably one of them."

"We're going to question everybody who ever knew Zelda Greenless before we're through." To Dwayne again: "Weren't you a member of the Centre Gang yourself?"

"No."

"Never?"

"No, sir. Never."

"You go to Don Mills High School?"

"Yessir."

"What grade?"

"Eleven."

"Do you know Dreamer?"

"Yes."

"Who else in the gang over in the plaza?"

"I know some of them. Some of them have dropped out of school, but a couple still go to Don Mills."

"Did Dreamer go to Don Mills?"

"No. He's been out of school a long time now. I think he went to Danforth Tech., on Greenwood Avenue in the city."

143

"Which of the gang members go to Don Mills High School?"

"Roy Milling does, and I guess Cathy Edgars does. The others have quit school. No, Bruce Corcoran still goes occasionally."

McDumont glanced at Detective Smith who was putting the names in his notebook. He asked Dwayne, "What are the names of the others?"

"The only ones I know are Steve Robichaud, Len Shillig—"

"How do you spell that?" Tom Smith asked him.

The boy spelled out the name. "I guess the only other regular gang member I know is Patty Finlayson. There's others but they come and go, like."

"Did they all go to Don Mills High School at one time?"

"No. Some of them went to Victoria Park Secondary, and others still went to the same schools they'd attended in the city or up in Willowdale maybe."

"They're the only ones you remember, the ones whose names you've given us?"

"Well, there was Drop Kick Drewson, who was a good football player before he began shooting shit—"

"Dwayne!" Doris Hardley stared sternly at her son.

"Speed?" asked Inspector McDumont.

"Yeah, speed and finally smack."

"Where's Drop Kick now?"

"The reformatory. Guelph. Stole a Corvette." (He was almost gloating.) "It took four of your squad cars and two provincials to get him. He was clocked at a hundred and twenty on the freeway. Wrecked a Metro squad car."

"So that made him one of your folk heroes?"

"Well—no."

"Then don't gloat about the son of a bitch," McDumont told him. "To me that kind of person is just a strung-out punk. In my days on the force I've met hundreds of dope addicts who could shoot you, Drop Kick and that frizzy weirdo Dreamer into Kingdom Come. You punks are just joy-poppers who'd be dead in two hours if you turned on just half their regular daily intake."

144

Dwayne said nothing.

"Hey, Hardley, are you proud your son is a head and a speed freak?"

"Of course I'm not."

The inspector pulled the steak knife from his pocket and held it out. "Any one of the three of you ever see one of these before?" He pushed it into Doris Hardley's hand, and she promptly let it fall to the floor.

Dwayne said, as if as an afterthought, "I never shot speed, I just dropped it."

The inspector said, "You won't stay taking it orally. Some day you'll want a rush so bad you'll shoot it. Then it's heroin and good-bye."

Bill Zotas picked up the steak knife and handed it to Hardley.

"You ever see one of those, Hardley?"

"No!" He was so emphatic that all the policemen knew he was lying.

The inspector turned to Dwayne. "You've seen them though, haven't you? Some of the Centre Gang wore them as a gang badge or a talisman to keep off the sweats and yawns. They'd been cut down though and made into daggers. You had one yourself."

The boy nodded.

"You damned little fool!" his father exclaimed.

Everyone, including Doris Hardley, stared at the man.

"Why did the gang members boost them from the Coach'n Four?"

"I dunno. It's better to have something you've worked for than something you've bought."

"None of you punks know anything about work. Do you think lifting restaurant flatware is work!"

Dwayne shook his head.

"How'd they wear them, in a leather sheath on their belt? How did you carry yours?"

"In a leg sheath, strapped around the calf of my leg on the inside."

"Give me your key to Mrs. Greenless's apartment."

The boy took the key from his pocket and handed it to the inspector.

"Where's your knife now?"

"I lost it."

"Where? When?"

"Don't remember."

"Maybe later we can jog your memory at head-quarters."

Hardley said, "Listen, Inspector, that boy's only seventeen—"

"I don't care if he's only fourteen. Like we used to say about the Eyetie girls in the war, 'If she can carry two pails of water she's old enough.' How did you know I was an inspector, Hardley?"

"I—I—just knew that's all."

"I guess you had your ear pressed to the door there when we were questioning some of the other tenants. What do you know about Anton Zutach?"

"Nothing."

"How about you, Mrs. Hardley?"

"He reminded me of a little shaggy dog running around at the edge of a pack following a bitch in heat. He was always hanging around the Greenless woman's place."

"Did you ever visit Zelda Greenless. Maybe to tell her to lay off your little boy?"

"No I didn't. I never spoke to her in my life."

"We found two liquor glasses when we searched the dead woman's apartment. Both bore lipstick stains. The Forensic Lab will be able to tell us what kind of lipstick it was."

"I'll save them the trouble. Neither one of them was mine. Probably Eleanor Jacton's next door."

"I take it you didn't or don't like Eleanor either?"

"No I don't. I quit going to the Bon Beauty Boutique when she began working there. I get my hair done at the Consino Cosmetic Parlour."

"Is that in the Don Mills Centre?"

"Yes."

"Your move must have saddened a lot of people," the inspector said dryly. "That's all for tonight. Thanks for offering us chairs. We'll be back again."

"You may not get in at all the next time," Hardley said.

"We'll have a warrant," said the inspector. "Maybe

146

an arrest warrant." Without asking the Hardley's permission he walked over, picked up the phone and called the Don Mills police station.

"Hello. This is Detective Inspector McDumont . . . Who, Maury?" He grinned. "Staff Sergeant Maurice Grantham then. Howya doing, you old flatfoot. So they've got you in mothballs on the night desk up here eh? . . . No, still the same. She's fine, fine . . . Yeah, listen, can you send a squad car over to ten-forty-nine Don Mills to pick up three stranded Homicide men? How's Mickey? Remember years ago I told you not to marry any girl with a boy's name like Billy, Mickey or Georgy? . . . No, I know Mickey's okay. Has she had her hysterectomy yet? Yeah, I know . . . Okay, Sarge."

Without even a glance at the Hardleys McDumont opened the hall door and followed by the detectives walked to the elevators.

Going down in the elevator he said to Zotas, "Tomorrow, Bill, I want you to try and talk to Gerald Robinson in five-o-two, directly under Zelda's apartment. He's a retired public school principal."

Zotas put the man's name and apartment number in his notebook.

As they waited in the lobby for the yellow squad car to arrive, the inspector asked, "Where do you live, Bill?"

"Steeles Avenue and Keele Street."

"Too far out of our way to drop you off."

"I've got my car parked behind headquarters anyway."

"Okay then."

A 33-Division car pulled up in front of the house.

Chapter 10

Inspector McDumont had read all the daily reports from his men, had written comments on the bottom of some and had initialled and filed the others. He had also filed some correspondence after writing his replies in longhand for Marge Craiglie to type and file in the morning. Some routine letters from other police departments he had placed in his desk drawer to be studied in the morning. Most of these had mug shots and fingerprint forms, ard these he attached to the letters with paper clips.

One of these, from a police homicide detail captain of the Cleveland Police Department, was a warning that a child-molester and child-murderer being sought by them was believed to have slipped across the Canadian border at either Buffalo or Niagara Falls, New York—present whereabouts unknown. The inspector read the man's data sheet, "Thomas Stokes, alias Thomas Stokely, alias Tobias Stonehem, 34, Caucasian, height 5' 4", weight 130 lbs., brown thinning hair, brown eyes, scars from gunshot wound on left biceps, last permanent address 2667 Wyandotte Avenue, Akron, Ohio. Wanted for the strangulation murders of 3 girls, 1 boy, all under the age of ten. *Modus operandi*: picks up child at skating rink or swimming pool, offers ride home. Drives to outskirts of city or town, rapes child then manually strangles victim. Occupation, rubber-tire pressman. Bisexual."

McDumont had stared at the mug shot of the child-murderer, arrested in 1970 on a charge of indecent assault, charge dismissed for lack of evidence; arrested in 1971, child-molestation in movie house, sentenced to six months Cleveland House of Detention. He found himself comparing the police photograph of the small, timid-looking man with his mind's picture of George Bullay in Don Mills.

He carried the hand-written letters to Marge Craiglie's desk and placed them under a paperweight, then returned to his office. He glanced at his watch and saw that it was 11:30. It would soon be time for Sergeant Prust and Larry Helmont to check in and be relieved by Sergeant Ed Soley and Bill McQuaig.

Now that he had the department to himself he spread out the yellow blanket he had caught Zutach trying to hide in the garbage hopper, and taking the Coach'n Four steak knife from his pocket inserted it into the hole ringed with dried blood. It passed completely through, handle and all. This strengthened McDumont's belief that the knife had been jabbed into the murdered woman's back after the body had been covered with the blanket and, because the blanket hole freely admitted the much thicker handle, that the knife had been used to make a larger wound in Zelda Greenless's back than a straight stab with the blade would have done. He placed the blanket on top of his pistol and holster in the bottom drawer of his filing cabinet. It could be sent to the lab in the morning.

He merely scanned the reports of the 33-Division detectives and uniformed men, and placed them in a new file which he labelled "Zelda Greenless." The stabbing weapon, along with the other evidence sent back to headquarters with Clary Roundy earlier, had been sent to the Forensic Lab by Sergeant of Detectives Eric Manders, his second-in-command.

Tom Smith's and Bill Zotas's reports were concise, and their lists of names and addresses given during his questioning of the apartment house neighbors were carefully written down. He placed these reports in the "Zelda Greenless" file also. Detective Roundy's report was written with a ballpoint pen in beautiful calligraphy. He had questioned the superintendent of the Gamble Avenue apartment house, who had told him that Eleanor Jacton had moved away, date unknown, about two years before. At the time she was living alone, and the superintendent did not remember any man answering Wilfrid McMulley's description. Zelda Greenless had also lived alone until she married Danny Greenless; then he moved in with her and they lived together for a few months. They separated then, and Mrs. Greenless began dating younger men as she had done prior to her marriage. She had entertained some members of a motorcycle gang, and the superintendent, name of Joseph Lederrers, had received so many complaints from the other tenants in the house that he had been forced to give Mrs. Greenless ten days' notice and terminate the lease, which still had four or five months to run. Lederrers said that the tenants had complained of the loud gunning of the motorcycles late at night and early in the morning. Here Clary Roundy quoted the superintendent verbatim: "It was just the motorcycle noise, nothing else. The management, or I, don't care whether our women tenants sleep with their dog or a gorilla as long as they don't wake the other people in the house."

McDumont chuckled.

He placed his own men's reports in the file.

Then he emptied his pockets.

Besides the carefully collected scraps of pink writing paper he had gathered in Zelda Greenless's apartment, he laid on his desk assorted notes and the Eaton delivery slip addressed to Piet Langenzent. Though Langenzent had told him he had just arrived from Ottawa that afternoon, the delivery slip was dated June eleventh. Presuming that the parcel it had been attached to had been delivered on the eleventh or the twelveth, and presuming too that Langenzent had taken it in and had thrown out the slip before Bill Zotas had checked the garbage chute and container earlier on the thirteenth, the man had been lying about arriving back that afternoon. The inspector put the delivery slip, attached to a noted reminder, into a drawer of his desk. Then he set about assembling the torn scraps of pink paper.

The words on the paper, childishly printed with a black felt pen, were difficult to decipher, so the inspector walked out to Marge Craiglie's desk and returned with a container of white library paste. With this—

stickily—he began pasting the paper scraps on a sheet of typewriter paper, fitting them together like a disturbed jig-saw puzzle. When he had finished the message was clear. It read: StoP fooling WitH DwayN. No mores warneNGs. Yu NOW who!"

It was impossible for the inspector to make out whether it had been printed by a man or a woman, but he knew from a long career of deciphering such notes, from suicides, blackmailers and unrequited lovers, that its pretended illiteracy was the work of a literate person. Though the printer of the note had been literate, he or she hadn't been smart enough to realize that anyone knowing Dwayne well enough to care about his liaison with Zelda Greenless or, jealous of it, would not have left the terminal E off his name. He wrote the name of a graphologist, who was frequently hired by the Department, at the bottom of the sheet of paper upon which he'd pasted the note, and placed it in the file.

There were male voices coming from the direction of the homicide squad doorway, and McDumont stepped out of his office. Two of his regular men, Lorne Gardner and Willis Arnop, who were on the 6 P.M. to 2 A.M. shift, were just entering the office. They both greeted him, but with some surprise.

"Where've you been, out on Runnymede?" the inspector asked.

"Yes, Walter," Gardner said. "We staked out the house all evening but nobody answering Turner's description went in or out." The detective hesitated a moment then went on, no longer looking the inspector in the eye. "Near midnight we were admitted to the house by the landlord, and he told us a young woman had come earlier and had picked up Turner's flight bag and things."

"We checked the room, Inspector, and it had been cleaned out," Arnop added.

"You guys bucking to go back to a patrol car?" asked McDumont. "Didn't it enter your heads that Turner might send someone else to pick up his clothes?"

"There were people going in an out all evening, Insp—"

"Coming out carrying bags?"

"Bags, parcels, sure, Walter, some of them."

"Those big rooming houses are as busy as the Union Station."

"Sergeant Stuart and Sam Chisolm will have to begin all over again on square one," the inspector said dryly. "You two go into your cubicles and call the Mississauga Police and tell them to have their men keep an eye out for Turner at the Airport—one of you do that while the other calls the dispatcher and has a couple of cars sent down to the Union Station."

"It's too late for the station, Walter," Detective Gardner said, glancing at his watch. "The last train to leave there at night is the Ottawa train at eleven-thirty."

"One of you call the Mississauga Police then. The other one go downstairs and—what time did the young woman pick up Turner's things?"

"About nine o'clock," Arnop said.

"Go downstairs and find out what trains besides the one to Ottawa left after nine-thirty," said the inspector. "Then have Turner's description sent out to all their destinations and intermediate stops. Check the airlines too." Angrily he stepped back into his office.

Inspector McDumont spent the next twenty minutes removing the photographs of young people from Zelda Greenless's photograph album and comparing the names on the back with the names of the Centre Gang given to them by Dwayne Hardley and copied down by Detective Smith in the Hardleys' apartment. There were snapshots with the names Roy Milling, Bruce Corcoran, Len Schillig, Cathy Edgars and one bearing the name George Drewson on its reverse side, dated Oct. 19, 1973. He matched it with the sobriquet "Drop Kick," the punk who was now serving a stretch in Guelph. The only names he couldn't match with a photograph were Patty Finlayson and "Dreamer." After finishing this the inspector had a half-dozen photos left over. He placed them all in an envelope and the envelope in an inside pocket.

He read the letters addressed to Zelda Greenless: from male and female friends in and out of the city, a

152

note from Dr. Hugh Rutsey almost begging her, for her own sake, to continue the psychotherapy sessions, two friendly and loving letters from her late husband Danny Greenless, and a two-year-old Christmas card from "Your ever-loving Aunt Liz and Uncle Peter." The postmark on the Christmas card envelope was Crow Lake, Ontario. Zelda had then been living on Gamble Avenue.

The inspector tipped back his chair and placed his feet on the edge of his desk. What have we got? he asked himself. Zutach, the Hardleys, father and son, maybe Piet Langenzent, the members of the Centre Gang, the writer of the note on pink stationery, person or persons yet unknown, male or female.

Somehow his policeman's intuition told him that the murderer *and* the person who had stabbed the dead woman both lived in the apartment house, providing they *were* different people. Why would a poisoner, knowing that the poison he or she had put in the dead woman's drink, and knowing too that it had worked, then stab the body in the back? *If* it was the same person, why would he or she not have gotten rid of the glass containing traces of poison? To stab a corpse, then twist the dagger in the wound, showed an almost pathological hatred of the victim by the killer. Craig Hardley? Anton Zutach? The writer of the threat on pink stationery?

The inspector heard Detective Sergeant Prust and his partner Larry Helmont enter the outer office. He took his feet off the desk and glanced at his watch. Twelve-o-eight. Then Sergeant Soley and Detective McQuaig came in. The detectives talked together near the front of the office, and the inspector sensed that Gardner or Arnop had warned them of his presence, and of the mood he was in. He smiled to himself.

Jumping up from his chair he stalked out of his small office, past the group of detectives with a curt nod in their direction, and down to his car parked behind the building. Maybe Gardner and Arnop's sloppiness would keep Soley and McQuaig on their toes the rest of the night.

When he reached his bungalow in Scarborough he

tiptoed in from the front door, only to find his wife and daughter playing cribbage in the kitchen.

"Here I am entering like a bloody burglar so's not to waken the kids, and I find you two up playing cards," he said.

"There's a pot of fresh tea on the top of the stove, Walter," his wife said, before counting her hand.

Chapter 11

Walter McDumont woke up at six o'clock in the morning, lying on his living room sofa, wearing yesterday's shirt, socks and shorts and covered with a Hudson's Bay blanket placed over him by his wife the night before. There were two things on his mind, a blanket and an empty apartment. He'd realized at the moment of awakening that the yellow blanket he believed had been used to cover the body of Zelda Greenless while being pushed along the apartment house sixth-floor corridor was not a full sized one, and that what better spot to place a corpse where it would not be found than an empty apartment.

He pulled on his trousers and sneaked into the bathroom. When he emerged he found himself facing his twice-removed, fifty-five years younger replica, Jamie Taylor, his daughter Beatrice's second child.

"Hello, you young Sassenach," he said, smiling down at the little boy.

"Hello, Grandpa."

"Don't be too long in there now; grandad's got to take a shower."

"You use funny words, Grandpa," the small boy said, laughing. "Why do you call yourself grandad, and call me a Sass—?"

"Sassenach? 'Cause that's what you are, James Taylor. Your father's father was an Englishman, and his mother too."

"Do you hate Englishmen, Grandpa?"

"No, sonny. I'm just fooling around when I call you that."

"Well, you're not my grandad, you're my *grandpa*," the boy said victoriously, shutting the bathroom door behind him.

The inspector's wife was in the kitchen.

"Morning, Jean."

"What are you having for breakfast, Walter?"

"Bacon and eggs and half a grapefruit. And toast. But first get me a clean shirt, my blue-striped tie, clean socks—black—and a clean pair of shorts. I don't like going into our room while Beatrice and the kids are sleeping there; I'm liable to wake the baby."

"Do you want your gray suit?"

"No. It's going to be hot today, and the one I'm wearing is the only summer suit I own. Anyway I'm not a TV personality that has to change his suit every day."

After his shower and breakfast, and wearing clean accessories with yesterday's suit, McDumont played on the living room sofa with his baby granddaughter, while the others ate breakfast in the kitchen.

"Here, Jeannie, grab grandad's fingers and I'll pull you up," he said to his granddaughter.

Just then his two grandsons rode along the hall and into the living room on Jamie's tricycle.

His daughter strode in after them, wearing her mother's bathrobe. "How many times do I have to tell you kids not to ride that thing around the house?" she asked. "Both of you together are too heavy; look at the tire marks you've left on grandma's hall floor."

Tire marks!

McDumont said, "Beatrice, come here and take the baby." He kissed the little girl, gave a peck on the cheek to the two small boys, and went into the kitchen. "I'm off, Jean," he said, giving his wife a dutiful peck on the mouth.

"It's only a quarter to eight!"

"The early bird catches the worm," he said. He shouted over his shoulder, "So-long, Beat."

"Goodbye, Dad."

He went out the side door to where his Ford LTD was parked behind his daughter's small station wagon, got in, and without letting the engine warm up even a trifle backed into the street and headed towards Don Mills two miles to the west.

Anton Zutach opened his apartment door to the inspector after answering his buzz from the vestibule and tried to smile as he said, "Good morning, Inspector."

"Good morning, Mr. Zutach. Did I get you up?"

"No, I been up since ha-pas six."

"May I use your phone?"

"Sure t'ing, Inspector. Over there by dinette."

McDumont walked to the telephone, noting as he did so that the painting Detective Zotas had mentioned on Zutach's living room wall had now been taken down. He dialed headquarters, gave his name and asked for Homicide.

"Walter McDumont, who's that? . . . okay, John. Did you and Chisholm just get in? . . . yeah. They lost Turner last evening . . . oh, he's been picked up? Where? . . . Cobourg? . . . good. Have the plainclothes pool send a couple of men down there to bring him back this morning. Okay. Listen, when the IDENT men come to work send them both up to Don Mills . . . they know the house, ten forty-nine Don Mills Road. Okay, Sarge, send them up right away then. I'll be down there in an hour . . . yeah."

Hanging up the phone the inspector turned to the building super. "Thanks, Mr. Zutach." As he headed for the door he said, "Stick around. I'll want you to open the door of another apartment soon. I'll be up in number six-o-two."

"You want I let you in, Inspector?" Zutach asked.

"No thanks." McDumont held up one of the keys he'd had made the day before. "When the other policemen come, in case they buzz your apartment, come up with them to the sixth floor."

The superintendent nodded blankly.

The inspector caught the super's wife, Zenia, peeking around the kitchen door frame, her hand covering her throat.

McDumont pressed the elevator UP button, and waited for one of the two elevators to come down to the lobby. When the first one arrived two young women got off, followed by Cecil Gilcrest.

"Hello, Mr. Gilcrest," the inspector said.

"Hello, there. Oh, hello, Inspector! I've got it right, "Yeh. Walter McDumont."

"I was still pretty groggy last night."

"Did you cure it?"

"Still a few butterflies alive down here." He patted his belly.

"Could I have a minute of your time, Mr. Gilcrest?"

"Go on, Inspector."

"How long did the Hardleys stay at your party?"

"I'd say about an hour."

"Do you remember what time they left?"

"Early. I guess they arrived about eight and left about nine."

"That was before Pat—?"
haven't I?"

"Pat Enderby?"

"That was before Pat Enderby took a ride on Anton Zutach's cart?"

"Yep. Quite a long time before, I'd say, Inspector."

The inspector looked to the glass door connecting the lobby with the corridor leading past the superintendent's apartment. "Was Zutach carrying anything in his arms, do you remember?"

"No, I don't think so. No. Definitely not, Inspector. I remember now because he tried to stop Pat jumping on his pushcart."

"Okay. Thanks, Mr. Gilcrest. Have a good day."

"You kidding, Inspector? Bye."

The young man left the lobby by the rear door leading to the parking lot.

One of the elevators came down from the top floor, and the second one from the third. From the first elevator to arrive stepped two women and two men, one of them George Bullay. Without seeing the inspector, Bullay walked to the rear door, while the other passengers crossed the lobby and went out into the street. The second elevator let out a young man who followed Bullay to the parking lot door.

The inspector took one of the elevators to the sixth floor. On the way up he glanced at his watch. It was 8:25. Well, Bullay hadn't lied about the time he left for work.

When McDumont let himself into the dead woman's apartment the first thing he noticed was that the painting, a mass-produced shopping center landscape, as

Zutach had said, "a picsha of mounting an forest," was back in its place on the wall. All right, he *knew* the superintendent had stolen the picture, but what he didn't know was *why*. Zutach must have brought it back from his own apartment after he knew the police had left. He'd bet a year's pay that the superintendent had also stolen Zelda's good 35mm. camera. He began looking into drawers and cupboards, hoping Zutach's crazy greed had forced him to keep it, and that he or his men would find it later in the superintendent's place.

The living room and kitchen drawers and cupboards didn't yield anything resembling a camera, nor did the linen closet or the clothes closet in the bedroom. However, when he approached the dresser he noticed that one of the drawers had been left slightly open. This not only outraged his neurotic sense of neatness but, as he had been the last person to search the dresser drawers the day before, where he had found the elector' list and the assessment notice, it showed him somebody had been into the drawer since. Without touching either of the two small knobs that could be pulled to open the drawer, he forced the point of his pen between the drawer and the dresser front, making a space large enough to allow him to slip a hand in and open the drawer that way. He parted the clothing carefully, and there lying at the bottom of the drawer was an expensive German 35mm. camera. Without touching it or closing the drawer he walked back into the living room, sat down, and lighted a cigarette.

Given time and a small push of fear or apprehension in the perpetrater, most mysteries had a way of resolving themselves, he thought. First the stolen painting, now the stolen camera, both returned to their original places by the thief, who could be no one else but Zutach. Among the mysteries remaining were the identity of the owner of the twin-size blanket that had covered the body, the inexplicable theft of the cheap landscape print, and the reason the superintendent had not taken the elevator with his handcart after the girl had ridden it, but indeed had wheeled it to the staircase? Its very weight and noisiness argued against choosing the stairs rather than the elevator—again why?

When the vestibule panel button beside the apartment door buzzed McDumont rose and said into the small grilled speaker, "Yes, who is it?"

"IDENT."

"Who's that, Russ?"

"No, Don."

"Okay come up to six-o-two."

He unfastened the apartment door and waited.

The inspector led Don, the fingerprint man, into the bedroom and had him brush the knobs on the opened drawer. The young man caught some prints.

"Okay, Don," McDumont said, carefully lifiting out some articles of female clothing. "Get all the prints you can from that camera. It's very important."

He and the photographer Russ watched as his partner brushed the top of the camera, picked up several prints, then carefully lifted it from the drawer with a pair of tweezers placed at the base of its strap, turned it over, brushed its bottom and sides and took off some more prints.

"Are they good ones, Don?"

"Perfect."

After the job was done, the camera photographed, and the print strips carefully put away in the IDENT man's black bag, the inspector said, "That's all for now in here, boys. Let's go along to apartment six-ten and see what we can find." He placed the clothing back in the drawer and closed it. Then following the two young men he locked the apartment door behind him. Making a thick bulge in the side pocket of his jacket was the expensive camera.

The doorknob of No. 610 yielded no prints at all.

"It's been wiped clean, Inspector," Don said.

"Okay. Leave your stuff here, will you please, and go downstairs to one-ten and bring up the superintendent."

The inspector and the photographer talked about

sports, the photographer knowingly and the inspector amateurishly.

When Don returned with Zutach in tow, the inspector said, "Mr. Zutach, will you please open this apartment for us?"

"Why? Is empty. Tenant move away."

"I know that, Anton my boy, but we'd like to take a look inside."

With a resigned shrug the superintendent placed his master key in the lock, turned the doorknob, and pushed open the door.

McDumont said. "All right, Mr. Zutach, that's fine. Thank you very much." Taking the little man by the shoulders he turned him in the direction of the elevators. "If we need you later, we'll give you a call," he said.

Zutach walked to the elevators, pressed his thumb on the button, and the door of the elevator he and the IDENT man had come up in opened. With a bewildered glance back along the hall at the policeman, Zutach stepped inside and closed the door behind him.

"All right, Don, hurry and get his thumbprint off the elevator button," the inspector said.

The fingerprint man picked up his bag and walked to the elevators. When he returned McDumont asked, "How did it look?"

"Pretty good."

"All right, now get his prints off the doorknob."

Wielding his brush carefully and skilfully the young man brushed several prints into view. The photographer and the inspector were able to see them with the naked eye.

"I'd like you to try and match the prints you've just taken with all those you took yesterday," the inspector said, as the fingerprint man wrote his particulars on his tapes. "Now, Russ, I'm not certain but I think that on the floor of this apartment we're going to find the tracks of a small rubber-wheeled, two-wheeled pushcart." Kneeling down, the inspector peered into the vacant apartment, lowering his eyes almost to floor level. With a creak of a knee he stood up again. "You try to see them, Russ."

The young photographer took his equipment from his shoulders and dropped on his hands and toes to the carpeted floor of the hallway, gradually lowering himself by bending his arms.

"It's forty years since I've been able to do that," McDumont said to the fingerprint man. Then he asked, "Do you see anything, Russ?"

The photographer sprang to his feet. "Yes, Inspector. There's a slight cover of dust on the floor, and I think I spotted tracks through it, both going and coming, or at least two pairs of them."

"Do you think you can get some pictures of them?"

"I don't know, Inspector, but I'll try."

He fixed up his speed graphic, changed its lens, covered it with a filter, got down on the floor again and aimed it along the apartment floor. He took two shots with the filter and another two without it. Leaving the larger camera where it was, he picked up his 35mm. and stepped carefully into the apartment living room, on which the front door opened. McDumont and the fingerprint man watched him circle to his left, close the flimsy drapes on the front and side windows of the room, and begin snapping photographs, some with a flash and some without.

From the middle of the room he said, "Inspector, there's some good rubber tire marks on the hardwood in here. I think I've got them all. A heavy two-wheeled vehicle was wheeled in here, then turned around, and wheeled out again."

"Good. Can we come in now?"

"Sure."

The inspector and the fingerprint man entered the apartment.

McDumont said, "Don, will you dust the inside doorknob?"

This was done, but nothing showed up. "This one's been wiped clean too, Inspector."

McDumont said, "Russ, bring your big camera in from the hall, will you please?"

As the photographer was doing this the inspector was staring down at pairs of black wheel marks on the floor. After the photographer had come inside, and the

162

window drapes had been pulled back, two sets of rubber tire marks could be plainly seen on the floor of the room. The photographer took some more pictures.

"They're like narrow skid marks on a highway," McDumont said. "No wonder my daughter gave my grandsons hell for riding together in the house on their tricycle."

The two young IDENT men stared at him.

The inspector bent down and studied a wiped-up spot on the floor where the small wheeled cart had stood. He took the foil from his cigarette pack, scraped up some waxy dust with his nail file from a floor crack and placed it in the rolled-up foil. "Looks like blood," he said.

The inspector then walked through the empty rooms. In the kitchen sink he found two cigarette butts that were now dry had been browned with water. He placed them in the folded foil with the floor scrapings. Returning to the living room he took the camera from his pocket and handed it to the photographer. "Here, Russ, will you see if there's a film in it, and if there is take it out and develop it for me as soon as you get downtown."

The photographer inspected the camera and said, "There's been four exposures made on the roll, Inspector." He wound up the film to its end, sealed it tight and placed it in his pocket.

"Okay, boys, that's all for now. Thank you both very much."

"Okay, Inspector."

They parted in the lobby, the two IDENT men going out to the street where their car was parked at the curb, and the inspector leaving by the rear door to where his car was parked in the parking lot.

When he drove out of the driveway the IDENT car was gone. This time the inspector turned right and drove north to Lawrence Avenue and east along it to the Don Valley Parkway. He suddenly remembered "Julius Caesar" and his scheduled appearance in drunk court. Looking at his watch he knew it was too late now to make drunk court. He consoled himself with the thought that the big lawyer's lawyer would have got

163

the case remanded anyway. He'd make sure that when the case came up both he and Clary Roundy would be there. He made a mental note to have Marge Craiglie phone the crown attorneys' office about it.

As he swung into the overpass leading to the Bloor Street ramp from the Parkway, his mind went back fifty years to a time when he and the other kids from his neighborhood used to swim in the Don River just about there, naked, at a spot they called Red Bridge.

Naked!

Which reminded him. What had happened to Zelda Greenless's clothes, the ones she'd been wearing when put to bed by Eleanor Jacton?

He should read his own homily, framed on the wall of his office:

Don't Try To Be Smart, Just Try To Work Harder.

When the inspector arrived in the homicide squad offices he placed the blanket and the other things, including the dust from the crack in the floor of apartment six-ten and the cigarette butts (which he placed in vials suitably tagged) into a plastic bag and sent them off to the Forensic Science lab. Then, after reading the reports of the detectives on the 6 P.M. to 2 A.M. and the ones on from midnight to 8 A.M. he held individual conferences with Sergeant John Stuart and Sam Chisolm, assigning them, along with Bill Zotas and Tom Smith, to Don Mills. He told Sergeant Stuart that Zotas would fill him in on what had happened the day before, and that he wanted the retired school principal Gerald Robinson in apartment 502 questioned about what he had heard during the last few days from the apartment above him. He also told Stuart to get the cooperation of No. 33 Division and to question any of the Centre gang who might be in or around the shopping plaza during the day.

He also told Stuart that some of the male gang members might be carrying handmade daggers strapped to the inside of their calf, and showed the sergeant the knife from the Coach'n Four from which they'd been made. He suggested to the sergeant that the two

164

probabtionary men might do the shopping center while he and his partner, Detective Chisolm, concentrated on the house. If any gang members were found with one of the daggers they were to be charged with carrying a concealed weapon and brought down to headquarters. He also suggested that Stuart and Chisolm question Mrs. Doris Hardley in apartment 606, and her son also if he was at home. Then as an afterthought he added Mrs. Norma Dryburg in 607.

After the detectives had gone the inspector took his own notes and those written by Detectives Smith and Zotas from the Greenless file and read them over, making a short list of names on his desk pad. Then he took the phone off the hook and Marge Craiglie answered.

"Marge, I want to speak to Pat, or Patricia, Enderby, a nurse at the Toronto East General Hospital." He spelled out the name. "Maybe you'd just better get me the number. Also, from Information, get me her home phone number. She lives in the Envoy Apartments, ten-fifty-five Don Mills Road. Also Ruby Susanna, at Our Lady of Compassion Separate School in Scarborough. She lives on Broadpath Road, Don Mills. Also Miss Monica Smith. She teaches at Overland Drive Public School, and lives at nine Woodcliff Place in Don Mills."

Marge said, "Inspector, it's time for the morning meeting with the staff superintendent."

"Eh? Oh yeh. I'll go right in. Leave those women's numbers on my desk, Marge."

In the outside hallway he met Inspector Lange of the Break and Enter Squad and together they walked down the hall to Superintendent Randall Ford's office.

After the regular morning meeting with the staff superintendent, which McDumont always referred to, derogatively, as "The Sales Conference," he chatted for a couple of minutes with the inspectors from the Fraud and Holdup squads.

When he reached his own office again he found on his desk the official findings of the Forensic Science Centre and Dr. Ed Mainguy's autopsy report. There was also a list of the three young women's names and phone numbers from Marge Craiglie.

His phone rang, and it was Bill Zotas calling in from the Don Mills Centre.

"Yeh, Bill?"

"I'm with Sergeant Semons of Number Thirty-three Division, Inspector. There's none of the hippie gang around yet. They don't usually arrive, according to Semons, until after the noon hour."

"Good. Listen, Bill, I want you to go to the Bon Beauty Boutique and ask Eleanor Jacton to call me here at my office."

"Okay."

"Can you identify the painting that was stolen from the dead woman's apartment, and has now been returned to it?"

"Returned to it!"

"Yeah. It was there this morning. Have you got a key to apartment six-o-two?"

"Yep."

"Okay, go back there and see if you can identify it as the one you saw on Zutach's wall yesterday."

"If it's the same one, I can identify it. I scribbled my initials on one corner of it when Zutach and his wife were out of the room yesterday."

"Good. Good man. Take it down off Zelda's wall and put it in your car or Sergeant Stuart's. But first get Mrs. Jacton to call me."

The toxicologist's report from the Forensic Lab stated that the victim, Zelda Greenless, had been poisoned by ingesting (along with large doses of ethyl alcohol) a salt, or ester, of potassium antimony, probably several hours before death. Fatal dose was 0.2 to 0.3 grams. Because of its lack of smell it would go undetected in alcoholic drinks. Syndromic signs consisted of metallic taste, odor of garlic on breath, burning pain throughout gastrointestinal tract, vomiting and purging, dehydration, shock syndrome, coma, convulsions, paralysis and death. There was a slight cyanosis apparent in terminal poisonings.

The inspector did not bother to read on about the poison. The lab had also discovered that the two drinking glasses had been used by the same person, namely Zelda Greenless, the lip prints being identical as was the type and color of the lipstick. Only one of the glasses had contained minute traces of potassium antimony, presumed to be one used several hours before the second one. The fingerprints on both glasses had been identical and matched the fingerprints taken from the corpse during the autopsy.

Dr. Mainguy's report backed that of the lab in stating that death was due to a toxic substance, probably ingested some hours before death, camouflaged in an alcoholic drink or drinks. There was no semen found in the vagina, and the blood level of alcohol was very high, indicating complete alcoholic intoxication. Other than the damage due to the toxic substance the physical condition of the corpse before death seemed to be very good. There was no indication that death had been caused by alcohol alone or by cardiac, renal or other organic dysfunction or disease.

The knife wound in the back was obviously a postmortem stabbing, the knife being wielded by a member of either sex. The blade had penetrated the body to a depth of nine millimeters into the pleural cavity, the pleurocentesis causing slight pleurorrhea. There was more blood than normal around the wound due to the dagger's being twisted after insertion. The blood however was clotted venous blood, mostly from the subcutaneous area of the wound. It was the coroner's opinion, from the state of rigor mortis and other postmortem signs that the victim had been dead between ten and twelve hours before its discovery at 8:30 A.M. The stab wound had been inflicted within two hours of death.

Inspector McDumont called the coroner's office, was told that Dr. Mainguy had left an hour before, and called him at his home.

"Hello, Ed," he said, when the doctor answered the phone. "Walter McDumont here."

"Hello, Walter. Get the lab report yet?"

"Yes, and yours too."

"What did the lab have to say about the two lipsticked glasses?"

"Both belonged to—and had been drunk from—by Zelda Greenless."

"Mmph. Thought we had something there, Walter."

"No. Eleanor Jacton, her friend in the next apartment, told me last night that she thought Zelda had used both glasses, probably in drunken bewilderment or stupefaction."

"Could be. She'd drunk enough."

"The lab says the lip and fingerprints match, and also match those of the dead woman."

"Just another of an old man's hunches shot to hell, Walter."

"I guess so, Doc."

"What was she poisoned with?"

"Antimony."

"Thought it was that or one of the oxalic acids."

"What are the commercial uses of the stuff, Ed?"

"It's used in some lead compounds I believe, Walter. You'd better get that information from the forensic toxicologist."

"Okay, I will. There were no signs of recent sexual intercourse, you stated in your autopsy report."

"That's right. I'll state that flatly."

"What if her lover, rapist or whatever had used a condom?"

"In that case I wouldn't be able to prove she *hadn't* had intercourse on the day of her death."

"We found several dozen condoms in her apartment."

"Several *dozen!*"

"That's right. She bought them wholesale, I guess."

"But why?"

"Well, I've had one explanation from a friend of hers. I'm going to question some of her lovers later."

"You mean she had several sexual partners?"

"Yes. Teen-age boys mostly, I think."

The doctor laughed. "The longer I'm on this job the more immune I become to surprises about the sexual habits, peccadilloes and preferences of the public at large. Actually I wouldn't have thought that our Zelda's sexual preferences ran in that direction at all." He gave an audible sigh. "*Chacun à son goût.*"

"What!"

"I merely said, everyone to his—or her—taste. Teen-age boys, eh? Strange as it seems I used to be a teen-ager once myself. I remember a landlady I had when I was taking my pre-med course— Hell, I'd better keep my memories to myself, especially when talking to a cop."

The inspector laughed.

"So long, Walter."

"So long, Ed. I'll be seeing you."

"It must be great being a teen-ager today, in this permissive society. Especially with woman friends like Zelda Greenless."

Laughing, the inspector hung up the phone.

The phone rang and Marge Craiglie said, "There's a Mrs. Jacton says you want to speak to her, Inspector."

"Put her on please . . . Hello, Mrs. Jacton. Inspector McDumont. Do you think that you and Wilf could go down to the coroners' building on Lombard Street after work and officially identify Zelda Greenless? . . . That's great! I know it's not very pleasant, but they'll just pull down the sheet and show her face. Do you know the Stantons in Crow Lake? . . . Yes, her aunt and uncle. Could you phone or wire them and ask them to arrange for her burial? I figured she'd want to be buried beside her baby that's all. Tell me, Mrs. Jacton, where did she get the seven thousand dollars she has in a Royal Bank account at the Coxwell and O'Connor branch? . . . oh, I see. From Danny Greenless? In his will? Well, you might as well reverse the phone call to the Stantons. Tell them they've inherited seven grand, less the funeral expenses. How are you feeling today? . . . That's good. I hope going down to the morgue won't upset you again. Okay. Thanks for calling, Mrs. Jacton."

It was noon before he called Patricia Enderby. He got her at her apartment.

"Miss Enderby?"

"Yes, who's that?"

"Police Inspector McDumont, Miss Enderby. I'm calling about the woman who was murdered in the Doncentre Apartments the night before last. I wonder if you could tell me what time you left Cecil Gilcrest's party?"

"Ten o'clock or thereabouts."

"I understand you took a ride to the elevators on the superintendent's little cart?"

"Yes I did."

"Was the man disturbed?"

"Well, he wasn't very happy."

"Do you remember if he was carrying anything in his hand, a rolled-up blanket, anything like that?"

"No he wasn't."

"You're sure?"

"Yes, sir, I'm sure."

"And you're sure of the time?"

"Perfectly. It was around ten. I had to get down to the hospital at midnight. I'm on emergency surgery, nights, all week."

"I see. So you were sober?"

"Yes. I only had two bottles of beer."

"Thank you, Miss Enderby. My name's McDumont of Homicide. If you remember anything else later, please call me."

The inspector dialed Monica Smith at Overland Drive Public School, only to be told she was home ill. He called her home number on Broadpath Road, but there was no answer.

He had better luck with Miss Ruby Susanna at the Scarborough Separate School. After a short delay she came to the phone.

He told her who he was and what he was calling about. Then he asked her what time she'd left Cecil Gilcrest's party.

She seemed to be cupping her hand around the phone as she whispered, "Too late, Inspector. I'm afraid I didn't leave until quite late in the morning."

"Go on."

"There were only four of us left at the party then. Cec and I and Monica Smith and a French-Canadian guy. Cec was asleep, and so were the others I guess. Boy, what a head! I just took the elevator down to the front door and let myself out. I walked all the way home."

"What time was that, Miss Susanna?"

"Promise not to tell! Around four o'clock."

"And you didn't see anyone in the hall or lobby of the Doncentre Apartments?"

170

"Believe me, Inspector. I didn't *want* to see anyone at that hour."

The inspector laughed. "Okay, thank you very much." Then he asked, "I don't suppose you'd hear anything anyway from the bedroom?"

"What bedroom? Listen, Inspector, Cec Gilcrest is the kinda guy who gives up his bed for a friend. *We* had to make do with the sofa cushions on the dinette floor. Sorry, I didn't hear anything."

The inspector dissolved in laugher. "I wondered who had been using *them*," he said. "Good-bye."

He called the Forensic Lab and asked for the toxicologist.

A young male voice said, "Raymond here."

"Could I speak to Dr. Hurst? I'm Inspector McDumont of Homicide."

"Dr. Hurst is on vacation, Inspector. I'm his assistant, Dr. Martin Raymond."

"You know the viscera tests you did last night on Zelda Greenless?"

"Yes, Inspector."

"I have it here before me, but has the poison any other name?"

"Yes. Tartar Emetic. Its full chemical or pharmacological name is potassium antimonyl tartrate." He spelled it out for the inspector.

"Has it any commercial uses, Doctor?"

"Well, tartar emetic in various compounds and dilutions is used by the medical profession. It only takes fifteen one-hundredths of a gram to be fatal. The world uses about one hundred thousand tons of antimony a year, I would say, so its commercial uses are fairly wide."

"Could you be a little more specific, Doctor?"

"Most metallic antimony is alloyed with lead. The lead used in roofing, lining and cable sheathing may have up to 6 per cent of antimony added. Forms of antimony trisulfide are used as pigments, components of matches, primers for cartridges—and the pentasulfide is used as a vulcanizing agent. Antimony trioxide is used as a component of enamel. Some compounds of antimony find application as mordants—"

"What are *they*, Doctor?"

171

"Metallic compounds that combine with the organic dyes in dyeing. Antimony is also used in the manufacture of fireproof textiles and flame-retarding paints."

"That's enough, Doc," the inspector said. "I wish now it *had* been a stab wound."

"But the stab wound in the murder victim last night was nonfatal, as a matter of fact was made postmortem."

"I know it, Doctor. Thank you very much."

Inspector McDumont made his way from his small office, told Marge Craiglie he was going out to lunch, and as he walked up Jarvis Street to Bloor was thinking of the one murderer in the world he was seeking, who had access to three-tenths of a gram of the poisonous ingredient from a substance of which the world used up to one hundred thousand tons annually.

Chapter 12

When he returned to the Homicide Squad office after lunch Inspector McDumont found himself facing a phalanx of newspaper, TV and radio police reporters.

"Yes, gentlemen?" the inspector said, pushing his way through them, then turning to face them.

"How come you lied to us about the Don Mills woman being stabbed to death?" asked one, the representative of a TV network. He was a stripling with a college degree who constantly used the plural "media" as a singular noun in his broadcasts.

"I didn't lie to you," the inspector said. "Zelda Greenless *had* been stabbed, and it wasn't until a couple of hours ago that I received the lab reports and the post-mortem findings."

"But you *knew* she'd been poisoned, didn't you?"

"No I didn't *know* anything. In my business we need facts not speculations. Both myself and the duty coroner, Dr. Edmund Mainguy, reasoned that she'd been poisoned, then stabbed after death, but until the doctor and the crime lab had verified it it was only an educated guess on our part."

A reporter from one of the morning dailies said, "Up until now then, Inspector, you've been following a will-o-the-wisp?"

"Not at all. I felt that if we found the post-mortem stabber it might lead us to the poisoner."

"And has it?" asked another reporter. "And what poison was used?"

"To the first question, not yet. To the second, tartar emetic."

"Do you run your murder investigations on, quote,

educated guesses, unquote, Inspector?" asked the same TV reporter who had opened the questioning. "Are the police educated enough for that?"

"Yes, educated guesses, speculations, common sense, thirty years of police work, widespread questioning, 'latent clues and prints,' as the TV detectives say. The police are educated enough for that, and *their* education didn't come from books, son. We also rely on luck."

"Has your investigations regarding the stabbing of the corpse brought you any success yet?" asked the *Globe & Mail* man.

"Sorry, no comment on that. For obvious reasons."

"Walter, have you rescinded your ban on newspapermen at the scene of the crime?" asked the *Star*'s long-time head police reporter. He was the only one who would have dared address the inspector by his first name.

"Yes. Any of you can visit ten-forty-nine Don Mills Road and question anyone you wish, Jocko."

"Can we get pictures and drawings?"

The inspector nodded.

"How many men have you on the case?" asked the CBC reporter.

"Twenty. Twenty-one, counting me. The whole homicide detail are always on every murder."

"Any prime suspects, Inspector?"

"Everyone who knew the murdered woman."

"There's a rumor, Inspector, that the dead woman was pushing dope," said the *Sun* reporter. "Anything on that, Inspector?"

"Up to now, the result of my questioning along that line has been negative. We believe, however, that her apartment was used by some users of methadrene, cannabis, hashish and barbiturates—the so-called soft drugs—as a stash."

"Have you any evidence of that, Walter?"

"Yes, but I can't disclose it at this time. It's my belief that Zelda Greenless was an alcoholic but not a head, speed freak or drug addict. She probably smoked some pot, in a social way."

"No smack, Inspector?"

174

"The coroner's report showed she didn't shoot heroin. We found none in her possession either."

"Walter, Dr. Morris Franczic, her employer, told me that the dead woman had filched a pad of his prescription forms? Have you anything on that? Did she forge his name on any of them, or have any of them dispensed?"

"We're working on that now, Jocko." Christ, he thought, I'd forgotten all about the prescription pad.

"Have you any idea, Inspector, when you'll come up with the murderer?" asked the CTV network reporter.

"Eventually—and inevitably," answered the inspector. "That's all for now, gentlemen."

There was the glare of a photoflash as a photographer took a grab shot of him.

"Anyone want some *good* pictures, I've got some in my drawer," McDumont said.

"No thanks, Inspector. The public wants pictures of its cops on the job."

There was some laughter as the inspector watched them troop out of the office.

Marge Craiglie, who had been sitting at her desk taking in the interview, said, "Inspector, Sergeant Stuart called. He'd like you to call back as soon as you can. He's in the dead woman's apartment."

"Okay, Marge, I'll do it right away."

In his own office the inspector called the apartment, and Detective Sergeant Stuart answered the phone.

"Hello, John. Walter here. You called me?"

"Yeh, Walter. Detective Zotas came back here to the apartment about an hour ago and found a prowler. He'd turned the place upside down. Tells us he was looking for his camera."

"Who is he?"

The sergeant was obviously reading from his notebook. "Name of John Kapett, fifty years old, lives in apartment seven-o-five upstairs here. Shipping and receiving manager of Wallace-Roberts Paint and Dye Products, two hundred Adelaide Street West. Bachelor."

"How'd he get in?"

"He had a key, he says."

175

"Bring him down here, John. Charge him with trespass or something. In the meantime—by the way which of the other men are around?"

"Zotas, Smith and Chisolm."

"Tell Smith to count how many of Dr. Franczic's prescription blanks are still on the pad there, then phone the doctor's office and ask the doctor's secretary to count the number on an unused pad. It's obvious Zelda wrote some scripts and had them dispensed."

"Yeh, Walter."

"Then tell Smith to take one of Dr. Franczic's prescription blanks to every drug store in the Don Mills Centre and go through their prescription files. Every time he finds one of Franczic's forms tell him to have the pharmacist tell him what drug was dispensed. If any of them were for bennies, dexies or barbiturates, I want them brought down here. Tell him to give the druggist a receipt for them, okay?"

"Okay, Walter. I'll send Kapett down with Zotas."

"Right."

The inspector then asked Marge Craiglie to call Mrs. Flora Debler, the graphologist, and ask her to come down to the office.

Flora Debler had a South-of-England accent and the eccentric clothing and mannerisms to match. She was a tiny woman, wearing a green Robin Hood felt hat, a tweed skirt, red blouse covered with an open, checked cardigan and a pair of sand-colored ankle-length desert boots.

She stalked into the inspector's office, flopped into a chair, took off her hat, fanned herself with it, replaced it on her cuckoo's nest of hair, and said, "Well, Inspec, you've got a job for me?"

"Yes, Miss Debler. I've got a stuck-together hand-printed note that I want you to examine for me." He handed her the piece of paper on which were arranged the torn pieces of pink writing paper.

"Printed, hey? I'm a graphologist, not a magician, Inspec. I analyze writing not printing."

"Then you can't do it?"

"Who said I can't? What do you want, a character analysis, age of the wri—the printer, what?"

"Both of those, plus the printer's sex."

Miss Debler put on a pair of square Benjamin Franklin glasses and began inspecting the pink felt-pen-printed note.

"Do you mind, Miss Debler, if I put you in another office to do your analysis? I'm expecting one of my men in any minute, and I want to talk to him here."

"Anything you say, Inspec."

McDumont led her to one of the small cubicles along the wall and seated her at its desk. She took a small six-inch ruler, graduated in millimeters, and a large circular magnifying glass with a short handle from her nondescript purse, and went to work.

The inspector had just finished hiding her away when Detective Bill Zotas came along the main office at the side of the man the sergeant had called John Kapett.

Zotas brought an extra chair into the inspector's office, and the two men sat down across the desk from McDumont.

Kapett looked a little younger than fifty, his hair in a long cut that curled over his ears and just above his collar. He wore a gray seersucker jacket and blue flared slacks with white buck shoes. His clean-shaven face showed signs of youthful good looks, and his soft blue shirt, its collar worn above his jacket collar, showed his attempt to hold onto or define his long-gone youth.

"You're Mr. John Kapett?" the inspector asked, without leaving his chair.

"That's right."

"And you found Mr. Kapett in the Greenless apartment?" he asked Detective Zotas.

"Yes, Inspector."

The inspector stood up. "I've got something to straighten out," he said, walking to the doorway. "Smoke if you like. I won't be long." He shut the door behind him as he left.

Looking into the cubicle occupied by Flora Debler he asked, "How's it coming, Miss Debler?"

She looked up. "Strange, Inspec. Very strange."

"I'll drop in again in a couple of minutes. Just wait here for me."

He made his way out into the corridor of the police building and down the hall to Staff Superintendent Randall Ford's office. Without wasting any time he asked the super if he could get him search warrants for two apartments in the murdered Don Mills woman's house.

"Whose apartments, Walter?"

"The Hardley's. Craig Hardley, apartment six-o-six, and one rented by John Kapett, apartment seven-o-five."

The staff superintendent said, "God, Walter, I can't give you indiscriminate search warrants. Have you any definite evidence against these people?"

"Of course not. If I had I wouldn't need search warrants."

"What have you got?"

"A hunch that I'll find evidence in one or the other of the apartments, maybe both."

"A hunch! Christ, Walter, I can't get you search warrants on a hunch!" the staff superintendent said. "Anyhow, read this." He passed a sheet of police stationery across his desk.

McDumont took it and began reading it aloud, his face hardening as he did so. "A charge by Mr. Stallings Telford, Q.C., O.B.E., that I and Detective Clarence Roundy did unlawfully place under arrest the said Mr. Telford in the Don Mills Shopping Centre on the afternoon of June 13, 1974. Also that the said Mr. Telford was subjected to public ridicule by Detective Inspector Walter McDumont and Detective Roundy, and driven to No. 33 Division station, where he was insulted and assaulted by McDumont."

"There's to be an inquiry tomorrow," Ford said.

"That fucking Julius Caesar, O.B.E.! What did he get the O.B.E. for, flogging army issue to the black market? The Order of The British Empire isn't a fighting soldier's medal; he must have been in the Service Corps or Ordnance!"

178

"I hope you've got a defense, Walter."

"I've got a defense, *and* evidence, for that son of a bitch!"

The inspector swung on his heel and stalked out of the superintendent's office. He found Flora Debler still at work on the note.

"Well, Miss Debler, is it a man or a woman?"

"It could be either or both, Inspec."

McDumont crossed to his own office and closed the door behind him.

The inspector sat down and faced the two men across the desk. He noticed that Kapett had smoked a cigarette down to the filter.

"Mr. Kapett, I know the detectives up in Don Mills have asked you some of the same questions I'm going to ask, but just answer them anyway please. You were discovered by Detective Zotas here as you searched Zelda Greenless's apartment?"

"Yes."

"You knew she was dead, of course?"

"Yes."

"What were you searching for?"

"My camera."

"How did you get into the apartment?"

"With a key."

"You knew Zelda Greenless well, then, to have been given a key?"

"I wasn't given it by her, I borrowed it."

"Who from?"

"A man who knew her."

"What is his name?"

There was no answer. Kapett burned his finger and thumb pressing out his cigarette butt in the ashtray.

"What was the man's name who gave you the key to Mrs. Greenless's apartment?"

"I can't answer that."

"Was it a man or a boy, Mr. Kapett?"

The man's faced blanched.

"What was his name—for the last time? Was it Roy Milling, Bruce Corcoran, or was it Dwayne Hardley?"

"It was Dwayne. The woman had given him a key."

The inspector stood up, opened a file cabinet drawer and removed a file folder. "Where's the key now, Mr. Kapett?"

"One of the detectives took it from me."

"Here it is, Inspector," Zotas said. "Sergeant Stuart told me to bring it down here."

"Is this the key you let yourself into the apartment with?" McDumont asked, tossing it across the desk.

Kapett picked it up. "It looks like it," he said.

"And you got it from Dwayne Hardley?"

"Yes."

The inspector sat down again, opened the file folder and pulled out an identical key with a tag attached. "What does the tag say, Kapett?"

"Dwayne Hardley."

"Do you think he'd have *two* keys, Kapett?"

"All right, all right! I got it from the building super-intendent."

The inspector took the pair of identical keys from where Kapett had dropped them on the desk, picking up the untagged key by its stem, carefully avoiding the loop which had been held between Kapett's thumb and forefinger. He placed both keys in the file and closed it.

"How come, Mr. Kapett, that Zelda Greenless had *your* camera?"

"She'd borrowed it."

"So you did know her?"

"We had mutual friends. I didn't really know *her* that well."

"I see. What are the names of your mutual friends?"

"Well—"

The inspector repeated, "Well? Well what? Dwayne Hardley was one, wasn't he?"

Kapett's upper lip was becoming beaded with sweat. "Yes. Dwayne."

"Any others?"

"The young people of the Centre Gang."

"Was Dreamer a friend of yours?"

"Good Lord, not *him!*"

Detective Zotas and the inspector exchanged knowing looks.

180

"Excuse me, Mr. Kapett," the inspector said. He picked up his phone and said, "Marge, did you get the message through to Stuart and Chisolm? Good. Phone Stuart and cancel it. All right—put him on as soon as he calls—who, Flora Debler? All right, as soon as you type up her report—in triplicate—bring it down to my office. The paper with the scraps attached you keep yourself for now. Okay."

Turning to Kapett the inspector asked, "Was today the first time you ever visited Zelda Greenless's apartment?"

"Yes. Absolutely."

"I see. Let's get back to the camera. Was it an expensive one?"

"Yes. It cost me almost three hundred dollars, American, in Germany."

"When was this?"

"Three years ago."

"Where in Germany?"

"Stuttgart."

"You were there on a holiday?"

"I was visiting a trade fair, for my company."

"Can you identify your camera, Mr. Kapett?"

"Yes. It's a Zeiss. A two-lens automatic Reflex f/3.5."

"Do you know the serial number?"

Kapett, his fingers all thumbs, took his wallet from an inside pocket of his jacket and extracted a piece of paper. "The serial number is 6674983."

"You must have been very much attached to your camera to have jotted down the number before lending it to Dwayne?"

"Yes I was."

"So it was Dwayne who borrowed it from you, then lent it to Zelda?"

"—Yes."

The inspector opened the bottom drawer of his filing cabinet and took out the camera. "Is this your camera, Mr. Kapett?"

Kapett took it, opened the back, and read out the serial number. "Yes, it's mine."

The inspector took it back from him and replaced it in the drawer.

The phone rang, and the inspector said into it, "Yes, Marge. Tell Stuart and Chisolm to question everyone on the floor again, just to show we're still on the job . . . oh they did? Then bring them down to my office please." After hanging up the phone he said to Detective Zotas, "Bill, it's hot as hell in here. Bring me a glass of water, will you, please?" He asked the man across the desk, "Will you have one too, Mr. Kapett?"

Kapett nodded.

"Make it two, Bill."

Marge Craiglie appeared in the doorway and handed the inspector a sheaf of fingerprint forms and a 6½-by 9½-inch brown envelope. There was also Flora Debler's report, typed in triplicate.

"Thanks, Marge," the inspector said. To the man across the desk he said, "Excuse me a moment, Mr. Kapett." He glanced through the fingerprint forms from IDENT, placed them in the Greenless file, and began reading Flora Debler's report.

Detective Zotas returned and handed Kapett and the inspector each a glass of water. Kapett drained his thirstily. As if making room for something he was going to lay out on the desk, the inspector interrupted his reading and moved the ash tray and Kapett's empty tumbler to the top of the filing cabinet. Then he finished reading the graphologist's report.

"Close the door, Bill," the inspector said. "Well now, you know that your camera's safe, Mr. Kapett. Where is it you work, again?"

"Wallace-Roberts Paint & Dye Products."

"Oh yes. And you're the shipping and receiving manager I believe?"

"That's right."

"What, specifically, do you ship and receive, Mr. Kapett?"

"Oh, pigments, dyestuffs—we wholesale to small companies—linseed oil, various oils in fact, things of that nature. Paints and dyes."

"Esters, things like that?"

Kapett stared at him.

The inspector wrote a few words on a piece of paper,

folded it, and handed it across the desk to Zotas, moving his head in the direction of the door. "Shut it after you, Bill."

The detective left the office.

"I suppose, Mr. Kapett, that you ship and receive many kinds of chemicals?" He consulted a note in the Zelda Greenless file. "Do you handle antimony trisulfide for instance, or compounds of antimony used as mordants?"

"I—I suppose so. I'm not a chemist, Inspector."

"Of course not. I don't suppose you handle straight tartar emetic?"

"I wouldn't know that."

"Who *would* know at Wallace-Roberts?"

"The company chemist, I guess. But why're you asking me about things like that?"

"Because Zelda Greenless was poisoned with tartar emetic."

"And you think *I* might have done it? How could I? Anyway I thought she was stabbed?"

Bill Zotas entered the office and handed the inspector a note. The inspector read it, crumpled it up, and threw it in his wastepaper basket.

"Okay, Mr. Kapett, you can go. You're charged with simple trespass, so you can expect a summons soon."

Without a word Kapett got up from his chair and left the office.

"Has he gone, Bill?" asked the inspector.

The detective looked around the door frame. "Like a bat outa hell, Inspector."

"Who did you talk to at Wallace-Roberts Paint & Dye Products?"

"The shipping foreman. A guy called Skinner. I was a nonexistent company whose order was late. I asked him if Kapett was around, and he told me he hadn't been in for a few days, had been home with the flu since the eleventh."

The inspector picked Zotas's note out of the wastebasket, straightened it out, and placed it in the Greenless file.

"By the way, Bill, will you take this key—" He picked

183

it out of the file by its stem. "—and this glass— "He spread his fingers inside it. "—up to IDENT for finger-printing?"

The dectective picked up both objects gingerly and carried them from the office.

Sergeant of Detectives Eric Manders came to the open doorway.

"Hi, Eric. Where've you been all day?"

"Working on that girl's disappearance up in the Weston area, with Colabra and Smith."

"Anything new?"

"Zilch, Walter."

"Come in and rest your feet."

McDumont filled him in on everything he could think of on the Greenless case, and also about being up on the carpet the next day on charges laid by Stallings Telford. "Goddamit, Eric, he was stoned as hell. Clary Roundy found a half-bottle of Chivas Regal under his car seat. *And* he wasn't in the parking lot, but out in the southbound lanes of Don Mills Road."

"What about the public humiliation?"

"Strictly by the book, Eric. I made him try to walk a painted line in the parking lot."

"And the assault at the station?"

"He was mouthy as hell, and wouldn't take a Breathalyzer. I ruffled his hair."

Manders said, "That *does* constitute assault, Walter."

"I know. I'm not thinking of denying it, Eric."

The sergeant of detectives, who was thin, balding, wore glasses, and looked anything but a thirty-year career policeman, sat in deep thought for a moment. Then he said, "Wasn't it this Telford joker who defended, unsuccessfully, one of the Italian mobsters who bombed the Italian bakery a year or so ago? Cunietto? Sure it was. He's Upper Canada College gone to seed. Owns a joint half as big as Buckingham Palace up on The Bridle Path."

"High Point Road," the inspector said.

"What's the difference, it's the next fancy street.

184

That neighborhood's full of money that's either inherited or stolen."

The inspector managed a feeble laugh. "The hell of it is, Eric, he's got enough clout to have his own charge squelched and make those against me stick."

"How the hell can he? You've got his half-bottle of liquor. He couldn't walk the white line. He refused a breathalyzer. You've got Roundy as a witness."

"Yeah, I know. Jeez, Eric I've got to get this Greenless case clewed up! I've questioned enough pathological liars in that apartment house to form a quorum of the city council."

"Listen, Walter, I'll go up there with you tonight, and we'll scare hell out of somebody who'll tell us the truth."

"Thanks, Eric."

"Thanks hell! Weren't we the best homicide team on the force for more years'n I care to remember? Just hang loose till I phone the wife 'n tell her I won't be home for supper." The sergeant of detectives left the office.

When he returned the two detectives sat at the inspector's desk and looked over the four prints that the IDENT man had made from the exposed film in the camera. The first two were clear and focused, and made with a flash bulb. One was a photograph of Eleanor Jacton and Wilf McMulley sitting at a kitchen table, smiling, and with their glasses raised in a toast. The second was of Zelda Greenless and Eleanor Jacton sitting with their arms around each other at the same kitchen table.

"Both taken a few minutes apart, I'd say," the inspector said. "See, Eric, that burning cigarette lying on the side of the ash tray is the same in both pictures, but burned shorter in the one taken of the two women than it was in the one of Mrs. Jacton and Wilf McMulley."

"Huh-huh."

The third print was lopsided and out of focus, and no flash bulb had been used.

"Zelda must have been drunk when she snapped this," the inspector said.

"Totally bombed," agreed Manders.

The fourth photograph seemed to have been shot surreptitiously from the kitchen. It showed a human being sitting on the living room ottoman.

"See, Walter, somebody shot this from the kitchen. See the door post. Is it a man or woman do you think?"

The inspector stared at it. "I think this was taken by the murdered woman, when she was very drunk or very sick. It could be a woman, but to me it looks like a man wearing a beret."

"By Christ, you're right, Walter!"

There was a knock at the door.

"Come in," the inspector said.

Detective Zotas entered carrying some fingerprint forms.

"Did the IDENT people match the prints on Kapett's glass or the key to any they took at the murder scene?" the inspector asked.

"No. The camera though—the outside of it at least —was covered with Anton Zutach's prints."

Do you know if they've been able yet to match the thumbprint on the toilet handle with any others they've taken?"

"I don't think so, Inspector. Don, the fingerprint man, said to tell you that several prints fail to match any in the department's files."

The inspector said, "Bill, phone home and say you're working late tonight. Sergeant Manders and I'd like you to come with us up to Don Mills. But first go up to IDENT and tell Don to send all unidentified prints to the FBI in Washington. We'll see if they can match them. Also send a set to the RCMP in Ottawa."

"Okay."

"Will it put you out to work tonight?"

"No, Inspector."

After the young detective had gone Manders asked, "Why did you mention the FBI before the Mounted Police, Walter?"

McDumont laughed. "It was a Freudian slip, Eric. I was thinking of a young American who lives in apartment six-o-eight, along the hall from Zelda Greenless. His name's Cecil Gilcrest and he's an immigrant from the States."

186

"While you're looking over those forms, Walter, I'm going to drop out for a coffee-and. Would you like me to bring you something back?"

"Yeh, a guy in a beret." He laughed. "Get me a cheeseburger, with the works, a Danish, and a cup of coffee—a double, double cream and sugar."

Manders patted his belly.

"Quit bragging," said the inspector.

He phoned Marge Craiglie and told her to get hold of the men in Don Mills and tell them to report back to headquarters. Including Detective Smith. "Then get me Madam McDumont, Marge."

After talking to Jean, and telling her he wouldn't be home until very late, if at all, he phoned Dr. Raymond, the assistant toxicologist at the Forensic Lab. He caught the doctor just as he was about to leave for home.

"Doctor, this is Inspector McDumont of Metro Police Homicide, I'm sorry to be such a nuisance but I wonder if you could tell me if tartar emetic can be made outside a laboratory or a pharmaceutical company?"

"It could be, I suppose. It's a comparatively simple poison to make. It's prepared by warming three parts of antimony oxide or powder of algaroth with four parts of cream of tartar in water. It separates from the filtered solution in colorless octahedra—"

"What's that, Doctor?"

"Octagonal—eight-sided—crystals, which gradually lose their water and become opaque. It's soluble in fourteen and a half parts of cold and one-point-nine parts of hot water."

"Cream of tartar is—can be bought by anyone, can't it?"

"Yes."

"How about antimony oxide?"

"I suppose it can be purchased by anyone having a legitimate commercial use for it."

"Could I go into a drug store and buy some?"

"I don't know, Inspector. Why don't you try?"

"I might just do that. Thank you, Doct—"

"Just a moment, Inspector, Dr. Leavis of the pathology lab has something to tell you."

"Hello."

"Hello, Dr. Leavis?"

"Yes. I just thought I'd tell you that the bloodstains on the yellow blanket and those mixed with the floor scrapings match the blood type of Zelda Greenless. To my mind they are undoubtably hers."

"And the stains on the carpet fibers that were sent down earlier?"

"Same thing, Inspector."

"Okay, Dr. Leavis, thank you very much."

"Oh, Inspector, there were also minute bloodstains on the two-wheeled cart that was sent down to us. They match the others perfectly."

"Thanks again."

After he hung up the phone he restudied Flora Debler's graphological report. To Inspector McDumont graphology as a pseudoscience ranked somewhere between astrology and teacup reading, but he knew that Miss Debler's skill in handwriting analysis couldn't be matched by anyone else in town. Her rather eccentric report read:

To Inspector Walter McDumont. June 14, 1974.

Note, childishly printed on pink letter paper, reads as follows: "StoP fooling witH DwayN. No mores warneNGs. Yu NOW who!"

In the first place this note was written by a person literate in the English language, as indicated by its pithy, grammatically correct sentences. In order to pretend illiteracy the printer began by mixing up his upper and lower case letters, but by the end of the second sentence had decided that misspelling was needed to give the note an illiterate authenticity. He overdid this in the final sentence, reverting to literacy with his use of the exclamation point. On the original note the configuration of the letters, primarily the capitals, shows a definitive male hand, accentuated by the capitalization of the terminal letters, P in stoP, H in witH, and N in DwayN. However female forces were at

*work in the below-line curling of the stems
of the lower case letters g and y.*

*Though I have attributed the printing of this
note to a male, there is a definite female influence at work throughout, as manfested
by the exaggerated slope of all the lettering,
especially the up and down strokes. This is
also attested to, in my opinion, by the grad-
ual pressure of the felt-tipped pen being increased towards the end of each individual
word. The printer was right-handed, and
was a male with barely suppressed female
tendencies.*

(Signed) *Flora Debler*

The inspector put the report aside and began a
mental characterization of the men he had met so far
in the Don Mills apartment house. He dismissed Wilfrid McMulley and Raymark Osler out of hand as
possible jealous lovers of Dwayne Hardley, had re-
servations about George Bullay, which left him with
Cecil Gilcrest, Piet Langenzent, mainly because they
were bachelors, and John Kapett. Kapett could be a
homosexual who kept his outwardly noticeable tendencies in check, a "closet queen" in other words. And
why did he know the members of the Centre Gang, and
lend his camera to Dwayne Hardley? To suppose that
John Kapett was the printer of the threatening note
to Zelda Greenless—indeed, to suppose Kapett was a
homosexual—was not enough. It took a hell of a lot
more than supposition to convict anyone of murder, as
McDumont knew very well. And why had the Hardley
boy pretended, in front of his mother and father, that
he visited with Mrs. Greenless? Maybe it was a cover-
up; far better to let them think he was sleeping with a
woman than with a man. Was Dwayne Hardley a
homosexual? A sodomite to an older pederast? There
he was slipping into suppositions again.

Eric Manders arrived with a bag of take-out orders
from a lunchroom on Jarvis Street.

"I thought I might as well bring mine out too," he

189

said, as he began separating the wax paper-covered orders on the top of the desk.

"Do you call that little sandwich a meal?" McDumont asked. "No wonder you stay so skinny, Manders."

"And healthy. Look at the size of that cheeseburger, *and* a double coffee with double double. *And* a Danish the size of a saucer."

"I don't intend to starve to death in Don Mills tonight."

Detective Zotas came to the door and announced he'd taken the instructions up to the IDENT department.

"Okay, Bill. Go out and grab yourself a supper. We won't be leaving here before six."

"Right, Inspector."

After Zotas had gone the inspector said, "Here's a graphological report on the note I assembled from Zelda Greenless's trash can."

"What note?" asked Sergeant Manders, masticating a sardine sandwich.

"Oh hell!" The inspector phoned Marge Craiglie. "It's okay to bring me that put-together note on the pink stationery now, Marge."

After the secretary had brought the note, Sergeant Manders read it, then began reading the graphologist's report. "I see you're still hiring old Flora," he said.

"Yeah, Eric. In some ways she's crazier'n a bedbug, but she comes up with some pretty challenging ideas. Read her report."

After he'd read it Sergeant of Detectives Manders said, "Can you fit anybody to her assessment, Walter?"

"Yes. A man I had down here this afternoon. John Kapett. He was found prowling the dead woman's apartment. Said he was searching for his camera. He knows young Dwayne Hardley, and claims he lent the camera to him, and the Hardley kid lent it to Mrs. Greenless. He's a bachelor."

"Which makes him suspect?"

"Not necessarily, though he did try to lie to us today. He lives on the seventh floor. There's two bachelors on the sixth floor too."

"Which probably means that the Hardley kid's

lover is a married man with four kids on the third floor," Manders said. "That's presuming that young Hardley is a fag, that Flora Debler is correct about the note, and that, what is it, Kapett?" The inspector nodded. "That Kapett is a closet queen but not closet-queenish enough to ever write on pink stationery."

"I know, I know."

"How are you approaching this whole mess, Walter?"

Between bites of his cheeseburger the inspector said, "I'm thinking that Zelda Greenless was poisoned with a dollop of tartar emetic on the afternoon of June twelfth, that's Wednesday. Her poisoner was in her apartment, and spiked her drink with it. She didn't become too sick until evening, but she was desperately sick when her friend Eleanor Jacton, from next door, visited her when she came home from work. Mrs. Jacton also visited her later and put her to bed, fully clothed. Up to then she hadn't been stabbed. Later on Mrs. Jacton looked in on her and found her lying in bed, 'breathing better' as she puts it, so she didn't disturb her. Sometime later the stabber entered Zelda's place, took her out of bed, undressed her, and stabbed her in her living room."

"Why?"

"That's what *I* want to know. I think that the stabber and the poisoner are two different people, but both with the same motives, or at least with the same intentions, that is to kill Zelda Greenless. Perhaps the stabber wasn't aware that she was already dead—and I'm only presuming she was—when he entered her apartment. He might have been going to have sex with her before stabbing her—we found an unused condom beside her bed—"

"The stabber's?"

"We don't know that. She had a box full of them on a shelf in her bedroom closet. It may have been lying there for a week."

"Go on, Walter."

"Wait till I finish this burger; it's going cold."

Manders laughed, then sipped his paper cup of tea.

The inspector swallowed the last bite of his cheeseburger, wiped his mouth on a paper napkin, and went on. "There were no bloodstains in the bed or in the bedroom, so the body must have been carried into the living room before the stabbing took place. Eleanor Jacton had put Zelda to bed fully clothed, but whether she still was or not when Eleanor looked in we don't know, and neither does Eleanor. According to her Zelda was completely covered with the bedclothes.

"Now, where or when the clothing was taken off the dead woman we don't know, or what happened to her clothing, either."

"How do you know she was stabbed in her own living room, Walter?"

"I cut some snippets of carpet from the living room rug, and according to the crime lab they contained bloodstains matching Zelda's blood type."

Manders nodded.

"Now, after the woman was stabbed the body was moved from her apartment to an empty apartment, number six-ten, at the other end of the hall, and was later placed, naked, in the garbage disposal closet, with the knife in her back. I'm pretty sure the body was transported on a small two-wheeled cart owned by the apartment house, and that she was pushed down the hall, and maybe later into the disposal closet, by Anton Zutach. The crime lab have found her bloodstains on the handcart, and I had the IDENT boys take photographs in the empty apartment, which show conclusively that the handcart, weighted down with her body, was pushed in there, turned around, and pushed out into the hall again."

"This guy Zutach is the janitor?" Manders asked.

"Yep. A frightened little liar. I've got plenty of his fingerprints, and Cecil Gilcrest and a girl was was at a party at his place the night of the murder, met him pushing the empty cart along the hallway. In fact the young woman, Pat Enderby by name, a nurse at the East General Hospital, took a ride to the elevators on it.

"Zutach also stole a painting and a camera from the dead woman's apartment, and had the painting on the wall of his own living room—he lives on the main floor—the next day. Bill Zotas spotted it, wrote his initials in a corner of it."

"Is it still there?

"No. Zutach got scared or his wife got on to him and he returned the painting to the dead woman's apartment after we'd left."

"What about the camera, Walter?"

"He'd also taken that back and shoved it into a drawer of her dresser. I know it was stolen and then returned, because I'd searched all the dresser drawers myself, and there was no camera there. The IDENT men made plenty of Zutach's prints on the camera and the dresser handles."

"Do you think he might be either the poisoner or the stabber?"

"No, he's too stupid. Do you think a murderer or a would-be murderer would take a picture down from his victim's living room wall and stick it up on his own?"

"Is it a valuable painting?"

"No, that's the funny part of it. It's only a shopping mall landscape in oils. Cost probably seven ninety-five, worth two bucks."

"I wonder why he took it down?" Manders asked. "What about the camera?"

"It *is* expensive. I have it here in my filing cabinet. Those photos we looked at earlier were on a roll in it when I found it in the dresser. The four exposures were developed up in the IDENT lab."

"Anything else about Zutach?"

"Yes. The body had been covered at some time with a small-size yellow woollen blanket. Personally I think it was covered with the blanket when the stabbing took place. Anyhow, I caught Zutach trying to stomp it into the bottom of the garbage hopper. The knife hole in it was enlarged, as if the stabber had twisted the knife after inserting it in the back of the corpse. The blanket could have been removed without pulling out the knife. I sent the blanket down to the crime lab, and the bloodstains on it were Zelda's."

"Why don't we just pinch Zutach, Walter? With the

evidence against him he's got no other out than to squeal on the stabber."

"I know, Eric. We can snap him any time on an accessory-after-the-fact charge, but in the meantime we'll just scare off the poisoner."

"We might get the identity of the poisoner from Zutach. Hell, he might be the poisoner, stabber and transporter of the corpse himself."

"I don't think so, Eric. He was either being paid or was frightened into helping the stabber. Anyway, I'll let you see him for yourself."

"Good enough, Walter."

The inspector called the police switchboard. "Susan? —I want to make a long distance call," he said.

"Sure, Inspector. Where to and who to?"

After receiving the information he had asked for on the first call, he made another, feeling however that whatever information this one turned up it would only muddy the waters of his preconception. But hell, he, who had discarded preconceptions many times in his past, knew that only on occasion did they lead to trial evidence.

He picked up Sergeant John Stuart's report dealing with his questioning of Gerald Robinson in apartment 502 and Mrs. Norma Dryburg in apartment No. 607. Robinson's remarks and answers had been a reiteration of what he had told the police earlier, but Mrs. Dryburg's evidence was calm, solid and devastating. According to the woman, who was 67 and lived alone, she spent at least part of her day sitting in her living room (which opened from the hallway) knitting things for her children and grandchildren. When the weather was warm she often opened her hallway door a couple of inches to allow cross-ventilation between it and the window, but during the evenings she locked the door and didn't answer it at all. Over tea, which she insisted Stuart share with her (the inspector smiled) she had told the sergeant that during the afternoon of June twelfth she had seen a male figure, whom she couldn't identify from a back view, admitted to the Greenless apartment, coming out again "ten or fifteen minutes later." She had watched this in an ornamental mirror that hung on the east wall of her living room and gave her a full view of the hallway from the Derymore and Hardley doorways to the door opening into the front stairwell. She was positive that the man had been wearing a head covering of some sort, but what kind or color she didn't remember.

The inspector told his secretary to get him Sergeant Stuart and a police stenographer immediately. When his phone rang and he answered it he found it was Sergeant Stuart reporting in from Don Mills. The inspector told him to wait for the arrival of the stenographer, then to re-question Mrs. Dryburg, getting an official statement. After her statement was typed up he wanted it signed by the woman.

The inspector handed Manders Sergeant Stuart's report. "What kind of men wear hats or caps this time of year, Eric?" the inspector asked.

"Well, uniformed policemen for one, some delivery men, gas and electric utility men, old men, some who are not so old but only old-fashioned, guys going to play golf or sail their yachts, some bicyclists, and baldheaded men who are sensitive about their baldness."

"Thanks," the inspector said, as Sergeant Manders began to read Stuart's report. "You can certainly narrow things down to fit a conjecture."

Sergeant of Detectives Manders smiled.

Chapter 13

The inspector and Sergeant of Detectives Manders drove up to Don Mills in a Homicide Squad D-car, while Detective Bill Zotas drove his own Dodge Dart behind them. The inspector had told him he might as well drive up in his own car, which would save him driving back downtown later.

When they reached the Don Mills Centre the inspector parked the homicide squad car in a parking space in front of the big supermarket, and noticed that Zotas had taken his own car farther into the lot and had parked it near the street corner and the lunchroom called The Coffee Spot.

McDumont got out of the car and said to Sergeant Manders, "I won't be a minute, Eric. I've just got to return something to a restaurant in here." He pointed to where Bill Zotas was sitting in his car. "Maybe you could go over and join Zotas. You might catch sight of some of the heads and speed freaks of the Centre Gang from there. Zotas can point them out to you; some of them anyhow."

The inspector walked to the Coach'n Four and entered, to be greeted by Mr. Crawford, the manager.

"Hi, Inspector! Any luck with the knife?"

"Yeh, the dagger that stabbed Zelda Greenless was ground down from one of your steak knives all right." He handed Crawford the knife he'd borrowed. "Tell Boukydis I returned it; I'm probably the only person who ever borrowed one just for lends."

The manager laughed. "That's for sure! Listen, Inspector, I wouldn't like it known around that a murder was committed with one of *our* knives. You know what I mean, some people might be a little put out cutting their steak with a—a prototype of a murder weapon."

196

"As far as we, meaning the police department, are concerned nothing will be said of it, at least until the stabber is brought to trial. Anyhow nobody was murdered with one of your cut-down steak knives; the dead woman was poisoned."

"Yeah! I read that in tonight's *Star*. How come, Inspector?"

"You'll be able to read everything about it in the *Star*. It was *their* head police reporter who found out about the poisoning for himself, and by the way things are looking he might even discover the murderer before we do. Anyhow, Mr. Crawford, thanks for your cooperation."

The inspector walked out of the steak house, took one of the short shopping mews or lanes and came out facing a parking lot on the west side of the shopping plaza. He strolled along the street, glancing into some store windows, until he came to the lane on which The Coffee Spot was located. He peered inside, along the counter and along the booths, but failed to find any of the Centre Gang, or those he knew to be members. He rejoined Eric Manders who was sitting in the rear seat of Bill Zota's Dodge.

"See any of the gang around, Bill?" he asked.

"Not a sign of them, Inspector."

Turning to Eric Manders he said, "We don't want to go over and question Zutach or anybody in the apartment house just yet, Eric. How about taking a stroll with me over to 33 Division. I want to check on that drunken shyster we ran in. An old friend of both of us, Maurice Grantham, is on the desk this shift."

"Old Maury! So he made staff sergeant, eh? Sure, let's go over and see him."

"Wait for us here, Bill," the inspector said. "Just keep your eye out for any of the gang members." He took his series of snapshots that Zelda Greenless had taken, and handed them over the seat to Zotas.

The two detectives crossed the parking lot and The Donway West and walked down the side of it to the short street that held No. 33 Metropolitan Toronto Police Division. From a pair of glass doors they climbed a short flight of steps to a large room across which was the Desk. Behind it there were two young police officers sitting at phone desks and the figure of their old friend Maurice Grantham, the desk sergeant.

The sergeant looked up, saw them, and his face broke out in a wide grin. "Well, look what we've got here, the downtown sleuths!" he shouted.

"Hello, Maury," said Manders, stepping forward and shaking the desk sergeant's outstretched hand. Walter McDumont also shook hands with Grantham.

"You two guys partners again?" asked Grantham.

"Just temporarily," the inspector answered.

"It's a pretty high-priced team isn't it? A detective inspector and a sergeant of detectives?"

Manders said, "I see you're a staff sergeant, Maury. How come you never phone anybody in our squad?"

"I do sometimes but you guys are always out for coffee." Lowering his booming voice so that it could only be heard a mile south on Eglinton Avenue he added, "I guess you're working on the apartment house murder?"

Both detectives nodded.

"I read in the papers that the woman was poisoned."

"Yeh. We were trying to keep it a secret but the newspapers queered our pitch."

"You knew it, Walter?"

"Sure, both Dr. Mainguy and I knew it as soon as we viewed the body. The face was slightly cyanosed."

"What's that?"

"A crossword-puzzle word meaning the skin turning blue because of lack of oxygen."

"How's old Doc. Mainguy?"

"Oh he's still up and around between binges."

"Next time you see him tell him I was asking about him will you?"

"Sure thing, Maury," the inspector said. "And thanks for sending the car last night to give us a lift back to headquarters."

"Any time, Walter." The desk sergeant looked at Manders. "You're not getting any fatter, Eric."

"No, and I don't want to."

McDumont said, "Yesterday afternoon myself and a young detective ran a guy in here for drunken driving. Name of Stallings Telford."

"I know, a lawyer. Lives on High Point Road."

"How come you know him, Maury?"

"It's not the first time he's been brought in here bombed."

"Did Ernie Willis charge him yesterday?"

The desk sergeant flipped back the pages of his ledger. "Yes, he was booked, Walter. He was bailed out in less than an hour."

McDumont told him that he, McDumont, had been informed by Staff Superintendent Randall Ford that he was to be called to the carpet the next day to face charges laid against him, and Detective Clarence Roundy, by Telford.

The desk sergeant nodded. "This guy Telford's got a lot of clout down at City Hall, Walter."

"Did he appear in drunk court this morning?"

The desk sergeant searched yesterday's charge sheet. "I don't think so."

"Why in hell not!"

"Don't get mad at me, Walter; I don't run the station."

"What's Ernie Willis's home phone number?"

"It won't do you any good. He left this afternoon to go up to his cottage on Squaw Lake, northwest of Bracebridge. He has no phone there."

McDumont unclenched his teeth and asked, "Maury, where do you keep the confiscated liquor?"

The desk sergeant crossed the space behind the desk and opened a cupboard. In it could be seen a pint bottle of either gin or vodka and a bottle of cheap rotgut wine.

"Is there a half-bottle of Chivas Regal in there, Maury?"

The desk sergeant walked over and peered into the cupboard. "No, Walter."

"When is Willis coming home from his cottage?"

"He's not due back until July second, Walter."

"Does that son of a bitch think I'm going to face a police inquiry without his testimony or the half-bottle of evidence we brought in here! That scared shit! Goddamit, if it hadn't been for the amalgamation of the police forces of the suburban boroughs with the city force Willis would still be riding his bicycle out in Etobicoke chasing kids out of market gardens or trying to catch chicken thieves. What's the matter with that guy!"

"He's up for his pension soon, Walter."

"He'll be up for more'n that if he doesn't report down to headquarters for this kangaroo court that shyster lawyer Stallings Telford has had called! If you can get in touch with him at all, tell him that!"

The two young policemen were staring at the plainclothes inspector.

"I'll tell him, Walter," said the desk sergeant.

"What're the rules up here? If a guy lives on Bayview or in the Bridle Path neighborhood, and is falling-down drunk, I suppose you send him home in a squad car? If he's some working stiff from the city who buys a bottle of derail and gets drunk, I suppose you book him, keep him in a cell overnight, then send him to drunk court in the morning!"

Staff Sergeant Grantham said nothing.

Eric Manders asked, "Is this guy Telford the same guy who lost the Italian bakery bombing case some time ago?"

"I don't know anything about that, Eric."

McDumont said, "Let's go, Eric, we've got some *police* work to do." More in sorrow than anger he said, "So long, Maury."

The two detectives turned and left the station.

McDumont was ominously silent all the way back to Zota's car, and Sergeant Manders respected his angry silence.

"Any sign of any members of the gang, Bill?" the inspector asked the young detective.

"I think some of them, two or three, went into The Coffee Spot a few minutes ago. I'm not sure who the others were but one of them was definitely the guy with the blond Afro called 'Dreamer.' "

"Okay, Sergeant Manders and I'll go in and talk to them. You wait a minute or two then come in and take a seat at the counter near the door. Okay?"

"Right, Inspector."

The two older detectives walked into the lunchroom, spotted two of the youths sitting in a booth near the back, and walked over to them.

"I'm Detective Inspector McDumont, and this is Sergeant of Detective Manders." He flashed his badge.

"Hi, Inspector, Hi, Sergeant," said Dreamer. He was freshly washed and wore a clean blue denim shirt with his greasy Levis. "You gents are wasting your time if you're looking for shit. We're clean."

"We're not from the narcotics squad," the inspector said.

The other, better dressed, sat across the both from Dreamer.

The inspector asked him, "What's *your* name, Milling or Corcoran?"

"Neither. I'm Clifford Drakes."

"Where do you live, Clifford?" asked the inspector, sitting down beside him. He pointed to the opposite seat, which Sergeant Manders took.

"I asked you where you lived?" the inspector repeated.

Drakes looked over at Dreamer, who nodded. He answered, "Twenty-seven Tremont Crescent."

The inspector said, "I don't think I have *your* picture. Are you a member of the Centre Gang?"

"No."

Dreamer said, "Cliff's the boy friend of one of our chicks, Cathy Edgars." Both detectives noticed his palsied hands and voice tremor.

McDumont asked the Drakes boy if he knew Zelda Greenless.

"No."

"He doesn't know her, Inspector," Dreamer said in his high voice. "He ain't a member of the gang. Both him and Cathy is square."

"What's your real name, Dreamer?"

"Milford Black. Now you know why I prefer being called Dreamer. I mean, a name like that can ruin your social standing, right? Who the hell you ever meet before called Milford?"

"Nobody."

"See!" He put his hands beneath the table to hide their shaking.

"Where do *you* live, Black?"

"Forty-three Parkwoods Village Drive. Away northeast of here, near Victoria Park Avenue. Our apartment house is government subsidized housing."

The inspector caught Bill Zotas's eye and motioned him to come over. The young detective left his coffee on the counter and came over to the booth.

"Give me the pictures, Bill," the inspector said.

Zotas handed over the dead woman's snapshots. "Bring your coffee over here," said the inspector. Then he riffled through the photographs, but failed to find one of Clifford Drakes.

"Put this in your notebook," McDumont said when Zotas returned. He pulled out his book. "This young man's name is Clifford Drakes and he lives at—what's the number?"

"Fifty-eight Southill Village," Drakes said.

"Got it, Bill?"

Zotas nodded.

"All right, Clifford, you can go now. We've got something to talk over with Dreamer."

The inspector stood up and allowed Drakes to leave the booth. Then he moved over on the seat, making room for Detective Zotas.

"Well, you guys've certainly got me boxed in," Dreamer said.

"*You* knew Zelda Greenless, didn't you?"

"Yep, Inspector. I knew her when she lived on Gamble Avenue. She was the reason I began hanging around this plaza. When she moved up here I moved over from the Parkway."

"What Parkway?"

"The Parkway Plaza. Corner of Victoria Park and Ellesmere."

"How did you meet her on Gamble Avenue?"

"I was a member of the bikers. The Devil Dealers

Motorcycle Club in them days. All of us knew her."

"Did you know Eleanor Jacton too?"

"Yeah. Not too good, but I knew her."

"What was Zelda Greenless to you?"

"A lady," was Dreamer's surprising answer. "I dug her."

"That's all?"

"That's enough. I don't call too many broads her age ladies, Inspector." He shuddered perceptively. "Christ, I need a hit!"

"How come she didn't have a snapshot of you?"

"She had one once but I tore it up. As you people probably know I got a drug record. I also got an assault record, and a coupla other things. I don't like having my picture took."

"Did you ever go to bed with Mrs. Greenless?"

"No."

"Did any of the other young guys?"

"Yeh, I guess most of them did."

"Then why not you?"

"Inspector, the way I been for the past coupla years I couldn'ta gone to bed with no chick. Man, I been in the joint, I been hassled, I been stoned on acid, hash and speed, and mostly strung out."

"What did the other members of the gang think of her?"

"Most of them thought of her as a ball freak. Not me. She wanted me to ball her but I never did. Like, man, the broad was old enough to be my old lady nearly, but all I got was a coupla hits of crystal from her, and some hash."

The inspector passed him the snapshots, and Dreamer glanced through them.

"Do you know these young people?"

"Most of them. Some might be guys and chicks she knew before I met her. McClure and Henderson were bikers. So was Halliday."

"Was she a dealer or a pusher? We found some hash at her place. Did she have anything else there?"

"Like what, Inspector, smack?"

"Was she a dealer?"

203

"No. She only dealt it to friends that were strung out or coming down off a high. Only pot, hash, meth, acid when she had it."

"Didn't she get methamphetamines sometimes on prescriptions she forged, and barbiturates?"

Dreamer thought for a moment. Then he said, "Yes she did. Now that she's dead I guess it don't hurt to talk. She forged some of old Franczic's prescriptions for Seconal, Amytal, Nembutal. She'd get you some Librium or Valium to bring you down from a bum trip. Man, she was a one-woman first-aid station. That's why I called her a lady. She'd even straighten out juice heads."

"But she put out to boys?"

Dreamer shrugged. "I guess you know all about that. Don't ask me why she did it, or why she hated old dudes. It was her personal trip. In some ways, like you just said, she was kinda strange."

"Who would hate her enough to kill her?"

"I dunno. Some chick who found out she was balling her boy friend, some dude that she turned down. Hell, Inspector, it coulda been one of them old broads in the apartment house or some dude that lives there."

"Is Dwayne Hardley a gang member?"

"Jesus, man, we might be heads and freaks, and we might do some crazy things like the time I shot Drano, but we're not fags!"

"How about Hardley?"

"Strictly a fucking fag, Inspector. A real Wellesley Street gearbox."

"So he didn't hang around with you or your gang?"

"I don't say he mightn't come around here in the plaza and rap around with us, but he wasn't one of us. We duked him outa the price of fixes of speed now and again, but we're strictly straight pussy, Inspector." He was clenching his teeth to keep them from rattling.

"Where did the Hardley kid get his money? From his old man?"

"I don't think so. I think he got it from some dude he was putting out to. He could always score a saw-buck somewhere."

"He went to Don Mills High School, and so do some

of the other kids whose pictures I showed you. Are there many users at the school?"

"Not too many, hardly any in fact that can score for smack or Charlie. Most smoke pot and hash, a few shoot speed, but most of them drop goofballs."

"Are drugs hard to buy up here in Don Mills?"

"Don't be so heavy man. Everybody around here turns on."

"Do you know anything, Dreamer, about tartar emetic?"

"What's that, one of the new ones?"

"No. That's absolutely the last one. It's what Zelda was poisoned with."

"Poisoned! I thought she'd been stabbed."

"She was stabbed after she was dead."

"Jesus Christ, and they call me a weirdo!"

"Do you remember boosting the four steak knives one time from the Coach'n Four?"

"We used to carry fancy daggers made outa steak knives."

"Where's yours?"

"At home. On the wall of my room."

"Do you live with your parents?"

"With my old man. My mother split years ago. Ran away with a guy that was running the Tupperware caper in our neighborhood."

"What does your father do?"

"Draws a war pension and gives it back to the Legion."

"What branch?"

"I don't know. Sometimes at Kingston Road and Woodbine, sometimes at the Baron Byng at Coxwell and Gerrard. We used to live on Ashdale Avenue. That's where my old lady made the walk."

"Who else but you had one of the daggers you used to wear in leg sheaths?"

"You know about that! I don't know nobody else that had one."

"Don't spoil our conversation by beginning to lie to me."

"I was stoned the night we boosted them from Diana's."

"But not too stoned that you don't remember it. Don't tell me you guys can afford the prices at the Coach'n Four?"

"We could *that* night. Hardley made a heavy score from some dude."

"What did he do, roll him?"

"I don't know nothing about that, Inspector." He was trembling all over now and his words were slower.

"We've already questioned Dwayne Hardley and he admits having one of the knives. Where were they ground down and honed?"

"Victoria Park Secondary. In the machine shop."

"That makes two of them, yours and the Hardley kid's. Who else had one of them?"

"George Drewson."

"Drop Kick?"

"Yeah. You guys've got that one. The fuzz found it on him when he totalled somebody's wheels on the freeway."

"How about the fourth knife?"

"I forget, Inspector. I can't think so good the condition I'm in. I gotta get me some meth, Inspector. That kid Cliff Drakes was good for a deuce. I was gonna put the hammer on him for the price when you come in."

The inspector pulled some bills from his pocket and handed Dreamer two dollars. "This isn't stool money, Dreamer," he said. "Jesus, I wouldn't want to see a dog in your condition. Can you get a fix around here?"

"There's more dope in the plaza than fucking food, Inspector. I can get myself straightened out so long as you guys don't tail me."

"We won't tail you," the inspector said. He stood up to let Dreamer out of his seat. "Hurry back, will you? I want you to go out to your place with Detective Zotas and give him your dagger. Otherwise we'll treat you as a stabbing suspect."

"Okay. Give me ten minutes." Dreamer, looking like a blond Zulu, walked away from the booth, then returned. "Thanks, Inspector," he said.

"When he comes back, you drive him up to Park-woods Village, Bill, and pick up the ground-down

206

steak knife." He pulled the police car keys from his pocket and gave them to the young detective.

"Do you think he'll come back?" Zotas asked.

"You answer him, Eric," the inspector said.

Manders explained to Zotas that most drunks and hypes treated the police with the same respect they received from them. "Personally I'd trust a guy like Dreamer a hell of a lot more than I'd trust some square john-citizens I've met," he said. Speaking to McDumont he asked, "Where do we go from here, Walter?"

"Well, some time this evening we're going to snap Zutach. He'll spill everything once he's charged."

"With what?"

"For starters with theft of a painting and camera from the Greenless apartment. That's enough to hold him on. I don't think he had anything to do with poisoning Zelda, but he sure as hell had plenty to do with the stabbing and the moving of the body from the apartment."

"He was pretty careless about fingerprints," Manders said.

"At first he was careful. It was only after he knew that we knew he was implicated that he became scared enough to get careless."

"Do you think he stabbed the woman?"

"No. In the first place I don't think he's got the guts, and in the second he had no motive, unless it was sexual frustration. It was something more than that that made the stabber sink that dagger blade as deep as he did and then twist it. And placing the body in the garbage closet was a symbolic act of pure hatred."

"By the murderer, do you think, Walter?"

"No, I don't think so. I think the murderer would have used the dagger in the first place, and not bothered poisoning Mrs. Greenless. There's two different people involved, Eric, and though I don't know who they are yet I have the feeling that I've met them both already."

"You don't think the fact that she was stashing so much hash in her place had anything to do with her being killed?"

"No, Eric. I'm certain none of the kids around here

207

had anything to do with it. Dreamer called the apartment the day the body was found, and Detective Tom Smith took the call. Dreamer was still on a run at the time, and he gave Smith his name. No matter how far out he was on meth or anything else Dreamer's too intelligent to leave his name at a murder scene. Anyhow he didn't know that Zelda was dead, I don't think."

The two older men talked about their coming vacations. Eric Manders said he was going to have his cottage winterized and move into it permanently after he was pensioned. "It's the thing now, Walter. You winterize your summer cottage and then move into it after you leave your job. Retirement homes they call them."

"Christ, Eric, I can see you living up in the bush!"

"Why not? Dorothy's all for it, and we can always drive down here to see the grandchildren. There's a curling rink and a Legion hall in Craig's Hollow, only five minutes drive from my cottage."

"Providing they plow the roads during the winter."

"Dreamer's back," Bill Zotas said.

Dreamer, his eyes staring, but not shaking as much as he had been, sat down beside the inspector.

"You're looking better than when you left here," the inspector said.

"I'll feel better later on. I scored a spike of methamp —MDA—from a guy. Man, I'm just beginning to hang loose. I was really strung out before."

"Okay, you go with Detective Zotas here out to Parkwoods Village and give him your ground-down steak knife."

"Right." Dreamer stood up, as did Bill Zotas. The young man hesitated.

"What's up?" Sergeant Manders asked.

"I haven't got the price of my coffee," Dreamer said.

"Here, I'll pay for it,' said Manders. He handed Dreamer a quarter.

"Thanks, Sarge. I'll pay you back the next time I score." Looking at McDumont, he said, "You too, Inspector."

"Keep the change," Manders said.

After the others had gone the two detectives walked out into the shopping plaza. This being a Friday evening the Don Mills Centre was busy with shoppers; the stores all open, and the parking lots jamming up.

"Let's take a walk along here to Diana's Artifactory," McDumont said.

"What's that?"

"A bar and grill. Sort of a cheaper young brother to the Coach'n Four, both of which are owned by George Boukydis of the old Diana Sweets restaurants."

"Really! I used to take Dorothy to the Diana Sweets on Bloor, west of Avenue Road, when we were younger. There's one yet on Yonge north of Queen."

"They're the ones."

They paused and looked into a men's clothing-store window.

"Look at that," Sergeant Manders said. "A hundred and eight-five bucks for a suit!"

"I used to outfit myself for a year on that," said McDumont.

"And get a pocketful of change back."

"You said it." The inspector glanced across the parking lot. "Oh-oh!"

"What's up, Walter?"

The inspector pointed. "See that little old guy there. There, just coming up the sidewalk. Wearing gray slacks and a blazer."

"Yeh?"

"His name's Raymark Osler, and he lives on the same floor as Zelda Greenless lived on. He's a black sheep of *the* Osler family. They've been lawyers and judges for generations. Old Raymark used to live in a shanty on the banks of the Don when this was farm country. Quite an interesting old bastard. Come on, I want to talk to him."

The detectives hurried between the parked cars and intercepted the old man before he entered the Artifactory.

The inspector said, "Evening, Mr. Osler."

The old man peered up at him before his face lit up. "Hello, there."

"Meet Sergeant Eric Manders. Mr. Raymark Osler, Eric."

"How are you officers! Great night, eh?"

The policemen nodded.

"Just going for a few gin-and-tonics," the old man said. "Will you join me in one, officers?"

"We can't right now, sir. Thanks just the same," the inspector said.

"You people have stirred things up quite a bit at the apartment house."

"Yes, we're sorry about that, but we have to do our work."

"Just what I told them. I think it was the newspaper people that bothered them most. Newspaper, radio, TV, what they call the media. A hell of a word."

"Who's they, and what were they saying?"

"The ones circulating the petition. Mrs. Bullay and Mrs. Hardley."

"Take a minute, Mr. Osler, and tell us about it," the inspector invited, his face hardening.

"They've circulated a complaint against you officers for being rude, impolite and for needlessly bothering innocent people."

"Did they get many signatures?"

"Quite a few, from every floor in the building. I told them the police department would laugh at them. I wouldn't sign it."

"I don't think it'll bother us much," Sergeant Manders said.

"Of course not. Well, I hope you find the person who killed Mrs. Greenless."

"So do I," the inspector said grimly.

"See you later, officers."

The little man crossed the sidewalk and entered the Artifactory.

The inspector said, "You know, Eric, it wasn't even our men who questioned the people on the lower floors or on the seventh floor. It was a pair of divisional detectives and a couple of uniformed officers. I've got to get that son of a bitch Ernie Willis back from his holiday! Maybe this petition will do it for me."

"He's really got you steamed up, Walter."

"Not only him, Eric. Why the hell wouldn't Randall Ford give me a couple of search warrants? With them I'm sure I could clean this thing up in half the time."

"We've cleaned up tougher cases, Walter. Let's go over to the scene of the crime. That's a place I want to see."

Chapter 14

Inspector McDumont pressed the superintendent's buzzer and a woman's voice answered.

"Mrs. Zutach?" the inspector asked.

"Yes?"

"The police, Mrs. Zutach. Will you let us in please?"

The door latch buzzed and the two detectives entered the apartment house foyer.

Xenia Zutach, her small son Rudolph in her arms, came from her apartment to the front of the elevators.

"Mrs. Zutach, this is Sergeant of Detectives Manders."

The little woman smiled shyly and nodded.

"Anything new going on around here?" the inspector asked.

Mrs. Zutach shook her head.

"Where's Anton?"

"He go to owner of house. Mr. Rubins of Martin-Rubins Development."

"Where does *he* live, Mrs. Zutach?"

"Come." She led the two policemen through the glass door that separated the north ground-floor apartments from the foyer. When she reached the open door of 110 she motioned them to go in.

"I get name and address for you," she said, seating the baby on the living room rug. While Sergeant Manders bent down and spoke to the baby, McDumont glanced at the wall that had held Zelda Greenless's painting. It was now the receptacle of an equally banal piece of shopping center art, a framed reproduction of a vase of gaudy flowers.

The little woman returned from the telephone with

a name, address and phone number written on a piece of shopping bag, handing it to the inspector. It read: Jerry Rubin, 205 Sultana Ave., 772-7272.

"Thank you very much, Mrs. Zutach," said the inspector.

The woman picked up the little boy. "Gentlemens— Anton not do noddings. All dat man's fault. Troubles all time wit dat families."

"What family, Mrs. Zutach?" the inspector asked.

The little woman began to cry, and the baby began crying also.

Sergeant Manders tried to humor the baby, which only made it cry more and bury its face in the mother's neck.

The inspector said, "I promise you, Mrs. Zutach, everything's going to be fixed up." As soon as he'd said it he realized it had been the wrong thing to say.

The little woman walked back to where the telephone stood on a small table outside the kitchen. She came back carrying a sheet of blue-lined legal-size paper, and handed it to the inspector.

McDumont read the fifteen or so signatures on it, each with the number of the signer's apartment written beside it. Above the signatures was typed: THE UNDER-SIGNED WISH TO BRING TO THE ATTENTION OF THE PROPER AUTHORITIES THE INVASION OF PRIVACY, RUDE-NESS AND LACK OF PROFESSIONAL COMPETENCE ON THE PART OF THE METROPOLITAN TORONTO POLICE DURING A DOOR-TO-DOOR SERIES OF INTERROGATIONS FOLLOW-ING A CRIME WHICH TOOK PLACE IN THE APARTMENT HOUSE AT 1049 DON MILLS ROAD ON JUNE 12, 1974.

The signatures were led by those of Doris Hardley, Craig Hardley and Dolly Bullay. George Bullay had not signed it.

Inspector McDumont led the way into the hall. Through the glass door leading to the foyer he caught sight of a figure stepping out of one of the elevators, and he hurried along the hallway. By the time he reached the front door the male figure had descended the steps to the sidewalk and had walked north out of sight on Don Mills Road.

"Who was it, Walter?" asked Eric Manders, coming up behind him.

"Piet Langenzent, from apartment six-o-three," the inspector answered. "He told us he had just arrived from Ottawa yesterday. He was supposed to be going back today."

The elevator took them in slow mock-opulence to the sixth floor. The inspector led the way to the door of apartment 602, and opened the door with his key.

"Who the hell lived here, the Bey of Tunis?" asked Sergeant Manders.

"It's wild, isn't it, Eric? Go take a look at the bed."

While the sergeant was in the bedroom McDumont dialed the phone number Xenia Zutach had given him. The phone was answered by a woman.

"Could I speak to Mr. Jerry Rubin please?"

"Just a moment." He could hear the woman calling, "Jerry!"

Yeah. Rubin here."

"Jerry Rubin?"

"Yes."

"The police, Mr. Rubin. Is Anton Zutach there?"

"Yeah. You want to speak to him?"

"I want to speak to both of you. This is Inspector McDumont of the homicide squad. Could you and Mr. Zutach come down to ten-forty-nine Don Mills. We'll be in apartment six-o-two."

"Sure, Inspector. Right away."

"Okay. Thanks."

He hung up, and told Manders that both the apartment house owner and the superintendent were coming down.

"Say, Walter, that's some bed," said Manders. "I wonder how they got it in there."

"Or how they're going to get it out. Thank God that's not *our* problem. We've got enough of our own."

"Walter, what do you think the super's wife meant about it being 'that man's fault,' and 'troubles all the time with that family'?"

"I don't know, Eric, but we're going to find out from her husband." He spread out the signed complaint on one of the tables and both policemen read it. "There's a funny thing about this thing," he said. "The person who typed it up knew the murder had taken place on the twelfth, but it wasn't discovered until the thirteenth. Either I or one of my men may have given this away, and again we may not have."

"Mmmph."

"The only people I questioned, who have signed the petition or whatever you'd call it, are Mrs. Dolly Bullay and the Hardleys. The others were all questioned by 33-Division men, plainclothes and uniformed." He took some papers from an inside pocket and extracted from them the Preliminary List of Electors that he had found at the bottom of a dresser drawer in the apartment earlier. "Look at this: *Mrs. Sally MacAlpine, Apt. 304.* On the electors' list she's listed as a psychometrician. What the hell's that! In one of the apartments on the fifth floor there's a Rita Heppelthwaite, listed as a confidential secretary, and next door to her a Margaret Cruikshank, who calls herself a financial analyst. Christ, I'll bet the two of them are stenographers." He ran his finger down the electors list to those on the sixth floor, and began to laugh. "*Apartment six-o-one, Dolly Bullay, educator.* Not a teacher but an *educator!* 'The word teacher is too, too plebeian, m'dear!' And wait! Doris Hardley has not listed herself as a housewife, but as a journalist! Her husband told us his wife has never had to work. Let's see what he's called himself. A floor trader. Well, he was honest there. So Doris Hardley is a journalist, is she? I wonder if she's the one who typed up this squawk about police lack of professional competence? The names on this petition run the gamut of the phony suburban upwardly mobile jerks in this town, Eric."

"Yep."

The inspector, suddenly remembering something, stood up and walked over to the cheap landscape hanging on the wall. In the bottom righthand corner of it he could see the initials W.Z. "Here, Eric, these are Bill Zotas's initials that he put on this painting when he found it down in the Zutach apartment."

"Yeah, I see them, Walter." The sergeant of detectives threw himself down on the sofa. "What I can't understand is why the superintendent would bother to steal such a cheap lousy thing and hang it on his wall?

215

Personally I don't think he lifted it on purpose but *for* a purpose."

"Such as?"

"You think that Zutach pushed the body of the dead woman down the hall to the empty apartment at the other end sometime during the late evening of the twelfth or early in the morning of the thirteenth, right?"

"Right."

"On one of those little two-wheeled trucks, like a flat wheelbarrow, with two curved handles?"

"Yeh. We've got it down at the crime lab. There were bloodstains on it matching Zelda's."

"Suppose he'd have met somebody in the hallway?"

"Then it would have been game over."

"Not necessarily, Walter. You figure the body was covered in a yellow blanket, a small-size blanket?"

"Yep."

"If you, say you lived on this floor, stepped off the elevator or came out of your apartment and found the building superintendent pushing what was obviously a dead body covered in a blanket on his little handcart then, as you say, it'd have been game over. Supposing however that instead of just the body laid back against the slats of the handcart—in my opinion rigor mortis would have set in by then—you met him pushing something covered by the blanket that from the front looked like a rectangular frame or box, and tied to the cart. You probably wouldn't have savvied that there was a body behind the frame would you?"

"The painting?" the inspector asked.

"Sure. The painting. He had to find something to disguise the body with, and what better thing than the big painting hanging there on the wall, as it is now? As it happened, let's suppose he *didn't* meet anybody in the hallway. In the empty apartment—what is it, six-ten?—he removed the rope or whatever that he'd used to tie his cargo, and what was he going to do with the painting? Leave it there for us to find, so that we could reconstruct what had happened. No. What I would have done if I'd have been him is remove the blanket and the painting and get them out of the way. Apartment six-ten is at the back of the building six flights of

216

stairs above Zutach's apartment. They're the back stairs, and probably seldom used. He carried the blanket *and* the painting down to his place. Where to hide the painting? The most obvious place, of course, on his living room wall."

"By God, you're right, Eric! Thank goodness you're not slowing down as much as I am in my dotage."

"Hell, Walter, my mind is clear. I'm fresh on the job. You've had a thousand things to think of since yesterday morning."

"What about the handcart?"

"There was nothing wrong with leaving that in the empty apartment, overnight if necessary. But he'd have been taking an unnecessary chance carrying the painting back to the dead woman's place."

"I think you've come up with approximately what happened, Eric, and believe me I'm grateful. There's one thing though that bothers me."

"What's that?"

"I'm almost certain Zutach wasn't the stabber."

"Then they may have worked in concert. If it wasn't Zutach, then it was the stabber who wheeled the body down the hall, into the empty apartment, and then carried it across the hall—the garbage closet *is* across the hall isn't it?"

"Almost."

"And the stabber then placed the body in the garbage closet, probably later at night or very early in the morning."

"I'm of the opinion that Zutach probably wheeled the body, disguised in the blanket and placed behind the painting, along the hallway to the empty apartment sometime during the evening, as you've surmised. He then removed the blanket and painting and carried them down the back stairs to his own apartment. Later on he returned to apartment six-ten and removed some blood that had dripped on the floor from the naked body, and also removed the handcart. It was while he was taking the handcart back to where he usually keeps it that the young people came out of the apartment where the party was going on, Gilcrest's apartment, and the young nurse took a ride on the handcart as far as the elevators. That was at ten o'clock."

217

"He may have been bringing it along to this apartment then."

"But he took it through the door leading to the staircase."

"Probably until the coast was clear, before pushing it into this apartment later on."

"Yes. Say, Eric, I'm going next door to see Mrs. Eleanor Jacton for a minute, if she's in. Why don't you go along the hall and see for yourself how far it is from apartment six-ten to the garbage closet."

Eleanor Jacton answered Inspector McDumont's knock at her door.

"Hello, Mrs. Jacton."

"Why, hello there. You're still on the job I see."

"Yes. Did you officially identify the—Mrs. Greenless?"

"Yes we did, Inspector. Won't you come in?"

"Thanks. My partner is just down the hall. I only wanted to ask you whether you arranged for your friend's burial?"

He entered the apartment and was shown to a chair.

"Yes I did. I phoned her aunt and uncle, Elizabeth and Peter Stanton in Crow Lake, and they arranged with a Toronto undertaking parlor to ship the body up there for burial. A small firm out on Dundas West— McComb and Greeley. They've hired a lawyer too."

"That's good. Is Mr. McMulley in?"

"Yes. He's lying down. Do you want to speak to him?"

"No." He stood up. "You were pretty shaken up by what had happened to Zelda the last time I was here. I don't suppose you have anything to add to what you told me then?"

"Nothing I can think of."

"Then I'll be going."

They said their good-byes at the door.

Back in apartment 602 Eric Manders was staring through the window. When the inspector came in they both sat down, and McDumont lighted a cigarette.

"It's only a couple of steps from the door of six-ten to the door of the garbage closet," the sergeant said. "A body, especially that of a slim young woman, could have been dragged across without any trouble. I don't think the person who sat the body up in the corner, whether it was Zutach or somebody else, would have needed the handcart by that time. In fact it would only have been a hindrance."

"You know, Eric, the more I think of this whole thing—a person gone crazy with hate for the Greenless woman, and wanting to show his or her loathing for her, would not have taken the chance of moving the body to the garbage closet very late at night."

"I'm listening, Walter."

"The whole idea of placing her body in the closet was to illustrate to as many people as possible that she was filth, garbage, scum. Why would the person who inflicted his (I think it's a 'him' so I won't mention a 'her' again) totally psychotic stabbing in a corpse's back—and took the terrible chance of being detected while doing it—bother to move the body first to an empty apartment and later into the garbage disposal closet unless he wanted as many of her neighbors as possible to see it?"

"Huh-huh."

"Let's presume that the stabber was Zelda Greenless's potential murderer, which I think he was. It was his intention to stab Zelda to revenge himself on her, or to right a wrong he felt she had inflicted on him or on someone close to him. It's crazy, but the person who does these things is crazy. All right. He lets himself into her apartment with a key—and Christ knows there were enough keys around that he didn't have to make one—and there he finds his victim already dead. He's psychotic, insane, crazy, depending on whether we're talking about him in medical, legal or man-in-the-street terms. Finding that somebody else (or even 'natural causes') has beaten him, he's going to become twice as crazy as he was before finding the body. It was in this state of pure, frenzied insanity that he decided to get the revenge so far denied him by the actual poisoner—and he doesn't know that she *has* been poisoned yet—by placing her naked body in a place reserved for trash and garbage. Everything that followed was motivated by sheer insanity."

"I agree with you, Walter but, if Zutach wasn't her stabber, what was his part in this macabre seeking of revenge?"

"That's what I'm waiting to ask him, Eric."

"And the apartment house owner is bringing him down here?"

"Right. They should be here soon."

The front door buzzer made its high, buzzing sound.

"This is probably them now," the inspector said. He spoke into the small grill beside the door. "Yes?"

"Bill Zotas, Inspector."

"Okay, Bill." The inspector pressed the button that unlocked the front door.

When the young detective arrived he threw a plastic-handled dagger, identical to the one that had been used to stab Zela Greenless, down on the ottoman. "Here's Dreamer's dagger." Throwing a leg sheath down beside it. "And here's the sheath."

"Where were they?"

"Just where Dreamer said they'd be. Hanging on the wall of what you'd call in a normal household the living room."

"What do you mean, Zotas?" the sergeant asked.

"Sergeant, I haven't been on the force that long, by either your standards or the inspector's, but I can truly state that Dreamer's apartment is the filthiest shithouse I've ever seen. Before becoming a detective I was in a squad car in 14 Division and later in 52 Division, but the apartment occupied by the Blacks, Joseph and Milford—father and son—is worse than any Spadina Avenue hippie commune, Sherbourne or George Street wino pad, or King Street rooming house I've ever set foot in."

Both older detectives nodded. The inspector said, "I figured it would be, Bill."

"Christ! On the drive out to Parkwoods Village I was beginning to almost *like* Dreamer. On the high he was coasting on he sounded quite sensible, and we talked about the drug scene. I asked him why he didn't get a haircut and a job. He told me he'd been an apprentice lithographer, things like that. After I saw and smelled the joint he lived in, though, I *hated* him. I can understand now why policemen beat up those kind of freaks!"

The sergeant said, "It gets to you sometimes, Bill. Maybe that's why social workers become callous, and psychiatrists have such a high incidence of suicide."

The inspector said, "Bill, put that dagger in its sheath, and take it and this painting down to the car." He lifted the cheap reproduction from the wall and handed it to the young detective. "By the way, where did you park the car?"

"In the parking lot behind the house here."

"Good."

Sergeant Manders asked, "Where did you leave Dreamer?"

"Flaked out on his kitchen floor. He was probably better off there than on any piece of furniture I saw in his joint. He passed out cold as soon as we got to his place."

"After you put these things in the car trunk you can come back here and wash your hands."

"I won't feel clean again until I take a shower tonight and send my clothes to the cleaners," Zotas said as he left the apartment.

Before the young detective returned there was a knock at the door, and the inspector admitted Anton Zutach and another man.

"Inspector McDumont?" asked the young man who had accompanied Zutach, looking from the inspector to the sergeant and back again.

"I'm McDumont," the inspector said. "This is my partner, Sergeant of Detectives Manders of the Metro Homicide Squad. You're Jerry Rubin, I take it?"

"That's right." They shook hands all round.

"I guess we may as well all sit down," the inspector said.

Rubin and Zutach sat down on the sofa, the sergeant on the ottoman and the inspector on one of the two chairs. As they took stock of one another McDumont noticed that Zutach had put on a shirt and tie and was wearing what the inspector took to be his best suit. Jerry Rubin was darkly Jewish, his black hair styled carefully, half-covering his ears, intelligent-looking, and, the inspector thought, probably a third-generation Canadian. He was wearing an expensive navy blue gabardine suit, highly polished black laced brogues, light blue shirt and plain dark blue necktie.

"Well, Mr. Rubin, I'm sure you know what happened in this apartment the other day?"

"Yes, Inspector."

"We happen to think that Mrs. Zelda Greenless was poisoned by someone—in fact we *know* she was from crime laboratory examinations—and was later stabbed, after she was dead, by a person unknown. As a matter of fact both the poisoner and the stabber are unknown to us at this time."

Rubin nodded solemnly.

"However, we feel that we are in possession of enough evidence now to pull in the person, or one of them, who were accessories after the fact of Mrs. Greenless's murder. I'm speaking now of the stabbing."

"I take it you are still looking for the poisoner?"

"Yes, we are."

The door buzzer sounded, and Sergeant Manders jumped up and pressed the front door lock button.

"That is one of our men who has taken some evidence out to the car," the inspector said. He went on. "I have always felt, and I'm speaking personally now, Mr. Rubin, that the poisoner—that is the real murderer —and the stabber are two different people. However, I will tell you this, I believe both of them to be tenants of this building."

Rubin nodded again. "We're unable to guard against accepting murderers, prostitutes, alcoholics, drug addicts or morally indefensible people as tenants in our buildings, Inspector."

The inspector nodded. "We're aware of that. We also know, or feel, that you, as the building's owner, are just as anxious that unwanted tenants such as you've mentioned be apprehended and taken off your property."

"Yes."

"Are you the sole owner as well as the president of Martin-Rubin Development?"

"No. A former partner of my father's, Mervin Martin, is deceased, Inspector. However, we have kept the corporate name. My father, Abraham Rubin, is a silent partner who now lives permanently in Florida. Under our corporate set-up he bears the title of chairman of the board. I am the president and my brother, Roland, is secretary-treasurer."

"Do you own other apartment buildings in the city?"

"Four in the borough of Scarborough and two in Mississauga."

Detective Zotas came in, and was introduced to Jerry Rubin.

"Excuse me, I have to wash my hands," he said, and disappeared into the bathroom.

The inspector laughed. "He's been visiting a place a couple of miles from here that almost turned his stomach."

"I know what you mean," Rubin said with a smile.

"Now, Mr. Rubin, did you call Mr. Zutach to come and talk with you this evening?"

"No, sir. Mr. Zutach called *me*. I think he has a great deal to reveal to you about the person who stabbed Mrs. Greenless, and—" He looked at Zutach, "about his own participation in what happened."

"All right, Mr. Rubin, I don't want to hear it now. I'm afraid Mr. Zutach will have to accompany us to police headquarters, where he can make an official statement which will be taken down stenographically." To Zutach he said, "Do you understand that?"

"Yes. I know."

Bill Zotas came out of the bathroom and sat down in the other chair.

Jerry Rubin said, "Inspector, when the time comes I'm willing to go bail for Anton here, who I feel has been taken in, because of his lack of knowledge of English and so on."

"That's fine, Mr. Rubin, if bail is allowed. That, of course, is out of my jurisdiction."

"I understand."

"You may be interested in reading this," the inspector said, handing the young man the signed complaint given him by Mrs. Zutach.

Rubin read the statement, then went down the list of signatures. At times he shook his head and once he said, "Hell, this guy owes three months rent, and is being evicted." When he handed it back to McDumont he said, "After you hear Anton's story a couple of these signatures may make you wonder."

"Not if they're the ones I think they are."

"Oh, Inspector, the rent for this apartment is paid up until the end of the month; but has there been any move made to get the furniture out of here?"

"Yes. An uncle and aunt are burying Mrs. Greenless, and their lawyer will be in touch with you soon, I'm sure."

The detectives stood up, followed by Rubin and Zutach.

"Sergeant Manders will go with you, Mr. Rubin, and you, Mr. Zutach, to your apartment. Tell your wife, Mr. Zutach, that you may be in custody a day or two before Mr. Rubin can get you out on bail. Bring your toothbrush, razor and things if you like."

Zutach, looking down at the floor, nodded.

"Incidentally, are the Hardleys at home?"

Zutach said, "No. They leave this afternoon. In car. Gone away till Sunday."

"How about their son? Did Dwayne go too?"

"No. Just old peoples."

"Okay." The inspector said to Sergeant Manders, "Better have Anton change his clothes. If they put him in the slammer overnight he won't want his good suit going through the delouser."

When they reached the main floor, Zutach, Rubin and Sergeant Manders went towards the Zutach apartment, while the inspector and Detective Zotas went out to the car.

In a squad room down at headquarters Inspector McDumont and Sergeant of Detectives Manders sat across a wide table from Anton

Zutach, now wearing slacks, shirt and cardigan, but no necktie. A male police stenographer with a shorthand pad sat at the end of the table. Before each was a paper cup of coffee. Detective Zotas had been sent home from Don Mills, with the reminder by the inspector to be sure to take a shower.

The inspector said to the stenographer, "Joe, Mr. Zutach doesn't speak perfect English, but don't try to take his declaration down verbatim. Put it in as good English as you can without changing its meaning."

"Right, Inspector."

"Okay, Mr. Zutach, tell us everything, right from the beginning. Understand?"

"Yes. I unnerstand."

"And you're sure you don't want an interpreter?"

"No, Inspector."

"You understand that you'll have one in court?"

"Yes."

"What language?"

"Serbian."

"Serbian is your native language, but you speak Croatian to Xenia, right?"

"Yes. Xenia is Croat."

"Okay. You understand that you're not being questioned on a murder charge, but the relatively minor one of doing an indignity to a dead body, or whatever it's called in the Criminal Code?"

"Yes, Inspector."

"How did you get yourself involved in the stabbing of the dead woman?"

Zutach hesitated a moment then the words began pouring out, almost too fast for Joe, the stenographer, to translate into police jargon. "On night of June twelve I get call from apartment on this floor. I come up, and Mr. Hardley wait for me at elevator. He is carry dagger under his sweatercoat. He tell me that Mrs. Greenless is whore that should be done away with—"

"Did he tell you why?"

"He say she—"

"Corrupts?"

"Yes. That she corrupts young boys. We should make her move out of the house."

"But he didn't say he intended to kill her?"

"No. I not even know he had knife under his sweater-coat."

"Go on."

"Mr. Hardley had key to Greenless apartment. We go in—"

"Was Hardley drunk?" Manders asked.

"Crazy drunk. Act like real crazy man."

The inspector motioned to him to go on.

"We go into apartment and place is filled with empty whiskey bottles and stuff. Mrs. Greenless is lie on bed. She have her clothes on but not shoes. Hardley slap her face but she not wake up. Then he take, what you call it, rubber? from box in closet and he say to me, 'Zutach, I'm going to give her a man's fuck.' He pull back bedclothes and strip her naked."

"And you just watched him?" Manders asked sarcastically.

"I am too surprised to do nothing. I am scared too."

"Of Zelda Greenless or Hardley?" the inspector asked.

"I not want to be there at all. I know it is crime to do things to a woman like that, but when I tell Hardley I leave he pulls out that knife from under his sweater-coat and says he will cut my throat if I try to run away. He tell me too that I am in it as much as he is now, and that I can't run away. He turn woman on her back and drop his pants, eh, then I say to him, 'She too sick for fuck.' 'She not sick she dead drunk,' he answer. I go over to Mrs. Greenless and feel her wrist—"

"Her pulse?"

"Yes. There is no heartbeat in her wrist. I feel her neck too, no sign of heartbeat. I tell Mr. Hardley, 'Mrs. Greenless is dead.' He not believe me at first, but then he feel her—pulse?—and he know too she is dead."

"How did you know about taking a pulse beat in her neck?" Manders asked him.

"During Hungarian revolution I see much dead body, and I know about that."

"Then what happened?"

"Mr. Hardley drop rubber on floor. He tell me he is get blanket from his apartment and we take her down to garbage chute where she belong. He pick up camera from dresser, eh, and give to me. He tell me this is something I can have. It is very good German camera, and I take it. All time he has knife in his hand, and I know he will stab me if I don't do what he says. He is crazy, real crazy.

"He go to his apartment and come back with small blanket you find in garbage container, Inspector. When he come back he carry Mrs. Greenless into living room, cover her wit blanket and then stab her in back."

"Why didn't you call the police, Zutach?"

"I am afraid then. All time Mr. Hardley tell me we are in dis thing both together, and we both go to jail if we don't do as he tell me."

"And you believed him?" Manders asked, unbelievingly.

"Yes. I just got citizenship to Canada. I not know laws here. I am afraid to not do what he want. I am also afraid of Mr. Hardley's knife. I know that he stab me in a minute if I get him mad. I tell you peoples he is crazy like a madman."

"He had given you the camera," Manders said.

"Yes."

"What else did he give you, or promise you?"

"He tell me he give me one hundreds dollars."

"And you were willing to take part in a crime for a camera and a hundred dollars?"

"No! Not for camera or hundreds dollars, but he tell me I am guilty like him, and he wave knife in my face."

"That was before he buried it in Zelda Greenless's back?"

"Yes."

"What time was this, Zutach?"

"Maybe eight o'clock."

"After Hardley had taken Mrs. Greenless's body into her living room, covered her with the yellow blanket and stabbed her through it, what happened then?"

"He is crazy! He stick knife through blanket, then he twist it. He tell me that is for what she do to Dwayne."

"His son?"

"Yes."

"What *did* she do to Dwayne?"

"She give him drugs. She take him to bed."

"How do *you* know she did, Zutach?"

"She have young boys in her apartment plenty time. I seen them come up. She give keys to some boys."

"Did you ever see Dwayne going into or coming out of her apartment?"

"No. I seen other boys."

"So you believed Hardley when he told you she'd had his son in her bed?"

"Sure."

"Supposing I told you that Dwayne Hardley was a homosexual. Do you know what I mean by that?"

"He go with men not ladies."

"Right. Have you ever seen him go into a man's apartment in the building?"

Zutach didn't answer.

"I asked you a question, Zutach!"

"He was friend of John Kapett on seven floor of apartment house."

"And Kapett loaned him his expensive camera. You've seen him visiting Kapett?"

"Yessir."

"How often?"

Zutach shrugged. "Some time. I not go up to seven floor every day."

"Didn't it occur to you that Hardley stabbed the wrong person? That it wasn't Zelda Greenless who was corrupting Dwayne Hardley but men like John Kapett?"

"I not know that Dwayne was—"

"A homosexual?"

"Yes."

"Did he visit other men in the apartment house?"

"I not know that."

"Where do you think he got the money to dress as he did, from Santa Claus?"

"Excuse please."

"Forget it. You seem to have known every other goddam thing that happened in the Doncentre Apartments, but you dummy up when I mention Dwayne Hardley, why?"

228

"I not know."

"Did *you* ever have relations with Dwayne Hardley?"

"No! I am happy married man."

"Did you know?—let me put it another way—Dwayne Hardley is looked upon by the male members of the Centre Gang as a flaming fag. They stood him sometimes, and let him spend his money on them, but they really had no use for him. They're a bunch of young crazies, but at least, as far as I know, they're heterosexuals. Now, for the last time, what other men's apartments did Dwayne Hardley visit in the Don-centre?"

"I swear to you, Inspector, I not know that."

"Did you know that Craig Hardley, Dwayne's father, has a bank account of less than a hundred dollars and that he's been playing the middle-class swinger on nerve and gall and money borrowed from the Benevolent Finance Company?"

Both Zutach and Sergeant Manders stared at the inspector. Manders thought, Just when I'm ready to believe Walter's slipping he comes up with facts that no other detective on the force would think of getting.

"Zutach, did you get your hundred dollars from Hardley?"

"No, Inspector."

"Well, I'm telling you now to kiss it good-bye."

Zutach shrugged.

"Now, let me reconstruct what happened after you'd covered Zelda Greenless's body with the blanket and Hardley had had his fun and games with his son's knife in her back. When I'm wrong, you interrupt me. Incidentally this is Sergeant Manders' version, but I think it's the right one." He paused, lighted a cigarette, then went on. "Hardley sent you down to get your handcart, right? You brought it up to Apartment six-o-two and between you and Hardley you placed her body, covered with the blanket, on it. By this time Hardley has sobered up somewhat, and he's also scared out of his wits at what he's done. So are you. Even under the blanket anyone who sees you pushing the handcart along the hall will know you're pushing a body. Either you or Hardley realize you have to hide the fact that it's a dead body you're pushing along the hall, so one of you gets the bright idea that the best way to hide it is to place something in front of it, such as a picture, tie the whole thing on the cart and anyone you happen to meet will think you're moving some household effects. Don't forget that Cecil Gilcrest is having a party, so there's more than an even chance you might meet somebody. Am I right so far?"

Zutach nodded.

"The thing that puzzles me is *why* you wanted to take the body out of the apartment at all?"

"It was Hardley. He want to show Mrs. Greenless in garbage closet. That is his—revenge, eh, for what he think she do to his son."

"Okay. You tie the body and the picture you take down from the wall onto the handcart. Right?"

Zutach nodded again.

"Who pushed it along the hall, and why did you take it into the empty apartment at six-ten? And what did you do with Zelda's clothes?"

"I push it," Zutach said, beginning to cry. "Clothes down garbage."

"It's too late for crying now, Zutach," the inspector said, handing the little man a Kleenex. "Why did you push the cart into six-ten?"

"Some peoples going to party at Gilcrest get off elevator. Is impossible to put body in garbage closet. I take it to six-ten."

"Then what?"

"I take ropes and painting off hand cart, also Mrs. Greenless' body. Then I take picture down to my apartment."

"What about the camera?"

"I take camera too. It is hanging around my neck on strap, eh."

"What did Xenia say when you arrived down at your place with a cheap painting and an expensive camera?"

"I tell her I am mind them for somebody upstairs."

"Did either you or Hardley use the dead woman's toilet?"

He shrugged—then thought for a minute. "No. Me and Hardley not go in bathroom."

"What did you do then?"

"I go back to six-ten, wipe up some blood from floor, take blanket and put it down garbage chute. Then I push handcart along hall to take down elevator. Girls come out of Gilcrest apartment, and Gilcrest, and one take ride to elevator on handcart. Then I take to front stairway where I keep it till hallway is clear, then back to elevator and down to basement."

"When did Xenia find out about the painting and the camera coming from Mrs. Greenless's apartment?"

She hear news on radio next morning, late next morning."

"And?"

"She call me every Croatian swearing word. Then she pray. Then she call me more swearing words. In afternoon after you and detectives have gone I take painting and camera back to apartment six-o-two. I put painting back on wall and camera in dresser drawer."

"Okay, that's it," the inspector said. "Oh, by the way, where was Hardley all this time?"

"He go with Mrs. Hardley to Gilcrest party. After party over, I don't know what time, he take body from six-ten and put in garbage closet."

"I hope you slept well."

"I never sleep all night, Inspector."

The inspector turned to Eric Manders. "Eric, take him down and book him, will you? The desk sergeant will know the charge, something about indignity to a dead body, something like that. Have them mug and fingerprint him and then take him out to the Don Jail. I don't want *you* to take him out, I mean the regular paddy wagon. We've got some more work to do tonight, up in Don Mills."

"Okay, Walter."

Zutach began to wail.

"Wipe your nose on that Kleenex and shut up!" the inspector told him.

The prisoner and Sergeant Manders left the office.

The inspector said to the stenographer, "Can you make a quick transcript of your shorthand notes, Joe?"

"Sure, Inspector."

"Make it in three copies, get Zutach to read one of

231

them and sign it before they ship him out to the Don will you please?"

"Sure."

"Tell the desk sergeant to hold him for a later shipment if necessary."

"Okay, Inspector," the stenographer said, leaving the office.

Chapter 15

Walter McDumont and Eric Manders drove back to the Don Mills Centre. They talked of how Anton Zutach had suddenly been so willing to talk and give a complete deposition of his part in the stabbing of Zelda Greenless.

"Hardley used him for a fall guy," Manders remarked.

"Yeah, but it was his wife Xenia who straightened him out. We're going to snap Hardley as soon as the son of a bitch arrives home. In the meantime I think I'll stop off and reassure Xenia Zutach. Luckily they've got a good boss in Jerry Rubin. He'll probably furnish bail for Zutach, and send a man down to the house to do the heavy work while Anton's in the slammer."

"When do the Hardleys return home, Walter?"

"Sunday. Right now though I'd like to question some of the kids who knew Zelda Greenless. You know, Eric, one of the strange things about this case is that I've yet to find anyone, excluding Dolly Bullay and Doris Hardley, who really hated the dead woman. That's why, at first, I thought the poisoner was a female, poison being a female murder weapon.

"We may be looking in the wrong direction, Walter, and for the wrong motive."

"Yes, we might be," the inspector said as he pulled the car into the almost deserted shopping centre and parked it facing the sidewalk west of the government liquor store.

"There's a small coffee shop just up that short stretch of street where most of the Centre Gang seem to hang out."

"Any prints from the liquor bottles, Walter?"

233

"Plenty, mostly Zelda's. The one piece of real evidence we've got is the mock-illiterate note sent to Zelda on the pink writing paper. I'm sure that the poisoner destroyed what was left of the poison and its container, so we're out of luck there. Dr. Martin Raymond, the assistant toxicologist at the forensic lab tells me that tartar emetic can be bought across a drug store counter, and the purchaser doesn't even have to sign the poison book. He was quoting the provincial pharmacy act."

"How is it usually bought, Walter?"

"By the ounce, he says."

"Has it any commercial uses?"

"Not that he or I know. It's that old cliché poison that you've read about in a hundred murder mysteries. The guy who poisoned Mrs. Greenless either lacked imagination or had enough of it to know how easy it was to purchase. It gave him a few hours after administering it in a drink to get away and find himself an alibi. I wish to hell he'd have used oxalic acid or something that I could tie down commercially. Oxalic acid needs fifteen to thirty grams for a fatal dose, but tartar emetic needs only 0.2 to 0.3 grams to be effective."

"Did you check out the drug stores here in the plaza?"

"Sure. Tom Smith checked every store in the neighborhood, but there was nothing on their books or in the memories of the pharmacists about anyone buying tartar emetic. Zelda had forged some prescriptions though."

"It makes it a guessing game."

"Yeah. Hey, there's one of the divisional detectives!" The inspector opened the window and shouted, "Hey, Brad! Brad Semons!"

The detective came over to the car. McDumont introduced him to Sergeant Manders. Then he asked, "Any of the Centre Gang around, Brad?"

"There's three or four in the coffee shop."

"Do you people up here have any members of the police youth bureau working this neighborhood?"

"Yeh. There's a first class constable named Tom Johnson and a woman cadet called Sandra Pope."

"Are they in the coffee joint?"

"As a matter of fact they are, Inspector. They're sitting with the kids. They had a baseball game in the high school field tonight; they beat a team from Scarborough."

"Bring them out here to the car, will you, Brad?"

The divisional detective went away and returned in a minute with a young policeman and an even younger policewoman. Both of them were wearing hippie-style civvies.

"Hi, man!" Johnson said as he walked up to the car.

"Forget that lingo!" the inspector said to him. "I'm Inspector McDumont of the homicide squad, and this is Sergeant of Detectives Manders, my second-in-command. You'll address us by our police titles, okay?"

"Why yes, Inspector. Sorry about the slip."

"What's your name again, Miss?"

"Sandra Pope, Inspector."

"Have both of you always worked out of this division?"

"Sandra has, but I was down in the Lower Ward before being posted up here. Peter Street, McCall Street, Niagara Street."

"There's a big difference in the neighborhoods I guess?"

"Tremendous, Inspector."

"What do you do around here mainly?"

"Well, we try to keep the kids in line, off drugs, watch them pretty carefully, line up sports and entertainment, things like that."

"Do you ever make any arrests?"

"Not too many," the policewoman answered. "They're a pretty good bunch around here."

"If they're so good how come Dreamer was taken to his apartment over on Parkwoods Village Drive by one of my men tonight, stoned out of his gourd on speed?"

The police youth bureau couple exchanged startled glances.

235

"There's not much we can do with a guy like Dreamer," Johnson said.

"Do you know whereabouts in this shopping plaza he picks up the stuff?"

Both shook their heads.

"Don't you think you should know? Starting right now, and for the rest of the evening, I want you to leave the social work to the Salvation Army or the Y.M.C.A. and become policemen. Miss Pope, forget about playing Zsa Zsa Gabor among the well-to-do and those who pretend they are, understand?"

She nodded.

"Did you both know Mrs. Zelda Greenless who lived over at ten-forty-nine Don Mills? The woman who was murdered?"

"I only saw her a couple of times," the policewoman said.

"I knew her pretty well, Inspector. Some of the kids called her the First Aid Lady. She was really a wonderful person; she'd work with a kid to bring him down off a bummer, whether it was acid, speed, or what."

"And you don't know anyone who would want to kill her?"

"Not at all, Inspector."

"Do either of you know Dwayne Hardley?"

Both nodded.

"What sort of kid is he?"

Johnson said, "He's a homosexual, Inspector."

"Which would sort of shove him out of the gang, I suppose?"

"He was never really a member of the Centre Gang. They'd take him for his money when they could."

"Where did he get the money?"

"Off his father I suppose. His old man works in an executive job at the stock exchange."

"Did Dwayne ever have relations with gang members?"

"He could have had, Inspector. It's my belief that he had older male companions."

"Such as who?"

"I don't know their names. Occasionally I'd see him in the company of older men—"

"More than one?"

"Yes."

"Can't you even name one of them?"

"I think I've seen him with John Kapett, who lives in the same building. And another man who generally wears a light blue beret."

"And you don't think he had a sexual relationship with Zelda Greenless besides?"

"I'd seriously doubt that, Inspector. He liked her, as all the kids did, and he might have gone to her place to smoke the odd reefer, but he was strictly fag. I think their relationship was platonic."

Sergeant Manders said, "Will you two people go into the coffee bar and bring out whatever gang members are there now?"

"Yes, Sergeant," Johnson said. To the girl he said, "I'll go and get them, Sandra."

Johnson returned with two youths and a girl in carefully patched jeans. He introduced them as Abe Gordon, Bruce Corcoran, and the girl as Patty Finlayson.

"You three people knew Zelda Greenless?"

"Yes," Gordon said. The others nodded sulkily.

"What did you think of her?"

"She was a fine woman," Gordon said.

"How about you others?"

"Right on," Corcoran said. The girl just nodded languidly.

The inspector asked the young Youth Bureau policeman, "What's the matter with her? Is she high on something or what?"

"She's been on a run with meth and dexies for several days, Inspector."

"And you people haven't done anything about it?"

"What could we do? We've tried to bring her down with tranquilizers."

"Where did you get them?"

"Zelda Greenless forged a prescription for thirty Valium tablets at the One Stop."

"What's that?"

"The local drug store, or at least the biggest one in the plaza."

"One of my detectives checked their scrip files. He found that the dead woman had forged at least a half-dozen of Dr. Morris Franczic's prescriptions. Now you tell me, that you, a policeman, aided and abetted a crime!"

"No, Inspector. She had them when Sandra here and I found out about them. We didn't know they'd been bought on a forged prescription then."

"But you didn't think to check them out?"

Both Youth Bureau officers were silent.

"Maybe I should give Inspector Fern Alexander your names tomorrow. She could probably give you the pedestrian crossing job on Queen Street between Eaton's and Simpson's stores, and put you, Johnson, up into an undercover job at Rochdale College."

Sergeant Manders said, "Sandra, take this girl up that mews alongside the wine store and give her a complete search. Pockets, handbag, everything. If you find any pills or capsules on her bring them back here."

Patty Finlayson screamed, "I'm not carrying any shit, you fucking fuzz!"

"Take her away before I puke," the inspector said to the policewoman.

After they'd retreated up the short lane or alley that connected the main parking lot to the one north of the plaza, the inspector asked Abe Gordon if he was a gang member.

"No, sir. I'm in pre-med at the U of T and I sometimes help bring gang members down off bum trips."

"Where do you live?"

"East of here, on Cassandra Boulevard."

"And you're in a pre-med course at the university?"

"Yes sir. I'll be in my second year in September."

"You're Jewish?"

"Yes sir."

"We don't find many Jewish young men attached to *goyim* gangs."

"No, sir. As I said, I'm not a member of the gang but, to be immodest, I'm interested in helping these kids when they're on a bum trip. It's not totally altruistic. I'm learning quite a bit about the drug scene, and also," he laughed, "something about cultivating a cool bedside manner with some very difficult patients."

"Where exactly is Cassandra Boulevard?"

"You turn north from Lawrence at the first stop light east of the Don Valley Parkway."

"Did you ever visit Zelda Greenless's apartment?"

"A couple of times. We cooled out a couple of kids who were on bummers."

"Did you ever have any sexual relations with her?"

"No, sir. On both occasions it was strictly business; all we were interested in was bringing the kids down."

"And you liked her?"

"I think she was a fine woman. She was an anonymous social worker without the social worker's presumptuous arrogance."

"How do you get over here from where you live?"

Sometimes I hitch a ride along Lawrence, but tonight I have my father's car." He pointed to a blue Thunderbird parked not too far away.

"Incidentally, do you have a key to Mrs. Greenless's apartment?"

"Yes, sir." He extracted a key from a keycase and handed it into the car to the inspector.

"Do many of the young people around here have keys like this?"

"Too many, I'd say."

"I'd better get the house owner to change the lock or the next tenants might find themselves in bed with a stoned-out hippie."

Gordon laughed.

"Do you know Dwayne Hardley?"

"Yes. He's a mark for most of the young people around here."

"Where does he get the money?"

"It's my bet he gets most of it from his older friends."

"Women?"

Gordon smiled and gestured turning his open hands back and forth. "I don't think women are Dwayne's trip, sir."

"Okay, Mr. Gordon. Thank you. Would you call him a male prostitute?"

"No, I wouldn't say that. I think he receives gifts from some of his male friends, that's all."

"Okay. Take your father's T-bird home, and drive carefully."

"Goodnight, sir," Gordon said, striding away.

The inspector motioned to Corcoran to come over to the car. "Your name's Bruce Corcoran?"

"Yes." He was still sullen.

"Where do *you* live?"

"Along Lawrence there. Nine Woodcliffe Place."

"And you go to Don Mills High?"

"Yes."

"What grade?"

"Ten. It's my second year in Ten. I failed my exams."

"Why?"

"School bores the hell out of me."

"And you knew Zelda Greenless?"

"Sure. Didn't everybody?"

The inspector reached through the open window and grabbed Corcoran by the lapel of his denim jacket. "Listen, you punk, *I'm* asking the questions here, and I want straightforward answers not fucking sulks and shrugs. Understand me?"

Corcoran nodded.

"Have you got a key to her apartment?"

Corcoran took a key ring from his pocket and after some considerable difficulty took an apartment key from it and handed it to the inspector.

"Did you ever visit Zelda Greenless?"

"Plenty of times."

"To get dope, juice or what?"

"Nookie. She was known all over Don Mills as a ball freak."

"Did she give you any drugs on these occasions?"

"A little weed maybe, but that's all."

"Do you shoot or drop anything else?"

"I've done a couple of hits on crystal."

"What's that?"

"Meth. Methadrene."

"Did you drop it?"

"No, I made a mix and shot it."

"No wonder you failed your Grade Eleven exams. And I don't suppose you'd be much of a sexual athlete after shooting meth. What happened when you did?"

"Once I shook it off at home, another time Zelda and that guy Gordon brought me down at her place."

"What does your father do for a living?"

"He's a retired army lieutenant colonel."

"What does he think of his son the speed freak?"

Corcoran shrugged. "Don't be so heavy, man. Everybody around here turns on sometimes."

The inspector called Constable Johnson over. "Take this guy up the alley and give him a complete frisk."

"Yes, Inspector."

When they were gone, Sergeant Manders said, "I don't think any of them, boys *or* girls, had anything to do with the Greenless woman's death, Walter."

"Neither do I. I wanted to get a partial consensus of what the young people thought of her, that's all. Even that creep Corcoran showed about as much admiration for her as he's capable of showing anybody."

"I forgot to ask you before, but did IDENT match the prints found on the toilet flushing handle in the dead woman's apartment?"

"No. All we know is that they weren't anybody's whom we've questioned so far, or at least anybody whose prints we've managed to get."

"What do you make of it?"

"Obviously, to me at least, they were made by the last person to visit her before she died of the poison. With the left thumbprint so outstanding—and there were partial fingerprints beneath the handle—they were made by a man who had carelessly urinated before leaving Zelda's place. The toilet seat was up, and though he'd been careful to erase his prints from everything else he touched, including the glass into which he'd poured the poison, he'd made that one fatal error. I think we'll have him when we get his prints and also get some evidence tying him to the threatening note he slipped under Zelda's door or gave to her in some way. My guess is that it was slipped under her door, for he sure went to great, if stupid, lengths to keep his anonymity."

The inspector reached into his jacket pocket and pulled out a Xerox copy of the note. "This was printed on pink notepaper, not from a writing pad, but from a memo pad perhaps." He handed it to Sergeant Manders.

The sergeant read the printed note and said, "The writer's an amateur. He or she doesn't realize that it's harder for an educated person to try to write like an illiterate than it is the other way round."

"Yeh. Flora Debler says much the same thing. She couldn't tell however whether it was printed by a man or a woman."

"I'd say a man, judging from the pressure on the felt pen, but I'll bow to old Flora's expertise."

"Me too."

The young policewoman and Patty Finlayson returned to the side of the car.

"She was clean of drugs, Inspector. The only pills I found were these, and they're birth control pills."

"Okay. Where do you live, Patty?"

"Norden Crescent."

"I have the number, Inspector," Cadet Pope said.

"Okay. Call a squad car from the station and take her home."

"Suppose I don't wanna go home?" the girl asked belligerently.

"Then we'll take you down to the mental hospital on Queen Street west and have you locked up until they bring you down from your high, cold turkey. What does your father work at?"

Chastened now the girl answered, "He's a preacher; an evangelist."

"I see." To the policewoman cadet, "Call a squad car, Sandra, and make sure you deliver her to her parents."

"Will do, Inspector."

Officer Johnson brought Corcoran back from the alley where he'd searched him. "Nothing, Inspector," he said.

"All right. Go on home, Corcoran."

The young man hurried away along the alley past the wine store.

The inspector thanked Brad Semons and Tom Johnson. When they left he backed the car out of the parking slot and drove across Don Mills Road to the Doncentre Apartments. Leaving Sergeant Manders in the car he went inside and rang the Zutach apartment.

"Hello," came the frightened little voice of Xenia Zutach.

"Inspector McDumont, Mrs. Zutach."

She pressed her buzzer and opened the door for him.

He walked down the hall to her apartment and she met him at the door wearing a nightgown and bathrobe.

"I'm sorry to get you up, Mrs. Zutach, but I just wanted you to know that Anton is okay. He'll probably have his preliminary hearing in a day or two, after we arrest Hardley. I'm sure Mr. Rubin will get him out on bail, and you don't have to worry about losing your jobs here. Mr. Rubin will be sending a man to attend the boilers and take out the garbage and any other heavy work."

"Thank you, mister," she said, smiling through her tear-swollen face.

"It's nothing, Mrs. Zutach. As it says on the police cars, TO SERVE AND PROTECT. This is part of our service. Good night."

On the way downtown Eric Manders asked, "Are you going to call it a night now, Walter?"

"Not yet. I've got a dope sheet to start that's going to be as big as the telephone directory before we're finished. I'll work on it most of the night so that Marge can type it up in the morning."

Chapter 16

On Sunday morning Inspector McDumont was in his office by seven-thirty, having got up, made himself a pot of coffee and left the house before Jean was aware he'd gone. He left her a note propped against the sugar bowl on the dining room table.

In his office he brought the dope sheet on the Zelda Greenless murder up to date. It was a thick bundle of pen-written notes, beginning on the morning of June 13 when the body had been found by George Bullay, and continuing to the present time. In it were the names and comments on all the people he had interviewed about the case, including those young people in the Don Mills Centre, whose addresses he had received from the Youth Bureau police couple, Tom Johnson and Sandra Pope. There were also the photographs and fingerprint files from IDENT, and a copy of Dr. Mainguy's autopsy report, backed by the findings of the Forensic Laboratory. Anton Zutach's confession had been neatly typed by the stenographer who had taken it down in shorthand, and it too was included.

Most of the fingerprints had been identified, but those taken from the toilet flushing handle had not been matched yet, even though the RCMP files in Ottawa and the FBI files in Washington had been checked against them. Whoever the poisoner was (and the inspector had no doubt that it was he who had left the prints in the bathroom) he had no known criminal record in North America. The clumsy, illiterate note that had presumably been slipped under Zelda Greenless's door had been Xeroxed, and the inspector had several copies of it. He was almost but not quite sure

that it had been given to her before the poisoning occurred.

But who had written, or printed it? Had it been
Craig Hardley (who had been insane enough on the
night he and Zutach had taken the stabbed corpse into
the empty apartment at number six-ten)? It was a possibility. The Hardleys were staying with friends in a
cottage out of town that apparently had no phone, and
the inspector didn't even know its location. If he *had*
known he would have had the Hardleys picked up by
the Provincial Police and brought back to Toronto. As
it was he had to wait for their return.

For some time the inspector had entertained the idea
that the poisoner had killed Zelda Greenless through
jealousy, and after finding that Dwayne Hardley was a
homosexual his thoughts had centered on the male
lovers the boy had had. His knowledge of these was
skimpy; the only name he had received so far being
that of John Kapett. Kapett's fingerprints had been
found in the apartment, presumably when he had been
searching for his camera, and the RCMP had matched
them with some taken during World War II when he
had been in the Air Force. They hadn't matched those
on the toilet handle.

The only other older male who seemed friendly with
Dwayne Hardley was a man who wore a light blue
beret. Who he was the inspector didn't know yet, but
finding him should be relatively easy.

This case was unlike most murders (which were
largely domestic or made during robbery getaways) in
that it required not only intuition but also a great deal
of personal research on the part of the Homicide
Squad. And it was one which the murderer, if he hired
a first-class law firm, was likely to win. All the evidence, except that in Zutach's confession, was frag-
mentary and inconclusive.

Since the inspector had joined the police force, and
especially since becoming a Homicide Squad detective
after World War II, he had relied on his own common
sense and personal analysis in cases such as this one.
He had made mistakes as in the one several years
before that the papers had named "The Sin Sniper

Case," in which the wrong man had been shot by a divisional plainclothesman. The case had been dismissed by the Police Commission, however, as the policeman had given the fleeing man the regulatory warning, fired a shot in the air, and done everything by the book. Besides, the fleeing man had been guilty of an attempted rape of a juvenile a short time before he was killed, and so was a guilty fugitive fleeing a crime. At the time the inspector had put a stake-out on the house where the slain man had lived, and as it happened the real Sin Sniper, a psycopath who gunned down prostitutes on the street, had lived in another house just behind the one occupied by the crippled evangelist who had been shot. Also, the evangelist had been carrying the Sin Sniper's rifle.

At the time Inspector McDumont had worked out an intuitive theory that the Sin Sniper was moving north from his first murder, and he had been right, though Eric Manders had not believed him. This time the inspector's intuition had told him that the murderer of Zelda Greenless lived in one of the apartments at 1049 Don Mills Road. He had been wrong, in the beginning, in thinking it was a woman, mainly because poison is largely a female murder weapon; but since learning from so many sources that Dwayne Hardley was homosexual he had come to the conclusion that the murderer of Mrs. Greenless was one of Dwayne's male lovers. He knew for a fact that the boy had received either fees or gifts from some of them, including the loan of the expensive German camera from John Kapett, but further than that he was unable to go.

His thoughts were interrupted by the arrival of Detective Sergeant John Stuart and Detective Sam Chisolm, who were on the eight to four shift.

"Hello, Walter, what are you doing in so early on a bright June Sunday?" asked Stuart.

"I had a lot of things to write up on my dope sheet, John."

"How is that Don Mills murder coming along?"

"Well, we've pretty well wrapped up the stabbing part of it. The apartment house janitor gave us a complete confession down here last night, and he's now in

246

the Don. His accomplice, or rather the half-insane leader of the pair, is away until sometime later today. We're going to pick him up as soon as he arrives home."

"The woman was poisoned first, wasn't she? How are you making out on that angle?"

"Nothing so far. I have a couple of suspects in mind but no presentable evidence about either one."

"Would you like a cup of coffee, Inspector?" Sam Chisolm asked.

"Yeah. Would you get me one, Sam? A double coffee, cream and sugar, and an egg sandwich." He pulled a bill from his pocket and handed it to the detective.

"A toasted sandwich?"

"No, just plain brown bread, Sam."

After Chisolm had gone, the inspector asked the sergeant what his team were working on at the moment.

"Really nothing, Inspector. We were in court most of last week with that guy from Etobicoke who killed his wife and her boy friend with the two-by-four. He copped a plea of guilty on a manslaughter charge. He's to be sentenced on the twenty-fourth. Has anything come in this morning?"

"No, it was a quiet night. Soley and McQuaig left when I arrived."

"Is there anything in Don Mills you'd like Sam and me to do, Walter?"

"No thanks, John. I've brought the dope sheet up to date now, and it's only a matter of waiting until later in the day to pick up the actual stabber. Hell, he's not even a suspect any more after the detailed description of the crime from the janitor."

"What are they going to be charged with?"

"What's that law about inflicting indignities on a dead body? I rather think though that the Crown Attorney's office might lay a heavier charge."

"I know the one you mean. They sometimes snap young girls on it who have tried to burn, or placed in garbage cans, their stillborn babies."

"Yeh, that's the one. Do you know what Lorne Gardner and Will Arnop are working on, John?"

"No I don't, Walter."

"Well, maybe later on in the day you and Sam could come up with me to Don Mills. I know you're off at four, but if you've nothing important to do tonight I'd appreciate it."

"We'll come, Walter."

"Thanks."

When Sam Chisolm brought him his coffee and an egg sandwich the inspector sat at his desk and went over the Preliminary List of Electors for 1049 Don Mills Road, copying down the names of all the single men in the building.

This done, he called up 33 Division. A young officer answered the phone.

"I'd like to speak to the man in charge there today," the inspector said. "I'm Inspector McDumont of the Homicide Squad."

"Just a minute, Inspector."

An older, gruffer voice came on the phone.

"Inspector McDumont here. Who am I talking to?"

"Staff Sergeant Leo Murphy, Inspector."

"I don't think we've ever met, have we?"

"I don't think so."

"Would you be kind enough to call Tom Johnson of your Youth Bureau and have him come down here to the Homicide Squad room?"

"Sure, Inspector."

"As soon as possible, Staff."

"I'll get on it right away."

The inspector strode across the office and looked in on Sergeant Stuart and Sam Chisolm, who were busy writing out dope sheets.

"A quiet Sunday morning allows us to get our paperwork done," the inspector said.

"Yeh, we're lucky, Walter," Stuart answered.

Sam Chisolm said, "A hell of a lot luckier than the Break and Enter Squad, Inspector. They had thirteen break-ins last night, five commercials and eight private houses."

"Any holdups?"

"I haven't checked, Inspector. There were two rapes

248

and an attempted rape in York Borough, and a battle royal, a real Donnybrook, at the Zanzibar Club on the Yonge Street strip."

"What happened there?"

"Some drunk called a Newfy a cod-tail eater."

"In other words a normal night."

The inspector went down to the main floor and asked the desk sergeant if there was a justice of the peace on duty, as he wanted to get a couple of arrest warrants.

The sergeant looked up his duty roster. "Today it's Mr. Ben Sleet. He'll be here soon. He usually starts at the Regent Street drunk tank, then comes up here."

"Okay, Staff, send him up to my office when he arrives, will you?"

"Right." The sergeant made a note against the man's name.

The inspector returned to his office, placed his head on his arms, and took a five-minute snooze.

He was awakened by a man's cough. When he opened his eyes he saw Officer Tom Johnson standing in the doorway, not dressed in his working denims but in a pair of green slacks and a brown tweed jacket.

"Hello, Tom. Today you look like a young policeman. Sit down, will you."

Johnson took the chair across the desk from the inspector.

"I guess everybody in Don Mills knows you're a cop?"

"Pretty well everybody."

"Don't you think it's impaired your efficiency as a policeman?"

"I suppose it has, but part of our job, Inspector, is police public relations. We *want* the public to know that the police force are not only heavy on criminals, but are also out to help the people in a neighborhood."

"And do you think you've helped the young people of Don Mills?"

Johnson hesitated. "Perhaps not as much as I should. I overlooked plenty of dope trips by the kids for instance."

"Don't you think you'd have done them more of a favor by finding out who's pushing the stuff? I *know* one of the main sources of the so-called soft drugs is right in the Don Mills Centre. Last night Dreamer was really strung out, and I gave him the price of a speed fix, just to get him back on his feet so that he could cooperate with us. It only took him five minutes, so he couldn't have gone very far. Tomorrow morning, at Superintendent Ford's seminar, I'm going to bring up the subject and ask that the Narcotic Squad and the RCMP infiltrate the Centre for a few days in the hope they can wipe out the dealers and pushers. You know, of course, that pushers have sold drugs on the Donway East to kids going to the high school? Everything from meth to acid."

"Yeah, I know that, Inspector."

"Didn't it occur to you to notify the narc squad?"

"I *have* done, Inspector. They always seemed to have more important places to check out than Don Mills."

"How about the juice joints? You've known, I'm sure, that kids under eighteen have gotten themselves phony ID cards and are drinking in some of the places."

"Again, Inspector, plenty of times they were accompanied by their parents."

"Don't you think you could have had the parents snapped for contravening the Contributing to Juvenile Delinquency law?"

"Yes I could have, Inspector."

"Why didn't you?"

"I don't know—I really don't know."

"Are you happy with your job in the Youth Bureau?"

"Not really."

"Would you like to get away from your Sally Ann sociology and your volleyball teams?"

"I think I would."

"Well, as you know, it's not up to me to put your case to your inspector, Fern Alexander. Why don't you have a talk with her yourself?"

"I think I'll do that, Inspector."

"Good, Johnson. Now this afternoon I and some of my men are going to be up at ten-forty-nine Don Mills to make an arrest of a suspect, maybe more than one. What kind of car do you drive?"

"A Volkswagen."

"Good. I'd like you to become a policeman again. At four o'clock I want you to park in the Doncentre Apartments parking lot, dressed as you are now. Go upstairs and draw yourself a walkie-talkie." He scribbled a note on a piece of paper. "You sit in your car, parked inconspiciously in the back lot, and you report to us upstairs when the Hardleys arrive home. Do you know them well enough to recognize them?"

"I know Dwayne's old man by sight."

"Do you know what kind of car he drives?"

"No."

"Well, it's a green Oldsmobile Cutlass. He's three payments behind on it, so it won't be his much longer. Anyway he won't need it in the joint. He'll probably be accompanied by his wife. As soon as they leave the car, give us the message over the walkie-talkie, let them get into the house, then go around to the front door and press the buzzer to apartment six-o-two where we'll be. We'll let you in, and you come up to six-o-two, got it?"

"Yes, Inspector."

McDumont got up and called through his doorway, "Sam!"

Sam Chisolm came out of his cubicle.

"Sam, this is Constable Tom Johnson. You two are going to be in communication by walkie-talkie this afternoon. Take him up to the Communications Centre and there you will draw a gizmo apiece. Then, to make sure they're working, one of you go out and sit in one of the cars and contact the other who'll be here in this office."

Chisolm nodded. He led Johnson out of the Homicide Squad office.

At 3 P.M. Inspector McDumont, Detective Sergeant John Stuart, Sam Chisolm, Sergeant Joe Grant and Detective George Wilson, were on their way up to Don Mills in two Homicide D-cars. One of them parked on the street outside the apartment house and the other was driven into the parking lot. Johnson's Volkswagen hadn't arrived yet, and neither had the Hardleys' Cutlass. The policemen were admitted by Xenia Zutach and they went up to 602, where McDumont opened the door with his key. Sam Chisolm had his walkie-talkie turned-on, waiting for a preliminary call from Johnson from the Volks; in the meantime they sat around, smoked and talked generally about where they were spending their vacations.

The inspector got up and walked down the hall to the Hard'ey's apartment and knocked gently on the door. There was no answer to either his first or second knock. As he was passing Piet Langenzent's door on his way back he heard a radio voice saying:

". . . And now our own Gordon Lightfoot's 'Sundown,' played and sung by the Canadian master himself—yessir! Your number four on the pop singles this week and climbing—I said *climbing*, folks!—right up to the top of the sales charts. Gordy Lightfoot and 'Sundown'!" There was the sound of a strumming guitar.

When he reached apartment 602 the inspector said, "There's somebody listening to rock music in six-o-three." He told Detective George Wilson, "George, go and listen at the door and see what you can get. I have an idea there's somebody in there with Langenzent." To Sergeant Stuart he said, "John, go downstairs to apartment one-ten, the superintendent's, and get the house master key from the little woman there. Identify yourself and she'll give you the key. We don't want to kick in any more doors than we have to; the owner is a nice guy."

Wilson and Stuart left the apartment.

Sergeant Joe Grant asked, "What make you think Langenzent wasn't alone, Inspector?"

"He didn't sound to me when I interviewed him like a guy who likes rock music. This was one of those hard rock stations like CHUG or CALL. Langenzent is the type who listens to musical interpretations or chamber music on the CBC. What he really is is an accomplished liar. We're going in there and see what he's still doing in his apartment when he was supposed to be going back to Ottawa. I don't believe much from a guy who wears a beret. I wonder why he stayed over in his place when he was due back in Ottawa today."

Detective Wilson came back to the apartment. "I think there's only two people in there, Inspector. One of them an older guy and the other sounds like a kid. Even though they left the radio on they sounded like a young couple going through the talking preliminaries to making love. I heard the young guy say, "Oh, darling, do I have to?"

"Have to what?"

"Christ, Inspector, I don't know. Personally I think I listened in to a pair of queers."

"You probably did. As soon as Sergeant Stuart brings back the master key we're going in to find out. I want you to stay here with the walkie-talkie, Chisolm."

"Right."

"Check it again with Johnson out in his car."

Detective Chisolm turned on his speaker. "Johnson, do you hear me?"

"Loud and clear, Sam," came the voice of Johnson from the parking lot.

The inspector picked up the gizmo. "Johnson, I want you to keep the line open all the time. Give Sam the word as soon as the Hardleys arrive, and afterwards. I want you to be ready for anything, understand?"

"Right, Inspector."

"If you get further orders from Sam Chisolm they're coming from me. I want you to execute them promptly. Understand that?"

"Yes, Inspector."

"Okay."

As soon as Sergeant returned with the master key, the inspector led Stuart, Sergeant Grant and Detective Wilson across the hall to Langenzent's apartment door. They listened as the radio voice droned on, ". . . and it's 'The Streak', kiddos—Number *One!—numero uno!* —with Ray Stevens! . . . How about that! Only six weeks on the best-seller list of pop singles and already *Number One!* You can't keep the goodies down, eh?"

The inspector placed the key silently in the lock,

turned it, and threw the door open. The four detectives stormed into the apartment, Wilson kicking the door shut behind him.

Lying naked in each other's arms were Langenzent and Dwayne Hardley, both breathing hard from the exertions of coition. The soft bed had been pulled out and they were uncovered.

Langenzent sat up and shouted, "What the hell is this! What are you people doing here!"

"You'll find out," the inspector said.

Langenzent reached for his trousers, which were lying on the floor.

"No you don't," the inspector said, kicking them away, then picking them up.

"You're supposed to be cops, but you don't know the law. Don't you know that what happens in the nation's bedrooms is nobody's business any more?"

"Listen, you smart-ass, the law reads that whatever happens in the nation's bedrooms *between consenting adults* is no longer looked upon as a crime." Dwayne Hardley lay with his arms behind his head, an insolent grin on his lips. "Anyhow I'm not running you in on a buggery charge."

The inspector asked the Hardley kid, "How old are you, Hardley?"

"Eighteen."

McDumont took from an inside pocket a small piece of paper. "You're a goddam liar, Hardley. I had my secretary check out your birth date at the Registry Office, and you were born—"

Langenzent tried to get off the couch.

"Lie down, you stupid hick, or I'll have Joe Grant here deck you. He used to be heavyweight champion boxer of the Metro Police. If you want a thick lip *and* a broken nose we'll see you get it."

Langenzent lay down again. "I just wanted to get something to cover us with, Inspector."

"You weren't covered when we arrived, so you can stay uncovered. Though you're a disgusting sight to all of us here, you'll stay uncovered until I tell you to put your clothes on."

"Now, as for you, Hardley, your birth certificate

reads, 'Dwayne James Hardley, born Toronto, Ontario, to Craig and Doris Hardley of fifty-four Howard Street, January twenty-first, nineteen-fifty-seven.' Now how old does that make you?"

"I don't know; you tell *me*," Dwayne drawled insolently.

The inspector reached across a cringing Langenzent and slapped Hardley's face, hard. "Now, wipe that grin off your mouth and answer my questions. You only became seventeen on January twenty-first last, right?"

Dwayne, half crying and rubbing his cheek, nodded.

"That makes you a legal infant, and makes you guilty, Langenzent, of contributing to juvenile delinquency among other things the Crown will think up." He turned once again to the sobbing Dwayne Hardley. "How long have you been a practicing homosexual?"

Dwayne shook his head. "I don't *know*."

"Don't get girlishly modest with me. We know you've had relations with John Kapett upstairs, and I would think your illicit relations with so-called men goes back at least two years. It's more than a year now since you had a certain schoolteacher from the high school fired when you were both discovered in—let's call it a compromising situation—in a classroom after school by a janitor. Is that true or not?"

Dwayne nodded.

"You pleaded youthful ignorance then, and claimed that the teacher had attacked you. Your old man and some shyster lawyer even laid your case before the school principal and the North York School Board. Like the slippery little bastard you are you got away with it. While you were having your assignations with Langenzent, Kapett and anybody else you could attract with your beautiful blonde girlish hair and hip-swinging walk you'd tell your parents you'd been in Zelda Greenless's apartment. Your old man, without even trying to check out your goddam lies, believed you. He believed you because in his heart of hearts he knew you were a faggot and he also knew that it was himself and your mother who had made you that way.

"Now tell me, and tell it true, did you ever have sexual relations with Zelda Greenless?"

"No. I visited her sometimes for the odd reefer, that's all."

"But it was more respectable to let your old man and old lady think you were having something with the woman next door than with a man across the hall?"

"I guess so."

"It was also to save your fairy pride that you gave your old man the key to Zelda's apartment, and also your steak-knife dagger when he was so stoned he'd have stabbed Christ on the Cross, right?"

"He made me give them to him."

"Save that for the court. Your old man, knowing that Zelda was stoned out of her gourd, went into her apartment with your key and, with the building superintendent to use as a patsy if they were caught, stripped Zelda in her bed and was going to have sexual relations with her, except that she was already dead. Did you know that?"

"Not at the time."

"But you know it now?"

The boy nodded.

"Did you know that Piet Langenzent thought he was your only lover?"

"He seemed to think so."

"But you told him too that you spent most of the time away from him in Zelda's place, and let him believe you were bi-sexual or something and were having an affair with her. Why? To make him jealous?"

The boy shrugged.

The inspector spied a blue Basque beret thrown on a chair. He picked it up and pocketed it.

Langenzent began to sob. He cried out tearfully, "You cheating little bitch! All those others while you made me think you loved me; that I was the only one in your life!" To the blank-faced detectives he said, "He was the only person I loved. I wanted him to move to Ottawa with me. We could have been so happy there together, for a while."

The inspector said, "Langenzent, I've been in touch with your timekeeper in Ottawa; you left there on the twelfth. And you were only a government project engineer, not a landscape architect. You bought two ounces of tartar emetic at McIver's Economy Drugs in Rockcliffe—I've already had this checked out by the Ottawa Police. You told the pharmacist on duty, a man named Charles Gaudin, that you wanted to use the poison, in solution, to kill bugs that were infesting the trees on the new campus.

"When you arrived home, on the afternoon of the twelfth, you visited Mrs. Greenless's apartment. She was bombed out of sight. You poured some tartar emetic into her drink, and were going to drive back to Ottawa to strengthen your alibi, but you changed your mind. Why?"

"I refuse to say anything else at this time."

"Maybe you were more anxious to see lover-boy here than to establish an alibi? Or maybe you thought the subsequent stabbing of the dead woman gave you an out? When we questioned you on the thirteenth of June, after Zelda's body had been found, you told us you'd just arrived home that day. You also received a parcel from Eaton's store on the twelfth, and it was propped against your door until you picked it up later the same day. It was seen, and has been sworn to, by an eyewitness. I'm in possession of the parcel tag which was recovered from the garbage. Do you deny all this?"

"No comment without the presence of my lawyer."

The inspector took Langenzent's wallet from a buttoned-down back pocket of his slacks and spread all the cards and papers it contained on a small table.

"You can't get away with this illegality!" Langenzent screamed. "You haven't got a search warrant!"

McDumont reached into his other inside pocket and pulled out two warrants. He wrote the name "Piet Langenzent" on one of them and gave it to Sergeant Grant. "Give this to that poor skinny closet queen, Joe. And notice, Langenzent, that it isn't a search warrant but a warrant for you as the murderer of Zelda Greenless."

Langenzent read it, his face dead white and his hands trembling.

"You're under arrest for murder," the inspector said. "Don't worry, it's perfectly legal, signed this morning by a justice of the peace." He turned to the cards and

257

papers spread out on the table. "You're even more foolish than I thought you were, Langenzent. Here's a gas credit slip from a freeway gas station, an Esso station, on the 401, dated June 12, 1974. I presume you drove down highways Seven and Fifteen to the freeway, and there's only one Esso stop from there to Toronto, somewhere around Trenton, isn't it? And here's something even more incriminating, sales slips for various drugs and toiletries from McIver's Economy Drugs. I was almost certain that whoever the murderer was he'd have the common sense to throw away such evidence. Maybe our pretence that we believed Zelda Greenless had died from a stab wound in the back paid off; you didn't realize that the coroner and the Forensic Lab would find the *precise* cause of death. As a matter of fact neither the duty coroner, Dr. Edward Mainguy, nor myself believed that the stabbing had killed Zelda. I think we were both rather surprised, though, that the stabbing had occurred post-mortem."

McDumont said to Detective Sergeant Stuart and Detective Wilson, "Go and give the kitchen and bathroom a thorough search for a two-ounce bottle of tartar emetic. It'll have a McIver's Economy Drugs label on it. According to the Forensic Lab it's a white liquid."

The inspector busied himself making a list of all the credit cards, automobile license, automobile ownership, calling and business cards and every other piece of typed or written material from the wallet. He then went over to a small antique roll-top desk that he hadn't even noticed on his previous visit to the apartment, and found it unlocked. He removed Langenzent's Bank of Montreal savings account book, a checking account book and a checkbook from a pigeonhole. Turning to the shuddering Langenzent he said, "You won't be needing any of this stuff for a long time." From another pocket of the slacks he removed the accused man's apartment key and his automobile keys. "After you're formally charged, your lawyer'll be able to pick this stuff up," he said.

Sergeant Stuart came back to the living room carrying a small bottle half-full of a whitish liquid. "Here's your poison, Walter," he said. "Stupid there tore most of the label off, but didn't destroy it. It was stashed on an open shelf in his medicine cabinet."

"Thanks, John," the inspector said. "Jesus, he used about an ounce of this stuff!" To Langenzent, "How much did you put in Zelda's drink?"

No answer.

"It only takes two- to three-tenths of a *gram* to constitute a fatal dose, you know."

Langenzent turned on his side, his face away from the room, and pushed Dwayne away from him.

As he placed the poison bottle in his jacket pocket the inspector said, "Gentlemen, we're witnessing the end of a love affair."

The door opened and Sam Chisolm shoved his head in. "They've arrived, Inspector," he said.

"Okay, Sam. Tell Tom Johnson, over that gizmo of yours, that I want him to park his Volkswagen sideways at the top of the driveway so that nobody can get in or out of the parking lot. Tell him to take the keys out, put on the parking brake, and lock all the doors too. Okay?"

"Right."

McDumont said, "Wilson, I want you to stand guard over this pair of lulus. If either one of them makes a suspicious move, shoot him." To the two detective sergeants and the detective McDumont said, "We'll give them time to get inside before we break in. I want you, John, and you, Joe, to be ready to move in with me. We'll let ourselves in with the master key."

He walked to the door, opened it slightly, and stood staring towards the elevators.

In less than a minute one of the elevator doors opened silently and Craig and Doris Hardley emerged. Craig Hardley was carrying a cheap bag of golf clubs hanging over one shoulder and what appeared to be a woman's middle-sized suitcase. His wife was carrying a pair of raincoats and a Loblaws' shopping bag that seemed to hold damp swim wear.

They entered their apartment, and the inspector heard the click as the apartment door was locked.

"We'll give them a minute or two," he said.

Looking over at the two naked male figures on the

pull-out bed he noticed that Dwayne was lying on his back, his mouth pulled back into its former insolent grin. Langenzent was lying on his side, his face turned away.

"Take care of them, George," the inspector said to Wilson as he and the other two detectives went out into the corridor, leaving the door slightly ajar.

They crossed the hallway catty-cornered, and Mc-Dumont inserted the master key in the lock, turned it, and gave the door a shove. It banged open to reveal Craig Hardley, stripped to the waist, sitting on a chair and changing his shoes for a pair of slippers. Doris Hardley was making a pot of tea in the kitchen.

"Who the hell invited you guys here!" Hardley asked, getting up and adopting a belligerent attitude.

McDumont walked over to him and handed him the second warrant he had brought with him. This one already had Hardley's name typed on it. "You're under arrest, Hardley," he said.

"What the hell for! What did *I do*?"

"We know that you stabbed the body of Zelda Greenless. We have a full confession from Anton Zutach, besides the evidence we picked up. Zutach is in the Don Jail, which is where you're going."

"I demand the right to call my lawyer!"

"You haven't got a lawyer, Hardley. The only lawyers you know are from your creditors. You'll be getting letters from a couple more of them for the car dealer where you bought that high-priced prestige car you now owe three payments on, and probably one from the Benevolent Finance. Put your shirt on."

"I don't have to do anything of the sort!"

"You don't seem to realize that you're under arrest on a serious crime. From now on you do what we tell you to do. If you don't want to put on a shirt, we'll take you the way you are. Come on, I want you to see something across the hall." He said to Sergeant Joe Grant, "Bring him over to six-o-three."

"You're not taking him out of here, you fucking bulls!" Doris Hardley screamed.

"Your wife's a real lady, Hardley," McDumont said. Turning to her he added, "And if you don't keep your

260

mouth shut we'll take you down to headquarters too, as an accessory." He turned to Sergeant Stuart. "Stay with this harpy who's been passing condemnations of the police around the building, John."

Sergeant Joe Grant grabbed Hardley by a wrist and shoved him into the corridor, with the inspector following. Hardley tried a bit of struggling, but Grant bent his wrist so that he shook his head with the pain.

The inspector opened the door to Langenzent's apartment, and the two detectives shoved Hardley inside.

"There's your son, the way we found him with his lover, Hardley. What do you think of that! And don't ever forget that you and your bad-mouthed wife made him that way."

Hardley sagged, and had to be held up by the detectives.

McDumont shouted, "Langenzent, turn this way so Hardley can see the type of woman his son has been sleeping with!"

Langenzent, his mouth twisted into a sneer turned his head.

Hardley said, "Why, you rotten perverted son of a bitch!" He tried to make a rush at Langenzent but the detectives held him back.

"Have you anything to say to your father?" the inspector asked the boy.

"I've never had anything to say to him," Dwayne answered.

"Dwayne, Dwayne," Hardley said, dropping his head to his chest.

"You stabbed the wrong person, Hardley," said the inspector.

"I didn't kill her, I didn't kill her. She was dead, I tell you, when I went into her place."

"We know all that. We have a deposition from Zutach. You're just lucky she *was* dead or we'd be taking you downtown on a murder rap. Seen enough now, Hardley, to know what your son is? Or didn't the fact that he was caught once before with the schoolteacher convince you that between that wife of yours and you you'd managed to bring up a homosexual?"

"Oh, God!" Hardley said, turning away.

"Take him back to his place," the inspector said. "Make him put on a shirt and a pullover or a jacket. It's pretty chilly in the Don."

After Hardley had been led away, McDumont said, "All right, you two, get up and put some clothes on."

"Have you got a small airline bag or something to hold your razor, toothbrush and things?" the inspector asked Langenzent.

"Of course."

"You'd better bring it with you; you might be held a few days before you'd be able to arrange to have them sent to the jail." To Detective Wilson he said, "Go with him, George, and watch what he puts in the bag."

"What is this, a B movie?" Langenzent asked.

"I'd say it was class D, with all you fools involved."

There was a loud cry from the hall, "Watch out! Hardley's escaped!"

The inspector opened the door just as Hardley passed him heading for the front staircase. In his right hand was what looked like a .22-caliber target pistol, and in his left a police .38. He waved the .22 at the inspector as he passed him, but didn't fire. There was the loud report of a pistol from the direction of the Hardley's apartment, but the bullet missed Hardley, and he opened the stairway door and disappeared. The inspector let Sergeant Joe Grant, pistol in hand, pass the doorway, and go into the stairwell before he crossed the hallway to apartment 602.

He said to Sam Chisolm, "Get Johnson on the walkie-talkie."

"Johnson, Chisolm here, can you get me?"

"Yes."

The inspector took the walkie-talkie. "Johnson, are you armed?"

"No."

"Hardley's pulled a split. He's got a .22 pistol and a police .38. He's coming down the front stairway and will probably try to make it to his Cutlass. Now don't try to be an unarmed hero. Is your car parked the way we told you to park it?"

"Yes."

"Then hide behind one of the other cars. Let Hardley

come out of the back door—Sergeant Grant is following him down the stairs with his pistol—let him get into his car, understand?"

"Yes."

"Hardley'll panic when he finds he can't get out of the lot, and you may have a chance to grab him and disarm him through the window when he's stopped. However, if Sergeant Grant is down there, let *him* do the disarming, and shooting if necessary."

"Yes."

"Good luck."

Detective Wilson handcuffed Langenzent's hands behind his back and shoved both him and Dwayne back on the daybed. He stood over them, with his pistol drawn.

There was the muffled sound of two shots from somewhere downstairs.

"Lock this door behind me," the inspector said as he headed for the elevator. "And make sure who you let in."

McDumont took his pistol from its holster and held it in his right-hand jacket pocket, waiting for the elevator. From the corner of his eye he could see Raymark Osler and Norma Dryburg peeking around the corners of their door frames. The elevator seemed to take an hour, but when it arrived he pressed the first-floor button and made a quick trip down.

The lobby was deserted. He ran to the front stairs and looked up into the deserted stairwell, calling, "Joe, are you up there!"

There was no answer.

He drew his pistol from his pocket and ran to the back door leading to the parking lot. Joe Grant had Craig Hardley in a bear hug at the left-hand open door of the Cutlass. His revolver and the two that Hardley had been carrying were lying on the asphalt. Tom Johnson was running towards them behind the line of parked cars. Grant twisted Hardley around and gave him a right cross to the chin, and Hardley collapsed back into the front seat of the car. Then Grant pulled him up and gave him a solid left to the nose and mouth.

The inspector called, "Johnson, pick up the guns!" before he sat down, winded, on the steel back-steps. He watched as the Youth Bureau policeman picked up the three pistols, then helped Sergeant Grant to handcuff Hardley's hands behind his back. He replaced his own pistol in its holster and said a short Presbyterian prayer of thanks that nobody had been shot.

Then he walked over to where Hardley was lying on the asphalt, with the two policemen standing over him. Blood covered half of Hardley's face.

"Good work, Joe. Good work. And thanks, Johnson for what *you* did."

"First good punch out I've had in months," Grant said. "Caught him just as he was opening the car door. He didn't have time to swing around and fire before I hugged him tight enough to break his ribs."

"Who owns the police pistol he was carrying?"

"John Stuart. This guy's wife went into the bedroom to get him a shirt and pullover, and she hid the target pistol in the sweater. As soon as she gave it to him he covered John and disarmed him. I ran into one of the bedrooms, pulled my own gun and waited for the son of a bitch to show his face around the doorpost. Then I realized he'd taken off, and I came out, pushed his old lady aside, and saw him disappearing through the door to the stairs."

"Was it you who shouted out, 'Watch out! Hardley's escaped!'"

"No, I think it was Stuart."

"What about the two shots I heard coming from down the stairwell?"

"They were his, very careless and very wild. I think he was hoping for a lucky ricochet, or maybe just trying to scare me off."

"Okay, Joe. As I said it was one hell of a job you pulled. Will you carry Little Lord Fauntleroy there to the D-car, put him in the back and sit there with him until we bring that foul-mouthed bitch Doris Hardley down to join him. I'll tell her to bring some Kleenex to wipe off his face. I'll send John Stuart down to drive the car, and take them both to the homicide squad room. No, first have him mugged and printed. I'll make the formal charges later."

"All right, Inspector." Sergeant Joe Grant, who was probably the most powerful man on the force, picked up Hardley under one arm and threw him into the back seat of the police car, then straightened him into a sitting position, though he was still unconscious, his head fallen on his chest.

"Johnson, will you put your car back into one of the empty parking slots, then I'd like you to get a knife from Langenzent's apartment and look for the two .22 slugs that Hardley fired into the walls of the front stairwell. If you find any casings bring them along too."

"Right, Inspector."

"Come on, we may as well go up in the elevator together."

At the Hardleys he gave Sergeant Stuart his pistol, and had him handcuff himself to the Hardley woman. Then he sent them down to the car parked in the lot, telling Stuart to take both Mr. and Mrs. Hardley down to headquarters.

"What about this fucking door? Don't tell me you're going to leave it open?" Doris Hardley asked.

The inspector pushed her into the hall, where Sergeant Stuart took her along to the elevators. Then he locked the door with the master key.

Raymark Osler came hurrying along the corridor. "I'm glad you got them, Inspector," he said. "I thought it was them all the time."

"You did? Then why in hell didn't you say so when we questioned you on the evening of the thirteenth?"

"I'm a lawyer; I can't make unsubstantiated accusations against anyone."

"Beat it, Osler," McDumont said, entering Langenzent's apartment.

He said to Detective Wilson, "I want you to take these two birds out to the D-car that's parked on the street and take them down to the squad room. I'll have Sam Chisolm come over and give you a hand."

"Why *me!*" wailed Dwayne Hardley.

"Because you're not only the instigator of this whole jeezly mess with your screwed-up sex habits but also because of your infidelity towards your—your paramours. You also let everyone think you were having an affair with Zelda Greenless, which got her killed. You have the morals of a homosexual mink. Now I'm not trying to put you down because you're a homo; I've known some good homosexuals; but I have no use at all for you as an immoral little bastard. I'm going to do everything I can to have you placed in the Clarke Institute to undergo psychotherapy, not that it'll do you the least bit of good, but maybe one of the headshrinkers there will be able to get inside your birdbrain and show you a little about yourself and what makes you tick. Your mother and father have been taken to headquarters, both on criminal charges, so you may as well join them."

The inspector called across the hallway, "Sam Chisolm!"

Sam came to the door of six-o-two. "Yes. Inspector."

"Bring your walkie-talkie and come over here and give George Wilson a hand taking these two down to the car parked in the street. I'll lock the door afterwards. Take them down to headquarters and make sure that Langenzent is mugged and fingerprinted right off. Got it?"

"Got it, Inspector."

The inspector gave the D-car keys to Detective Wilson. "You drive and let Chisolm sit between the two prisoners in the back seat, okay? I wouldn't want them to try to make love, handcuffed or not, in the back of a police car on a Sunday afternoon. It'd look bad for the force."

"Do you have to be so insulting?" Langenzent asked.

"You've got a lot of gall, Langenzent. You, a dumb social misfit and a woman-poisoner to boot, call *me* insulting?"

"All you have is circumstantial evidence that won't stand up in court."

"That's all we need. Nearly all murderers are convicted on circumstantial evidence; we seldom find a witness to an actual murder. Even a person with *your* intelligence should know that."

Wilson and Chisolm took the two suspects to the elevators. Chisolm was handcuffed to Dwayne Hardley.

When they had gone the inspector locked the doors to apartments 602 and 603, then crossed to the Hard-

266

ley apartment. He gave disgusted glances at a cushion cover from Mammoth Cave, Kentucky, and an alligator pennant from Crystal Springs, Florida, and went along the inside hall to the linen closet. The deep bottom shelf was piled with unwashed clothes. He said to himself, Not only a foul-mouthed bitch but a lazy one. From the closet he removed sheets, towels and pillowcases and, hidden at the back of the topmost shelf, he found a yellow blanket that was the twin of the one Hardley had used to hide the Greenless woman's body. Looking into the Hardley's bedroom he saw that the twin beds were without bed covers. He unfolded the blanket and found that it fitted one of the beds. Folding it up again and carrying it under his arm he locked the Hardley's door behind him and again crossed the hallway to Langenzent's apartment. He went through the small roll-top desk, ignoring the small pigeonholed stack of receipts and cancelled checks, but picking up a black felt marking pen, which he shoved into his already bulging pocket. He untied the string around a bundle of letters, most bearing a Netherlands postmark and stamp, and halfway through the pile found a thin pad of pink notepaper. He shook his head at Langenzent's bewildering stupidity.

Then he sat down at the telephone and called Jerry Rubin.

Rubin answered the phone himself.

"Hello, Mr. Rubin, Walter McDumont of the police."

"Yes, Inspector?"

"We made a clean-out of some of your worst tenants this afternoon, Mr. Rubin. Incidentally Anton Zutach gave us a complete confession last night."

"Good, Inspector. Who did you pinch today?"

"The Hardleys in six-o-six, Piet Langenzent in six-o-three."

"Do you mind if I ask on what charges, Inspector?"

"Langenzent on a murder charge for poisoning Zelda Greenless, Dwayne Hardley on a charge that the Crown will probably prosecute as being an accessory, Craig Hardley, his old man, on whatever charge the Crown lays for his post-mortem stabbing of the Greenless woman, and Doris Hardley on possible charges of being an accessory to the Greenless crime, obstructing police, and smuggling a small pistol to her husband with which he almost made a getaway. Craig Hardley will also be charged with shooting with intent to kill a policeman—God knows the Crown can fill a page of individual charges."

"So now you're finished with the Doncentre?"

"I hope so, Mr. Rubin. Incidentally, thanks for sending a man to help out Mrs. Zutach."

"No thanks needed, Inspector. Do you think they'll all go to jail?"

"With the evidence I've got. I'm sure of it."

"When will the apartments be cleared of their things, have you any idea?"

"Well, Zelda Greenless's apartment should be emptied pretty soon, as I told you the other day. Langenzent's will depend on his lawyers. I think that the Hardley place may be stripped by his creditors."

"Hardley owes me last month's rent, Inspector. Langenzent is paid up to the end of the month."

"Call me at my office in a couple of days. I'll try to give you the names of their lawyers then, and you can get in touch with them."

"Thanks, Inspector."

"Thank *you*, Mr. Rubin. I hope you try to spring Zutach when his bail is set."

"I'm going to. When will they appear in court?"

"I would think it would be either tomorrow morning or Tuesday morning, for a preliminary hearing. You can find out tomorrow with a call to the Crown Attorneys' Office."

"Okay, thanks again and good-bye, Inspector."

"Thanks for your cooperation, and good-bye."

He hung up the phone, then dialed a taxi firm and asked for a cab to be sent to 1049 Don Mills Road.

When he reached headquarters, after returning the master key to Mrs. Zutach and telling her, briefly, what had happened and of his phone call to Jerry Rubin, the inspector emptied his pockets of the felt pen and pink note pad, and placed them with the matching blanket on his desk. He also placed the blanket used in the stabbing with the other, the bottle of tartar emetic, and the original threatening note to Zelda Greenless. Then he called in Sergeant Alvin Prust, who was working the four to midnight shift.

"Alvin, I want all this stuff—better put it in a bag or something—taken down to the Forensic Lab at the foot of Jarvis Street. There's bound to be some people on duty there. I want the felt-tip pen run under the spectroscope, and its printing compared with this torn-up note to Zelda Greenless. I want a thorough comparison of this pink paper pad with the piece of pink paper the note was written on. I want whatever lab tests they do to be carried out to show that this clean blanket is one of a pair, and matches the blanket covering Zelda Greenless when she was stabbed through it." He wrote a list of these things down on a sheet of paper, and placed the pasted-up threatening note in an envelope. "I also want the contents of this bottle analyzed; I think it's a deadly poison, tartar emetic, so be careful with it. I want you to stay down at the Forensic Lab, Alvin, until all this has been done, and you have official lab reports on all of it. Then I want you to bring everything back here. If there's no senior man or scientist down there tell them to get one, as I have to have all this stuff done early this evening. Don't worry about your regular work, I'll send out another sergeant with your partner Larry Helmont if there's any calls. Okay?"

"Sure, Walter."

"Don't take any shit from some junior snot-nose down there. Tell them this is murder evidence, we have the suspects in custody, and we have to have the official evidence before their lawyers get a chance to spring them."

Prust left the inspector's office, then returned with a plastic shopping bag into which he carefully placed the material from the inspector's desk.

After he had gone, McDumont called IDENT to see if they'd mugged and fingerprinted the suspects.

"Yes, Inspector."

"Have you matched any of the suspects' fingerprints with those found on the toilet handle in the dead woman's apartment?"

"Yes, sir. Langenzent's prints match."

"Good, good. Have you got a couple of minutes to bring me the stuff?"

"Right away, sir."

"Who are you?"

"My name's Jim Babbitt, Inspector. I'm the duty man this Sunday."

"Okay, Jim, I'll be in my office."

When the IDENT man arrived he placed copies of the mug shots of the Hardleys and Langenzent on the inspector's desk.

"Did you have any trouble with them?"

"Only with Doris Hardley. We had to get a police-woman to straighten her out before we could get our pictures."

"How about the prints?"

"No trouble, Inspector."

"Now show me a comparison of the prints taken from the toilet flushing handle with those taken here from Langenzent."

The IDENT man placed two fingerprint cards side by side in front of the inspector. "The most prominent print was that of the suspect's left thumb. Those taken from under the handle were only partial and consisted of only those from the first and second fingers of the left hand." The IDENT man, using a pencil, showed the main features of the thumb prints. "As you know, Inspector, fingerprint classification comes under four main categories, arches, loops, whorls and composites. The thumbprint found on the handle has a tented arch." He pointed this out, then pointed out the same arch on the department fingerprint card. "As you can see, sir, they're identical. There is no doubt at all that they were made by the same person."

"Yes, they look exactly alike."

"Now, in the case of the partial prints of the first and second fingertips of the left hand there are re-markable similarities between the man's prints taken here and those taken from the toilet handle. As I say they are incomplete, but I for one would have no hesitation whatever in swearing in court that the partial prints belong to Langenzent."

"It is apparent to you then that after Langenzent used the toilet nobody else flushed it?"

They couldn't have, Inspector. If they'd been wearing gloves, for instance, they'd have eliminated the prints and if they had not been we'd have had either a double print smeared beyond recognition, or a clear double print, which would have been equally useless for identification purposes. May I illustrate in a better way what I mean about the matching of the two partial fingerprints, Inspector?"

"Please do."

The IDENT man took from his pocket a small bottle of "Liquid Paper," the typewriter correction fluid. "What I'm going to do, Inspector, is wipe out the parts of the prints taken of the first and second left-hand fingertips taken here at headquarters in the approximate pattern that the missing parts of the prints did not show on the toilet handle. This will give you a better idea of the similarities of what is left on the original prints taken by Don Weaver in the dead woman's apartment."

"You have copies of these upstairs?"

"Yes, Inspector, several. We have a complete file on the Greenless case. These I brought down, including the mug shots, are merely extra copies."

"All right. Go ahead."

The young man—what was his name again?—Babbitt, Jim Babbitt—took the stopper brush from the bottle of Liquid Paper and carefully obliterated part of the headquarters' prints of the two left-hand fingers from the card, following an almost identical line with that on the card holding the prints that Don Weaver had taken that day in Zelda Greenless's apartment. When the Liquid Paper had dried he handed the two print cards to the inspector and said, "Now, what do you think of the similarities?"

The inspector studied them carefully. "They match perfectly," he said. "Thank you very much, Mr. Babbitt."

"Just Jim, Inspector."

"And I can keep these?"

"Yes, Inspector, they're all yours."

"Thanks again."

After the young man had gone the inspector sat back and re-compared the prints, marveling as he had done the day Bill Zotas had reconstructed the name "Wilfrid McMulley" on the cut-up credit card found in the garbage. He thought, There's no doubt about it, the young guys are smarter than we were at their age, some of them at least. He placed the mug shots and finger-print cards in his desk drawer and walked down the hall to the squad room.

Sitting on chairs, still handcuffed as they had been when they left Don Mills, were Doris and Craig Hardley, Piet Langenzent, and Dwayne Hardley, who alone had had his handcuff removed. Detective Sergeant Stuart and Detectives Wilson and Chisolm were sitting across the table from them, and a young policewoman in uniform sat on a chair in a corner.

McDumont said to Stuart and Wilson, "Boys, move that bench over there to the far wall."

The detectives picked it up and placed it against the wall farthest from the door.

"All right now, remove the cuffs from the suspects."

Sergeant Stuart unlocked the handcuffs from behind the backs of the two men and the woman, who immediately began flexing their arms and rubbing their wrists.

The inspector said, "I want the four of you to sit on that bench against the wall, Dwayne on my left, Mrs. Hardley next to him, then Langenzent, and you Hardley on the far right."

They left their chairs as slowly and languidly as they could and sat down on the bench.

McDumont said to Sergeant Stuart, "John, handcuff Dwayne's left wrist to Mrs. Hardley's right, her left to Langenzent's right, and Langenzent's left to Hardley's right wrist."

Doris Hardley said, "Jesus Christ, my wrist is hurting like hell as it is."

The inspector ignored her, but watched carefully as Sergeant Stuart and Sam Chisolm completed the handcuffing.

"All set, John?" he asked Stuart.

"Yep, Walter."

The inspector looked at his watch. "It's five-thirty now. If you like we'll send out for coffee and sandwiches for you all. What will you have, Dwayne?"

"A Coke, some French fries and a hamburger, no onion."

The inspector made a note of it on his pad.

"Mrs. Hardley?"

"Stick it up your ass!"

"Langenzent?"

"I'll have coffee and a tuna fish sandwich on wholewheat."

The inspector noted it.

"Hardley?"

"A cheeseburger and coffee and slice of apple pie."

The inspector noted Hardley's order, then said to Detective Wilson, "George, will you go up to Bloor Street and get these orders?" He handed Wilson a bill and the sheet torn from his note pad. "You police officers will be spelled off for supper as soon as the suspects are fed."

He strode from the room.

In his office he began work on the day's activities at the Doncentre Apartments for his dope sheet. After twenty minutes had gone, and his writing hand was beginning to cramp, he placed the dope sheet back in his filing cabinet and strolled along the hall to the squad room. The suspects were eating their sandwiches, all except Mrs. Hardley of course. Langenzent was having a hard time trying to lift his coffee or sandwich to his mouth, for Doris Hardley would give his hand a jerk every time he tried to take a bite or a drink.

The inspector said to Sergeant Stuart, "John, unlock the handcuff between Mrs. Hardley and Langenzent, will you?"

This was done, and Langenzent was able to eat his tuna sandwich and drink his coffee.

The inspector said, "Mrs. Hardley, you're the most intransigent prisoner here. You're not only foul-mouthed and uncooperative but to me you're a thoroughly distasteful woman. This afternoon you gave your husband a pistol with which he could have shot any of my men. You are facing a serious charge. I think it's best for all concerned that you be taken to the city jail now, and I hope your attitude changes. I'd like you to know that your—and everyone else's here—conduct as well as the crimes they have committed or abetted are filed in a report that is going to the Crown Attorneys' office tomorrow. From this report the various charges you will face will be determined."

"You won't get nothing out of me!" Doris Hardley said.

"Perhaps I won't need to."

The inspector motioned the young policewoman from her corner, and whispered something to her. She left the squad room.

"We don't usually keep suspects in handcuffs down here, but because of your conduct this afternoon we have had to do it. I know that being handcuffed is not the most pleasant way to be, especially to eat, but you forced us into it. Any complaints you have you can give to your lawyers tomorrow. Now, I see that you, Hardley, are finished eating and you too, Langenzent. We are going to leave you cuffed together until later." He said to Stuart, "Sergeant, unlock the cuffs fastening Mrs. Hardley to Dwayne."

The sergeant unlocked the cuffs.

"Mrs. Hardley, please stand up."

"I like it better sitting down."

"You're going to have plenty of time for that where you're going."

"You should have eaten something, Doris," her husband said.

"You go to hell."

In a couple of minutes the young policewoman accompanied by a colleague, both wearing full uniforms and hats, entered the squad room.

"Did you arrange things out at the jail?" the inspector asked.

274

"Yes, sir."

"And you have a paddy wagon outside?"

"Yes, there's one ready in the parking lot."

"Cuff Mrs. Hardley's hands behind her back, John. She's going for a ride." He said to Doris Hardley, "If you want to say good-bye to your son and husband, go ahead."

"I'll see you both soon. Good-bye," she said, not kissing either of them.

The two policewomen led her out of the squad room.

Take the cuff off Dwayne there," the inspector said.

"Whose cuffs are they, anyway?"

"This pair is mine, Walter," said Sergeant Stuart. He placed them on the back of his belt.

"All right. Leave the pair connecting Langenzent and Hardley as they are." Turning to the bench he said, "Dwayne, if you're finished eating, put your cup and French fries box in that wastebasket there. While you're at it, put your father's cup and also Mr. Langenzent's in the wastebasket too."

The boy did as he was told.

"John, I want you, Sam and George to stay here with these suspects. However you can give your orders for something to eat to one of you, and he can go out for it. If either prisoner wants to use the bathroom he's to be handcuffed to one of you detectives. I'm taking Dwayne to my office for questioning." He led the boy out of the room.

In his office McDumont pointed to the chair across the desk from his own and told Dwayne to sit down. He sat down also in his own chair. Taking out his cigarettes he asked Dwayne if he wanted one.

"Yes please."

The inspector lighted both cigarettes.

"As you know, Dwayne, I'm not a psychiatrist but a hard-nosed old cop. I'm not going to talk to you about your homosexuality any more because I'm not competent to talk about it. What your mother and father have been arrested for is for your father's stabbing of the dead body of Zelda Greenless and the placing of it in the garbage closet."

The boy nodded.

"You were in your apartment before your father took the dagger and went into the Greenless apartment?"

"Yes."

"Just a minute." The inspector picked up the phone and dialed the headquarters' switchboard. He said, "Who's that, Ethel? This is Walter McDumont. Fine, thank you. Have you any male stenographers on shift tonight? Who, Joe? Great, put him on." There was a short period of silence, then the inspector said, "Is that you, Joe? Listen, can you come up here to take testimony from three people connected with the Zelda Greenless killing? Good. Have you eaten yet? Great. Incidentally, that was a good job you did for me with Zutach. Two minutes? Fine." He hung up the phone.

He said to Dwayne, "There's a police stenographer coming up to take down whatever you tell me. I want you to try to remember everything in chronological sequence, don't embellish it and don't use what you say to get revenge on anybody, understand?"

Dwayne nodded.

"I'm not sending you to the Don Jail. I've been in touch with the Clarke Institute out near College and Spadina. I'm sending you there until the trial. I wouldn't want to send you to the Don, where I'm sure they'd have to keep you isolated from the other prisoners for your own protection. In the Clarke you'll be locked up but not in an individual cell. You'll probably have access to any recreational facilities they have there and the use of a common room during the day. Whether they'll put you in a dorm or a room I have no idea, but we'll find out more about that when the doctor comes to get you later. His name's Bob Macpherson, and he's a Scotsman like me. I think from his voice over the phone that he's a young guy. Now, I think they'll go into your history much more thoroughly than I'm going to go into it here, and because they're doctors whose job it is to bring people, some with your problem, many with other neuroses, back to what we think of as normalcy, you'll probably have private therapy sessions and group therapy sessions. It will depend on you whether you accept the help they'll offer you or not.

276

That's out of my jurisdiction. Anyhow, you'll be much better cared for than you would be in the city jail. What do you think of it?"

"I think it's super of you, Inspector. Thank you."

The figure of Tom Johnson appeared in the doorway.

The inspector said, "Come in, Tom. Did you find the slugs and cartridges?"

"I dug the two .22 caliber slugs out of the walls of the stairwell, Inspector, but could only find this one cartridge." He laid the two mashed bullets and a .22 cartridge on the inspector's desk. "I think the second cartridge is probably in the breech of the target pistol."

"It probably is. Now Detective Sergeant Alvin Prust is down at the Forensic Lab with some stuff I want analyzed right away. Do you know where it is? It's at number eight Jarvis Street, right down at the bottom. There'll be somebody there, I expect, who'll be able to make ballistic comparisons. If there isn't, get Prust to have them bring a man in." The inspector unlocked his filing cabinet and took the .22 target pistol from the bottom drawer. He broke it, counted the rounds in the chamber, and said, "You were right, Tom, the spent cartridge is still in the breech. I'm sorry as hell I didn't check it before having you search all over for it." He clicked the pistol closed again, put on the safety catch, and handed it to Johnson, who slipped it into his pocket. "Okay, Tom, I'm sorry to be spoiling your Sunday night, but I've got to get these things done. As soon as you reach the Forensic Lab ask for Sergeant Prust, and explain things to him. Okay?"

"This was a work night for me anyway, Inspector. Thursday was my day off."

"Okay, don't leave the place until we get a ballistics comparison and report on those slugs." He handed the two slugs and the cartridge to the young officer, who placed them in his pocket and left the office.

McDumont took out his cigarettes and offered one to Dwayne, who shook his head. The inspector lighted his.

"Did you expect all these things to happen, Dwayne?"

277

"No. It's left me both scared and very surprised."

Joe, the stenographer, arrived with his pencils and shorthand book.

"Bring a chair in from one of the other offices, Joe, and sit down at the end of the table."

The young man came in carrying a chair and sat, pencil poised, ready to take notes.

The inspector asked Dwayne, "What is your full name?"

"Dwayne James Hardley."

"Your address?"

"Apartment six-o-six, ten-forty-nine Don Mills Road, Don Mills, Ontario."

"You were home on the afternoon of June twelfth, nineteen-seventy-four?"

"Yes."

"Were you at school that day?"

"Yes."

"What time did you arrive home?"

"Around three-thirty."

"Who was there?"

"My mother, Doris Hardley."

"What time did your father arrive home?"

"Around five or five-fifteen."

"What is his full name?"

"James Craig Hardley. He never uses the name James. My mother has always insisted that Craig is a— a poshier name than Jim, and so for years he's just called himself Craig Hardley."

"Do you love your mother?"

A hesitant, "No, not any more."

"What kind of woman is she? Describe her briefly."

"She's dominating and domineering. She has sort of taken over the male role in the family. She is always threatening my father."

"With what?"

"Divorce and a large alimony settlement, things like that. She's also told him of brief affairs she's had with other men."

"How did you hear these things?"

"Lying awake in my bedroom when I was younger, and even up to a short time ago. Sometimes when she was in one of her tempers she'd say these things at the table."

"In front of you?"

"Yes."

"What would you do?"

"Sometimes, like, I'd run out of the apartment, other times I'd pretend I didn't hear her."

"What did your father do?"

"*He didn't do anything!* Just took it, like a beaten little dog. I began to hate him for this when I was maybe ten years old or so. My mother would watch TV all afternoon, then open cans of stuff for supper, or packaged meals. My father never complained. I hated him for that, and as I grew older I knew that he—"

"Submitted?"

"Yes, submitted to these humiliations."

"Do you know why?"

"I do now. My mother had made my father marry her. I was born six months after the wedding. So in a way I began to think that I was to blame for the way things were. Sometimes my mother would hint to me that it was my birth that had put her in the position of being married to a failure, a man who was always in debt, who drank too much, who couldn't seem to get the advances he should have in the companies he worked for."

"What were your mother's social aspirations?"

"I beg your pardon, Inspector?"

"Did your mother pretend to be better socially than she actually was?"

"Yes. She mixed with women she'd met at the beauty parlor or some place who had far more money than we did. She pretended to them that my father was an executive with a stockbroker's office, and tried to keep up with them socially. She'd drag my father to parties, even though they couldn't afford them, and we'd take car trips all over the States and Canada, so she could drop names like Las Vegas and Fort Lauderdale into her conversations. My father once had a car repossessed because he couldn't afford the payments. He used to have to humiliate himself at finance companies to get enough money to carry on the act."

"How did he pay off the finance companies?"

"When I was younger and we were still living on Howard Street, he'd have to take evening jobs, like working in a Bloor Street haberdashery, things like that. Once he went on the night shift at the Dunlop Tire Company. He couldn't drink then, of course, and he'd come home as soon as he could after the stock exchange closed, sleep, then go to work at Dunlops."

"What was your mother's background, do you know?"

"She was born on Allen Avenue in the Riverdale district, though she told everybody she'd been born on Logan above Bain Avenue, which was a little classier. One time when I was maybe twelve or so I found a chocolate box in her drawer and I read everything in it. There was her birth certificate, marriage licence, and her graduation certificate from Queen Alexandra School on Broadview Avenue. She never went past Grade Eight. Through reading these things I sort of put things together, and I knew she'd been living a lie all her life."

The inspector nodded.

"Do you know how your father met her?"

"Yes. She was a waitress in a lower Bay Street restaurant where he used to have lunch. She was attracted to him, I guess, by his looks and by the fact that he worked at the stock exchange. Then I came along, and she forced him to marry her."

"It's happened that way in a million cases, Dwayne. It was no fault of yours."

"No, but when you're a little boy and your mother throws it in your face you think it's your fault." He began to cry, and took a handkerchief from his pocket, blew his nose and wiped his eyes. "Sorry," he said.

"That's all right, kid. Don't try to be a Spartan. God knows you've been given enough things to cry about."

Joe sat at the end of the table waiting for the interview to continue.

The inspector said, "Joe, would you go down to the coffee machine and bring three coffees? I'm regular, cream and sugar, and how do you like yours, Dwayne?"

"Black please, with sugar."

The inspector handed Joe a half dollar. "Get one for yourself, Joe."

"Sure, be right back."

McDumont said, "While Joe's away, because this has nothing to do with this interview, what do you think of Dolly Bullay in six-o-one?"

"She's the same as my mother. Luckily for some unborn kid she never had any."

"How about her husband, George Bullay?"

"The exact same as my father. The poor stepped-on twirp."

"She's a friend of your mother's, isn't she?"

"Yes."

"Do you know where *she* comes from? Bright Street in lower Cabbagetown. I'm a Cabbagetowner myself, but I've never tried to hide it. She has. Bright Street is even worse than Allen Avenue used to be. As we used to say, 'There isn't a house on the street that would make a good Chinese laundry.'"

Dwayne smiled, finished wiping his eyes and put his handkerchief away.

Joe returned with the coffees, accompanied by Sergeant Prust carrying his bag of evidence. He handed the inspector the reports from the Forensic Lab.

The report and analyses of the evidence that Prust placed on the inspector's desk confirmed that the two blankets were a pair, had been purchased at the same time and that their fibers matched perfectly.

"Take this down, Joe," McDumont said. "Ready?"

"Yes, Inspector."

"Do you recognize these twin-size blankets, Dwayne?"

"Yes. They were used as covers on the twin beds in my mother and father's bedroom. She cut the labels off because they weren't classy enough."

"Okay, Joe, and you too, Dwayne, drink your coffees while I look over the rest of this report. By the way, Alvin, did they have to send out for some experts down there at the lab?"

"Not for the stuff I took. They had some people on duty who could handle them. They had to send for a ballistics man when the young policeman—Johnson?

281

—when he brought in the .22 slugs and the pistol. They weren't finished with him when I left. They were firing test shots with the pistol I believe. They shouldn't be long making the ballistics comparison."

"Fine, Alvin. There's been no calls while you were away, so you can carry on with whatever you were doing."

The Forensic report stated that the torn-up note that the inspector had assembled had been made on the same paper that formed the thin pad of pink paper McDumont had found in Langenzent's desk. The black felt pen was also the same one with which the threatening note had been printed. There were references to a broken tip at the end of the felt and it had been compared with the original printed note by spectroscopic analysis, micro-analysis and X-ray diffraction. The bottle of liquid was definitely tartar emetic.

The inspector put everything, including the lab reports into the bottom drawer of his filing cabinet and locked it.

"Cigarette, gentlemen?" the inspector asked, offering the package to Dwayne and the stenographer. Both shook their heads.

"Joe, you have that stuff about the pair of blankets, haven't you?"

Joe read his shorthand notes, and repeated them to the inspector.

"Good. I haven't much more to ask you, Dwayne."

Dwayne nodded.

"Where did you live after you moved from Howard Street, and when would that be?"

"We moved into a flat in Rosedale, on Standish Avenue, backed up against the CPR main line. It's not a *Rosedale* street, Inspector, if you know what I mean. The rich people in their mansions lived farther south, away from the main line railway track and the constant noise of passing freight trains. But it was *Rosedale*, don't you see? That's what made it important to her."

"Did you live there until you moved up here?"

"Yes. We were evicted for nonpayment of rent on Standish. We lived in an upstairs flat."

"Was your father doing any extra work at that time?"

"Sometimes, but he could never keep up with my mother's spending. I remember one year he worked for a tax consultant in the evenings, making out tax returns, and another time when he worked in the booth of a city parking lot north of Bloor Street."

"After you were old enough to get by on your own, and believe me there's plenty of seventeen-year-olds who are doing it, why didn't your father just walk out?"

With a wry smile the boy answered, "Believe it or not, Inspector, my father loved my mother."

"Was it reciprocated? Did *she* love *him*?"

"No, I'm sure she didn't. I don't think she loved me either, but it was part of the game she played, at least among her friends, that she loved us both. Don't let me say what I want to say about her, Inspector!"

"All right, I won't. Let's go back to the afternoon of June twelfth. Your father came home drunk between five and five-thirty?"

"Yes. He'd been drinking with some friends from the Exchange at the Cork Room on Bay Street."

"Now, in sequence, tell me what happened."

"First she cursed him for being a drunken bum, then she told him if he wanted supper he could make it himself. She told him she was going out to see a friend."

"Female or male?"

"She didn't specify, Inspector, but I think both my father and I figured it was some man. She was dressed up in a spring suit, and she left the apartment. Oh, before she left she said, "What the hell kind of man are you anyway, letting your son sleep with that whore in six-o-two? If you were any kind of man at all you'd do something about it!"

"And then she left?"

"Yes."

"Was your father very drunk at this time?"

"He was more drunk than when he'd first arrived home. He'd had a couple of shots of cheap rye after arriving home. I'd have to say he was crazy drunk."

"What did he do then?"

"He twisted my arm until I gave him my key to Zelda's apartment."

"Go on."

"Then he asked me where my gang dagger was?"

"And?"

"I told him I'd thrown it away."

"What then?"

He twisted my arm up my back until I thought he was going to break it. I guess I must have screamed with the pain, but it didn't stop him. I finally told him it was in my dresser drawer. He went into my room and came back with the dagger, which he had taken from its sheath. He then tried to dial Mr. Zutach's number but couldn't, so he pressed the knife in my back and made me dial the number for him."

"What did he say to Zutach?"

"He told him to come up to the sixth floor right away."

"And then what?"

"He went to wait for Zutach at the elevators. He had the knife stuck down the front of his pants, hidden under his cardigan."

"What did you do?"

"I listened at the door as he and Zutach passed on their way to Zelda's. Mr. Zutach was protesting that Mrs. Greenless was very sick and should be left alone, but my father said he had to teach her a lesson she wouldn't forget. As soon as they let themselves in to Zelda's apartment, I took the elevator down to the first floor, and ran across to the shopping plaza."

"Just where did you go?"

"To The Coffee Spot."

"Did you have money?"

"Yes, I had a dollar and change."

"How long did you stay over there?"

"I don't know, Inspector. It must have been eight or so when I went back home. Both my mother and father were out. My mother had changed from her suit to a dress, and I could hear the noise coming from the party in the Gilcrest apartment. I could hear my mother laughing in there."

"At that time you didn't know what had happened to Zelda Greenless?"

"No I didn't. I still don't know where she, or her body, was at that time. I was almost certain though that my father had killed her, in fact I believed he had until I heard from some of the Centre Gang the next night, I guess it was, that she'd actually been poisoned."

"Where did you spend the night of June twelfth?"

"Sleeping on the back seat of my father's car in the parking lot."

"And you didn't return to your own apartment after your father had gone into Zelda Greenless's until when?"

"I had a breakfast of toast and coffee at The Coffee Spot before my father came down to the car to go to work. I went home about lunch time."

"And you stayed in until we came to question your family that evening?"

"Yes, sir."

"All right. That's all for now. Joe, take his testimony down on your typewriter and type it up. We'll have to have him sign it before he's taken to the Clarke Institute. Three copies please."

The stenographer left.

"Aren't you ashamed of yourself letting your old man and old lady think you were sleeping sometimes with Zelda Greenless?" the inspector asked.

"I'm very much ashamed," the boy said, his head bowed and his eyes cast down.

"She'd always treated you well, hadn't she?"

A whisper. "Yes." Then louder, "Really, Inspector, even though my old man was crazy drunk like I said I didn't think he had the guts to do what he did. It was the first time in my life I'd ever seen him show any courage at all."

"It didn't take much courage to stab a dead woman in the back."

"Neither my father nor I, nor even Mr. Zutach knew she was dead at the time they went into her apartment."

"When did you get her apartment key back from your father?"

"The next evening when he came home from work."

"When and how did you get rid of the dagger sheath?"

"I guess it was the day after Zelda's body had been found. I put it in a garbage bag and shoved it down the garbage chute."

"When did you know Langenzent was back from Ottawa?"

"I guess we, that is my family, were aware of it when my father listened to you detectives coming along the hall questioning the tenants. I knew for certain at noon today when he called me, and asked me to come over."

"He didn't tell you he'd poisoned Zelda though, did he?"

"No."

"But he knew you'd visited her in her apartment?"

"Yes, sometimes he'd go into a towering rage over it. Tell me I was not to see her again. He'd tell me he loved me so much he could kill anyone who got in his way. Sometimes he'd cry and call me a little cheat. He'd bring me presents from Ottawa, and give me money. Sometimes he'd ask me to forgive him, but he couldn't help his jealousy."

McDumont sat with a curled lip across the desk. "Okay, that's enough. I'll throw up if I hear any more fag love confessions."

Detective Larry Helmont came to the door accompanied by a short fat young man with a full beard. "This gentleman wants to see you, Inspector. His name's Dr. Robert Macpherson of the Clarke Institute."

The inspector stood up. "How'dy do, Doctor. Here's your patient, Dwayne Hardley."

"Hello, Dwayne. I'm sure we're going to get along fine over at the institute. You'll meet a lot of young men your age over there, and you'll learn to fit in with our program I'm sure."

The inspector looked down at him, thinking, like all shrinks he's a fucking Boy Scout counselor at heart. He said, "Okay, Dr. Macpherson, take him away."

"I thought we two Scotsmen would have a short chat about him first."

"Never mind about the Scotsmen malarkey. I have two more people to interrogate tonight, and I only had three hours sleep last night. We'll just wait for the stenographer to bring up the typed deposition he's given me, then you take him away and question him yourself. He's a homosexual, and he's deeply involved in the murder of a young woman who didn't need to be murdered at all. If you want to try and reform him and change him back to an acceptable heterosexual, good luck. As for me I'm finished with him. Did you drive over?"

"No, as a matter of fact I ride my bike to work. I took a cab."

"Well you'll be going back to the Clarke in a Homicide Squad police car, with a detective, an armed detective, at the wheel."

"We don't believe in harsh treatment or intimidation, Inspector."

"Well *we* do, Doctor, when it's necessary or advisable. This guy's father not only stabbed the corpse of a dead woman, but tried to shoot one of my sergeants today. Once he's delivered to your custody at the Clarke front door he's your little patient, but until then he's ours, understand?"

"Of course," the psychiatrist said, seemingly crushed.

Joe, the stenographer, came with the three copies of his typed confession, and the inspector had Dwayne Hardley sign them all. Then McDumont went to his door and called, "Alvin, Larry!"

The detective sergeant and the detective came out of their cubicles.

"I want you two to escort this suspect to the Clarke Institute along with Dr. Macpherson. Larry, handcuff yourself to him. You drive, Alvin. I want you to take him in to the admitting office and get a receipt for him from whoever's in charge. Okay?"

"Right, Inspector."

"This is outrageous!" Macpherson said.

287

"You don't know what the bloody word means, Macpherson," said the inspector.

Larry Helmont handcuffed himself to Dwayne Hardley, and the four of them left the Homicide Department.

The inspector followed them through the door, and entered the squad room down the hall. Langenzent and Hardley were still handcuffed together on the bench against the wall. The detectives were sitting in their chairs, talking together.

"Cut Hardley loose, Sergeant," the inspector said to John Stuart. To Hardley he said, "Follow me down to my office, Hardley. You, John, follow us and don't hesitate to shoot if he makes one small step out of line. Sam, cuff Langenzent's hands together behind his back."

In his office, the inspector told Hardley to take the chair across the desk, and told Sergeant Stuart to bring a chair and sit in the doorway.

"Well, Hardley, I've got two confessions there in my filing cabinet, one from Anton Zutach, whom you conned into being the patsy in your stabbing caper, and one from your son Dwayne, who has filled me in in detail about the events leading up to your going to Zelda's place 'to teach the whore a lesson' or words to that effect. Now you and I know you were crazy drunk when you came home from work that night, and with your sweet wife egging you on, and putting your manhood down, you felt you had to show her, and yourself, that there was more to you than a business and financial failure who owed a month's rent to Jerry Rubin, three payments on the Cutlass that you couldn't afford to buy in the first place, and God knows how much to the Benevolent Finance Company.

"Ever since you left Howard Street, and even while you were living there you had to take evening jobs to pay your debts and augment your salary. Your son told me that you'd worked for an income tax consulting firm, as a parking lot attendant, and once as a night-shift worker in the Dunlop Tire plant. Now believe me, Hardley, those are things in your favor as a man. What isn't in your favor is the fact that you allowed yourself to be domineered by a conniving woman who forced you into marriage, then, though she'd only had a Grade Eight education and was a waitress when she snared you, tried in every way she knew how to make you both socially acceptable in a segment of society that you just couldn't afford to join. Surely as a man who has worked with figures all his life you knew the percentages were against you. Why didn't you rebel?"

Hardley shook his head, staring down at the desk.

"Now as far as the stabbing of Zelda Greenless was concerned it's my belief, and this ties in with Zutach's testimony, that you fully intended to rape and then kill Zelda Greenless. You stripped her of her clothes, and not knowing she was already dead until Zutach told you, you took a condom from a box of them on her closet shelf and dropped your pants. Isn't that true?"

Hardley nodded.

"Say yes or no, Hardley, this is being taken down stenographically."

"Yes. As you've said though, Inspector, I was crazily drunk."

"I believe you, and you can use it as part of your defence at your trial. Do you want me to let you read both your son's and Anton Zutach's evidence?"

"No, I'd rather not."

"Even with your wife Doris bitching at you the night of June twelfth when you came home drunk, and hinting that she had a date with another man, that shouldn't have been sufficient reason to go stab Zelda Greenless and stack her in a corner of the garbage disposal closet to show your neighbors that you looked upon her as garbage. You know that Dwayne is homosexual; you've already had a schoolteacher discharged from the high school because of him being caught with your son. Is that right?"

"Yes."

"We've sent Dwayne over to the Clarke Institute. If he'd gone to the Don Jail he'd have been gang-shagged by every weirdo and wino in the joint, you know that don't you?"

"Yes, Inspector. Thanks."

"Knowing what your son is, what made you think he'd be having relations with a woman?"

"I don't know, Inspector. As you've said, I was crazy drunk that night, and with Doris bitching at me and everything I just didn't know what I was doing."

The inspector unlocked his filing cabinet and pulled out the two blankets. "Do you recognize these, Hardley?"

"Yes, they're off our twin beds."

"The dagger is down in the vault, but do you remember stabbing Mrs. Greenless's corpse through it, then twisting the dagger?"

Hardley nodded.

"Yes or no, Hardley!"

"Yes."

"And do you remember giving Zutach a German camera to keep him quiet, and offering him a hundred dollars?"

"Not exactly, but if he said I did, I guess I did."

"You used Zutach as a Patsy, threatening him with that goddam dagger, but you weren't that drunk that you didn't think of disguising the body on his handcart with the picture you took off Zelda's wall. I'm leaving the figuring out as to how drunk or sober you really were to the judge or jury at your trial. What time did you take the naked body of Zelda Greenless from apartment six-ten and carry it into the garbage disposal closet."

"It was very late at night; I don't remember."

"But you admit you did it?"

"Yes, I did it, Inspector."

"I want you to know that we have an eye witness who saw you coming out of Zelda Greenless's apartment. That was before you and your wife whooped it up at Cec Gilcrest's party. Mrs. Norma Dryburg is going to testify against you, Zutach *and* Langenzent, whom she saw going into Zelda's."

"Okay, okay! Christ, Inspector, I've admitted everything now."

"This afternoon your wife smuggled you a .22 caliber target pistol and you disarmed one of my men with it and fired two shots at another. Do you deny that?"

"No, I admit it. By today I knew the game was up, not only in regard to the crime I'd committed, but maritally, financially and every other way. I was actually hoping Sergeant Grant would shoot me in the parking lot."

"All right, take him back to the squad room, John, and bring back Langenzent. Handcuffed as he is. Who's in there with him now?"

"George Wilson and Sam Chisolm."

"Tell them they can check out. Let's see, get somebody from the pool to look after this guy until we question Langenzent. That still leaves you, Stew, and me, until Prust and Helmont come back from the Clarke."

"Okay, Inspector."

Langenzent refused to answer any questions at all. Even to admit that he'd purchased the tartar emetic in Ottawa, or that he'd been jealous of Dwayne's friendship with Zelda Greenless.

The inspector called the downstairs desk and arranged for the two prisoners, accompanied by two detectives, to be taken to the city jail in a paddy wagon.

He was sitting back smoking a reflective cigarette when Tom Johnson arrived with the ballistics report from the Forensic Laboratory and the slugs and bullets fired with the .22 pistol. He also had microphotographs of the rifling marks on both the slugs and comparison bullets, and of the cartridges. The inspector placed them in his bottom file drawer and locked the filing cabinet.

In a couple of minutes two big uniformed policemen came into the Homicide Squad office. "You got a couple of prisoners to be taken out to the Don in the wagon?" one of them asked.

"Yes. There's this one here, and the sergeant will show you where we've got the other one stashed, in a squad room down the hall. The Sergeant and one of you men will ride inside with them to the jail."

"Okay, Inspector."

The uniformed men, Sergeant Stuart and Piet Langenzent left the office. The inspector walked to the corridor door and watched them bring Hardley out of the squad room. The lot of them went down in the elevator.

McDumont sat at his desk until Sergeant Prust and Detective Helmont returned.

Alvin Prust said, "You'd have thought we'd been checking somebody into the Four Seasons Sheraton. What a routine we had to go through! I had to show my badge before they'd issue us with a receipt for the kid. Then Dr. Macpherson led him down a hall with his arm around his shoulders."

"I know," said the inspector, laughing. "You should never trust a headshrinker with a full beard who rides a bicycle to work." He glanced at his time sheet under the glass on the top of his desk. "You two are on to midnight, I see."

"Yeah, Walter."

"I'm going home. Take care of the store, and no matter who gets shot, stabbed, garrotted or drowned in boiling Bromo Seltzer don't bother calling me 'cause my phone'll be off the hook until tomorrow morning. Alvin, see that the jail knows that Langenzent is being held on a murder rap will you? Good night, guys."

"Good night, Walter."

"—Inspector."

He rode down in the elevator with Tom Johnson. "Don't forget, Johnson, if you want to switch from the Youth Bureau, speak with Inspector Fern Alexander."

"Yes, Inspector."

McDumont drove along Bloor Street to the Don Valley Parkway, then along Lawrence Avenue to his house in Scarborough.

"Do you want me to make you a pot of tea, Walter?" his wife Jean asked as he took off his coat and sat down at the kitchen table.

He nodded.

The next time she looked at him he was fast alseep with his head on his arms. Like a good wife she undressed him to his shorts and rolled him under the bedcovers. He was sound asleep again before his head hit the pillow.

Postscript

No matter where an author finishes a short story or a novel, and if he's a professional in his trade he always finishes it at its logical end, there are readers who decry the fact that he hasn't continued it to show them "what happened to the people afterwards."

I have no intention of extending any of my novels into sagas, and am satisfied that I have shown my characters in the positions they occupied in a certain place at a certain time. However, to satisfy in a small way the "what happened to the people afterwards" crowd, here is a brief synopsis of what some of the people from *Death in Don Mills* are doing today.

CONSTABLE HUGH CHESLEY, the first officer at the scene of Zelda Greenless's murder, is still driving a squad car out of No. 33 Division.

INSPECTOR ERNEST WILLIS of No. 33 Division has been transferred to a desk-job sinecure at Police Headquarters, after being severely reprimanded for his men's conduct in their questioning of the occupants of 1049 Don Mills Road.

DETECTIVE SERGEANT BRAD SEMONS still works out of the Don Mills police station.

DETECTIVE ARTHUR ELLYS has been transferred from No. 33 Division to No. 14 Division, which handles the second-highest crime rate among all Metropolitan Toronto police precincts.

STALLINGS TELFORD Q.C., O.B.E. beat the charge of drunken driving brought against him by Detective Inspector McDumont, largely because of his lawyers' skill, and because he had been given back his half-bottle of Chivas Regal by Inspector Willis.

DETECTIVE WILLIAM ZOTAS, DETECTIVE THOMAS SMITH and DETECTIVE CLARENCE ROUNDY are now full-fledged members of the Metro Toronto Police Homicide Squad.

SERGEANT OF DETECTIVES ERIC MANDERS has taken a slightly reduced pension, and he and his wife have winterized their summer cottage and are living there. (His road to the highway is blocked many days during the winter with snow, but he accepts his isolation philosophically.)

DR. EDMUND MAINGUY, the duty coroner in the Greenless case, has retired, and has begun collecting sculptures of walruses (largely Eskimo carvings) and his living room now has the appearance of a stone zoo occupied solely by members of the genus *Odobenus*.

DETECTIVE SERGEANT JOSEPH GRANT, the detective who disarmed and put out of action the doubly armed Craig Hardley in the Doncentre Apartments parking lot, was awarded a medal and a Metro Police commendation, and is now an inspector in a suburban police precinct.

RUSS, the IDENT photographer, has left the police force and has taken up cinematography with a small Canadian cinema studio specializing in beer commercials and films of young girls skipping through fields of clover.

DONALD WEAVER, the IDENT fingerprint man, is working for his father as manager of a real estate development near Streetsville, on the outskirts of Toronto. His place in the IDENT Bureau has been taken by *James Babbitt*.

MRS. FLORA DEBLER, the graphologist, is still working freelance at her skill, and her occasional correspondence with Inspector McDumont is still filled with such expressions as, "line flow, relative slant, pen pressure, letter connections and spacing, line curvature, tremor, shading, proportion, and base alignment."

DR. HUGH RUTSEY, the sensible psychiatrist at the medical center on Wynford Drive still practices there, as does *Dr. Morris Franczic*, the urologist. Franczic has had three unsatisfactory secretaries since the death of Zelda Greenless.

DR. MARTIN RAYMOND, the toxicologist at the Forensic Sciences Centre, is still on the job.

JOHN KAPETT, one of Dwayne Hardley's ex-lovers, is still shipping- and receiving-manager of Wallace-Roberts Paint and Dye Company, and has moved from Don Mills to a downtown apartment house, where he shares an apartment with a 31-year-old male Pakistani.

THE BULLAYS, DERYMORES, MRS. NORMA DRYBERG, WILFRID MCMULLEY AND ELEANOR JACTON still occupy the same apartments on the sixth floor of 1049 Don Mills Road.

CECIL GILCREST has been moved by his company to Thompson, Manitoba, which is a hell of a long way from the King Edward Hotel. He has an Indian mistress called Lila Mooseantler, with whom he shares a company house.

ZELDA GREENLESS is buried in the Protestant cemetery in Crow Lake, Ontario, next to the body of her baby. Her aunt and uncle, the Stantons, being her only living relatives, inherited her small estate. They went down to Toronto and picked up some small pieces of furniture and the kitchenware. They called up the Salvation Army Furniture Salvage Department but when the driver and his assistant arrived, and saw the size of the bed, they offered to take only the living room stuff and the dresser. Peter Stanton got the Salvation Army Commissioner on the line and told him that if any Sally Ann Christers ever came to his door again asking for a donation, he'd kick them off his property. Finally the salvage truck from the Crippled Civilians came and removed the furniture, including the bed, which they had to dismantle. Peter Stanton kept them working with generous tots of Gordon's gin and Cocktail Mix.

PIET LANGENZENT is still being held in Toronto's Don Jail on a charge of noncapital murder. He had made the mandatory plea in such cases of "Not guilty." It is expected that his trial will be scheduled for the Ontario Supreme Court's next assizes.

ANTON ZUTACH is out of jail on $10,000 bail furnished by the apartment house owner, and is back with Xenia and his son Rudolph. All the apartments are rented, this being a time of housing shortages and a seller's market in housing. Apartment 610 is occupied by a retired United Church minister and his wife who deplore the casual matings of such people as Wilf McMulley and Eleanor Jacton and another young unmarried couple occupying Cec Gilcrest's old place. The Greenless apartment has a woman tenant, who calls herself "a spiritual mystic," and who knew Dolly Bullay when she lived on Bright Street and went to Sackville Street Public School. Dolly has denied this to the woman, who won't accept the denials. The Bullays are now searching for a condominium somewhere away from the mystic reminder of Dolly's proletarian past.

DWAYNE HARDLEY is still being held in the Clarke Institute, as the Crown Attorney's Department has decided that the stabbing trial should await the outcome of Piet Langenzent's poisoning trial. He fits in fine with the neurotics, psychotics and speed freaks in the institute, has learned to shoot pool and play euchre. Occasionally Dr. Robert Macpherson takes him with him to a cottage on summer weekends and to his Annex-district converted coach house when the weather is inclement. Whether "Doc Robbie," as Dwayne calls him, is interested in curing him of his homosexuality or not would be mere speculation on my part, so I won't go into it.

CRAIG HARDLEY is still in the Don Jail, having been unable to raise bail. He has had two visits with his wife, Doris, but both ended up in screaming matches on her part so he stopped them. He works in the jail kitchen, and rather likes his job. He has decided that when he gets out he is going to open up a Financial and Tax Consultant's office somewhere in a new upper-middle-class suburb, and live by himself. His Cutlass was repossessed by Simon & Enderby, a General Motors dealership in West Toronto. His furniture, as chattels, was taken by the Benevolent Finance Company. His own and his family's personal property is stored in a basement storeroom where it is slowly gathering dust.

DORIS HARDLEY, held as an accessory, is also in the Don Jail. She has been working in the jail laundry since her arrest, as her recalcitrance has already given

296

her three stretches of isolation, loss of privileges and severe condemnations from the woman chief turnkey. She has turned down two Legal Aid lawyers, calling one of them "a stupid little kike," and is currently without a lawyer.

RAYMARK OSLER died of a coronary attack on the late evening of Friday, August 16, while crossing Don Mills Road from the Odeon Don Mills cinema. Before the ambulance arrived his body lay in the roadway, stopping all northbound traffic, except that turned along the Donways East and West by a policeman from No. 33 Division. The brave, impatient idiots from Don Mills, Don Valley Village and such places set up a cacophony of hornblowing, thinking themselves safe, hidden in their wheeled signs of affluence. However, the police issued them all summonses for causing a disturbance, and all the cars north of the Donway, proceeding north, were held long after Raymark's body had been removed.

Osler was rushed by ambulance to North York General Hospital where a "Code Ninety-nine" was broadcast over the speaker system from the emergency department. Several doctors answered the call, including a cardiologist, but despite their expertise and untiring efforts were unable to save his life.

His son flew in from Vancouver, and found from his will that his father still owned a small piece of brushland on the west bank of the Don River, where his wife, Ethel, was buried. His name, birthdate and date of death were cut into the stone on Ethel's grave, and he was buried beside her. His son shipped some of his father's mementos to Vancouver, and sold the furniture for a small sum to a second-hand dealer. After all he's a lawyer, and they don't give much away.

MILFORD (DREAMER) BLACK had a real bummer of a speed trip in July, and was taken by the police to the Ontario Alcoholism & Addiction Hospital on Russell Street, where they pumped his stomach and put him to bed on massive doses of Valium to bring him down. He stayed in one of the third-floor clinical wards for eight days, then was moved up to the fourth floor for a thirty-day therapy and rehabilitation course. After a

week of bumming around up there under the "guid-
ance" of "some social worker stiff," as Dreamer called
him, he checked out.

He found himself a job in an Etobicoke plant making wax paper, and moved into the top suite of a dup-
lex out there, leaving his old man to cope with the
juice and his garrulous memories of World War II in
the Legion halls. He doesn't even smoke grass any
more, and the company made him shave off his beard
and get himself a shorter haircut. He's seriously considering a date sometime soon with a girl who works
in the wax paper plant.

PATTY FINLAYSON continued shooting and dropping
a wide variety of so-called soft drugs. In July she found
she was pregnant, by whom she had no idea, and she
stole some money out of her old man, the evangelist's,
wallet and began hitchhiking to Vancouver. In Wawa
she slept in a tent with two male American hitchhikers
from Grand Rapids, Michigan, and from then on she
slept with a variety of young men, and men not so young
who gave her lifts in their cars and trucks, and made
Vancouver late in August. The last time she was seen
and identified she was in the company of two black
youths in Vancouver's Gashouse district.

BRUCE CORCORAN was picked up by undercover men
from the Narcotics Bureau and the Royal Canadian
Mounted Police selling sugar cubes dipped in acid
outside the Don Mills High School. He received a sentence of two years less a day in the Guelph Reformatory on possession-and-dealing charges. He met Drop
Kick Drewson there, but Drewson was bucking for
parole and ignored him.

CLIFFORD DRAKES AND CATHY EDGARS were married
by a provincial judge in the old Toronto City Hall. They
moved into a single room and kitchenette on Brunswick Avenue. Drakes found a job as a shipper for a
plastics company, and Cathy Drakes became a clerk
in a FAST, FAST, FAST! film-development booth in a
shopping center. They are no longer drug users (Slif-
ford never was), and much of their evening relaxation
consists of walks to the movie houses around Yonge
and Bloor streets or taking part in the sing-songs or

watching the acts in the Brunswick pub. They ration themselves to three bottles of ale apiece most evenings.

ABE GORDON is still attending the University of Toronto, and stands very high in his class. A couple of his father's friends have tried to tout him into specializing in gynecology after he studies medicine, but his heart is set on two things: pediatrics and a pretty Jewish girl named Esther, whom he met at a child care center rally in East Don Mills. He seldom goes near the Don Mills Shopping Centre any more.

DETECTIVE INSPECTOR WALTER MCDUMONT is still the senior officer of the Metropolitan Toronto Police Missing Persons and Homicide Bureau, but he assigns more of his duties to the younger men of his squad than he did before. Following the Zelda Greenless case he was brought before a police disciplinary board on a charge of wilfully countermanding the orders of Police Superintendent Randall Ford, by arranging arrest warrants on his own initiative, after Ford had refused him search warrants a couple of days earlier. McDumont had faced Ford in front of the police top brass and had said, "Listen, you goddam traffic cop, we got the killers didn't we?" Everyone knew he was alluding to Ford's long career in the traffic division before being promoted to superintendent. McDumont also told the board that Ford's counter-investigative stupidity had held back the solving of the Greenless case. It had also caused one of his best men, Detective Sergeant Grant, to become the target for Craig Hardley who had been doubly armed. He had topped this off by telling the board, "Ford wouldn't know the difference between a killer and a guy parked in a no parking zone."

He received a loss of seniority and a severe reprimand, but refused to be transferred to a division or another squad. "You'll either dismiss me from the force right now," he said, "or leave me where I am." He was told that his job was administration and squad discipline, and was warned against going out on cases, which should be left to younger men. "Yeah, thanks!" he said as he was leaving the board room. "Don't worry, you'll need me again."